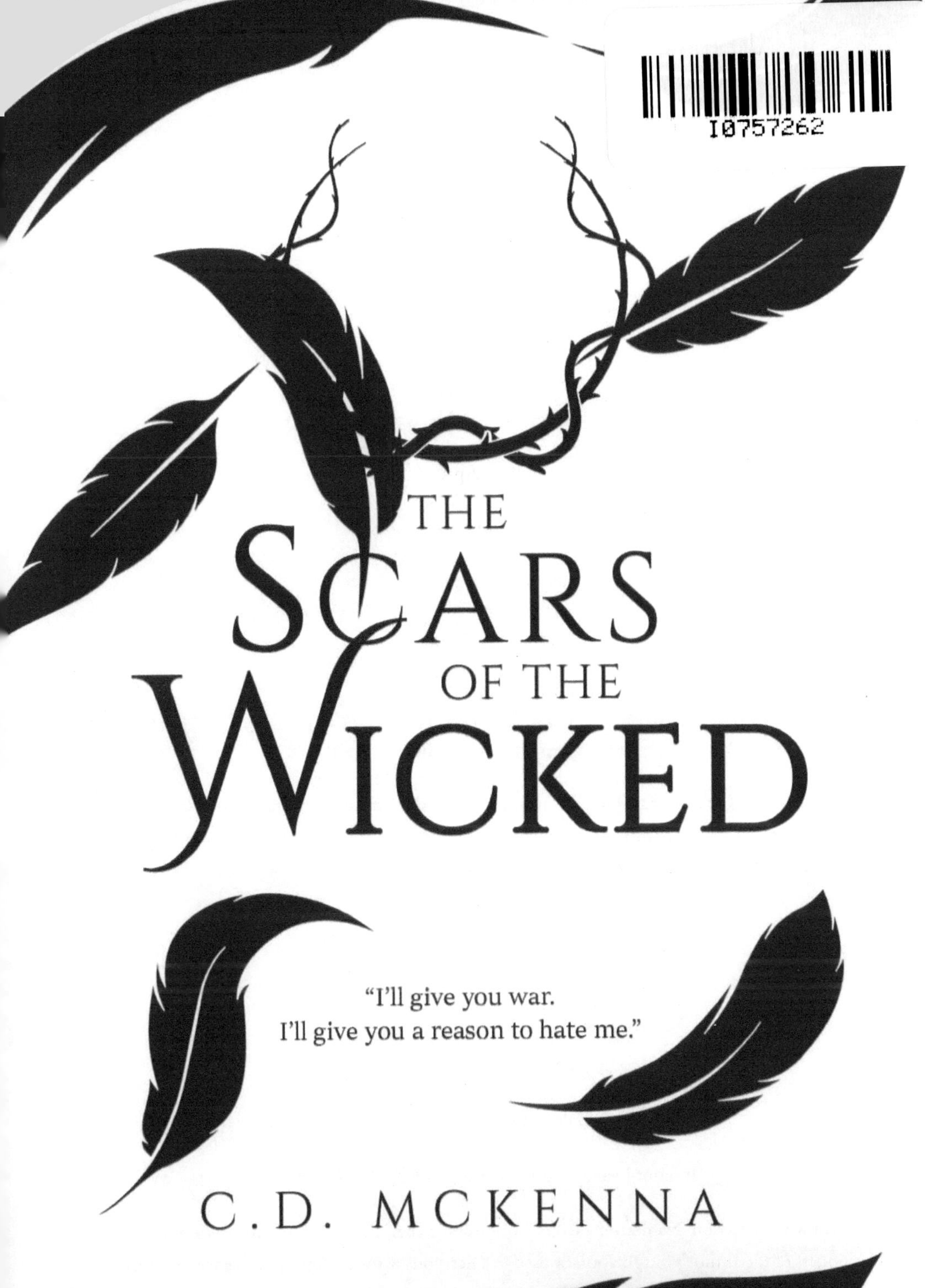

THE
SCARS
OF THE
WICKED

"I'll give you war.
I'll give you a reason to hate me."

C.D. MCKENNA

The Scars of the Wicked

The Vorelian Saga

Copyright © 2025 C.D. McKenna

Published by C.D. McKenna

First Edition: April 2025

Printed in the United States of America

eISBN: 979-8-9902901-5-0

979-8-9902901-4-3 (paperback)

979-8-9902901-6-7 (hardcover)

Library of Congress Control Number: 2025904128

www.thevoreliansaga.com

Cover Design by Cherie Foxley

Map Illustrations by Eve's Worldbuilding

Editing by Dylan Garity

Interior Design and Formatting by C.D. McKenna

Evil wears many faces—including that of a hero.

Sorréle
The Decaying Lake
Sorréleian River
Ferguson
Releuthian Mountains
Diemon
Uncharted Lands
No Man's Land
Merrél Sea
Gamer's Village
Hazar Desert
Geral
Easter's Port
Boldur Valley
Easter
N

Diyra
The Shade
Assane
Junok's Port
Junok
Merrél Sea
Mourdle Mountains
City of Liral
The Delfic Forest
Raveer
Whale Village
The Gulf of Beritisian
Crown Port
Jasper Village
Nighthunter Federation
Ronin's Port
N

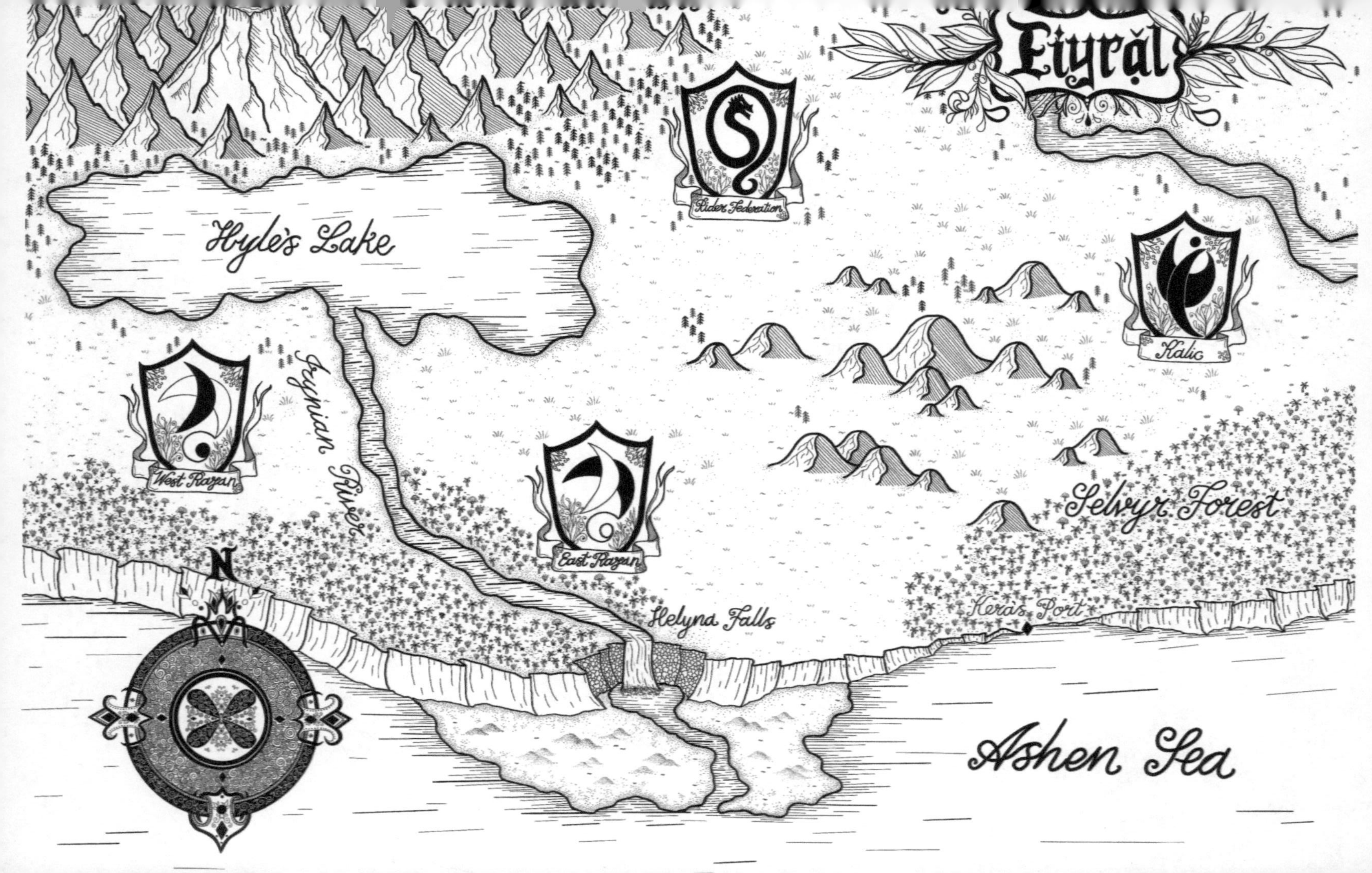

Eiyrăl
Hyle's Lake
Rider Federation
Kalic
West Razun
East Razun
Frynian River
Selvyr Forest
Helyna Falls
Kera's Port
Ashen Sea
N

Greitón
Greve's Point
Hil Islands
Delion's Port
Barnäl's Port
Tyrik Village
Warón Sea
Ruby Village
Delion
Saveen's Port
Saveen
Barnäl
Venkar City
Crescent Lake
Pynsole Mountains
Vor'Gal
N

Contents

PART 1

"Give man power, and he'll challenge the Gods."
~ The Vorelian Scrolls

Corrupted Gods

Present Day

The snow was almost gone. Syra stepped over a broken branch and admired all the new growth. She wasn't fond of the cold, and finally seeing green buds on the foliage around her felt refreshing. Many trees had withstood the tundra that the Mourale Mountains had become, but a few wide-leaf ones hadn't. Large stretches of ice still clung to the higher spots, including her little area that overlooked the valley. Soon, though, it would be gone. Dryl had told her it was only a matter of days now. She'd spent almost three moons staring at snowcapped trees—three moons since she'd seen Sekar and Dryl had taken his place as leader of the Infernol.

Last season, the Infernol had been prepared to seize Raveer in a race against Liral, who had also moved an army toward the weakened city. But the harsh winter had halted nearly all progress. No one would risk traversing the unforgiving conditions, cold enough for people to lose fingers or the tips of their noses. Visibility in the winter storms was also nonexistent. That hadn't stopped Dryl from sending scouts to observe Liral's activity, trudging through snow up to their waists. The small paths carved by brave travelers and traders were narrow, though—too small for any army to move.

Syra had spent most of the winter tucked in a fur cloak, continuing her training with Zarek. She and the Guardian had grown closer by force, but she welcomed it. She appreciated his reliability and stability. Zarek was predictable, even at the worst of times, and she could always bet he'd have something snarky to say. Banter was their language, and while their first moon together had been anything but friendly, they were learning about each other. They had to.

But Zane was still missing. Early scouts had brought no word of him, and Syra was starting to lose hope that the ex-commander of Raveer was still alive. Despite her protests, the search had ceased in order to provide more resources to monitor Liral. Few men were willing to venture into the brutal snowstorms, and even fewer would risk their lives for a man they hardly knew. Syra had admittedly spent many nights picking fights or insisting they weren't doing enough. Zane was a friend; to give up felt like she was failing him. Yet they had no leads, nothing to give the scouts any direction. They were fishermen casting too wide of a net, and now she feared she'd never get closure on his whereabouts.

Dryl was preoccupied with preparations for the Infernol to charge Raveer now that the seasons shifted. He hadn't been the same since returning, and Syra still struggled with that. This was a man she'd grown a deep affection for. Not in a romantic way like a bard might envision, but rather they needed each other. Dryl offered her peace, and she gave him purpose. Now, when she tried to seek out the comfort of their conversations, he was too busy or rushed. Sometimes, he wouldn't even answer the door when she knocked. Outwardly, she pretended she understood. In her heart, she was frustrated. The world he'd experienced after the Nighthunter Federation was a mystery to her, but she hoped to learn about it one day, when things settled. He'd saved her life more than once. He and Zarek had risked their lives and sacrificed everything for her.

Syra slipped underneath a large rock jutting out from the side of the mountain, ignoring the frigid ice. She scanned her surroundings, listening. A bird chirped, a rabbit bolted. Nothing seemed amiss. But it was, and she needed to figure it out fast or risk being caught. She was being hunted.

With the warm weather, she and Zarek had switched up their training. Syra was working on understanding her surroundings without the help of Chaos, because as the Guardian explained, she would not always be so lucky as to be able to harness that force. Gods were not invincible. They had weaknesses. Much like any Harvester, their strength could be depleted, or they could be injured by the slash of a sword. Gods bled like any mortal. Sekar appeared untouchable because he'd mastered Chaos, but he was as susceptible to a blade as she. Mother was everywhere and nowhere, unaffected by man. She was a vast resource for deities, but Syra couldn't solely rely on that. She was building skills in sight, sound, and smell—and most importantly, intuition.

Ice seeped into her pores, turning her hands numb, but she couldn't move and give herself away. She'd braided her hair down her back, trying to avoid any obvious giveaways—her red hair stood out like a sore thumb in this environment. They were dressed light—tunics, pants, belts, Death's Swords, and basic leather. They'd been doing this for a few days in a row, and she was currently losing. Zarek knew these woods like he'd lived in them for decades. She'd only won once—a mercy win—and she hoped to change that today. It was time to wipe that smug smile off his face.

Syra kept herself poised to run. Hands splayed wide on either side, muscles tense, she needed only a moment to get out from underneath this rock. Zarek weaponized his patience. If he waited long enough, sooner or later, she moved. That was how she'd gotten herself "killed" these last few days. Not again.

A twig snapped. Faint, but adrenaline filled her instantly. The sound had come from above. Without hesitation, she shoved herself free and ran. Avoiding the fallen branches was hard, and her boots smashed into a handful as she fled the scene. Zarek would have words about that later, but not before he admitted defeat.

Stealing a look behind, she saw movement. That was him. The Guardian slipped off behind a dense section of trees with trunks as wide as men. She slowed, breathing as steady and quiet as she could, but kept moving.

Syra took a sharp turn left and backtracked to where she'd originally been. The rocky portion gave her good opportunities to hide, and she had yet to attempt to trick him by returning to the same place. It was worth a shot.

She took care not to crunch the twigs beneath her feet. She kept to narrow paths reserved for wildlife, worn down and easy to use, listening to her surroundings and watching for any movement. Nothing. It was as if he were a ghost.

Back at the slab of rock she'd hidden under, she wasted no time and slipped beneath it again. She pressed her chest against the icy stone, her heart slamming itself against her ribs as she stuffed herself farther back.

Syra waited, tense. Her muscles started to protest. Zarek had to be close. Her hands were numb, her shoulders burned, and her ribs felt bruised. Nothing. Either he was toying with her, or she was getting close to winning the game.

Boots came into her line of sight, but they weren't where she was expecting. They were hanging. Annoyance filled her instantly. Zarek was sitting on the rock.

"Cozy down there?" he called.

No use in giving him the silent treatment. She'd wasted enough precious strength. Syra crawled out, sore, and shoved a rogue strand of hair behind her ear as she stood to face the Guardian. As usual, he looked pleased with himself. "How'd you know?"

"All criminals return to the place of the crime," he observed. He had his sleeves pushed up, and the Marking stretched across his forearms. "I expected a little better from you. That was pretty weak."

Syra crossed her arms, deflated and irritated. "Were you sitting here this whole time?"

"Almost." Zarek jumped off, bringing himself to his full height. "What did you learn today?"

And just like that, he was ready to scold her. "Patience is your weapon. You wait and let the enemy come to you."

The Guardian nodded. "Good observation. What else?"

She stared up at him, confused. "Don't return to the same place?"

"Don't ever assume."

Syra unclasped her sheath just as he pulled free Death's Sword. He swung without warning, and she ducked, unsheathing her weapon at the same time. Syra turned just in time to deflect, her bones jarring from the impact. Zarek was fighting with full strength.

As he delivered a series of blows, he said, "Don't ever assume you've got the upper hand. Don't ever assume you're cleverer than the enemy." He swung from the side, forcing Syra to sidestep. Leave it to the Guardian to try and kill her and call it training. Zarek never made it easy. Her foot twisted from the uneven ground, and she slipped off the rock. The fall was short, but it might as well have been from the ledge of a cliff. She landed with excruciating force against a trunk. Disappointment ripped through her, hard. Syra didn't even want to look Zarek in the face, so she closed her eyes.

She heard him approach and sheath his sword. "Know your surroundings, Syra. You will not always fight on flat ground or in an open field. The training rings are staged and intended for you to succeed. Out here, you are no better than the rabbit trying to outrun a predator."

But the training rings were where she'd gained so much confidence. She was better than ever before, able to hold her own against Zarek. They'd even earned themselves an audience on several occasions. That all seemed a lifetime away. She might as well have just picked up a sword with that reckless mistake.

"How's your foot?"

"It's fine," she mumbled. There was no pride in telling him that it felt bruised. She hadn't mastered Chaos—far from it—and she wasn't well equipped to handle a sword fight after this either. She was a mockery.

Zarek's presence didn't waver. She knew he was standing over her, waiting, but she wasn't ready yet. "Will I ever be ready?"

"What do you mean?"

He knew, but he wanted her to say it out loud. She knew Zarek well enough now to know when he was more interested in hearing her dig her own grave than settling whatever worries she had. "For everything. For holding my own in the Soul Realm, for protecting the realms, Shevana, all of it. When I was younger, they used to tell the children that Gods were invincible. They were the most powerful beings to exist, and yet"—she stretched her hands wide—"here I am."

"You're better off than you were two moons ago," he replied. "Gods aren't born all-knowing. If they were, there'd be hundreds of them. Chaos might deem a soul worthy, but that doesn't mean you have the knowledge to be successful."

"So the foolish and untrained Gods end up dead. Nice." His dry sarcasm was rubbing off on her. "And what happens when I come in contact with Dark Energy? I can't hold my own with a sword; I can hardly handle Chaos. If I encounter Dark Energy, I might as well tuck tail and run." All the irritation she felt was bleeding off her. They'd been given this time to train, and she was grateful for it, but it wasn't enough. Put her against anyone like Shevana or Henry, and she would be worthless. If Sekar was an enemy, it would be the shortest battle in Vorelian history.

The crunch of dirt met her ears as Zarek shifted. "Do you think so little of yourself?"

Dark Energy was far more dangerous than she'd realized. It was corrupted Chaos, as Sekar put it, capable of damaging a God's lifeforce and, in extreme circumstances, severing a God's connection with Chaos. Death. Before Sekar disappeared, he'd told her that Dark Energy, at its core, was the closest thing to Mother, but the souls bound to it—the restless dead—plagued the energy's purity. That included any beast, ritual, or object. If it was forged with Dark Energy, it was lethal. Any Harvester wild enough to mess with a force that not even the Gods would touch was damned.

"Hey." Syra opened her eyes and saw Zarek's outreached hand. "Come on. If we're late to Dryl's meeting again, he'll string us up."

At that, she sighed and grabbed his hand. Moping was over. Dryl was punctual. He hauled her up with ease, picking up her sword too. Syra sheathed it, sour about the turn of events. "Thank you," she mumbled.

"For what?" They started their long walk back to the Infernol. Syra ignored the bruised feeling in her foot. In her current mood, if it had been broken, she'd have kept walking to prove a point.

"For being patient with me."

Zarek didn't say anything at first. It wasn't often that she spoke like this with him, but she wanted him to know how much she appreciated his efforts.

Finally, he said, "In all this madness, it's nice to have a shoulder to lean on."

There Will Be War

A dozen men crowded Rhys's study, a space that fit five people at best. The stench of sweat failed to cover up the smell of the man Morei stood next to, who reeked as if he'd not bathed in days. The king of Caster glanced his way—tall, dirty, and unkempt. He shouldn't be so focused on this man's repulsive stench, but he could hardly think straight because of it. Ahead, leaning over the rich redwood desk, was the chancellor. His face was scrunched up, and a droplet of sweat rolled off his nose and onto the desk.

"Your Majesty," he said. The men around him parted, and Morei shuffled through to Rhys. He could have scolded the soldiers and commander for their blatant failure to give him his space, but that was not the type of king Morei was. He wanted his men to feel comfortable, bathed or not.

The king regarded Rhys. By the Gods, it was sweltering in this room, and it was only early morning. "Spit it out." The chancellor looked pale compared to his usual tan shade.

Rhys cleared his throat. "We've been threatened. Just a bit ago, I was summoned to the port, and when I arrived, a man was there. Pirate, obviously. He bore the Red Queens sigil on his hat, and he told me"—the chancellor looked like he wanted to crawl under the desk, a sight Morei didn't think was possible—"that time was up. I didn't know what he meant, and I tried to ask. Thought he'd lunge, so I drew my sword, but all he would say was that time was up." His amber eyes, so infuriatingly similar to Ezra's, met Morei's. "And then he slit his throat."

"No prisoners," Edwin mumbled from behind. "That's the way of the Red Queens."

Morei looked between the two. He'd been king of Caster for a *season*—three full moons—and now, he was faced with impending war on his front step. They'd discussed this already when he took the throne, that these pirates were upset because Drexis failed to keep his end of the deal, but he thought they'd resolved the issue. They'd sent a ship out to find the Red Queens and convey the message of a new king, hoping to meet. There'd been silence, but Rhys assured Morei that was normal. Out at sea, time moved differently. The chancellor was the proclaimed expert on pirates. He was an asset in that regard, and it was his confidence that pushed Morei to make a monumental decision in his first moon cycle here: the decision to conquer Ferguson.

The isolated kingdom had fallen within days of Caster's arrival. Morei didn't go—couldn't, under the strong advice of Rhys and the council because of the already unstable politics—but Edwin informed him that the king and queen had taken their own lives. Pathetic and unworthy of any respect, in Morei's opinion. A coward's way out of facing the new future. The Ferguson army hadn't even been prepared for the attack. Their daughter and son, too young to rule, were now under the parental care of their aunt, acting ruler. Queen Denesa was too old to start a war, and when he met her, he found her frail and dissociated. The Ferguson family was strained, complicated, and unreliable. Cousins refused to acknowledge their bloodline, declaring cursed lands, and Queen Denesa's son, Richard, was a councilmember. Probably the only one with a head on his shoulders—he actively tried to seek out Morei's acceptance through letters and invites. The king appreciated the gesture but was in no place to leave this city. Still, he'd extended the offer in return and was hopeful to finally meet Lord Richard soon.

Lady Lilly gladly took on the responsibility to sit on Ferguson's council. She was Lady Genesa's sister, having brought her on after hearing about her fierce nature. Having a Caster member was integral to keeping the control. The councilwoman was strong, and proven to be clever and cold—precisely what he needed. A small fraction of his army already lived in the northern city, reporting on any activity and teaching. Most of the Ferguson army was relieved to have any sort of structure and order. These men lacked proper training or guidance. A huge disappointment. Now he understood why Ferguson was so reclusive. Their swords were old, their armor chipped and rusted; their leather was cracked and falling apart. Promptly, he'd redirected Ferguson's finances into strengthening the army instead of the explorative campaigns they'd poured their coin into.

Few tried to run. Those who did were promptly killed. Morei wouldn't settle for prisoners or runaways.

Someone coughed, dragging the attention back to the obvious: the Festival of Seasons was days away. The event that would reaffirm his newfound title. Yet Rhys's encounter soured the excitement he'd felt just this morning. A dead man, no less a Red Queen, was grounds to halt all plans, but Morei couldn't. The chancellor and council had advised him early on that this was an iconic staple of the city's culture. People spent many moons preparing for this, sometimes for an entire summer. Cancel this and he risked losing the little loyalty he'd managed to earn, which was unstable but growing.

"How much time?" Morei asked. In the frenzy of the summoning, he saw that Isla was not among the crowd. She'd received the call, so where was she? Agitation flared. That was a mistake that would cost her. His trust in her commitment grew shallower by the day.

"Maybe a full moon, maybe two," the chancellor answered. "We don't know—"

"That's unacceptable," Morei snapped. "You're telling me this city lives and breathes for the sea, and you can't give me a prediction for an attack?"

"Your Majesty, the Red Queens are strategic," Edwin said. "That's exactly what they want."

The king swallowed his temper. In recent days, his violent impulses had returned with a vengeance, making it hard to concentrate. The ailment was worsening. "Then how do we predict? We can't go into this blindly, and we can't have men on guard for the next moon cycle. That would exhaust them and put the city on edge." He glanced at Rhys. The chancellor and he had come a long way, but they still were on guard with each other. He knew Rhys didn't trust him, and the same was true in return, but they needed each other to get what they both wanted. "You once told me a ship couldn't sail without its crew. You and these men are my crew, so tell me your best approach."

He wanted to do this. To place the responsibility on the chancellor. Rhys needed these moments almost as much as Morei needed to have control. It gave the chancellor purpose.

"Well." Rhys wagged his finger, lighting up. "Hold on." He opened a drawer and pulled a large scroll out. Immediately, Morei and the closest soldier helped clear the desk, setting almost everything on the ground next to their boots until Rhys had enough room to unroll the scroll. It was a map of the Merrél Sea with a level of detail that Morei had never seen before. Islands dotted the sea not accounted for on any world map, along with markings for where the currents were and the fastest travel routes. A circle was drawn north of the Caster coast with the word *vortex* written above it. This was a map for seamen, not the casual viewer.

Men leaned in from behind, and Morei got a strong whiff of body odor again. He wrinkled his nose and looked at the soldier who reeked. The man's mouth was decorated with sporadic silver teeth.

The chancellor pointed to a cluster of islands. "This is where I predict they're staying. This offers shelter from the harsh conditions and also gives them a place to restock any supplies, like meat. These islands are full of wildlife. This"—he pointed to the one closest to Caster—"is a steep volcanic mountain that stretches nearly a league. Nobody could see them if they sailed past the island."

"Or they could ambush," Morei observed. It was a good place to be.

"It's also likely what happened to our men," Rhys continued. "But we can't sail out there with an army. This is their territory. No land army would survive an attack at sea by the Red Queens. They know those waters better than any pirate. There's a reason they've ruled the waters for centuries. It's in their blood."

The king didn't like where this was going. "What are you suggesting?"

"Wait," the chancellor replied. "They'll come to us."

Edwin slammed his hand on the desk, startling everyone in the room. "No," he said, firm. "You don't know how many they're bringing. What if they bring ten ships? More? We'd be slaughtered."

"And what are you suggesting?" Rhys bit back. "Take our best ships and men and go out there to be massacred? They'd kill us before we even reached the island."

An argument started between the two men. Morei watched, appalled. The tension was immediate, saturating the room with a sticky heat that made a few soldiers shift uncomfortably. Edwin was determined to make his point clear about how he would command his men, while Rhys outright disregarded all royal code and overstepped to prove his opinion was better. Two wolves fighting over scraps of meat.

The king could see the soldiers eyeing him, waiting for his reaction. He wiped the sweat from his brow, hopeful the small act would gain their attention. When that didn't work, his anger won.

Morei was closest to Rhys, so he reached over and snatched the man by the collar of his blue tunic. The chancellor, startled, went to shove the hand away, but the king yanked him across the desk. Several remaining books went to the floor with a painful thud. The only thing keeping the chancellor upright was his iron grip on Morei's wrist. Edwin ceased all discussion.

"As much as I appreciate your passion, Chancellor, don't let it blind you." At that, he shoved Rhys back. Hot rage painted his face, turning his skin flush, but Morei didn't care. Rhys was temperamental, but he wasn't foolish.

The commander, however, was proud. Too proud for his own good, but Morei couldn't blame him. Edwin came from a line of well-respected warriors. "The same for you, Commander. I will not repeat myself."

An awkward beat of silence passed, but the king had his mind made up. "The chancellor is right. I will not pack up the men and send them off to the middle of the sea. We will prepare for the pirates to come here. Edwin, I want a report of all material, weapons, and the number of men readily available. I know our numbers aren't like they used to be, so don't give me that speech. I don't care if you gave me a report yesterday, I want a new one now. Give me your best strategies for creating a strong defense." He knelt and picked up the two books that had fallen. "You know what? Do a count on the Ly'rün too. We can utilize that for the defense."

His attention turned to the chancellor. "We need to warn the citizens but not make looming battle apparent. We have several options. We could withhold all information and leverage the surprise of the attack to our advantage. Villainize the Red Queens even more. Or we could post announcements around the city after the Festival of Seasons to ensure the citizens are aware that the city is in a defensive stance. If they wish to flee for the time, they can, and we will supply some of the funding for horses and wagons. If they choose to stay, that's their decision. Canceling is not an option. Preparations will need to be worked on around the festival. Your thoughts?"

Rhys opened his mouth, but Morei raised his hand.

"Great choice, Chancellor. We'll go with the second option. It shows loyalty to the citizens and reflects our priorities. Go ahead and get everything prepared. While you're at it, grab me a report of the city's finances. We can meet later to discuss the appropriate funding needed for the travel. I'll also trust you will pass the word to the council. As great as it would be to sit and chat, I'd rather gouge my ears out."

That earned him a few chuckles from the soldiers. The Caster council was a nightmare, and while Morei knew they were necessary, he couldn't stand most of them. They would back him. They had no choice.

Rhys's neck was flush. Morei wanted the chancellor to challenge him, to dig himself deeper into the hole he'd made, but he didn't. Shame.

"If there's nothing else, go," Morei ordered. Edwin nodded and turned without saying a word. The door opened, and men started to file out. It was hardly even early morning yet, and they were already under preparations. The king couldn't believe it. As much as he dreaded dragging this city into battle, he was thrilled to justify his burning impulse. He'd caged it since the day he took Drexis's life, knowing he would shatter any bit of trust if he slipped. But in war, there was no time to ask for forgiveness.

"Rhys," he said just as the man tried to leave the study, the last one out. His shoulders tensed as he slowly turned to face the king. "Close the door."

Rhys's jaw muscle twitched. Alone, the tension was palpable, and the king didn't make the first move to speak. He waited. The heavy silence didn't bother him—his goal was to get the chancellor to squirm.

But he didn't. He held Morei's gaze like a warrior staring Death in the face. It was honorable, and if the king hadn't been agitated by his outright disrespect for his title, he would have commented on it.

Speaking up the way he had without consideration for the king's presence was punishable.

"You can't replace me." The words were low. A bluff.

"I never said I did," Morei replied. "Do you think I'm that foolish?"

The question made the chancellor blink.

"You're impassioned, and I respect that," Morei continued, "but you're going to get your tongue cut out if you speak like that again while I'm in the same room. Do I make myself clear?"

Rhys chewed on his words. An inner battle was going on. "Spit them," Morei said. "Nothing you say will shock me."

They'd had their ongoing struggles since day one, and while the chancellor conformed to an active and engaging king, Morei knew he was trying to undermine him by acting outside his duties. Rhys felt he deserved more, but he had yet to prove that to Morei.

They were cordial, yes. But they were hardly friends.

Instead of speaking, Rhys reached over and shoved a decanter off its place on a small table. The glass shattered, spilling water, but neither man flinched.

"I hate my title. I hate being obligated to serve you. I am the man everyone forgets about. The man who does everything for people like you but with no recognition. People like you get all the praise, but all you do is run around and give a few orders." His voice rose as he spoke. Morei had known this day would come, but he was still surprised at the amount of anger. "You say a few things, and they hang on your every word. I could stand here and give a speech, and everyone would forget it by supper. Because I'm not a *king*." The word came out like he was repulsed by it.

"No," Morei answered, "it's because you're forgettable."

His face twisted into shock, then fury. It was the truth, though, and the king didn't care about the chancellor's emotions.

"You whine, complain, but you won't work for the respect you so desperately crave. You want power? Control? Then stop sneaking around like a spineless thief and stand up for your decisions. Work for it. Prove your worth to me, and I'll make sure the entire world knows your name for centuries. But if you can't, and you want to continue to sneak around behind my back, then I'll make sure this entire city knows what kind of scum you are."

They had bigger problems to deal with, and Rhys was having an identity crisis. Morei could care less, so long as the man fulfilled his word on what was requested, and the king knew he would. Rhys was too proud to ignore anything assigned to him.

Morei was determined to find Isla before his next appointment. She had abandoned her order, which irritated him more than this poor attempt of a man. But he wanted the chancellor to know just how much he was always watching.

He lowered his voice. "You are still working behind my back, and you really think I don't know about it. You want to know why *Ivory* was docked without being searched by my men? It's because I allowed it." The fire keeping Rhys fighting died. "Your trading with the illegal market does not concern me, Chancellor, but it's how you do business."

Fingers trailed the desk with meticulous care. The king knew he had Rhys by the throat. He'd been waiting for this moment, patient. One never attacked unless they were fully prepared, and Morei had an arsenal of information.

"I know your pockets are full of illegal coin, Rhys. I also know that you have forged documents under my name to get shipments delivered with the palace's finances." Morei let each word sink in, speaking slower and slower until he was certain the dead could hear him. Rhys looked like caught prey, frozen in disbelief but too proud to admit defeat. No matter. Morei didn't want to kill the chancellor just yet. He needed time—and Rhys's knowledge of the sea.

"So, you tell me you hate your title, that you want more, that you *deserve* so much more, but do you?" The king was genuinely interested in where he got his logic. "You should consider yourself lucky that I find your petty crimes amusing rather than insulting. I should publicly execute you. The people would remember you then."

The chancellor didn't reply, his tongue caught in whatever sludge he was stewing up. Morei was baffled. To finally speak as he had, and Rhys couldn't even admit to his crimes. Slamming his fist on the desk, he raised his voice and demanded, "Do you? Do you believe you deserve so much more after how much you've undermined me?"

Rhys looked anywhere but at the king. "It won't happen again."

Morei scoffed. "Come now, Chancellor, at least be an honest thief. Don't lie to me about your intentions." Rhys's Adam's apple rose and fell—pitiful. The chancellor knew his actions were against city law and was ashamed of being caught. "Look at me like the man you want to be." It was not a request he would make again.

Tension turned each movement into slow motion. The chancellor finally met his deathly gaze. "There he is," Morei remarked in a cold whisper. "The man who wants to be king. Your actions are unforgivable and insulting to the Caster name, but I will not do anything about it. You want to know why?" Rhys didn't give any answer. "Because a criminal is always a criminal, Rhys. The next time you work behind my back, think about this conversation. I will not tell you twice how I deal with thieves." He pointed to the door. "Go, before I cut your fingers off one by one."

The chancellor didn't move right away, but when he did, he bolted. Rhys mumbled something about being better, but the king didn't acknowledge it. He knew whatever the chancellor said was for show. Rhys wouldn't change. He couldn't. Much like how Morei couldn't change how much he adored the final glimmer of life he saw when Death took her next victim. But he could remind Rhys who was in charge.

Morei stood there, reining in his emotions. It would do no good to lash out at Isla when he went to find her. The woman was a thorn in his side, constantly poking at his patience. The princess's obligations were laughable, and she needed to start prioritizing where she put her time. He could only tell her so much. If she continued to fail to show up when she was supposed to, he would have to consider finding someone else more capable of the duties of a queen.

He fumbled with his pocket, needing to ensure it was still there. Sure enough, his fingers brushed against the cool metal. The Lirallian Ring was a relic he'd failed to harness, too uncertain about what might be waiting for him on the other side, but he still kept it close. Morei feared this ring would be used for all the wrong reasons if it ended up in the enemy's hands—while with it in his, he could do whatever he saw fit.

Destined for Worse

Syra and Zarek walked back to the Infernol, making no effort to rush. Based on the sun's position, they still had a bit of time before they would be late. The hidden organization was tucked up in the Mourale Mountains. People from all over the Vore World called the Infernol home. Some had come there to seek refuge after the fall of the Lirallian Empire, starting families and raising generations of Infernol members. Others still lived beyond the Mourale Mountains, acting as agents and reporting what they observed—people as far north as Kalic. These mountains had housed thousands for centuries, but Dryl intended for that to change once Raveer was taken. The Infernol needed resources, and if they didn't take Raveer, Liral would.

Small entrances were scattered, and one could only gain access if they knew where to look. A series of knocks against a gray slab of rock, or finding the trapdoor covered by fallen trees. The Infernol were clever, going as far as to utilize hawks to send messages. Syra now often referred to their home as a city—a small and hidden one—but it lacked the charm of one. Cities were stationary, surrounded by stunning landscapes, and while the Infernol had remained in one location for centuries, they were an order away from packing up and leaving. Dryl constantly reminded her of that.

"Would you stay?" she asked, breaking up the crunching of boots.

Zarek raised his brow. "Here?"

"Yes."

"In a different life, perhaps. You?"

"I'd miss the sea." Syra took in the expansive trees and the birds that hopped from one branch to the next. "It's beautiful, though."

The Guardian was quiet for a moment. "Have you had any dreams lately?"

The question didn't need to be explained. Zarek was asking about Morei, the dreaded king, one of the many reasons she struggled to find peace. Knowing he was out there, dangerous, made her restless. Sekar had been so angry at her because of what she'd been able to do. Knowing what she did now about Dark Energy and its effects, she understood his response. The God had made sure to train her better, gave her more control over Chaos by building up barriers in her mind to sleep at night. Dream walking could happen because Mother interacted with her while she slept, twisting visions into realities. With that training, Morei had disappeared.

Syra wanted to believe the best in Sekar. That was all she'd done for almost a season, but this was the longest they'd gone without seeing each other. The God didn't just vanish. Everything was intentional to him, and try as she might, she couldn't justify his actions. He'd promised to train her in exchange for her company, then fled once she'd grasped Chaos. Yet whenever the Guardians questioned her about it, she feigned acceptance.

On top of that, they had the realm fracture, which was causing energy fluctuations and strange occurrences. That was why this all had begun in the first place. "No," she answered. "Nothing. Just like yesterday."

The Guardian wasn't perturbed. "But your dreams are still . . ."

"Odd," she finished. "Vivid. Like I'm living memories from someone else's life."

"The energy fluctuations are becoming more extreme," Zarek said. "We're closer to the fracture, so are more exposed to those ramifications. Creitón probably won't feel anything for another few moons." That was the best they'd come up with. Trying to track down any knowledge proved almost impossible. This had never been seen before, so everything was based on theory. "I tried to harvest energy this morning. One moment, I couldn't even reach Light Energy. The next, I was drowning in it. We will have to let Dryl know, so that there can be an announcement. Harvesters will get themselves killed in no time."

Syra bit her lip and avoided a rock jutting out from the ground. "I've been thinking about something, and I want to hear your thoughts." She knew better than to bring a half-assed theory forward to this man. When she'd found time, she'd gone through what they'd collected thus far. Parchments with detailed notes, others with half-finished phrases, some old stories that dated back to the country's founding, and others. "We keep saying the realm fracture is causing Chaos to come into the living, to disrupt all the energies. But what if it was the opposite?"

Zarek slowed to a stop. She had his attention, and fueled with that, she continued, "Chaos devours all living things. We know this. That can't change." She knelt, needing to show him. With her finger, she started to draw three poorly constructed circles in the melting snow, overlapping. "Our realms are all connected somehow. Call it a veil or whatever, but this veil acts as our barrier. It keeps each realm exactly where it needs to be—the perfect recipe, right?" She looked up to see Zarek nod. She pointed to the circles. "But this realm fracture disrupts that recipe, and now our results are varying. If it's not Harvesters having problems, it's wildlife migrating south or unstable weather patterns. If this is happening to the living, then it's possible this is happening to the Soul Realm too."

He opened his mouth, but she held up her hand. "I know what you're going to say. The Soul Realm is already dying because of Ön'grusah. But does that mean it can't suffer from the same symptoms that the living is suffering from?"

Now, he tilted his head. Syra swept dirt over the circles and started fresh. Ön'grusah. The word still left a bitter taste on her tongue. Zarek had only recently told her about the sickened energy, tampered with by demons after they managed to combine Dark and Light Energy. The Guardians had been watching Ön'grusah for centuries, unsure how to resolve it and lacking resources. It was the primary reason the realm was the way it was—dead and blackened.

"I think our realms are much differently placed." Carefully, she drew the circles atop one another and then pointed to the top. "This is Chaos. The Gray Realm. Mother. The next is the Soul Realm, but notice how it overlaps with both Chaos and the living? It's also closer to the Gray Realm, which would explain why it's suffered the way it has in recent centuries. And now"—she pointed to the bottom—"we're next. Farthest from the Gray Realm, it has been able to avoid some of these issues, but not anymore, and I think it's because the realm fracture cuts through both realms, straight into the Gray Realm." She drew a line right through all three circles to prove her point and looked at Zarek.

The Guardian gave a single nod. He wanted her to continue.

"We theorized originally that the Gray Realm was pushing into this realm, but what if it was sucking life out?" Syra placed her finger onto the bottom circle. "As it draws life from this realm, that energy is dragged through the Soul Realm, disrupting an already fragile realm, and then finally into the Gray Realm. It's a crazy idea, I know, but it's plausible. Nobody knows exactly how Chaos functions, so we can't say whether she draws in or expands. All we know is that high fluctuations of Chaos cause massive disruptions to the behavior of Dark and Light Energy."

She fell quiet, biting the inside of her cheek. The idea was hardly complete, but it was a start. Zarek, like many others, was persistent in the belief that Chaos expanded and that the realms didn't overlap as she now displayed. Yet their behavior and structure had never been investigated before—there was never a need. Her theory was the first of its kind.

"So how do you explain the energy fluctuations the living realm is experiencing?" Zarek asked. No judgement or doubt.

"As life is sucked out of this realm," she replied, "Light and Dark Energy have less to cling on to. We know those energies make up the living and the souls locked here. But what we can't explain yet is their relationship without those. My guess is that souls are also considered some form of life to Chaos, so as she draws in to feed, Light and Dark Energy lose their bonds. This creates their volatility, which causes the fluctuations we're now seeing."

"And being that everything is connected in some way to energy, those fluctuations cause imbalances and odd behaviors," Zarek observed.

"Like the migrations, or even the strange behavior with the mice we saw the other day."

The Guardian scratched his face. This was the first time she'd seen him so interested in anything she had to say on the matter. "You mention the fracture starts in the Gray Realm. That would mean that to close this, we would have to go to the source." He sounded concerned.

Syra stood. "I know." This was the part she wasn't so sure about. "I haven't gotten too far on this part yet. The Gray Realm isn't like the others." She recalled her experience, remembering the orange hues and the charged feeling in the air. "I don't think the methods would be the same. But I do think there's a fracture in each realm. A connection point, so to speak. Or some varying level of disturbance in this veil that defines our realm that it would be easy to see or feel."

She waited for him to reply, but Zarek just stood there, arms crossed, studying her. His expression rested between annoyed and thoughtful, like he couldn't decide if she was hallucinating or on to something. Syra's cheeks grew warm, not because she was embarrassed, but because she was growing increasingly nervous about what he might say. This theory would change everything they thought they knew about the realms and the behavior of energy.

"Is it that bad?" she mumbled. Syra stepped away from the Guardian, trying to collect her thoughts. She was on to something. All her studying hadn't been for nothing. The realms were all anyone could talk about. Well, all Dryl, Bane, Zarek, and she could, at least. The Infernol commander, under Dryl's approval, oversaw and participated in the conversations. From the day Dryl showed back up, he'd been a part of their discussions. He was, to her knowledge, the only mortal to know what was really going on beyond just war and politics. How he managed to sleep at night was beyond her. She barely could when so much was happening.

Maybe the theory was stretching it too far. Maybe the realms didn't have to be positioned a certain way for this result. "Look, I think I got carried away."

Turning, she opened her mouth, but she stopped as Zarek's face dropped. She knew that look.

The winds shifted, bitter after the welcoming warmth of the day. The hairs along her arms stood on end, alert. A warning. Syra felt the cold sting of metal plunge its teeth into her back. The blade twisted, and agony blossomed across her chest, burning a path right down to her toes and fingers. Syra tried to gasp but found the air refused to enter. She reached desperately for the protruding weapon, but she couldn't find it. Someone kicked her knees in, sending her to the ground. Iron and gritty dirt coated her mouth, and broken branches poked her cheek. Kicking outward, she hoped to land a hit on the attacker but instead felt a boot connect with ribs. The weapon was yanked free from her back, merciless. Her whole body lurched, but when she tried to move, another boot settled onto her back, right where her injury was.

Everything was happening too fast. Zarek took one step, freeing Death's Sword. "This isn't necessary." In her panic, he still sounded as calm as the day they met. The Guardian moved toward her, but an arrow burrowed itself right above his heart, slick and black. The Guardian fumbled for it with one hand, never revealing any shock, but as he ripped the arrow out, a hooded figure dropped from the tree above.

Pale blue skin flashed underneath the iconic Guardian cloak. Syra's strength ceased, and terror turned her body into a statue. Zarek never stood a chance. The ambush was calculated, quick, without mistakes. The Guardian pulled free a short yellow blade and dragged it right across his neck. Zarek dropped instantly, landing hard against a slab of melting ice.

"No, no, no—" Adrenaline surged, forcing her to life. She rolled and kicked, ignoring the agony that seared the muscles of her back apart with every movement. Reaching for Zarek, she barely had a hand around his arm before she was dragged back like she weighed nothing. The sudden motion made her head spin, and she blinked furiously. That wasn't right. Her hands doubled, blurred; the ground swayed as she tried to get up again. Syra's vision turned gray. She tried to speak but found her tongue no longer obeyed. Her arms failed, and she collapsed face-first into the dirt. The last thing she saw was a black boot.

Leather and Sand

Cyrus admired the lapping waves. They dragged the sand back into the Warón Sea, only to spit it out moments later. Above, the sun was gaining strength as the morning aged, and the air was thick with the salty stench of the sea. Cyrus came to the beach frequently for the peace it offered. Housed in the palace of Delion, he was constantly inundated with staff, soldiers, and councilmembers who wanted his opinion, asked questions, or stared. Despite King Alaric's attempt to normalize Cyrus's presence, people still found a way to creep into his personal space. He'd learned to live with it, but that didn't mean he accepted this new way of living.

People from all over brought gifts. Cyrus hated it. He'd confessed to Alaric that he didn't want the gifts, and the king found a way to give them away without being obvious. He'd kept one—a new dark leather belt engraved with dragon scales—but nothing else. Cyrus had spent his life poor. The less he had, the more comfortable he was. That didn't stop Alaric from ensuring Cyrus had a new wardrobe with custom-fitted attire—boots, gloves, greaves, and bracers included. The leather was all engraved with different sigils from the Old Tongue. The bracers were fitted with short horns, a reference to dragons, and all layered to look like scales. His greaves were similar, though without the horns.

When Cyrus was first given these items, he refused them in front of the entire council. Alaric looked horrified, and Cyrus realized he'd spoken prematurely. He was not an expert at politics, but he was learning as fast as he could. That day, he learned that speaking out against the king was disrespectful. In private, it was fine, but not in front of the council.

When he wasn't the one asking a hundred questions and boring the king, he was stuck in the palace library with his nose in a book. Cyrus had read more in the last season than he'd read in his whole lifetime before. Anything he could find regarding Vorelian history, Dragon Riders, tales of beasts, and energy harvesting, he grabbed from the shelf and sat with at one of the many tables. One book, *The Lost Dragon*, spoke more in mythical nonsense than anything insightful, but a section of it broached the Rider Federation. It was just a few sentences—something called "Vinfali" was mentioned, but that was it. Curious, he'd spent far too much time trying to find anything else with that term with no luck. It was likely nothing, but next to Hyle, it was the closest thing to a world lost to him. The age of the Dragon Riders.

He reached over and dabbed more oil onto the cloth. The saddle that had been custom-fitted to Sozar was overdue for an oil. The leather master told him that if he hoped to reuse most of the leather once Sozar got larger, he had to take care of it. Cyrus was trying to do so now, but he wasn't skilled in this field. Jule had shown him how, but sitting here now, he knew he wasn't doing it right. A visit to the leather master was coming, he knew, and he could only imagine the disappointment on the old man's face once he realized how poor Cyrus's oil technique was.

Sozar lay in the lapping waves, partially in the water, partially out. The dragon was content with that position, and Cyrus teased him. A lack of commitment—the dragon didn't know what he wanted. Sozar only snorted, sending smoke upward. The dragon had grown so much in the passing season. He was approaching his first summer, which made Cyrus's stomach twist. The life he'd known so well as a miner was beyond his reach.

His harvesting skills were improving every day. His ability to connect to the energy around him intensified with his bond with Sozar. Hyle had told him that. A Rider who was also a Harvester was a dangerous combination, and it was important to identify the boundaries. The God explained that it was easy to draw on the dragon's lifeforce, but that didn't protect him from the consequences of overexertion.

A faint sound of sand crunching caught his attention, and he stopped what he was doing. Sozar blinked lazily. Whoever was coming wasn't a concern. That didn't mean Cyrus was eager for company, though. Alaric was speaking to tradesmen; he was not due for sword training anytime because he'd long since graduated from the daily rituals of that, so he couldn't think of anyone who might want his attention now.

Hyle. The word echoed through Cyrus's mind. He looked at Sozar, feeling the dragon's affection for the God. This man was their closest thing to a mentor, father, brother, and Dragon Rider. Dameon was crooked, twisted by a sick dream of war, and for that, Cyrus pitied him. That was no way to li ve.

The God settled into the sand to his left. The man looked no older than forty, but his silver gaze, decorated with the ghastly scar that cut over his right brow and cloudy eye, made him look centuries old. Hyle was dressed plain, even for a God, looking more like a commoner who worked the fields daily than a man born for the throne.

"It's peaceful here," Hyle said. He was cross-legged and wore boots that looked older than Cyrus. No weapons were present.

"You haven't been around," he replied. It had been a least a full moon since he'd seen the God. Without Hyle, he felt a bit like he was walking blind. The Rider-turned-God grounded him in this storm that was now his life. So many people wanted to use Cyrus and Sozar for their political statement, their strength, their reputation—even Alaric wanted something from him despite his kindness and offered sanctuary—but not Hyle.

The God inhaled deeply, the sound loud compared to the lapping waves. "I've been busy." He looked over at Cyrus, who knew he wouldn't get more information than that. "How have you been?"

A simple question, but Cyrus knew the real meaning. He loosened his grip on the cloth and saddle. "I still see him every night when I dream. Just standing there, holding that book." At the mention of Henry Junok, he grimaced. There would come a time when he needed to face that undead false God, but hopefully not soon.

"Have you considered that was what Henry wanted?" Hyle asked. "To scare you?"

"Of course," Cyrus countered. "But I can't help but think this is all some ploy. Like he's let me sit here."

Hyle raised his brow. "And have you just sat here?"

The sarcastic tone did not go unnoticed. "Well, no—"

"You've trained harder than ever before," the God replied. "You can harvest energy and swing a sword, and you have an extensive knowledge base on this world. You are more dangerous now than you were a season ago. Is that what you think Henry wanted?"

Cyrus pursed his lips, knowing the expected answer. Reluctantly, he spat, "No." When Hyle didn't say anything more, he added, "Then what did Henry expect? Me to sit around and carve wooden statues with a dagger?"

That made Hyle laugh, which made him look centuries younger. "Of course not. You know that. Henry knows you're doing everything you can to understand this war you've been thrown into. He expects it, I have no doubt. But what he won't anticipate is your motivation."

Cyrus's attention turned back to the oil project he was failing at. He started to rub the cloth against the leather again, watching the Old Tongue sigils shimmer under the new coat of oil. "Motivation still gets you killed," he muttered.

Silence. One so thick he felt he couldn't move. "Are you afraid to die?"

Such a direct question was not out of the ordinary for the God, but Cyrus was startled at his hesitation. He'd never thought of death so directly before. Sure, he'd been close to Death's embrace several times, but in the moment, he'd just wanted the agony to stop.

"I'm afraid that I won't be able to do everything I want," he answered. "Does that satisfy?"

The God raised his brow. "And what is it that you want to do?"

"Explore," he said. "Without being hunted or wanted. I want to see the Vore World." He wanted to see Zorya again. Wanted to apologize for the way he left things, make everything right, and clear his conscience, but that motive was between him and the sea that lay ahead. Nobody needed to know just how sorry he was for abandoning Razan to Dameon and Ashtir.

"Admirable." Hyle wasn't dismissive. "The more we know, the more attuned we are to those around us. What if I told you there was a chance for that?"

Cyrus's hesitated on the leather once more. "A chance to explore?"

"A chance for that freedom to explore," Hyle corrected.

He nodded slowly, unsatisfied. "Then I would say that you are trying to tell me something I don't want to hear."

"You learn fast," Hyle replied with amusement. "There is someone here who wants to speak with you."

Cyrus tried to stifle his discontentment. "Who?"

"You are the birth of a new era. While you might want to reject that and sit here poorly oiling your saddle like you've stuck your head in the sand, the world has awoken thanks to you and Sozar."

Even in the insult, the God was well spoken. The words were a cold slap to Cyrus, and he swallowed his humiliation. He'd run, escaped Geral, flown across the world, he'd survived Raj Delion and even exchanged words with Henry, but here he was, begrudgingly accepting the company of a God who had done nothing but help him. Simply because he'd finally gotten a sliver of normalcy in these passing moons.

"I'm sorry," he managed to say. "I didn't mean to sound like I'm ungrateful."

Hyle nodded. "I know. You never asked for any of this, and yet so many of us expect you to embrace this path like you were born for it. The tales of heroes never tell us just how reluctant that hero was to become who he needed to be."

Cyrus chewed on those words. Hyle hadn't pressed him on the matter of the Rider Federation or this talk of destiny, just guided and trained him when he was around. Told him tricks for when he rode Sozar, and even advised the dragon on several strategies for optimal speed and recovery during a fall.

He rubbed the cloth into the leather a bit harder, knowing he needed more oil but too annoyed to reach for it. Instead, he channeled all his emotion into the action. "Who is this person?"

"From Venkar City," Hyle said without missing a beat. "Her people have waited for you for a long time."

That made his motions slow. "Me?"

"Sozar too." The God winked. "He is the whole reason a Rider exists, after all." In response, the dragon snorted, and Cyrus could feel the smugness radiate off him in waves.

Keep it together, Cyrus commented dryly.

"When the Rider Federation fell, Riders struck a deal with Venkar. Information was shared, and the royal family promised to protect what was given to them until the time was right." Hyle motioned at Sozar. "That time is now. They have come to learn about you two."

Cyrus licked his lips, suddenly parched from the nerves. "Vikter?" He was careful about when to bring up the Rider that Hyle seemed so fond of, but he wanted more details. He was starved for them.

In response, the God motioned for his items. "You're doing it wrong," he scolded lightly. "Let me show you."

Relieved to be shown, Cyrus passed the large saddle over, along with the oil and cloth. Hyle got into a similar position, with the leather propped up on the legs, and then poured a bit of oil on the cloth before he started a slow circular motion. "Oiling leather is a test of patience," Hyle explained. "You learn to appreciate the silence of the task rather than rush it. The process takes time, and it's important to show the same level of care for every spot. Where leather meets scale, check for cracks." He set the cloth down and did so, his fingers moving with the ease of an expert. Hyle stretched and folded the leather in ways that made Cyrus's heart stop, certain he was going to tear it. "The slightest crack can be devastating on a long flight or fight." As he folded one of the straps, he ran a finger over the exposed tan leather, searching for any abnormalities. When it was obvious he was satisfied, he picked up the cloth again and started the same motions.

The silence between them grew. Cyrus fought for the right response, but none came. This was the closest he'd come to learning more about the Dragon Riders, and he was paralyzed.

Hyle sensed the trouble unraveling in his head. "Vikter was one of the Riders to strike a deal with Venkar. In time, you will come to know his story but only when it is right." He dabbed more oil on the cloth. "Vikter hated oiling his stuff. Used to drive the leather master mad. Always enjoyed the result, not the process. The Ny-gals would scold him because he would have the most rundown boots and saddle in a parade of Riders. Looked like a misfit among everyone else." Hyle chuckled, living a memory with Cyrus as a bystander. "The council finally decided to keep an extra saddle for Aythen and boots aside for just occasions."

Sozar hadn't spoken this whole time, a rarity for the dragon. Cyrus glanced over to ensure he was still there. Sozar blinked back, sensing his curiosity.

He lives in a world that has forgotten his name, the dragon mused. *The people know him for what the stories say, but nothing more. The least we can do is listen.*

I sense it is more than that for you, Cyrus countered gently. The dragon held a clear respect for Hyle.

"The woman who awaits you is from the royal family that have ruled Venkar for over one thousand summers. She is the youngest of the family, so she has taken on the role of ambassador, as her brother is due to accept the leadership title. Her older sister is promised to one of the White Horns."

The last part surprised him. "Pirates have arranged marriages?"

"Only the more respectful ones." Hyle examined the saddle in more detail, scanning the seat and the leather flaps where his legs rested. "This leather looks a bit aged."

Being scrutinized by the God wasn't what he'd hoped for. Cyrus stomached the shame festering in his chest. "Is she here now?"

Hyle beamed, proud. "She's on the alcove, waiting for you."

Startled, he swung around in his seat to see for himself. Sure enough, a dark-skinned woman covered in white tribal markings and dressed in gray leather stood there. Her black hair was braided down either side of her face, and when she saw him, she waved. Respectfully, he gave a wave in return and turned back.

You are no help, Cyrus told Sozar.

The dragon yawned and flashed rows of sharp incisors. *I saw them coming.*

No help. Cyrus turned his attention back to the God next to him. "You want me to go talk to her now?"

Hyle raised his brow and offered the cloth. "Unless you wish to do this?"

With a wave, he stood. When Sozar made no motion to follow, Cyrus shook his head. "Let me do the hard work," he commented, unable to keep the affection from his words. The dragon had a way of wiggling his way into his heart even when he was being stubborn.

"Do you remember what I told you on this very shore?"

Cyrus paused. He couldn't forget. Never would. "That whatever decision I make, I do it for Sozar. No life is worth living if it is alone."

The God nodded and turned back to the saddle. Their discussion was over. Cyrus let the sand suck his boots in, now more aware of the pull and tug as he moved to sturdier land. Ahead, Destiny awaited.

A Dagger and Silk

Morei despised mornings like this, where everything felt out of control. The Red Queens had sent a clear threat that he couldn't ignore, and now he was hunting down Isla Caster, the woman to whom he'd promised the opportunities of royalty, but who'd failed to show up after being summoned.

If she intended to be respected at all, Isla needed to start acting like a Caster. Everything reflected on him, so when she failed to show, the soldiers and council looked to him. He could do nothing in those situations but politely ignore the obvious: Isla was disrespecting his title.

The woman learned fast, he couldn't deny that. She had taken to her studies with incredible success. Isla asked all the right questions, made the right observations, and even made suggestions about historical events that could have been avoided if one action or the other had been taken. In their last session, she'd figured out that the strategic flaw in the Battle of Pearls was a lack of communication the night before between the king, commander, and army. The failure cost Saveen an entire fleet of ships, ships carrying enough gems to fund a generation. Now, those precious jewels lay at the bottom of the Merrél Sea. She even made several strong observations about the Ferguson family, including Queen Denesa's unwillingness to rule.

Morei knew that the council still held reservations about her because of their traditions—the princess was a firstborn, and as a woman, that made her bad luck in Caster culture. The longer he sat on this throne, the more he r-eflected on one of his first encounters with Emerald, when she'd declared that Caster possessed a daughter. At the time, he'd never believed her—no public records backed those claims—but now he wondered how she'd gotten the information. He'd failed to leverage her connections. Regardless, Morei was determined to prove them wrong. When Isla put her mind to something, she was impressive. When she boldly disregarded his orders, he wanted to stab her and leave her for dead on the shore for the crows. He'd done everything he could to keep his violent tendencies chained, but it was times like this that threatened to ruin the delicate façade he'd built.

He'd already faced challenges about having her reinstated. Even after the official declaration, some councilmembers, like Lord Varun and Lord Cayden, were adamant that placing Isla on the throne was a bad omen. The last time he'd seen them, after insults were thrown, he'd threatened to remove anyone who refused to change their mindsets. That had resulted in Isla getting up and leaving in tears. She didn't possess the backbone yet for politics, but Morei believed she could have one in time.

That was also the last time he'd seen the princess, and the more he thought about it, the more he was certain her avoidance was due to the council's behavior.

He turned the corner and saw a maid he recognized. Talia, he believed. Startled, she quickly greeted him.

"Have you seen Isla?" he asked.

She blinked and repositioned the basket in her hands, which was full of fresh grapes plucked from the garden behind the courtyard. "I saw her a bit ago. She was in the courtyard with an older gentleman. Sir Grayson, I believe."

Morei would never admit it, but there was a charm about the staff here that was far different from Geral. Both were friendly, but something special about the Caster staff caught his attention early on. They looked out for one another, had generations of family involved with the duties, and were quicker to treat Morei like a person than the staff he'd been raised by in Geral. Here, he felt at home, even if he was still an outsider.

"Thank you." He gestured at the grapes. "May I?"

"These? Of course." Talia offered him the basket, and he plucked a small strand of green grapes up. "If you don't mind me asking, Your Majesty, I haven't seen your bird in a while. Is everything okay?"

He nearly flinched at the question. Reyd. Eazon. Whichever the God preferred to be called, though Morei preferred to call him a waste of space. He hadn't been around for at least a moon cycle, and Morei wasn't sure if he was grateful or annoyed. The God's presence was of no benefit to him. Eazon didn't offer knowledge, advice, or anything. When he was around, he drank Kendell's Milk and bugged Morei. A leech. The king tried to get answers out of the God, like why he was there in the first place, but Eazon always avoided them. Morei didn't believe it was solely for entertainment like Eazon originally told him. In raven form, the God had quickly earned the affection of everyone in the palace. Many of the staff members, like Talia, brought him crackers and fruits, thinking he was just a bird. Nobody knew who he really was.

He pulled a grape free. "He's wild. Don't know what he sees in me, but he shows up every now and then. If he returns, I'll let you know." At that, he ate the fruit. The flavor was incredible. Geral's desert climate hadn't allowed the growing of grapes. Most of the fruit was imported from Diemon and elsewhere, but in Caster, everything was grown right in the city.

Talia looked disappointed, but he didn't wait long enough to discuss it further. He moved past her, bidding her farewell. As he walked, he ate the grapes, looking around. Pillars of marble, grand paintings of battles at sea across the ceiling, statues of ancient beasts and wolves, and large open regions where he could see the Merrél Sea. The marble floor was garnished with the gold wolves he'd seen the first time he stepped foot in this palace. That day felt leagues from this moment, but still within reach. All of it was under threat, and he hardly felt like he had his feet under him to manage it. Kingdoms he could grasp, but pirates were a breed of merciless warrior he wasn't accustomed to. Lacking information on them irritated him, but his mind had been elsewhere, such as scavenging for every book possible about dream walking. Syra still managed to live in his head, and it drove him mad. Whenever he had a chance, he'd tried to recreate the connection, but he hadn't succeeded.

At the entrance of the courtyard, he found her. Dressed in a flowy, pale green dress, she looked more like a commoner than royalty. Isla's hair was tied up in a bun with loose strands framing her face, and grime smeared her cheek from whatever she was doing. In her hands, she carried some dirty rags. She didn't look like a princess. She looked like a maid and smelled like she'd been rolling around in soiled hay. *This* was what she'd prioritized over the meeting.

"What is this?" Morei asked. Already, anger dripped from him. This was the third time he'd caught her since she was reestablished as royalty. She'd promised him this would stop.

Isla stared, mouth agape. "I was—I was helping Sir Grayson."

"And ignoring your summoning?"

"His barn hand, Paol, was sick. I offered." The tension of their last argument still mingled between them. He'd snapped at her for being so weak in the face of the council. In her studies, she excelled, but when in front of the council or soldiers, she struggled to maintain any authority or confidence. It was like talking to two different people sometimes.

"I don't care if a barn hand is sick, or if the stalls need to be cleaned by the dead. If I summon you, you come," Morei snapped. Someone walked by, and he could hear their footsteps speeding up as they passed. He gestured at her. "You look like you've been rolling in shit. You're royalty. I expect you to act like it."

Her cheeks were flush, her sea-blue eyes hard. "You can't expect me to throw away everything I know. It's impossible."

"And what is that, Isla? Enlighten me." This was escalating faster than he intended, but he couldn't stop himself. Seeing this woman stand here, ignoring her bloodline, while someone like Rhys walked around as a proud criminal with a title he didn't deserve—it infuriated him. If she didn't appreciate the second chance, then he would give it to someone who would. Isla was ruining his reputation by acting this way.

"Helping people!" she yelled. The intensity made him flinch. She'd never raised her voice at him. *Ever*. "You expect me to be like you? You expect me to walk away from the people I've spent my entire life helping? If that's the cost of your title, I don't want it."

When she tried to walk past him, he grabbed her arm and shoved her back. They weren't done. Isla stumbled. If she wanted to play tough, he would.

"Helping people is one thing. Ignoring orders is another," he stated. "You ignored the summoning to do servant work. I don't ask miracles of you, and I don't impede on your personal time. You've exceeded in your studies and continue to show me that you can think between those ears, but you cannot disobey me. That I will not tolerate."

He liked Isla as a person. He'd already seen what she was capable of in such a short time, and he knew she would make a fine queen one day, but not like this. Politically, that would be the next step to strengthen his rule. A queen didn't clean stables or do staff work. A queen appeared in the city and offered resources. She helped take care of the city's safety.

Isla's chest rose as she sucked in a large breath of air. "You know nothing about helping people." The words were callous, supposed to be cruel. "You are so busy trying to prove you're some great king when all you've done is throw this city into shambles."

That struck a nerve. "The taxes are lower than they've been in decades. Crime has dropped and continues to do so, taking Ferguson has given the people faith, and you want to tell me I'm hurting this city? You know what's hurting it? This." He motioned between the two of them. "Because I'm too busy finding you to get anything done. If you're so desperate to be a maid, then I'll let you. But you'll have to make a public announcement about it. We're days away from the festival, so I'll have to choose another dance partner because I'm not dancing with a *maid*. That's against tradition."

The princess's hands tightened on the bundle of rags. She was fuming. Good. "You'll be happy to know you missed an extremely important meeting. The Red Queens have threatened us, and there's confidence that they will attack by the next full moon. We're gathering reports now and will announce to the citizens to be prepared, while funding whatever we can to help their travel if they choose to flee. The festival will continue as planned—we must keep tradition alive to alleviate any distrust."

She didn't reply. "Still happy you mucked a barn, princess?"

That brought her to life. "Don't punish me for something I couldn't predict. Are we done here?"

The king was second-guessing having her a part of any of this. He debated whether it was a good idea to tell her anything. He wanted her to hurt, even if just a little. But he was also annoyed at himself for letting her get under his skin so easily. Not even Rhys did that, and the man was a lying thief. Isla came from a rich bloodline of royalty, and she didn't care. People across the world would sell their lives and loved ones for a position like Morei's. It was a disgrace for her to act so poorly.

"We're done."

Isla nodded, moving past him, but then she stopped. "Maybe you should muck a barn for once, Morei. It might teach you a thing or two about the people you want to lead."

The king didn't reply—couldn't. He was seething, and he knew damn well that anything he said now, he would come to regret later. She hadn't even addressed the Red Queens or the festival. Isla was more worried about proving a point that meant nothing.

He hadn't planned for these two, her and Rhys. They were fierce, highly opinionated, and constantly pushing boundaries. The entire city felt that way, to some degree. It was a far different culture than Geral's—hardheaded, stubborn, and self-preservative—and while he cherished the bright moments, like how the staff treated one another, he dreaded the volatility of such strong-willed people. It made ruling more complicated, and his temper left less tolerance for that with each passing day.

Morei stood there in the sun for a long while. People came and went, oblivious to the threat, acknowledging him. He leaned against the stone arch of the courtyard's entrance, arms crossed. The king was due to see the seamstress soon, and he had no desire to waste his time in the palace halls until then. The fresh air was much needed after this morning's events.

The people wouldn't generally see him here, but he didn't care. He was lost in thought about how he handled Isla. They hadn't gotten anywhere, and he still didn't feel he had a better hold on the woman. Morei wanted the city to succeed, and to be the heart of his empire, but he also needed to figure out how to get people like Rhys and Isla to respect him. If he couldn't earn the trust of his innermost circle, he would never be granted the respect of the citizens. And if he couldn't get that, he was on borrowed time, which petrified him.

Thorns of Blood

Syra's wrists hurt, and her neck and back felt like they were going to rip in half. She tried to move her head, but the muscles screamed. When she attempted to find her footing, her toes scraped cold stone. It was freezing, and chills racked her. Syra tried to move her arms, which were hanging at an awkward angle, only to realize she couldn't. Metal dug into the skin when she tried to shift even an inch.

Her breathing came ragged. The room was dark, and she couldn't see a window. She rubbed her toes against the stone again. It was dry. Forcing her head up and ignoring the pain, Syra traced heavy chains to the ceiling. She tried to move her arms left and right, but the chains were too tight to give her that mobility. Wounds along her arms lit up in fire. Those were new. Dried blood cracked from her movement, and more oozed freely.

The last she remembered was Zarek being ambushed and his collapse. They never had a chance to protect themselves, and she wasn't sure the Guardian was still alive. Never in her life had she seen someone drop that fast. Then she thought of Dryl. Her heart skipped a beat. He was supposed to be expecting them. The Guardian would have to know something was wrong when they didn't show.

In frustration, Syra yanked at the chains, but she felt skin break and hot blood run down her arms. The agony was immediate, and she inhaled sharply. Just as she did, her back lit up with a reminder of her stab wound. The deep throb came to life, her muscles spasmed, and a warm tear rolled across her cheek without permission. She hurt everywhere.

"Come on," she hissed into the dark. The Zyulë Bond was supposed to protect her, but here she was, strung up for slaughter.

"You're probably confused," a man said. Syra tensed, which only worsened the pain, as movement in the dark caught her attention. A large man stepped toward her, wearing the Guardian cloak and carrying the same pompous expression that all Guardians seemed to be born with. His coloring looked gray in the dim light, but his crimson eyes burned a hole right through her. "I'm here to give you a warm welcome and make sure you're not dead or dying."

"Thanks," she breathed, making the word as cynical as possible. "Could you spare me all that and tell me where I'm at?" Flashbacks of the attack wrapped ugly tentacles around her thoughts. Guardians of Death. The answer felt horridly obvious, as cold as this cell. Chest tightening, she pursed her lips and tried to keep her mind from spiraling into a frenzy. It would do no good if she lost her focus now.

"Those cuts along your arm are from the Syckl Blade. It possesses a toxin derived from a Cer'han, one of the handful of beasts that evolved from Dark Energy. Beyond Death's Sword, this is one of the few things that can kill us. Gods too, though you might have known that already. Guardians are executed with this blade in ceremonies, but you seem to be managing yourself just fine." The Guardian crossed his arms and regarded her. She tried to keep her face from revealing any worry. Dark Energy. She was right where she dreaded to be, where no God was safe. "I'm going to say you probably know the answer to your question too, Syra. What you should be asking is why."

Ah, so they all carried the same arrogant attitude. "Enlighten me." Desperate to take away the sharp pain building in her elbow, she tried to move again but was only met with even more discomfort. No position was right. Likely intentional.

He took notice. "Consider it a temporary arrangement." Now, he started to walk around her, methodical and slow, observing her like a farmer would in choosing his next pig for slaughter. "You're the one they've talked about nonstop. You're famous around here, did you know?"

Syra didn't answer.

"They want to absorb your lifeforce," he told her. "Strip you of your dignity by chaining you like a criminal, and then when you're at your weakest, plunge a blade through your heart. Don't worry, they've already thought about your Zyulë Bond. Sekar is in a similar predicament, though I must say you're faring a lot better than he. I'm curious about that."

If she'd had more blood to lose, it would have drained from her face. Her cheeks were numb, her palms sweaty, and her lungs turned to marble. "What?"

"I thought it was mad myself. Who could possibly chain a God? The God of Dreams and the Goddess of Death, no less." He was in front of her now, and he wagged his finger. "We know what you did with that boy. Brought him back to life, but don't worry, we took care of it. We around here are calling you that because of it. Certain laws cannot be broken without severe consequences. You are uneducated in the Order's laws for how we manage the dead. We could have had a horrible situation on our hands."

The memory of Erun traced her mind with a chilling finger, and Syra shivered. That was how she'd earned the discoloration on her hand—her scar.

"Where's Zarek?" she asked, wanting to change the topic. The Guardian's whereabouts were far more important than worrying about laws she didn't know.

"I'd probably say he's worse than either of you," he commented dryly. "A bit caught up in a lovers' quarrel. I tried to intervene, ease the tensions some, but Shevana nearly had my head for it. So I figured I'd be better off here, giving you a warm welcome. You don't want to meet some of the others. A little sick in the head, if you ask me."

Syra didn't believe him. Sarcasm was this man's gift. A Guardian trait. "Is she going to kill him?"

He hesitated. "He's not in good graces with her, if that's what you're asking." The Guardian leaned forward, almost nose to nose with her now. "You've got bigger things to worry about."

"Whose side are you on?" As tough as she was trying to act, her concerns were torn between Zarek and Sekar. The two men were complicated, but they were a large part of her life. She could not lose either.

The Guardian straightened. He was young, she realized. His features weren't as hardened as Zarek's or Dryl's were. Perhaps he was a part of the last generation of Guardians made before Shevana destroyed what they built. "They intend to harness your lifeforce along with Sekar's to disrupt Chaos. In doing so, they hope to leverage the energy and channel it into themselves."

"They can't." Syra wasn't even sure who "they" referred to. "Chaos is not intended for everyone."

"In purity, yes. In altered form?" The Guardian let that question fester between them, and Syra was starting to grasp the entirety of the situation. He wagged his finger as if scolding a child. "Your lifeforce is not pure of Chaos, only bound to it. Do you see where this is going?"

Syra wanted to melt into the ground, disappear, anything to avoid this. This had not been on her list of threats, and now she was scrambling for any idea of how to counter it. Escape was the only thing she could think of.

"Why are you telling me any of this?" she asked.

The Guardian shrugged. "You may call me Raid, Your Majesty." He offered a dramatic bow.

Humor was not what she was looking for. "Can you at least tell me exactly where I am?"

"The Guardians were built by Gods, did you know that?" Raid ignored her entirely, strolling around her again. "But it wasn't because they wanted to give souls a chance to cross into the Afterlife or do the right thing. That would be too sympathetic to think about. No. The Gods created the Guardians because we could supply Chaos an endless feast." He stopped, hands clasped behind his back. "The stories never tell of souls being sacrificed to keep the balance, do they? But that is the truth. A soul is the purest type of lifeforce that you can have. Energy feeds off that. Every season, we must select certain souls that wander this realm not to guide to the Afterlife, but to bring to another gateway. One that gives them no peace, no happily-ever-after, just nothingness. Everything that they are is sucked dry."

Raid faced her. "We were created to ensure Chaos never goes hungry. A backup plan. And now, with our Order crumbling and the realms fractured, Chaos seeks to feast in other ways."

Syra couldn't believe what she was hearing.

Raid approached the door. "A piece of advice, Syra. Don't do anything foolish. You're in Ashýon territory. The beasts out here spare no mercy for even your bloodline."

He would leave her, and she couldn't fathom being alone yet. "Wait." Syra watched his outreached hand steady over the door handle, if one could call it that. It was a curved metal hook poorly nailed to the door. "How long do I have?" A risky question—she didn't know how much she trusted the Guardian, but he'd given her some information, so she was willing to take the plunge.

They stood there, his back to her. There was a good chance he would lie. An even better chance he would leave without saying a word. Syra knew he owed her nothing. Whatever he told her wouldn't matter if she were going to end up dead, anyway, and she understood that. Raid could have been talking just to talk. Zane used to do that constantly.

"Days." That terrible, single word. "Is that all?"

Syra frowned at the question, but now was not the time to ask. "Is she here?"

Raid's chest rose and fell. "No."

Relief washed over her in hot waves. She wasn't ready to face the Soul Realm's leader. "Is Zarek here?"

"No."

Panic took over. "Where is he?"

"Sekar is here." The Guardian shifted his head, glancing over his shoulder. "There are much more dangerous things out there than Shevana. Some men here want you dead simply to prove their loyalty to that woman. You would do good to remember that."

At that, he left. Syra stared at the door, willing it to open so she could talk to Raid more. It was unclear what side he was on, but it didn't matter. He'd given her information she could use to get out of here alive. Or so she hoped.

The Rider's Promise

By the time Cyrus reached the alcove, he realized he didn't know the woman's name. The sand gave way to rock eaten by the salt from the sea, and he took care to step up without making a fool of himself. First impressions did count, and he did his best to never look like a moron, especially in front of a woman. When he reached the top, he positioned himself next to her. The youngest sister of the Venkar royal family was about his height, lean, and had eyes the color of a storm. She looked like a warrior.

The woman brought her hand across her chest and dipped her head out of respect. No matter how often that happened, it still made Cyrus uncomfortable, but he'd grown better at hiding it. When she raised her head, he nodded.

"You know Hyle?" He gestured at the shore, where the God was still working on the saddle. Sozar didn't move, and Cyrus knew the two were exchanging conversation. The privacy that the dragon placed between them was done out of respect, and he appreciated it. It gave him a moment with the woman.

"He has protected us through the centuries," she replied. Her accent was thick, each word pronounced in such a way that Cyrus strained to understand. "We honor him the best we can for everything he's done for us."

Cyrus's tongue struggled to form words. He wasn't sure what to say or how to say it. Hyle had told him these people had information on the Rider Federation, but he knew he couldn't outright ask here. It would be rude to initiate a discussion like that. What he needed to do was get to know her first.

"I didn't get your name," he managed.

"He isn't good at those." She must have meant Hyle, although Cyrus was curious how much the God interacted with these people to be spoken about in such a manner. "You may call me Chavi. My blood is of Qeranz descent."

The woman was proud. Cyrus wanted to show respect, so he dipped his head and said, "It is an honor to meet you." He was tempted to reach for her hand but refrained. He guessed that if he tried to be too formal, she'd stab him.

"The honor is ours," she replied. "The Dragon Blood flower has bloomed for the first time in centuries. When we saw that, we knew the age of dragons had returned."

"The Dragon Blood flower?" Cyrus hoped he didn't sound foolish.

A faint smile brushed her lips. "It exists in only two places in the world. Where my people are, near Crescent Lake, and in the ruins of the Rider Federation. The flower is only able to bloom because of the dragon."

He was lost. "I don't understand."

"The very ground beneath our feet gives energy, yes?" Nothing about her demeanor revealed if she was disappointed or entertained.

Cyrus nodded.

"So too does a dragon. Certain things in our precious world react to that energy. Dragon Blood is one of them. Without the energy of the dragon, these plants cannot thrive."

"Incredible," Cyrus said, and it was. Every day, he learned something new. "I would love to see it."

"And you will," Chavi said. "I am here to invite you and Sozar to return with me. You will meet the people who have kept your legacy alive all this time. You will be celebrated."

Hyle must have shared names. The woman spoke Sozar's respectfully, like it symbolized something beyond Cyrus's understanding. But he also cringed at the idea of a celebration. Too many of those in recent moons had left him feeling used for some political need or another. He didn't want to tell her no, though, afraid to disrespect her and lose out on information.

"I'm not one for celebrations." The answer felt safe.

That elicited a chuckle. "No Rider ever is. Only a few adored the attention."

She spoke as if she'd known them all. Cyrus shifted a little closer to her. It felt like she was the key to unlocking everything—everything that Hyle refused to. The God was reluctant to share. Cyrus didn't blame Hyle, but he still wondered the reasoning. Sozar said that with time, they would know, but they didn't have that luxury.

He wanted to know about Hyle, craved the answers to the God's demise as a Rider. And most importantly, why now? After all these centuries, why was it Cyrus who was destined to lead the change?

"There's a traditional story shared among my people. Every child is raised with it and entrusted to repeat the story when they have their own children." Chavi's fingers grazed over one of the white tribal markings on her wrist. The paint looked freshly applied. "When the first people arrived in this country, they did not seek tall palaces and great ships, they sought resources. Farther they traveled, until they found themselves before a body of water. But it wasn't normal. It glowed, rippled, and hummed. Still, starved for thirst, the people drank. And once they did, they discovered the truth about why this lake was what it was. They knew instantly that they couldn't let wanderers find it or they risked war." Her fingers traced over another marking on her hand. "My people, from the moment they called his place home, have defended this land. Centuries of commitment run in my blood, and I intend to ensure my children's children can still speak that story."

Cyrus swallowed, grasping at her meaning. Either Cyrus proved himself to her and her people, or he was an enemy. Venkar had protected its land for all this time. They would not risk losing it now, even for him. Whatever this lake held was important enough that no king or explorer in any history book he'd read about spoke of it. It was mentioned on the maps, but with no special note. No descriptions, markings, or indicators that the lake offered more than just quenching a thirst. Once more, he was in awe. The world grew bigger every day.

"This lake—" he began, hoping to learn more, but she tore herself free from the paintings on her skin and looked at him fully.

"The world calls it Crescent Lake. We refer to the lake by its original name, the Pink Waters. You will see for yourself, Sea Flyer. Only few have ever seen it, and we intend to keep it that way."

"You have my word," he told her, hoping she believed him. Cyrus would keep whatever secret they wanted so long as he got his answers.

"I am leaving this evening," Chavi continued, composed. "If you accept our family's offer, I will see you outside the gates, where the road splits into two."

She turned to leave, but Cyrus grabbed her wrist. "Wait." When she stared, he stumbled for his words. "Why? Why me?"

Chavi stopped. Her expression softened, and now she looked more like a friend who just found out about a tragic death rather than a fierce warrior who'd ended the lives of hundreds. She was beautiful—hauntingly so. All the tenseness of their interaction melted, and she let her guard fall. Her shoulders slumped; the arm that Cyrus had grabbed relaxed. She motioned with her chin toward the God on the shore.

"Him."

Cyrus was stunned.

"He speaks highly of you, Sea Flyer. He sees in you what he wished he could have been when the Rider Federation needed it most."

Her words might as well have slapped him—they stung just as much. "He doesn't tell me anything about what happened. Do you know?"

A sorrowful smile met him, so full of anguish that he let her go. "Everyone in Venkar knows his story, but only because he shared it with us. That's his right, not mine. When he sees fit, he will tell you."

Chavi's gaze lingered on the God, but only for a moment. Then she gave Cyrus one last nod and quietly made her way back to Delion. He watched her go. He was so determined to find answers. Finally allowed access to them, he couldn't have enough—he was a starved animal searching for scraps. The only problem was that everyone around him hesitated to tell him the hideous facts of whatever it was they were holding on to. Cyrus knew they didn't mean to, but couldn't they see that he *needed* these answers if he was going to be who he needed to be? Who the world needed him to be, or so they told him?

He had half a mind to march back to Hyle and ask *again* what his story was. Cyrus knew better, but he teetered with temptation. Kelise, the God's dragon, had been killed, and Sozar told him that Hyle still blamed himself for her death. Why? The Rider Federation had fallen from a political war, that much he'd gathered, but how was it all connected?

Reasoning won, and Cyrus remained where he was, still watching Chavi. She was small now, and on the edge of the hill, she stopped. She raised her hand and waved again. Cyrus returned it. And then she was gone.

He wanted to accept her offer. Hyle hadn't brought her here for just a chat. Needing a friend, Cyrus poked at Sozar's mind. The dragon immediately welcomed him in.

Well?

He turned toward the endless sea. The sun was still early, but the view took his breath away. A God sat on the shore—a Dragon Rider—next to the black-scaled dragon that had changed everything the day he hatched. The picture before him was perfect, and he wondered if Hyle cherished this as much as Sozar appreciated the God's company.

No—he knew he did.

Tonight, we fly to Venkar. Cyrus was confident in the decision. *Hyle has brought them to us. There is a reason for it. We owe it to him and ourselves to find out what that is.*

The dragon seemed pleased. *He spoke about Aythen with me. Told me about her and Kelise's bond.*

Despite nobody looking, Cyrus nodded. Sozar deserved those answers. That was his bloodline. *I'm happy for you. Did he happen to tell you if Aythen was as stubborn as a mule as you are?*

The dragon snorted loud enough that Cyrus could hear it from here. Hyle stopped and looked at Sozar before turning to him, grinning.

Cyrus started his way back to the duo on the shore. Alaric would want to know details, but he didn't have much to go on. The best he could tell the king was that Hyle was behind all of it. That should please the man well enough to send them off without too much concern.

Tonight couldn't come fast enough.

To Serve the Wolf

Arms stretched wide, back straight, Morei didn't move. Rose and her partner, Vera, were busy doing final measurement checks on his attire that he would wear at the Festival of Seasons. The room they stood in was simple for a master seamstress like Rose, but when he'd offered to give her something better, she refused.

A small table of folded clothes stood to the left. Behind him, hanging on countless racks, were fabrics and tools she used for measuring. Rose asked for one now, and Vera snatched a metal coil off a hanger and handed it to her. Across the walls were simple spiral designs that must have been hand-painted many summers ago. Flakes were now peeling off. The mirror before him was tall and wide, bordered by an ostentatious frame made of colorful gems. It was probably the most expensive thing here.

Save for his attire. The staff and council had spared no expense. Morei knew he would be dressed royally—that was the point—but never had he worn such bold and proud pieces. He wouldn't have to say a word for the citizens or any stranger to know he was king of Caster. Embroidered silver thread as thick as his finger was woven through the blue fabric of his shirt. The thread varied in size; along the sleeves, it was thick, but it networked throughout the entire blue shirt, becoming as thin as a strand of hair. It was like a web of silver, but it all met at the howling wolf on the back, which was massive. The collar of his shirt was embroidered with Old Tongue sigils—honor, commitment, loyalty—and the tail of the shirt fell to two points, which were also garnished in Old Tongue. His pants, sharing the same colors, were flawlessly fitted. This was who Morei was born to be, where he belonged. Royalty wasn't just about the title, it was looking and acting the part. Most commoners would never manage under all the obligations. That was what separated his bloodline from the citizens.

When Morei asked about the sword, Rhys looked mortified. While the city was known for its violence, it took tradition seriously, going as far as to abandon infants and set the dead on fire in the sea during certain times of the season. The king and his dance partner were not to possess weapons during the festival—it would be considered an insult. And with Morei trying to earn the citizens' trust, he needed to be careful. Going without a weapon was out of the question, so he would get creative. If he couldn't have his sword strapped to his hip, then he would have a dagger fitted to the inside of his boot.

He was still sidetracked about this morning. Right now, he didn't feel like a king. He didn't like it when he didn't have complete control—it increased the risk of something going wrong. When things went wrong, mistakes happened, and those were often costly. At that, Morei grimaced. The last time he'd lost control, he was standing underneath an Inere, the ancient Vore beast. Morei wasn't afraid now, but he had been that day. And little had come of that encounter. Scouts scavenged the land, only finding damaged areas where the Inere burrowed. It was hard getting men to search for the beast, though. Many shook their heads or walked out on him, and he'd finally had to pull his efforts. The world didn't take lightly to the unnatural.

He also couldn't forget about Sekar and Syra. His blood ran cold, and his vision narrowed. Morei hated Sekar's manic grin, and Syra was nothing but a threat. Gods and realms were out of his league, but that didn't stop him from trying to learn all he could. Finding direct information was near impossible to come by. He'd sent scouters dressed as commoners across the Vore World for old tombs, but he had yet to hear from any of them. With Eazon gone, he felt more and more like himself. He dreaded the day that man showed back up. When deities were around, the king doubted himself and his choices.

"Straighter," Rose ordered. "You're slouching again." To make her point clear, she patted his back.

Morei obliged. "Apologies." They'd been at this for half the afternoon already, and he couldn't figure out what was taking so long. "Are we nearly finished?"

The master seamstress raised her brow at him. "If you wish for me to be done, I can, but that means you'll be walking around the festival with a half-fitted shirt. Is that what you want, Your Majesty?"

He liked Rose. She was tough and didn't care much for titles. The only thing that mattered to her was her job. "Very well. Continue."

Rose nodded and told Vera to grab something else.

Morei stared at himself in the mirror. In this outfit, his ailment wasn't visible, which he was grateful for. When they'd originally fitted for the clothing, he'd told Rose that he didn't want any black veins visible, especially those rising along his neck. They'd worsened in the last season. Energy harvesting was responsible for that. Something about the force of Dark Energy exploited the demon he'd been bound to all those moons ago. That was his only running theory. With no information about this ailment available, he was grasping at loose straws. And he was admittedly too proud to request an advanced healer to see him. That would reflect weakness, which he couldn't afford in a new title.

Morei was fighting tooth and nail to tame his impulses. He didn't want to ruin his character, not so soon, and he was trying to be the best version of himself, but it wasn't easy. He'd nearly lost his temper a handful of days ago when a crook had snuck through the palace doors because a soldier had fallen asleep. Rhys had been there and intervened before Morei had the soldier's head.

He knew he couldn't control it forever. Eventually, the little bit of restraint he retained would be destroyed by the ailment festering in his mind and body. For now, though, he would try to fight it. And he hoped—even if it was a small hope—that he could find clear answers before it was too late. Emerald had once mentioned Guardian's blood, but he'd failed to validate that in any research, and he didn't put his trust in a woman who had taken advantage of him.

"Nearly there." Rose tugged at a sleeve and then pinned it. "What do you think? A little more fitted on the wrist, or some slack?"

Morei's attention turned to his shirt. He moved in it and rotated his wrist. "What about without the pin?" Rose took it out, and he repeated the same actions. The sleeve shifted more, revealing the veins at the base of his hand. "Pinned."

"You got it." Rose did another pin and then wrote something on the parchment she had laid on the table behind her with her small quill. She didn't ask questions about the ailment, and he appreciated it. "All right, I think that's it. We'll have it ready by tomorrow night."

"Perfect," Morei replied. The festival was in two days. "Is there anything else needed from me?" There wasn't, but it was polite to ask.

She shook her head. "Unless you're sewing, then no." She cracked a pleasant chuckle that warmed the room. In another life, she would have been a fantastic addition to the Geral community. The staff would have loved her. The thought grew, wrapping agonizing tendrils around the little content Morei had managed to find in these walls.

"We'll leave you to it," Rose said, then gestured to Vera to exit the room. Morei watched the younger seamstress leave. He didn't think he'd ever heard a word come out of her mouth.

When Vera was gone, he stopped Rose. "Does she speak?"

The master seamstress gave him a shrug. "She's mute."

"What?" How had he not known that prior? "How?"

Rose looked around, making sure they were alone. "Her family was slaughtered violently in front of her when she was maybe but four. The king—Drexis—took her in as an act of mercy. Call it one of the last nice things he ever did, but the girl never spoke again. A bit sad, if you ask me, but we do our best with her. She's a hard worker and well spoken with words on parchment." Rose shook her head. "Anyways, I have to go. Don't want her getting nervous out there. She doesn't like to be alone."

When the seamstress was gone, Morei changed out of his attire and into the clothes he'd entered with. A far simpler black button-up with matching pants. The fabric was lighter too. With the warming days, the heat was becoming unbearable again. Alone, he dared a peek at the black veins. They represented everything he didn't understand. Morei hardly recognized himself sometimes, and the more he thought about it, the more he realized that the man he was now was not the man his father had raised him to be. The king wanted to do right, to lead the people and give them a prosperous life, but his approach was less than admirable in the eyes of the rest of the world. They didn't understand what stress he was under. Violence had never been taught to him. A king led with his words, not his sword, and yet, Morei couldn't help but raise his weapon to prove his point—to have control. He wasn't sure what man that made him, and he feared what his father would say if he could see him now.

As he strapped his belt on, he heard a knock.

"Come in," he called.

Rhys appeared in the hall. The king was surprised to see the man so quickly after their heated exchange, but by the pale look on the chancellor's face, he realized they had a far bigger issue.

"We've got a problem."

Hearts of Sacrifice

S yra wasn't going to die here, and she sure wasn't going to hang here until *they* were ready to steal her lifeforce for some mad plan of control. Sekar had once told her the Guardians knew of her existence far before she was ever born—hopefully that still mattered. Every different thought she could muster, she dredged up. Big or small, she would try anything to stay alive.

She strained her gaze upward. The hook was long. When she tried to jump, her chains didn't make it even close to the edge. Agitated, she jumped harder and failed again. The Dark Energy toxin coursed through her, but she'd managed to stay mostly conscious. Raid had sounded impressed, but maybe she was just stubborn, or foolish, or both. The laceration on her arm stung, and every time she moved, blood droplets rained below. Her wound should have at least stopped bleeding, but she supposed that was an extra benefit when torturing people with the Syckl Blade.

Syra was a survivalist. She always had been. Being raised in Caster had taught her to never stop moving. Stopping meant she was as good as dead.

Her father used to walk her down the streets and point out people to be wary of, as well as hideouts and secret alleyways for kids her size. The world she'd known as a child was not friendly, and she felt like she was reliving everything now. Including the need to never stop trying.

"Come on," she hissed, and jumped. It took all her core to get any height. She couldn't use her legs. Hopefully, the training with Zarek paid off.

The longer she went uninterrupted, the stronger she felt. Syra wasn't skilled enough to expertly harvest Chaos or hold her own in a sword fight for long, but she wasn't stuck in a fog like she had been earlier. She didn't know how long she was hauling herself upward before she felt the chain catch on the edge of the hook.

An instant feeling of weightlessness filled her before she landed on her ass with bruising force. She sat there, stunned, then jumped up. The chains started to drag behind her, making too much noise. Syra dropped to her knees and wrapped the metal around one arm, then stood again. She approached the door and took several breaths. Chances were she would open the door to a Guardian or two, perhaps even Raid, and she had no way of defending herself in this state. The risk was worth it.

Her back ached constantly from the stab wound, and her steps were choppy. Now that she was on her feet, the toxin reminded her that she was still sourly compromised. Syra leaned against the door, head spinning. Her lungs burned, and she was pretty sure a trail of blood followed, but she didn't care. Syra needed to get out of here.

Opening the door, she hesitated. It glided with far too much ease. Nobody came in after her. Syra stepped out into the hall, baffled. This was not what she'd imagined—the ease of this all made the hairs on the back of her neck stand on end. A test, maybe, but that was twisted. Ignorance felt more like it.

Black vines were everywhere. The stone was hardly visible now that she looked more closely. A rotten smell intensified, and Syra wrinkled her nose, stifling a gag. Lanterns hung in close succession, lighting the narrow hall, but she wasn't sure they helped. The vines sucked in all available light, creating long shadows. And they were moving. She watched, horrified, as one along the ceiling shivered and stretched.

The floor was similar, and she shifted her foot away from a vine. Avoiding these would be important. Now where in Ashýon was she? Not that she was familiar with the region enough to know, but the lack of knowledge made her uncomfortable. She knew from discussions that this region was home to horrendous creatures.

Each step forward was followed by a pause to listen. All around, glaciers of ice jutted out from all angles. At least she knew why she couldn't get warm. It was deathly quiet, and that made her nervous. A slight scuffle against the wet ground traveled down the hall, deafeningly loud. Guardians patrolled, stopping occasionally to look around before continuing. None were Raid, and she pressed herself up against a wall each time to wait for them to pass. She only saw three, which made little sense. Two Gods locked away, and only a few Guardians to keep a lookout? Something wasn't adding up.

Syra kept to the main hall, stepping into the side halls whenever a Guardian was near. Raid had mentioned that Sekar was here—hopefully she could find him in one of these rooms. There was no sense of direction here. Every hall looked similar, the vines covered everything, and the lanterns all flickered like they might extinguish at any moment. The idea of being stuck here in the dark made her anxious.

Halfway down the hall, she heard commotion and froze. This wasn't the usual echo of boots. The door on her left was locked, leaving a slimy residue when she pulled her hand away. Up ahead, a junction. Syra bolted, narrowly missing a vine, and shoved herself against the wall as fast as she could. If anyone turned down this side, they'd see her.

The voices grew louder—two men, though they didn't quite sound normal—and they continued the way Syra had come. They looked ordinary, but there was an accent and scratchiness to their voices that she couldn't place.

Now that no one else was coming, Syra pushed forward. Her toes sank into a cold sludge, and she peered to see one of the vines lying across the floor. She shuddered. This place, wherever they were, was the epitome of every nightmare personified.

The doors that she came to couldn't open. A few did, but they were empty cells covered in slabs of ice. She could feel panic growing as she got farther away from her cell. Breaths came out in thick fog. If they found her now, she would be lucky if they didn't cut her hands off for a laugh.

She tried the next door, and it opened. Ice clung to the corners of the dimly lit room. Wiping her hand against her clothes, she scanned the chamber and stopped. There he was, hanging like she was, but in far worse condition than she would've thought possible for a God. Sekar was beaten, cut; blood dripped freely, and his royal tunic was shredded, hardly holding on. This was Dark Energy—what it could do to even the most influential Gods.

Carefully, afraid the wrong movement might cause him to startle, she approached. "Sekar," she whispered. If not for the faint wheeze of breath, she would have thought him dead.

Harsher, she said, "Are you awake?"

No response. Never had she seen him like this, *vulnerable*, and she wasn't even sure what to say. This was Sekar, the very God who had ripped her life apart. She didn't even know him if he wasn't making snarky remarks or stealing the show everywhere he went. The grating sound of his breathing sent a shiver down his spine—like he was choking on water.

"Sekar." Firm but soft. Blood pooled at the base of his feet. Lacerations covered him all over. The Syckl Blade, no doubt, used to torture. Whatever he'd done to earn such a beating probably involved a struggle, based on the injuries. Even a God as strong as Sekar couldn't withstand the lethal ramifications of Dark Energy. Yet right now, Syra desperately needed him to wake up or acknowledge her.

Dread stabbed her then. None of this was right. It was easy to justify ambushing her, but not a God like him. It couldn't possibly be real—any of this. A vision, perhaps, one conjured up by none other than the man who hung before her. Maybe this was his way of getting her attention, putting a little fear in her, his twisted way of having fun. In her head, she screamed to wake up.

Her mind didn't waver, nothing shifted around her, and the world was the same. Bleak. This was real. Syra didn't have all the answers she needed, and she couldn't worry about them now. She needed Sekar well. He was the only chance to get out of here alive. Nobody was as capable of harvesting Chaos as him, but he would be useless if he couldn't stand.

Grabbing his shoulders, she shook him. "Hey."

He groaned. She shook him even harder, panic melting into a frenzied frustration. Her decision to storm in here was looking less and less wise.

"Are you there?" she asked.

Sekar blinked and tried to move, but the chains kept him in place. "Well, where else would I be?" Bruising discolored his rich tan complexion, the left side of his face was swollen, and his teeth were stained red, but those dark eyes came to life at the sight of her, furious. "What are you doing here?"

Syra stared, confused. "I'm here to help." Strange—for her to be the one helping him.

"Get yourself killed?"

"Close. Help you out of here. What have they done to you?"

The God spit blood. "I got caught up in a disagreement."

Syra ignored him. "The chains. There's a hook up there. If you can jump, you can get out of here."

That made Sekar laugh, but it came out in a wheeze. "And go where, princess?"

She straightened and tried to get a good look. It all looked identical to what had held her. "I told you not to call me that." Syra saw some scuffs on the ground where Sekar's feet were. "What did they do to you?" She walked around and saw some whip marks along his shoulders, but underneath the fresh wounds were scars. Plenty of them. It was the first time she'd ever seen his back bare.

"Your arm," the God rasped, drawing her attention back. "Is that from the Syckl Blade?"

"Yes." Syra glanced at the door. She was getting nervous now. It was all becoming real.

"How are you standing?" he asked, exasperated.

She stood in front of him again. "I just am. I can't even fathom lifting you off those hooks." When he continued to stare, she motioned behind her. "I don't think we have much time. Zarek is in danger too. He was with me when they ambushed us."

The God didn't make any immediate movements. Syra presented her bound hands. "If I could do it myself, I would—"

"Corrupted Chaos," Sekar interrupted, dragging out the words. The grating sound worsened.

"Do you see yourself?" Syra asked. "I don't know why, and we don't have time to talk about it." Her intuition was screaming that they needed to move now or die trying. "Listen, if I sit underneath you, maybe you can shift your weight off the hook easier. I can't catch you like that, so—"

The door opened, and Syra spun around to see humanoid figures in the entrance. They stood on two legs and had two arms, but their faces weren't normal. Their mouths stretched up to their ears, which were points, and a line of curved teeth was exposed against dark, sickly gums. Their gray lips were complemented by black, vinelike skin that appeared to move. Bottomless pits, vacant of any clever thought, landed on her.

The demons let out a strange noise, which made her toes curl. It was like dragging glass against rock.

"Run," Sekar ordered.

She didn't ask or look back. Once the demons took a step in, she bolted for the entrance. A cold, wet hand tried to latch on to her, but she was too quick. Syra had no idea where she was going. Her instincts told her to go left.

Behind, screeching was followed by thundering boots. Everything looked the same, and she couldn't tell if she was back in the primary hall or somewhere else. Vines shifted all around her, coming to life with hissing sounds. Voices echoed, and she stopped. They were coming from ahead.

Four Guardians appeared, and her stomach twisted. Swords drawn, they looked exactly like what the old stories used to call them: Death's Knights. Their pale blue skin and black hair appeared ashen under the lighting. Syra didn't stand a chance against the four of them, even if she'd been armed. She tried to summon Chaos, but the energy slipped right through her fingers like sand.

The first Guardian approached, and when she stepped back, she felt herself hit something solid. Syra spared a quick look to see another Guardian. Raid. This close, she couldn't help but think how similar he looked to Zane. He didn't look nearly as thrilled to see her as her friend would have been.

"Well, hello," she mumbled, feeling small.

The Guardian before her hauled her up and over his shoulder without hesitation. Syra tried to roll off, but instead of landing on her feet, someone kicked her, and she ended up flat on her chest. The vines smushed and retracted, angry for the disturbance, and she heard one of the men snap at another, but the words were lost to her. The rotten scent of the place filled her nose, and her ribs felt like they'd just been struck by a galloping horse. Syra was hoisted up, and an annoyed Raid stared back at her, gripping the back of her tunic like she weighed nothing more than a sack of flour.

"Don't do that again."

Kings of Trouble

Cyrus's steps had an extra hop as he approached the throne chamber. The more time that passed since he'd spoken to Chavi, the more certain he was about leaving. Answers lay there, and he wouldn't get them behind the palace walls. He'd trained his mind and body, but now it was time to take charge of his destiny.

No more running, no more hiding. This was what he'd been waiting for. Cyrus had gotten too comfortable in the comfort of routine, but no longer.

Soldiers stood next to the grand doors. A carved ship plated in silver stared back at him, the door handles intricately carved to look like tentacles. Delion spared no expense with the designs and architecture of this palace. Cyrus had seen a few palaces now, but this one was by far the most prestigious build yet. He dared anyone to try and one-up Delion.

The soldier to his left greeted him. "Master Rider." He dipped his head in respect. Everyone called him that now, though Cyrus didn't feel like one. "His Majesty is speaking to King Jair."

Cyrus stopped, the air sucked right out of him. "Saveen?" he clarified, but he knew that answer already.

The soldier nodded. "Aye."

"Now?"

"Aye."

Nerves turned his skin hot. Dameon, prince and traitor, had fled the city when his father intended to force him into servitude after Ashtir hatched. That icy grin flashed across his mind. The prince was power-hungry, but underneath all that was a boy who'd been punished for his curiosity. Never had Cyrus thought he'd be here, on the other side of the doors, this close to the king of Saveen. But now that he was, he felt obligated to enter. King Jair needed to know his son was alive, but Cyrus also wanted the man to know exactly what he thought.

"Very well," he breathed. The soldiers made no reaction as he turned the handle and entered.

"—promised to deliver," Alaric said. They were in the middle of what appeared to be a serious and heated discussion. Both kings stopped and looked at him. Asher stood beside Alaric, ever faithful in his role as chancellor. Cyrus let the doors close behind him and kept his chin high as he closed the space between them. The blue rug that stretched from the doors to the thrones padded his boots as he walked.

"Cyrus." Alaric straightened and tugged at his sleeves. A habit he'd learned was the king's way of staunching his anger. A fair warning that many missed. Cyrus hadn't, although he assumed it was for Jair. The eccentric family had given Alaric troubles since the day he took the throne.

"Your Majesty," he replied, and stopped before them. It was respectful to refer to Alaric that way in front of outsiders. Others needn't know the nature of their friendship. "I heard King Jair was in and didn't want to miss the opportunity to meet him." Jair was wide, and just a bit shorter than him. But that didn't keep him from exuding enough dominance to tame a wild beast. His honey-brown skin looked like leather from countless summers in the sun, and his black hair was cut short, revealing neck tattoos. King Jair used to be a captain, Cyrus remembered.

Cyrus extended his hand to shake, even as Jair momentarily fumbled. That didn't surprise him. The strongest men could never quite keep it together when they met a Dragon Rider, and he supposed it was compounded by the fact that his son was one too.

"An honor," King Jair whispered, taking Cyrus's hand with a firm squeeze. His skin was as callused as it looked. "I have heard so much about you, but I can't believe we haven't met yet."

"I was going to say the same." When they broke free, he motioned at Alaric. "He speaks highly of you and the trades." It was a lie, but Cyrus's growing confidence made him bold. Asher's brow went up just enough to reveal that he approved.

King Jair nodded, flashing a grin that took summers off his features. "You don't say?"

Alaric jumped right into it. "I do. Our trade has continued to bring a wealth of culture into this city. My council was just informing me yesterday of the positive feedback they'd received from the gusak leather. You said you've got a treaty with pirates to hunt those things?"

The Saveen king nodded. "Aye. They never disappoint. It was their oils and innovation that made leather from the skin of a gusak, you know. They didn't hunt on land for long periods, and so would turn to the sea for all their resources. Clever people."

"Fascinating," Alaric commented. He didn't care. Cyrus could read right through it, but he also knew the king well enough to pick up on the small cues. Jair had no idea.

The two kings exchanged some words, and Cyrus took the opportunity to survey the throne chamber. The exterior was just as grand as the interior. The palace was built to last for an eternity. It would long outlive him. Carvings of waves came out of the walls, tentacles made up the crown molding. The detailed painting of a ship stood out to him. Alaric once told him that it was the exact ship that had first set sail from Delion's Port centuries ago. Whoever painted the piece had spent a great amount of time capturing the main deck and all the men and women who worked the ship. This was not just the first ship to set sail from this city but the country. The ship was endearingly named *Curiosity*.

Two thrones stood proud behind them. Iron tentacles made up the back and arms, and Cyrus was almost certain they'd never been sat in. The silver cushions looked untouched. He wondered if Alaric would ever take a queen. The king hadn't shown much interest in the idea when the council first presented it. In private, Alaric said that the courtship in Creitón was painfully long and admitted that he only refused to agree to a queen because he didn't want a princess. The royal women he'd met were all snotty, and the other kingdoms strictly wanted the power that came out of arranged marriage, but tradition was proud in this country, so Alaric kept his words quiet. When Cyrus pressed him more, he learned the king had secretly been seeing a commoner just outside the city. She didn't even know Alaric was the king, and he preferred it that way.

That was a moon cycle ago. Cyrus wondered if things had changed.

"—isn't that right, Cyrus?" Alaric asked.

He blinked and looked at the two kings. Whatever they'd said went right over him. "Yes."

The Delion king looked pleased at the answer. "You can't expect a Dragon Rider to pledge fealty to every family, Jair. Surely you see the faults in that reasoning, yes?"

Dameon's father wrinkled his nose like he'd just gotten a whiff of something sour. "I mean no disrespect."

"None taken," Alaric replied smoothly. The way he spoke when acting as king and behind closed doors—it was like two different people. He cleared his throat and stared like it was a life-or-death situation. "Cyrus has been granted refuge given the previous circumstances. We've been over this. I would hope you trust my word enough to not doubt my intentions or integrity." A pause. "Do you?"

Jair shifted on his feet. His boots looked like they'd never seen the sun. "You and I both know that your father's decisions severely damaged our relationship."

"Don't forget Barnăl," Alaric offered with a cold laugh. "You think I forgot?" Asher didn't move, hands laced together.

"Of course not," Jair answered coolly. "I'm just saying that sometimes to appease tensions, compromises need to be made. Wouldn't you agree?"

Alaric didn't miss a beat. "No. Issues outside our control caused these tensions—you and I both know that. That doesn't obligate anyone to make compromises." His fingers tugged at his sleeve again—he was well beyond his tolerance for this conversation.

Cyrus swallowed, tasting the bitter frustration. Two kings determined to prove their point without raising their voices or directly threatening one another—he lacked this kind of skill. He hadn't come in here to cause problems, but he did want to clear the air.

"King Jair, I wanted to speak to you about several things." At Cyrus's words, the Saveenian turned his attention to Cyrus. "Rumors have reached my ear that you and your council think I am a threat because I don't pledge fealty. Is that how you determine a man's loyalty, Your Majesty?"

He held his gaze, not wanting this king to doubt for a moment that he was serious. If Jair was so determined to play the predator, then Cyrus would make sure he squirmed. Being the one in control felt nice. Too often these arrogant rulers thought they could step all over him. It was starting to leave a bad taste in his mouth.

Sozar poked at his mind. *Don't be cruel about his son. We don't know the entire situation.*

I know.

"In tradition, that has been our way to show loyalty," King Jair replied. It was obvious that he was trying to remain collected. "Many of my people don't know how to cope without it. It's ingrained in our blood."

"I understand," Cyrus said. "I really do, and I respect those traditions. But would you believe me if I told you this was the fourth kingdom I've landed in? I spent the better part of a season running from men like you who want to force me into serving strictly their needs."

Alaric looked giddy. His chancellor, on the other hand, looked bored.

"And now, while I understand that each ruler has a certain amount of responsibility to maintain, I do think it's a tad short-sighted that you would assume my loyalty is strictly tied to the royal families of this world. What of the nomads, the exiled, those who don't have a city to call home? What of the citizens who have a ruler who doesn't represent them? Do you expect me to ignore the greater number of the world for the select few who claim their title by the purity of their blood?"

King Jair's mouth twisted like he was stifling vomit. Behind him, Alaric was a statue.

"In my readings, I've learned that the Dragon Riders never pledged fealty to the cities. In fact, the cities pledged fealty to the Rider Federation. I like to think they did that because they all agreed that certain matters, like peace, were far more important than the petty argument over who's got the better soldier."

You've said your peace, Sozar observed.

Cyrus inhaled deeply. "You should expect that I will never give my loyalty to one city or the other. My promises and loyalty are to the common people. As king, I'm sure you can respect that."

The Saveen king slowly nodded, realization dawning over him. He reached his hand out, and Cyrus took it. He was satisfied to have made his point. Jair would share this with his council, and they to Barnăl. But before they could break contact, Cyrus said, "Your son is strong-willed."

The color drained from Jair's face instantly. Once tough and dominant, now he looked like a man who'd seen Death and been running from her. "Excuse me?"

"I met your son, Dameon, a season ago, while I was in Eiyrăl. We exchanged words, and our dragons met. I didn't know at the time he was the prince, but he carried himself as one." He knew the king would be troubled, but the lesser of two evils was telling him that Dameon was still alive.

The king retracted his hand. "How was he?"

"Angry." Speaking this openly brought him peace. "But passionate about his beliefs." A silent exchange passed between them. Jair knew that Cyrus knew that the king was primarily responsible for what happened. "We left on different paths, but I suspect he's doing quite well." That part was a lie. Dameon and Ashtir were with Henry Junok, but he didn't have the courage to tell this man that his son was paired up with the most dangerous person in the world. Sozar agreed.

The Saveenian nodded weakly. "Thank you for telling me. I've spent many moons trying to locate him or get any sort of idea where he's at, but it's impossible."

Cyrus forced a smile. "Dragon Riders never sit still." Especially when they were running.

The earlier tensions were gone. King Jair, in all his fierceness, didn't seem to care much for anything now. His jaw worked back and forth as he glanced back at Alaric. "My apologies, Alaric, but I think I need to step out for a bit."

The Delion king didn't hesitate. "Of course. Take all the time you need. I will have you escorted to the courtyard. One of my staff members can give you anything you like. When you're ready to continue, let one of my soldiers know. I will be in my study reviewing some reports this afternoon but will stop to finish our business."

Jair thanked them both and retreated from the grand chamber. As the doors closed behind him, Cyrus felt the harsh slap of Alaric's hand against his shoulder.

"After that, I'm tempted to hand the crown to you! No politics." He scoffed. "You handled him like he was a fish flopping on the shore. Snatched him up and tore the head right off. Impressive work and, might I add, spares me from looking at him any longer."

Cyrus grimaced at that visual. "I couldn't listen to another accusation. I'm tired of people making assumptions about where my loyalties stand."

"You made that quite clear," Alaric replied. "Didn't he, Asher?" The chancellor nodded. For such a fiery man, he was quiet today.

Alaric flashed one of those wicked grins reserved only for private conversations. It was the kind of look that Cyrus was certain was the last thing his enemies saw. "So many fine lines we rulers have to walk, but you came right in here and said everything from the heart. I hope he chews on those words for the rest of the summer. I can't stand the man."

Cyrus didn't quite align with that thought, but he didn't say so. He hadn't interacted with Jair on the political level to make those kinds of conclusions, though he knew the Saveen king was hard to work with. He rubbed the back of his neck. "I was actually coming here to tell you something."

Alaric tilted his head. "What is it?"

A hundred different responses fought for release, mostly driven by eagerness. Venkar was nestled in some of the most breathtaking forestry in the world. Mountains jagged and steep towered high enough to touch the sun, and creatures that existed nowhere else thrived in the southern side of the country. Cyrus had heard so many wild tales of adventure and exploration from soldiers and staff alike that he'd started to envy them. And now, he could finally live that.

"I'm going to Venkar."

The Dead Sea

odies. They were everywhere. They crowded the shore for as far as
one could see on either side. Bloated, pale, and swarming with flies
and birds. Some had their eyes gouged out, most likely from the crows that
fluttered about, while others' stomachs were torn open. The body cavity
was cleaned out, devoid of any mucus, intestines, or blood to indicate these
people had ever been alive. They looked like stuffed dolls—piss-poor replicas
of the living and breathing individuals standing next to Morei.

"So . . ." Rhys tried to speak, but no more came out. Already, a crowd
of onlookers was starting to show. A few had already been here when they
arrived, surveying the growing landscape. The first body arrived just after
dawn, and no one had alerted Morei. Shipwrecks often meant victims, and
the city thought nothing of it. By late morning, several more floated in from
the sea, and when a dozen more showed up on top of that, it became clear.

Scanning the sea, he saw no sign of debris or a victorious ship. Morei stared
at the dead, trying to place them—mothers, fathers, soldiers, anything to

identify them, but not even that was clear. Their clothes didn't display any origin, no emblem of the wolf or armor to represent a family's colors. They were strangers, and when he took in the crowd's confusion, it was obvious nobody else recognized them either.

This day couldn't get any worse. Right now, he was tempted to turn around and walk away, but his title obligated him to stay and take charge. There they all were, gaping at the shore full of the dead, mumbling questions to each other. A few bodies drifted back to sea, while more washed up as they stood there. Whispers started, and some immediately turned around to wretch. The king couldn't blame them. The smell was repulsive, putrid, unlike anything he'd ever inhaled before. The Red Queens were masters of sending threats. If this was them, then he wouldn't deny the respect they deserved. If they wanted his attention, they had it.

"Sir?"

The meek voice came from one of the larger soldiers to Morei's left. He glanced over at the young man, noticing how discolored his skin was. The king should have felt something—disgust, perhaps—but he lacked even that. All he felt was building anger. It was all happening again. If it wasn't Grënyl or Cu'cel, it was this. If it wasn't Geral, it was Caster. He couldn't escape the madness.

Silence followed. Everyone wanted answers. The king took a step forward, but Rhys immediately grabbed his arm. "You don't know if they're poisonous."

Morei raised his brow, certain this behavior was all for show. "I need to see them."

The chancellor looked to consider this, but he quickly relented. Peter, his old chancellor, would have thrown a fit. Rhys knew better. Slowly, the king approached the closest body, an old woman. Her gray hair was sparse, most of her scalp visible, and her eyes were missing. What remained were dried-out sockets that looked clean enough to serve stew from. She was stuck on the shore, the waves lapping lazily against her body. Her clothes, torn and tattered, looked far too large for her small frame. But her stomach, cheeks, and feet were twice the size they should have been, like bladders ready to pop. He'd never seen feet or cheeks bloat like that. It was unnatural.

The king took a quick glance behind him. Nobody spoke, only watched. He couldn't blame them. They were just as curious as he was. Among them, he saw Isla. It was only fitting she would show when he least wanted her to. The princess's expression was somewhere between horror and morbid curiosity.

Looking back at the body, he knew what to do but still hesitated. It would be gross. Slowly, he reached forward and started to inspect the woman's cold and slimy skin. No skin should feel that way, and he stifled a gag. This close, the smell made his eyes water.

The sand sucked his boots in as he repositioned himself to pull at the ill-fitted sleeves. The fabric felt coarse, ready to tear at any moment, so he was careful not to. He wasn't sure why—perhaps some odd respect for the dead or an underlying fear that anything drastic might awaken the woman. He tugged the sleeve up but saw nothing. She was so thin her wrist bone protruded sharply from her translucent skin. Morei reached over and checked her other arm. Nothing. He didn't want to get near the stomach, certain that it might pop at the wrong motion. When he pushed her thin hair aside, though, her head lolled. A small gasp followed from behind.

Morei shot them all a glare.

Her mouth was open now and, more comfortable, he clamped his hand on her jaw, turning her head to his. He studied the expression as best he could. Severe stretch marks showed along her mouth. It was a strange sight, like how a mother's stomach was damaged during pregnancy. He poked at the cheek closest to him. It bounced back.

Something was inside.

When he tried to pry her mouth open, it wouldn't give. Rigor mortis had set in, turning muscles into stone. Morei, invigorated and more confident, pulled his dagger free from his boot. A shadow appeared behind him—the chancellor.

"My commander won't come by my side, but you will?" Morei observed without looking up. "I'll remember that."

"The people are scared. You can't blame them." Rhys knelt next to the king. "Some people are better off as sheep."

"Others as wolves," Morei finished. He'd heard that phrase several times since arriving in Caster. "Shall we?"

The chancellor nodded.

Morei pressed the dagger against the bloated cheek. The skin broke, but no blood came. The king's nerves were on high alert. "Is this normal?" he asked quietly.

Rhys cleared his throat. "What?"

"The Red Queens."

Silence. It was quick, but in the heat of the moment, it felt like an eternity. "They're usually more of the one-dead-to-send-a-message kind of crew." The answer came soft enough that the others wouldn't hear. "This is beyond my scope of knowledge."

That wasn't what he wanted to hear. If this was the Queens at work, he needed to know. Morei pressed the blade deeper into the skin until muscle gave way and it slid into the mouth. No blood, but he did feel the dagger press up against something. He froze.

"There's something in there," he muttered.

The chancellor didn't betray any surprise. "Should we tell the people to leave?"

Morei twisted his dagger until he tore more skin, making a larger hole. He pulled the weapon free, and the air that was trapped inside escaped with the blade.

"Or not," Rhys commented.

The king dug his fingers into the lady's mouth. He didn't like any of this, but he was too curious to stop. In the back of his head, though, he was frightened that this could be another cruel trick by the Gods he despised. If it was, he would rip Eazon's feathers out one at a time.

The lips parted, and the woman's jaw slacked. Morei stared into the gaping black hole, tense and ready to jump. The chancellor leaned in. In the lady's mouth was a network of what appeared to be roots. They were black, wet, giving off a shimmer when the sun hit them just right. He hesitated. Cu'cel brushed his thoughts, reminding him of his actions in Geral.

"Move back," he ordered.

"What?"

"There could be illnesses." Cursed ones brought on by the Gods. The king's hand loosened, halfway tempted to forget his wild curiosity.

Rhys didn't move. "I'm already this close. Go on."

Morei wanted to argue but didn't. If the chancellor wanted to take the chance, that was his decision. He took his dagger and plunged it into the woman's stomach. At once, air tinged gray escaped in a puff. Then the skin sagged. Rhys still stayed put, determined. He sawed the belly open, taking fabric with him, until he could pry the contents out.

More roots. No organs, and the bones that should have been there weren't. The king reached farther into the cavity of this woman's body. He felt for ribs but found none, and when he got to the place where a heart should have been, a jar was in its place. Morei froze, keeping his face plastered in the same expression to not give anything away to those who watched. His fingers slipped around the cold glass. It was small, and he easily surrounded the whole thing in his hand and tugged it out. Vines ripped free with a grotesque snap, and he positioned his hand behind the body, so that the people couldn't see what he was doing.

Rhys saw but didn't make it obvious. In fact, he shifted to help block the view. "What is it?" he mumbled.

Morei didn't answer right away. He unscrewed the cap. Inside was a folded piece of parchment. This was the sickest game of messenger he'd ever seen, but he couldn't deny the precision. Carefully, he plucked the parchment out and unfolded it without appearing obvious, even as he felt the color drain from his face.

I know what you did. King Nerius of Junok.

That was all, but Morei didn't need anymore. The past was finally catching up to him, but the timing couldn't have been worse. He shoved the glass under the dead body and slipped the note into his pocket as he tried to get a full breath. This wasn't pirates. This was a threat from Junok. He plunged his hand into the cavity again, hoping there might be more, but as his fingers skimmed over cold and slick vines, he found nothing.

Unbelievably, he wished it was the Red Queens. They were present, new, not a reminder of his mistakes. Without a word, Morei moved to the next body. The young man's pale skin was slicker than the woman's, and his grip on his dagger slipped as he dragged the blade across the bloated stomach. He was met with the same grotesque visual as he plunged his hand into the cavity and reached for where the heart should have been. Sure enough, his fingers tightened around glass. The vines held on to this one better, and he had to tug a few times before they relented, snapping.

Morei kept his back to the crowd, not wanting to betray how nauseous he was becoming at the crushing reality. He unscrewed the jar as discreetly as possible and pulled the small parchment out. Unrolling it, he stared at the same message. All the bodies must have held the same message. This was meant for him.

He tucked the parchment back into the glass and stuffed it back into the cavity. His arm and sleeve were stained, his confidence shaken, and he forced several breaths in before making his way back to Rhys, who still waited for an answer.

"Junok sends their regards."

The crowd was whispering, but he knew what they said: Was this because of him? They didn't need to know the panic that turned his blood cold. They didn't need to know this was the work of the Diyrăllian city either.

"A ship," he told Rhys. "We will tell them it was a wrecked ship, and these must have been the passengers. That should settle their curiosity."

A curt nod. He understood.

The king stood, his left arm dotted in a black, mudlike substance. From afar, the citizens could mistake it for blood, and he would lead with that. "A shipwreck," he said, louder and with as much confidence as he could muster. "A shame, but it will be cleaned up before dusk." In a lower voice, he told the chancellor, "Burn them on the shore."

Rhys raised his brow. "Not a proper burial."

"I don't care. Burn them," he repeated. Cu'cel graced his mind with a rotten laugh, and he swallowed. When in doubt, fire always worked. "We need confirmation the bodies are destroyed. You can't do that if you send them off."

People shared looks, but nobody dared to get close. Morei awaited questions, but none came. He shot Edwin a glare, indicating the crowd needed to move. The commander took the hint and ordered them away from the coastline. Soldiers followed the same motions.

Once most of the backs were turned, Morei added, "If anyone asks, it's precautionary. We can't risk illness."

"Fair enough." The chancellor scratched his chin. Morei could tell he wanted to ask more about what they'd just discovered, and why Junok was sending this kind of message. The people couldn't know what had happened to Emerald. Not the truth, anyway. Sure, rumors existed. It was common knowledge that the queen had been killed while in Geral, but the matter of how she'd died remained unconfirmed, and he intended to keep it that way. Only two people knew the truth: him and Sekar.

"I don't know," he said before Rhys could ask. "If I knew, I'd tell you now. Get the bodies taken care of quickly. Keep ears on the city. If people start talking, let me know. Until then, business as usual."

"Charming," the chancellor muttered. It was his favorite word to use when he wasn't entirely in agreement with the king. Morei didn't care.

A Scar Twice Earned

Syra hung in her dungeon again, right where she'd started. She'd earned another laceration for pulling that stunt. The Guardian responsible for the Syckl Blade hadn't said a word to her as he unveiled the ugly weapon. When he left, more Guardians arrived, carrying chains to keep her from moving too much. They were agitated that the toxin wasn't having the same effect as it was on Sekar. She'd tried to talk to them, but that'd earned her a slap, so now she kept quiet. Without food or water, she was running off fumes and adrenaline, but even that was starting to wane.

These men were not like Dryl. They were cold, devoid of emotion, hardly showing any expression. She'd heard stories from Sekar and Dryl about the dark nature of the Guardians, even been warned by Raid, but she hadn't seen it until now. One part of her wanted to believe that this behavior was exaggerated because of the current conditions, but another part feared Shevana had bred monsters.

The Guardian training was dead, destroyed centuries ago by Shevana, and now Syra knew why. Minimizing the number of new trainees meant that the leader could focus solely on manipulating and forging her perfect warrior.

When they left her, she tried to get free again. The weight of the chains strained her muscles, and that meant the spikes along the metal cuff dug deeper into her wrists. She managed to wrap her fingers around a chain link, holding herself up just enough to keep the thorns from obliterating her flesh. It hardly helped, though. The muscles along her neck and back screamed in agony, and she could feel the warm touch of blood coating her back now that the wound was reopened. If she wasn't killed for her lifeforce, the blood loss would see her to the Afterlife.

After several failed attempts at getting free, she resorted to yelling insults. Her frustration bubbled over, and she saw no direct path to an end. Syra hadn't come all this way, sacrificed everything, to be ambushed and forgotten about in some dingy cell for when the time was right. The realms were in danger, Zarek and Sekar needed her, and she refused to admit defeat. She frantically searched for any opportunity to leverage—a twig would have helped at this point—but found nothing. The cell was empty, save for her. The door and walls were all outside of reach.

When no one came in to tell her to shut it, she quieted down. Her energy evaporated fast, and her vision went in and out of focus. The toxin was finally doing its job. It was becoming harder to grip the metal. As slumber tore her apart, she felt the fleeting warmth of Chaos brush up against her mind. The presence engulfed her instantly.

Syra awoke to an incessant tapping. Adrenaline shot through her, but her muscles and body moved slower than she would've liked. Syra blinked, vision blurred and head swimming, but she picked up on the man sitting in a chair at the door, which was open.

"Rise and shine," Raid greeted.

In response, the ground shook. Adrenaline rushed her, but it moved with the thickness of mud and made little impact on her already sore and beaten body. Chains rattled, and the lantern hanging next to the door squeaked as it moved. Raid tensed, watching the ceiling for any cracks or dust. It was the first time that he'd appeared concerned. As the trembling settled, his shoulders relaxed.

"Nasty tremors. Those started a while ago."

As irritated as she was about the situation, Syra was relieved to see a familiar face, but her tongue failed to work right away. Things were moving too slow in her head. Raid didn't seem bothered by the wait.

"Toxin is doing her duties," he explained. He had a small dagger and was carving something with it. "Don't worry, it'll wear off soon enough, which is why I'm here. You've got a bit of an immunity to it, we've gathered. Probably the bloodline."

Raid's boots were propped up on the other side of the entryway. He looked comfortable, like he'd been sitting there for a while. Syra opened her mouth to speak, but he continued.

"You got good training under your belt. Who should I thank the next time I see them?"

Mouth parched, she whispered, "Zarek."

"Ouch." Raid stopped his carving long enough to look at her. "Apologies about that. Didn't realize we were bringing him up." The Guardian restarted, peeling layers of wood away. Or so it appeared. She wasn't sure.

"He's with Shevana back at the palace. Bit too far of a walk for you in this condition."

If she could have nodded, she would have. So Zarek was alive—but she didn't know how to get there or out of this current predicament, and she definitely wasn't sure what to do about Raid. "Thanks."

"No problem." The Guardian examined the piece, leaning over to get better light. Then he returned to his work. "I've been tasked to keep you company. Consider it your lucky day. Make sure you don't get a wild hair and try and jump again once your pride returns."

Speaking was coming easier now that she was becoming more alert. "I don't think I'd be able to. You have enough chains here to hold a dragon down."

He chuckled. "Oh, believe me, it would take a lot more than that."

"How much?" Syra wanted to keep the conversation going.

"Hm," he hummed. "In the era of the Dragon Riders, special chains were forged in dragon blood and energy to hold dragons if they were imprisoned, but that was rare. Everyone knew it was a dreadful idea to chain a dragon. It was the Riders who were punished, and usually the dragons obliged to protect their Rider."

Syra's elbows were on fire, and her head pounded, but she did her best to sound as normal as one could in this situation. "Did you have any involvement in the Dragon Riders?"

"Of course. Well, not me." He scoffed. "I'm one of the youngest here. A whole 267 summers old. Practically an infant to some of these elders serving the Order." Raid raised the item he was carving to her. "How does this look?"

Syra squinted, unsure what he was working on yet. "It looks great."

"Good." Raid returned to his carving, pleased. "Anyway, Guardians were involved with the Rider Federation, but only when necessary. The Dragon Riders were self-sufficient, knew right from wrong for the most part, but Guardians stepped in occasionally. Although, stories on that are vague. You know, with Shevana's whole 'burn history' approach."

Syra dragged her tongue over the roof of her mouth, tasting metal and sand. This Guardian wanted to talk, but she couldn't figure out why or what he was willing to share. Still, she took the risk. "Nobody speaks highly of her."

Raid leaned in and started making small cuts along the top of the wood. "Save for the fanatics. You met a few of them with your stunt you pulled. I nearly earned myself a stab for making sure they didn't beat you more than necessary back there. You're welcome." A fat gap of silence fell over them, but she didn't press. The strength she had was hardly worth bragging about, and she figured he would speak about something, but she was surprised when he expounded on his words.

"There are so few of us left. Eighteen, to be exact—almost half of those men loyal to Shevana. The other half . . . well, it's a bit of a dispute, really. The few of us in this forsaken mountain have big plans now that you're here, but it'll only work if you don't get yourself killed beforehand. Do you understand?"

Her head swam violently, and she squeezed her eyes shut. In response, blood shunted to her core, turning her flush.

Raid didn't show any concern. "The next time you want to try to escape, avoid the vines. It's not only Guardians in this place. You're dealing with demons and creatures too. They keep watch. Those vines alert us when there's any sort of attempted escape from a prisoner. Did you see the way they moved when you so graciously stomped all over a live one?"

She did, and weakly, she nodded.

"There's nasty little slime creatures that run around. They hide under thick sections of the vines and will come out in hordes when triggered. Don't let them latch on, either—there's a curved hook they use, and they're excruciating to get off. They want to eat your flesh. Not sure what anyone calls them, but I like to refer to them as bastards." He shivered as if to make a point. "Don't ask Jerun about it. He's got a nasty gash that's still healing on his leg."

Syra felt oddly grateful to have him here. His company was comforting, even if she was in agony.

"Shevana's mind isn't the same as it used to be. She's entrusted much of the security with the demons, too much faith in the remaining Guardians who cling to her, like the men you met back there. Those of us who challenge her rule don't speak up. It would get us killed, so we do our duties but try to keep our space whenever we can."

She wanted to know more. "If you aren't loyal, why do you serve her?"

"Waiting for the right time, my lady." Raid waved at the surroundings with his dagger. "This is our identity, being Guardians. We have nothing left in the living realm—certainly no family that lives. The idea of trying to end the last piece of what makes us who we are cripples the majority of those who remain, including me. We would rather live under a mad woman than end it all." He sounded somber.

"Why would it end?" Syra asked.

"The bloodline," he clarified. "The Soul Realm can't go without an heir for long, but nobody can just take Shevana's place. You see, your family's blood was the only one chosen by the Gods to rule. This realm burns in your blood. Without your lineage ruling, the realm will crumble. Hence, why some of us have waited for this." He lifted the piece to her again. "Look better?"

Syra thought it almost looked like a bird based on the narrowing of the head. "Getting there," she replied. The Guardian's words bothered her. She didn't know about that. It had always been about putting a stop to Shevana when the time was right, but she didn't realize the consequences of it. She was certainly in no shape to rule, and a variety of issues needed to be dealt with, including the realm fracture.

"The raven calls both realms home," Raid said, changing the topic. "It is our crest here, what we try to embody. Stay curious, stay fierce was a saying mentioned for many centuries. What the trainees were drilled with. It's not spoken much anymore, but if you ask any of the men where their honor lies, they will tell you the raven. You know why?"

She was too weakened to shake her head, and was glad when he continued.

"It is believed from old stories that a raven is a soul too stubborn to move into the Afterlife. They still had so much life to live, debts to be paid, or families to love that they couldn't find rest. In that turmoil, they were capable of extraordinary things, like shifting into a raven. Stuck in the Soul Realm, they flew higher and higher until not even the realm could bind them, and that was how they crossed into the living. A realm we once called the Gods' Realm, for that is where the Gods reside. Soon enough, more of these souls found a way out, flooding the living realm with what many now call the raven. But in Old Tongue, they were referred to as Rü'shane. A literal translation for God's soul."

Syra knew what he was carving now. The depiction was coming to life, the beak taking shape, the feathers earning details.

"So, you see, when a Guardian takes their oath, they give it to Rü'shane, because that is whom we wish to embody. That stubborn and ever-persistent curiosity that keeps the ravens alive. They represent everything we should be, and tell us that no risk is not without a little sacrifice and fear."

Raid stood then, pocketing the dagger in a basic sheath on his hip. Death's Sword was strapped on the other side. He looked at her now, regarding her without judgment. It was like they were two friends catching up. "Just trying to stretch my legs," he commented.

Exhaustion was bubbling up, but Syra fought tooth and nail against it. "Why are you telling me all this?"

The Guardian raised the half-done raven, studying it in the light the lantern gave next to him. "Everybody has the right to make an informed decision, Fräurune. You are at least owed that."

That was hardly an answer. Her head grew heavier, so she let it drop, no longer capable of keeping watch on the Guardian. Raid wasn't going to let her out; he was just here for a chat while he guarded her. She closed her eyes. It was nice to just rest. Her arms had finally gone numb.

"Sleep well, my lady."

Farewell to the Night

Alaric motioned to the staff member walking by with a bowl of mashed potatoes. "Give him a little more, will you? Don't want him starving to death before he leaves tonight."

Cyrus groaned into the plate. "I've got more than I need, Alaric." They were in the small dining chamber that the king used for more private events. The table was selvyr wood, imported from Eiyrăl, with a channel carved out of the center and filled with blue. Tiny ships were placed strategically in the blue, along with small replicas of the Krakí and other sea beasts. Cyrus spent more time studying the table than his food whenever he came here. The dark grains that cut through the silver wood reminded him of the desk he'd sat at when he first met Kyllian.

The ceiling here was vaulted with intricate crown molding, the walls painted a pale blue, and the floors polished silver stone. The room was a bit much for Cyrus's liking—even the seats were designed to look like thrones—but he didn't tell Alaric that.

"Nonsense." The king dismissed him with a wave of his knife. "Eat. I hear Venkar eats bugs and bark for their meals."

That made Cyrus's stomach lurch. "Really?"

Alaric flashed him a grin. "Only the Dragon Riders."

He leaned back in his chair as the woman piled more mashed potatoes on his plate. He didn't even stop her when she scooped more than necessary. They really were delicious, and he would manage to find room for them somehow. "You're lying."

The king raised his hands in submission. "Maybe." Then he dug back into the fish on his plate. It was fried. The skin was crispy, overly seasoned and buttery, and while Cyrus had turned his nose up to fish for some time after arriving here, this dish was delectable and tasted nothing like the sea.

The friendship that had formed when Alaric first showed Cyrus kindness had since blossomed. They found peace in each other's company, and Alaric spent more time dining with just him than attending council festivities. Asher occasionally joined them, but tonight, he was dining alone in his study, reviewing export reports. While he knew the king enjoyed the luxuries of attention and praise, he clearly avoided the council. Cyrus didn't blame him. They were hungry for arguments and spent more time tossing insults than being productive in the council meetings he had attended. Thankfully, Alaric told him those weren't necessary anymore. The council's obsession with Cyrus had faded some—not entirely, but enough to grant him the freedom of choice.

Yet underneath all that kindness was a darker side that Cyrus caught a glimpse of every now and then. Even today, Alaric hinted at volatile and impulsive behavior. A piece of his father, Raj, was always within reach. Alaric's pale hazelnut eyes never quite sparkled like others' did, and he often wondered what the king did when no one was looking. Cyrus had once caught the look of an animal when a prisoner was being questioned after trying to steal imports from a ship. The king's face contorted so quickly that he'd wondered whether he'd really seen anything. But he never did see that prisoner again. Cyrus was not a fool.

The king had been raised at the hands of a monster. It was hard to blame him for his tough demeanor after meeting someone like King Jair. Most royalty Cyrus had met were snakes.

A fork waved in front of him, drawing his attention back to the king. "Are you listening?" Alaric asked.

Cyrus reached for the wine. "Apologies. I was thinking about the travel." He drenched his tongue in the bitter taste of what was supposed to be the finest wine. Then again, he was not a wine expert.

Alaric stabbed some vegetables. "I'm thinking about constructing a dragon statue. Have the artists work their magic. Maybe something that looks a little like Sozar?"

He was drunk, Cyrus had no doubt. "That's unnecessary. He doesn't need a bigger ego."

"I think it would be iconic. Maybe even the birth of a new religion. Actually, I think a religion was dedicated to the dragons. Ah . . . what was it?" He waved his fork again, frowning.

"Lih'rel," Cyrus answered, recalling his reading. "And no, it wasn't just dragons. It was all the Vore beasts." He took a spoonful of mashed potatoes. "And he's just Sozar, Alaric. No need to make it anything else."

The king took another drink, downing the rest of the wine. He set the glass aside and motioned to one of the ladies standing along the wall. She grabbed the decanter and approached. Alaric leaned back. "He's not just Sozar, he's the *magnificent* Sozar."

I like the sound of that, the dragon intruded, smug.

Cyrus couldn't believe what he was hearing. *No. It's not happening.*

The dragon yawned, curled up in the palace courtyard. Alaric had ordered the construction of several dragon holds to accommodate Sozar. The original ones from the Rider Federation centuries ago had long been transformed into other palace sections. Only the massive dungeons beneath indicated the rich history with the Dragon Riders, a place Cyrus loathed.

The king believed they would be done in the next full moon. They would even have a place for Cyrus to stay, if he pleased.

"I will be back as soon as I can be." He changed the subject, glad when the lady checked on his wine to top it off. "Can I have some water, please?"

She nodded and left.

The king pursed his lips. "People will ask, especially the council. I will tell them that you've left to address some personal business." He waved his hand. "They need not know. If it is necessary, you will share." Alaric squinted. "Do you have any idea what it might be?"

That water couldn't come fast enough. The more Cyrus thought about what might lie ahead, the drier his tongue became. He kept thinking about what Chavi said. "Information—that's all I know. Perhaps something to help strengthen defenses?"

The king burst out laughing, so loud that the woman who returned hesitated to approach the table. Cyrus motioned for her and gratefully accepted the water. He drank half the glass in one gulp as Alaric wiped away the tears. Yes, he wanted to go—he was eager to be off—but he was also anxious about the dangers. Nothing ever came easy. He'd learned that much.

When Alaric finally recovered, he shook his head, still chuckling. "You sounded almost like a king there. Well done." He wagged his finger. "But no, I don't think it has anything to do with us. You and I both know that."

Reactive, speech clear, no sign of the drunken man he'd seen moments prior. When the woman returned, he said, "Give us some privacy, please."

They waited as the few women shuffled out of the room. Cyrus's fingers drummed the metal of his glass, creating a soft but inconsistent tune he couldn't quite figure out if he hated. The additional noise was an annoyance, so he stopped. So much to say, but he wasn't sure what should be shared and what shouldn't. The food stared up at him, ugly and nauseating. The mashed potatoes looked more like a cyst, and he pushed the plate away.

When the door finally closed, Alaric repositioned. He grabbed his drink, leaned back, and kicked his boots up on the table, narrowly missing the bread.

"Tell me what's on your mind."

All the courage seeped out of Cyrus's pores like sweat, and he slumped back in his chair, leaning his elbow on the arm. No longer was this the king speaking to him, but the man who had saved his life.

"I think they are going to tell me things about the Rider Federation."

Alaric instantly took on the appearance of a child receiving his first gift. "Really?" He took a drink. "What could they possibly say? The Dragon Riders have been dead for centuries"—he motioned at him—"well, until you came along."

"Don't forget Dameon and Ashtir," Cyrus reminded him. "I'm not the only one."

The king waved him off. "I haven't met them, so to me, they don't exist. Only you and Sozar."

That was ignorance speaking. "They are dangerous," he insisted. Alaric was unstable at times, but he wasn't a fool. He was one of the cleverest men he'd come to know. The alcohol was making his tongue loose.

The king raised a hand, his response slow. "I put my faith in you two. I know the other Dragon Rider is out there, and I hope that I never have to meet him or his dragon."

"Okay." He took another drink of his water. The king's gaze didn't waver. "It all sounds crazy, doesn't it? This idea that the Dragon Riders might be rebuilt. I don't believe it myself."

"Why?"

Cyrus struggled to find the right words without sounding insensitive. "How could they possibly be rebuilt? I found Sozar by accident. The Rider Federation, when the city fell, left everything in ruins. There's nothing left." Even as he said those words, he felt the bitter taste of shame on his tongue. Hyle had said otherwise. Had hinted a possibility existed. "I know what Hyle has said. You were there. But now I'm being told Venkar has these answers, and it seems unreal to me. That everything I could have ever needed was within reach."

Alaric inhaled slowly, the sound deafeningly loud in the silence that filled the space between them. Cyrus predicted a lot of questions. More importantly, the awe that came with the idea of the Dragon Rider resurrection. He was relieved to speak on the matter but reluctant to listen to all the far-fetched fantasies of what could be.

Instead, to Cyrus's shock, the king asked, "How do you feel about it all?"

That left him quiet for a long breath. "Nervous," he confessed. "There's so much change happening. And I know you and many others expect things from me that I'm not even sure I can do." It was terrible to admit that out loud. He hadn't even admitted it to Hyle. How could he confess to a God that he didn't feel capable of living his destiny? Hyle never had a choice—he was forced into a role he was hardly prepared for.

Don't fear the man you were born to be. Sozar's words were gentle, affirmative.

Alaric tilted his head, regarding him. "Sometimes the best leaders never wanted the position to begin with. Remember who you are, Cyrus, and don't forget that Destiny saw something special in you. You came here for a reason, and look where you've come—so far!" He leaned forward and raised his glass. "Isn't it worth being the Dragon Rider the world believes you are?"

The air was cool. Cyrus pulled the coat tighter around his shoulders to fight off the wind that tried to pierce his skin. The deule fur that tickled his neck was soft. The tiny creature only resided on the southern side of the Vore World, or so Alaric told him. He'd yet to see one, but he hoped that would change.

No extravagant goodbyes or parties saw him off, which Cyrus appreciated. He would be back, and Alaric ensured the departure was quiet. Asher was there to see him off, offering a nod and a word of good luck. The king promised to inform the council of their whereabouts the following morning—*if* they asked. Cyrus was glad about that. He didn't want to be bombarded with hundreds of questions when he returned. Without certainty as to exactly what he was flying into, he chained his hope. But that didn't stop the excitement of adventure from bubbling up.

Sozar kept low. The night was illuminated by the full moon, offering visibility on the ground below. Cyrus didn't need the light to know where they were going—he'd walked the dirt street hundreds of times. Behind, Delion was still alive. Small fires, lanterns, people walking about. They cheered when he flew over them, and Cyrus waved in return. Sozar let loose a large roar that he was sure the entire country could hear. If Chavi had questions about them coming, she wouldn't now. She would know.

As the dragon lowered himself to the approaching intersection soon after, Cyrus could see her. Standing there, no horse, and just a small pack over her back. She waved at them.

"Where's her steed?" he asked out loud.

I don't think she intends to get back on foot, Sozar mused.

The dragon flared his wings out, slowing the descent. Cyrus always tensed up on the landing. Core tight, hand on the horn in front of him, he waited until he felt the impact of talon and foot against the dirt. Sozar was getting better at softer landings, but it was still jarring.

Not too bad? Sozar asked as he tucked his wings in, and Cyrus swung his leg over to descend. The drop was getting higher, and he gratefully leveraged the dragon's front leg on the way down. As his boots struck the hard-packed ground, she spoke.

"It is an honor to serve you."

Cyrus looked at her fully. Leather reflected the moonlight, and her skin glistened. She was dressed only somewhat warmly, no doubt more acclimated to the cooler nights than him. "That's not necessary," he replied. "I don't want anyone serving me." Chavi stared at him, swaying from side to side and chuckling. "Your horse?"

The woman motioned at Sozar. "Your dragon will arrive twice as fast. What good is it if I cannot arrive to my own people to introduce you?"

See? Sozar observed.

Cyrus's gaze danced between her and the dragon. Nobody had ever ridden Sozar besides him. An intrusion of intimacy rippled through him, wiggling deep into his chest. Cyrus forced air in. This was appropriate, but the words came out slower than he'd like.

"You want to ride with me?"

Chavi nodded. "It will save us time. We can be there before dawn."

He understood, but he struggled to accept the reasoning. *Sozar,* he started, *are you okay with this?* As much as he wanted to be the one to make the decision, he wasn't, not here.

Sozar reached his large head around, meeting his gaze with his fiery own. *This is our path forward.*

He nodded. "All right." He rubbed the back of his neck. "Saddle might be a little snug for the both of us, but you said we'll be there before dawn?"

"Yes." Chavi took several careful steps toward Sozar. Raising a hand, she seemed to wait for permission, even checking with Cyrus. When the dragon snorted, she jumped but then laughed nervously. "Apologies." Now she placed her hand against his shoulder. "I've never been close to a dragon before."

"He gets that a lot." Cyrus came up next to her. "When you're ready." Hopping on the back of a dragon wasn't an elegant skill. It involved strategic foot placements and hoisting himself up with his upper strength. "I'll help."

The woman nodded and reached up. She latched on to the saddle, and as she did, Cyrus grabbed her waist and boosted her up. She was light, and she moved quickly. She threw her leg over and snatched the horn in front of her. Without wasting any time, he hopped up behind her, leveraging the saddle. As he settled in behind, he grimaced. This was a tight fit.

"Comfortable?" he asked Chavi. She was tense and hardly moved, even as she nodded. "Good."

Sozar started to move, and Cyrus realized he had little to hold on to. Reluctantly, he wrapped an arm around the woman. "Only while Sozar takes off." This was not his ideal travel setup. But more importantly, while he found Chavi beautiful, this was not the woman he'd have chosen to share Sozar with. Zorya was always on his mind—she should've had a similar opportunity first. He'd taken her for granted, was too confused with who he was, and shattered her life after his departure. If the princess—no, queen—didn't want anything to do with him, he understood. He just wished he could let her go, but he couldn't. He wouldn't. Cyrus still owed her an apology for the way he'd left things.

Fly as fast as possible. Sozar didn't need an explanation. Their thoughts always intermingled, even subconsciously. With a handful of steps, his wings flared, and he launched himself into the sky. The pull of the motions tugged at Cyrus, but he was familiar with it. Chavi wasn't. She immediately leaned back, and he had to keep him and her up. Every muscle in his core tightened, and when she finally regained her composure and straightened, he said a silent prayer of gratitude to the Gods.

Sozar gained altitude. The beat of his wings relaxed Cyrus, and he let go of Chavi but kept his hands on his legs, ready to grab her in case of any emergency. The last thing he wanted was to be the cause of her death before he even made it to Venkar.

Born to Reign

The festival was in two days, and Morei was nowhere he should have been. He should have already checked the final preparations, helped approve anything the staff required, and ensured everything was transitioning smoothly. The festival was going to be huge and would last several days. On top of that, they would have dancers and expect expensive imports this evening for the event. Morei, as king, should have been there.

Instead, he was in the underground tunnels he'd been told of in the first few days of rule. Down here, where stone cracks decorated the walls, few lanterns hung, and vast rivers flowed to the grand Merrél Sea, he could have peace. The king had never been fond of places like this—he was far more accustomed to the endless dunes of the Hazar Desert, where he could see for leagues. Dungeons too, which had long since been abandoned because of the superstitions that the people held regarding the dead, but Morei hadn't run into any spirits. At this point, given his encounters with Gods, a spirit would be the least of his concerns.

Morei never went far. He wasn't here to explore, though he'd done plenty of that in the past. He came here when the compulsion got far too strong, or when his thoughts spiraled. Nobody else came here, save for citizens trying to avoid city tax. The soldiers wouldn't even venture this way.

Tucked up against a cold stone wall, Morei stared into the dark. He could hear the small river but could not see it. If he crawled forward some ten paces, he would. Morei let his thoughts have their way. They had grown progressively more violent in the passing several moons. He'd known how borrowed his time was, but he'd hoped he had longer. He was a king, and his job was to ensure the people could trust him. After his merciless seizure of Caster, he treaded on thin ice, and one small mistake could cost him everything he'd worked for. Ferguson granted him a sliver of assurance. Now, he was dealing with the imminent attack of the Red Queens. The bodies from this morning still hung over his thoughts. He wasn't sure what to do.

Morei willed his spiraling thoughts to silence, but all he could see was the memory of Emerald lying there in a pool of her blood and Sekar's gleeful glare. That was the day his life fell apart. Until then, despite all the signs, he'd been certain there was a way out. That certainty had cost him his rulership—and Emerald's life.

The dead queen didn't earn his sympathy; she'd proven to him just how tragic affection could be. It was her murder that meant more to him. The worldwide political ramifications were undeniable. Morei thought—no, he believed wholeheartedly—that he could outrun those consequences. What he saw this morning proved otherwise. Nerius was her brother, but he'd abandoned the family some summers ago, trading in his silks for the harsh winds of the sea. That was what he'd held on to, but now Nerius was king of Junok, and he knew Morei's hands had his sister's blood on them.

It didn't matter if he knew the truth of Sekar's involvement. The note was a threat. Junok was coming for him. He didn't know when, but the threads of thought were coming together. Sekar had to be involved in some way. The God was toying with him again, trying to rip away the only bit of normalcy he had as king.

Morei bounced his fist against the cold slab of rugged rock. His heart was hammering. The people couldn't know. They couldn't afford an attack from Junok or the Red Queens, or both. It would destroy Caster.

Slowly, he slid to the ground, stone digging into his back. He needed to try again. Previous attempts had failed, but maybe it would be different this time. He focused on the readings. Old books spoke about dream walking like projection. If he focused hard enough, knew the person he was after, then he could connect with them. Morei understood enough to correlate with what he could do as a Harvester; entering people's minds while awake was not difficult, but it could be dangerous. The primary difference was that dream walking was meant for victims who were asleep. Sekar was an expert, and many over the centuries had tried to replicate that power. As far as Morei had found, nobody could quite get it right, and many died trying.

The king still didn't know why. He brushed off theories about the mind's activity during sleep and the sensitivity one had to the energies around them. They felt incomplete. Breaking into someone's mind was routine for some Harvesters, but it was nearly impossible when the individual was asleep. Morei had tried both during these sessions. He stretched his mind as far as it could go, desperate to cling to the smallest threads of consciousness that felt like Syra or Sekar. He knew he shouldn't—he should've been scared off, but the more time that passed, the more irritated he got that nothing was resolved. He couldn't figure out why their connection existed, why it had stopped, and why he couldn't reestablish it.

And now, with Nerius's threat, he was impatient to locate Sekar. Not having contact with the deity after all that had happened felt irresponsible—an obvious threat to his empire. Dreams of Syra still haunted him, but these were different. Hallucinations, scenes that blended his memories with her involvement, and crippling what-ifs. But he never saw her innocently. She was constantly responsible for something heinous in his dreams—and she always had Sekar with her.

He concentrated hard, sensing hundreds of things at once. At first, he'd been overwhelmed by all the lifeforces of the citizens and animals, but he'd managed to grow accustomed to it. Stretching across the sea, though, was impossible, so he focused on channeling energy into a call. It always gave him a headache, and he pressed his fingers against his temple.

Over and over, he tried. And again, like all the times before, he failed. The king expended strength, his muscles weakened, and he could feel his mind splintering. He broke the concentration before he overdid it. Last time, he'd woken up feverish in these tunnels, blacking out from overexertion. That was not a mistake he would make again.

He blinked into the dark, angry. He might as well have been a cow waiting for slaughter. The king slammed his fist into the ground next to him. Bruising pain flourished up his arm, and he flexed his hand in annoyance. What he needed was more information, but not even that was fast enough.

"You've got me," he mumbled. His words were directed to the God of Dreams, if he could hear. "Your rules, your game." The statement was sour on his tongue, and his muscles tensed. "You won't let me live my life, but you can't face me? Are you a coward?"

No response came. How infuriating.

"Are you a coward?" the king yelled. His voice carried through the tunnel until it faded altogether. Again, nothing.

The compulsion was hardly controllable. Morei laughed, scratching the stone with a short nail. He needed to get himself together, but the sensation that rushed him made him flush. This was a losing battle.

His head pounded, his muscles wouldn't relax, and his fingers twitched like he had an enemy in front of him. A sliver of reasoning knew this was unacceptable for a king. Morei would never make it if he couldn't take more control of his impulses, but he hardly knew how when it all stemmed from the ailment that he knew so little about.

And another part of him—the part gaining strength rapidly—didn't want to change. If this was what Destiny wanted, then she would have it.

Morei stood, shaking out his hand, which was still a bit sore. He wanted to get a drink and find some food. Sitting in here was not helping his thoughts any, and the king didn't want to give them any more leverage over him than they already had.

Hand on the hilt of his sword, Morei made the short walk to the heavy door. It was engraved with a large, howling wolf, the image now rusted and cracked. He hauled the door open and stepped out into the side of the courtyard. The night was chilly, the sky clear, and with the countless lanterns still burning, he could see everything.

Morei quickly made his way to the palace entrance. Soldiers stood there, chatting about some bet, but when they saw him, they stopped. "Everything all right, Your Majesty?"

He hoped he didn't look that bothered. The question came easy. "Actually, I need something." He motioned behind him. "Is there any report of long-term citizens living there?"

The one on the left, Geoff, shrugged. "Oh, by the Gods, I have no clue."

"Well, I thought there was," the other replied. Morei tried hard to place his name, but he couldn't. He was usually better at that. "I remember—well, he's dead now—but my mentor went down there, king's orders, looking for some people. I thought we found them, though. That was many summers ago."

"The dead live down there, so be careful. Although they might be afraid of you." The men chuckled and smacked each other. That would suffice. They wouldn't ask questions if they thought he was just a bit spooked.

"Thank you," he told them with a nod. "I'll leave you to it."

Morei entered the main palace halls and made his way toward the galley. It was late, but he wanted a snack before he tried to get some sleep. His adrenaline was still high, so he wasn't sure he'd be able to relax, but it was worth a try. A glass or two of Kendell's Milk might help take the edge off his compulsion. Actually, he was betting on it. He couldn't go into tomorrow feeling this way. Morei would kill the council before high noon at this rate.

The galley was massive—twice the size of Geral's—and he found several staff members prepping fruits and sharing drinks. They greeted him warmly, and he returned it. He motioned to a basket. "Are these today's leftovers?"

An older plump woman nodded. "Yes, Your Majesty."

He reached for it, noting how his hand trembled, but she quickly added, "Oh, no. Let us make something for you. Do you need something?"

The king waved them off. Nobody seemed to notice his deteriorating state. "Not at all. I just wanted something small." He pulled the cloth off and saw several pieces of bread, cheese, and a single terone, a small citrus fruit that only grew along the coastline. He grabbed it, along with the bread, and waved at the ladies. "Good night."

But as he turned to leave, he saw Edwin, who looked exhausted. "Your Majesty."

"Yes?" He held the items in his hands, hoping this was nothing serious, though his gut told him otherwise.

"We have apprehended Eli. His brother, Grant, was not with him, so we are still searching. I wanted to tell you immediately, but given the time, I can place him under surveillance until tomorrow morning."

The king glanced at the ladies, who quickly returned to their work. He looked back at the commander. This was the only Energy Harvester they could confirm was still alive, but by the time the king had requested the brothers, the young man was already out at sea. They'd been waiting for a ship to return since. After the threat, though, Morei was worried the Red Queens were involved with this timely return.

No sleep would come now, at least not soon. "Take me to him now. And Isla—"

"Has already been notified. She will meet you there."

Morei nodded and took a bite of the bread. It was from the morning, but it still tasted fresh. "Good," he said once he swallowed. As they fell into step, he added, "And one other thing."

Edwin raised his brow.

"If you ever refuse to come to my side again, like you did this morning, I will personally have your tongue, and then I will strip you and all future generations of your name of all honor."

A long beat of silence followed, filled only by their steps. In a low voice, the commander answered, "Yes, Your Majesty."

Courted with Blood

Only a few times had Syra ever felt this oppressive nature of being watched. The sensation ripped her out of slumber, clawing at her sense of peace despite her awful situation. She blinked, head heavy, stomach rumbling, but her mind felt sharper than it had before. The toxin was wearing off already, but she didn't want to give that away again.

The meticulous slow sound of boots stopped. "You are quite the talk around here." His voice had a razor-sharp edge to it, and she flinched. Every instinct told her to run, but she couldn't. The man approached, revealing a lock of closely kept blond hair, blood-colored eyes, and skin that looked gray under the dim light. He bore no weapon, and he was tall. "I couldn't wait to come down here to find out what all the fuss was about."

Syra tried to shift, but her muscles were locked, and she couldn't feel her fingers. "And you are?" Her voice cracked, dry.

"Your savior, your nightmare, your knight in shining armor." The man shrugged. His breath didn't turn to mist like hers. "I am known by quite a few names."

Syra didn't laugh. "And you are?" she repeated.

He approached, now so close that she could see the grayish tint to his skin along his jaw and fingers, complemented by thick networks of black veins. This was not a mortal man. His pupils were slits, and what she originally thought of as red irises were primarily black with bright red flakes. "They call us Ka-Geíons. We are the result of Ön'grusah. Quite a few centuries ago, our not-so-bright brethren, the Honuyál, did the unthinkable: they molded energy. Not just any, either. Dark Energy. They gave it continuous structure, changed the entire makeup of it. In that, a new species was born, the Geíons. But we weren't all alike. I'm sure you've seen some of the lesser. We like to call them Gor-Geíons—it's nice to give things a name. I'm sure you understand, coming from the living realm and all."

The demon smiled, as if flattered by his sympathy. As he did, he revealed rows of sharpened teeth. "You mortals—well, I guess you're not one anymore, are you? Sneaking in to be judged by the Eternal Flame . . . now that was clever."

"Not my first choice," she remarked. A shiver smacked her, and she hoped he didn't notice. What she wouldn't give for a fur cloak or blanket and some food. She was starved.

He ignored her comment. "How does it feel, Syra? That is what the living realm calls you, right? Here, you're known as the Light Bringer, Fräurune, although"—he picked up a lock of her dirty red hair and let it drop—"I dare say you're a bit far from that title, yeah?"

She stared, not sure what he was getting at. "I don't understand."

The demon motioned around them dramatically. "You're finally here! Isn't that what Destiny wanted all along? Don't you feel anything for that?"

"I feel uncomfortable—and in pain," Syra answered bluntly. "That's the best I've got." This demon's attitude was playful, a harsh contrast to the dungeon's conditions. Nothing bothered him. She wanted him gone.

His lips twitched upward, and his appearance shifted. A part of his face transitioned into dark gray, leathery skin. His mouth stretched up to his ear, decorated with curved teeth, and those black orbs met hers—cold, animalistic. As quickly as he revealed his true form, the image was gone, replaced by the mop of blond hair and ashen skin. Syra didn't flinch, but underneath her beaten exterior, she was afraid.

"Shevana has spoken about you for quite a while," he continued. "At first, I couldn't quite place my finger on why she was so interested in you. You were, after all, born a mortal and raised among the living—no offense." Syra frowned, missing the meaning. "Yet, over and over, things would go wrong for her. If it wasn't Kar—nice play on the name, by the way—it was Dryl abandoning the Order. She was pretty pissed about that one. But then Zarek?" He wagged his finger at her. "That broke her, Syra. And she won't admit it, but I think she's got a little grudge against you."

"You think?"

The demon chuckled. The sound made her skin crawl. "I want to know why the world is so fascinated with the little redhead from Caster. Sure, we can point the finger. Bloodline, Goddess, penchant for the dead, but what is it really that makes them mad for you?" He looked at her, curious.

"I don't know," she replied. If she could have shrugged, she would have. Preferably melted into the ground. This conversation already made her uncomfortable. He was searching for something, an answer she didn't have. "I spent most of my time running." It was like he'd never looked at anyone before, which was unnerving. Maybe he'd never seen anyone from the living realm, though she highly doubted that, given the form he took. Syra was beginning to realize he wasn't here to hurt her—at least yet. Maybe he could offer her information. She knew little about demons, save for what she'd been shown, but she hoped it was enough. What she really wanted was Raid back. He was strangely comforting, especially compared to what stood before her now.

The demon turned away, and she took the opportunity to ask, "What's your name?"

He paused. "Do you intend to earn my loyalty by wiggling your way into my undead heart?"

"What?" Syra scrunched her face as best she could. Even that motion hurt. "No, not unless you're feeling like undoing these chains and helping me, which I highly doubt. I just want to know what your name is. Feels appropriate, given you know mine."

"Hm." He stopped several paces away and regarded her. "Don't be so certain in your assumptions, Syra. You believe that because I'm here and you're there, I have a side in all this. Foolish. What do they teach you in the living, anyway? How to build with rock?" He shook his head, clearly appalled, and Syra felt a pang of regret. She wasn't thinking straight.

"You may call me Elyas," he finally said.

She decided to switch strategies. "What do you want?"

"Impatient," Elyas scolded. "All of you from the living realm have the patience of an egunsar. Pesky little things that try to eat your eyes out when you fall asleep. Absolute horrors. Your attitude reminds me of one—chasing after some end that you don't fully comprehend. What if I wake and smash you? You're dead just like that, but you can't even think that far ahead because you're too focused on the prize." He made a clicking noise in his throat, similar to an annoyed creature that had lost its meal. "I anticipated far more from the Light Bringer."

Syra bit her tongue. She didn't want to start an argument with a higher intellectual demon—a Ka-Geíon—when she couldn't even defend herself. Elyas was here for the games, he wanted a reaction out of her, and so the only thing she could do was stay quiet in his insults.

He reached out and let a frigid finger tuck some hair behind her ear. "I want to know what makes Syra tick. Why do you do what you do?"

She waited for him to pull his ghastly hand away, noting the blackened nails. They looked devoured by fungi. "Because it's the right thing to do."

Elyas scoffed. "Wrong. Nobody ever does anything because it's the right thing. No. They do it because they are driven by a power in here"—he painfully poked her chest with his nail—"not because of some flimsy, vague statement. Try again."

Irritated, she glared at him, but he seemed to enjoy it, so she stopped. "Because if I don't do anything, people like you will ruin the realms. You've already destroyed this one. I'd like to keep the living realm alive."

In response, the demon picked at his teeth with one of his nails. He looked bored. "Wrong again, Syra. Humor me, won't you? Dig a little deeper into that beating heart of yours. I'd do it myself but that would require me to rip it out of you, and I think you need it. Goddess or not."

That was not a bluff. Elyas wanted to get personal, and she couldn't figure out why. "I want to protect my friends—"

Her words were stolen as Elyas wrapped a hand around her throat. His demeanor shifted instantly, and he squeezed hard. "Wrong *again*. Tell me what makes Syra tick," he hissed.

Tears burned, carving a path down her cheeks. Her lungs screamed for air, and panic ripped through her body. A sinister sensation tumbled through her head, kicking her immediate thoughts aside and fumbling with the most secretive pieces she kept hidden. Elyas titled his head, narrowing his crimson gaze, as he dug deeper into her head. Every emotion became a feast for him. When he found the searing agony and terror, the corner of his lip twitched, and he got a little closer. His hot breath drenched her cheek. Another hand trailed up her arm, slicing skin open as his nail burrowed into flesh. She inhaled, trying to get air, but he squeezed harder, and the blackened claws of his mind peeled back the last layer of defense. He ripped the answer right out of her.

"Because I had no choice," she gasped. The demon's grip loosened, but only enough to give her the chance to speak. She wanted to stop but couldn't. The words forced their way out with his coaxing. "All I ever wanted to do was run. Get as far as I could from all the problems, start a new life, but I couldn't. Now, everyone tells me I'm all the realms have. I have a bloodline that I don't want, and the rest of you seemed to think I exist solely to reclaim a throne I never wanted in the first place."

Tears rolled, fat and hot, down her cheeks. She could hardly look at Elyas—he'd exploited her as easily as if he'd ripped apart a doll and peered inside. The tingling sensation of humiliation made her chest tight. Now that she had admitted that, she felt ashamed. Dryl, Zarek, Sekar, Zane . . . what would they say to her if they knew the truth? After all this time, after everything they'd devoted to her—the risks, fights, lies, training—all of it for a role and title she never wanted. Syra did want to do the right thing, she did want to help and protect those she loved, but she'd never imagined her life where it was now. And for that, she resented Destiny.

Elyas grinned like a proud father. "There you go." He removed his hand entirely, but not before brushing his fingers over her wet cheek. "Was that so hard?"

Still, she did not look at him. Instead, she watched the tears fall to the bloodied ground below.

His mind released hers, oozing out of her as if from a seeping wound. She shivered, nauseous from the encounter. Stomach knotting, she fought the urge to throw up whatever was left, though she suspected it wasn't much. Bile at best. This demon was dangerous, and she needed to be careful. If he'd wanted, he could have taken far more from her than just a confession. In an instant, he'd made her feel like she was the same girl who'd fled Caster—worthless, unable to defend herself, and irrational.

"Syra," Elyas prompted. "Don't feel so bad. Sometimes the person we don't want to be is the person we never knew we needed in the first place."

Syra snorted, but it made her throat hurt. She couldn't believe how fast her life had changed. Everything felt like it was in shambles. Mere days ago, she'd never have predicted this. At the worst, she might be oiling leather for soldiers, but not this. "Thanks for the advice."

"You're welcome," he replied. A stifling silence followed as he stood there, studying her like a buyer surveying a fine jewel.

One of his blackened nails trailed alarmingly close to the laceration on her right arm. She begged Raid to walk through the door now. Skin tender to the touch, she clenched her teeth, not wanting to show any discomfort. "You and I," he breathed close to her ear, "we could rule the realm together. We don't need Shevana. She is stuck in tradition. But you and I? We could create something extraordinary."

He pulled away, regarding her. Syra swallowed the rising bile. "I don't want anything to do with you."

Elyas didn't flinch at the rejection. "You don't even know what I want. Don't you want to?"

Emboldened, she said, "No."

It was exactly what he wanted to hear. "Your blood is fresh, new, and the realm needs that. But it also needs structure, which I can offer. We can provide balance by merging these traits. That sounds interesting, yes?" He waited until she made a feasible attempt to nod. "Good. I've gotten quite tired of the day-to-day, but with you? I see potential."

"You're a liar."

He stopped in front of her, offering her the most sinister chuckle she'd ever heard—short, hollow, and too loud. The teeth he flashed could cut glass.

"I'm trying to be kind," he whispered. To her, it sounded like he'd just yelled. "But I am not one with patience, so I'll jump straight to the point, to spare your little mind from getting too overwhelmed." Elyas took a step forward, too close now. "I want to spare your life because you're the last of the bloodline, and the realm needs that. Do you want me to kill you, Syra? Do you want your pride to be the reason this realm perishes?"

He was serious. Syra could see it through his wild gaze, and that made this entire encounter more disturbing. One moment, she was chatting with a Guardian, the next she was being courted. Not in the way young girls dreamed of; no, she was being threatened. He wanted her because her bloodline was all this realm had. Refusing meant he would kill her, but it didn't seem to matter, did it?

"You're going to kill me anyway. That's the reason you and Shevana—"

"Tsk-tsk," Elyas interrupted, his face faltering. "You think too much. I've said awful things, but I certainly don't mean them. I like you. I'm intrigued by you, and I think we can benefit each other. But if you prefer, I can rip your heart out too."

An ultimatum. Syra gaped at him, deflated. Hang here until she was killed, or agree to some demon's gracious plan to keep her alive, so that he could stay in control, and *hope* he kept her alive. Shevana didn't know what he was doing. That was obvious now. She couldn't fathom settling for either. There had to be another way.

"Tell you what," Elyas said. "Why don't I give you some time to think about it? Maybe somewhere a little nicer than here. What do you think? Big question, I understand, and I wouldn't feel good about forcing you into a decision you're not ready for."

He approached the door, and Syra was beyond relieved. His presence made her skin crawl, made her feel dirty. Then he stopped at the entryway, ruining her hope.

"Your mind is . . . different than your friend's." He sounded blissful, perhaps even crazed about it. A beast preparing to ravage a meal. "Why is that?"

His tone changed too fast for her comfort, like he couldn't figure out who he wanted to be. Did he mean Sekar? Or Zarek? She didn't like where this was going. "I don't know."

"Hm." His presence receded, and she looked up to see him inviting more Gor-Geions inside. Raid was nowhere to be seen, and her heart dropped. "You will find, Syra, that I'm not fond of 'I don't knows.' They tend to pique my curiosity." He leaned against the doorframe. "Don't struggle. I would really hate to make this harder than it needs to be."

The Pink City

Shadows stretched across the tropical landscape. The sun was barely over the horizon, painting the sky in a stunning array of oranges and reds. When the first light fell, Cyrus saw the massive trees with their wide leaves for the first time. He was used to the pine needles and thumb-sized leaves in Sorréle, but this was different. Leaves as wide as his body hung like curtains from trees that stood as tall as palaces. They were thick, covering the forest floor, and hugging mountains with jagged peaks. Crystal-blue water ran beneath them through narrow, carved rivers. Occasionally, they disappeared from the large trees but then would return. Birds with wild-colored feathers bolted from trees at the sight of Cyrus, cawing and screeching. Some had long necks with curved beaks, others large crowns made of feathers.

"Is there anything else that lives here?" Cyrus asked Chavi. They'd flown straight through the night as promised, and he could feel it in his legs and back. His shoulders twinged when he moved his head, so he refrained from any sudden movements. What he needed was a good stretch.

The woman had long since relaxed. At least her body offered some reprieve from the wind. "We call them umpels." Her voice carried easily to his ears, and he was getting better at deciphering her accent. "It's Old Tongue for tricksters. They run around on all fours but can climb. That's usually where you'll find them with your things. Once they have something, it's lost for good. They never return it." She laughed.

Cyrus smiled. He was excited. The farther they got from Delion, the more free he felt. Alaric was a friend, and the man who'd saved his life, but Cyrus was not cut out for politics. Out here, in the open sky, he felt more like himself.

"There." She pointed to the left. "Our city is nestled in the woods, but there is a clearing Sozar can land in."

The dragon steered in that direction without a word. He began his descent, while Cyrus strained to see anything that resembled a city. Nothing stood out to him. Just more trees.

Chavi seemed to sense this. "You won't see it. Venkar was specifically designed to be hidden. The only way in and out is through one path."

A glimmer peeked out through several trees, a pinkish hue that contrasted sharply against the thriving greens. "What's that?" Cyrus pointed ahead.

The woman didn't follow his gaze. "Crescent Lake. You'll see it once we're in the city."

Sozar hummed. The dragon couldn't hide his excitement, and the emotion seeped into his own veins. Cyrus should have felt nervous, but he only felt a thrill. In a season, he'd seen so much. As the trees stretched up around them, blocking out the view and swallowing them whole, Sozar flared his wings for the landing. Cyrus wrapped his arm around Chavi long enough to steady himself while Sozar set his weight down.

Cyrus slid off the saddle. His knees nearly buckled, and he caught himself with the dragon's leg. His muscles burned and protested, and his back was on fire. After so much flying, the ground felt foreign.

Chavi landed next to him with a huff. She too wobbled and swayed, leveraging Sozar to keep herself up. "Whoa," she mumbled.

"I know." He chuckled and patted Sozar, whose scales were warm and slick to the touch. "You don't get used to flights that long."

The woman did some stretching and walked around the clearing. Cyrus took in their surroundings. The trunks of these trees were at least two men wide. Foliage clung to their bases, sprouting tiny purple flowers. The ground beneath was sandy, almost beach-like, but more hard-packed. From everywhere, chirps and chatter echoed. Ahead lay a tunnel-like entrance made entirely of branches.

"That's . . ." He couldn't get the last words out.

"How we get in and out," Chavi confirmed with a nod. "Yes. Ready? I'm sure they've seen us coming already."

Cyrus wanted to ask how, but he already suspected the answer. "The trees?" he asked.

She beamed like a proud mother. "Let's go."

Sozar followed close behind, his hot breaths teasing the backs of Cyrus's legs as they moved. The intertwined branches and leaves quickly swallowed the little light that broke through the canopy of trees. The darkness was intrusive, and Cyrus peered back to the clearing they'd just been in. Sounds were muffled in here. The chirping birds died out, and the sounds of their own boots felt hollow to his ears. Ahead, he could see doors, but they were not made of stone, rather of vines tightly interwoven to appear solid. He reached out, more curious now, and let his hand graze the cold wall of leaves to his immediate right.

"How is this possible?"

Chavi picked up the pace. "Energy, Sea Flyer." The woman stopped at the doors, which stood three times their height. Tall enough for any dragon to get through. "The world you see is an illusion. But beyond these doors is a city that has protected your heritage for as long as anyone can remember. I welcome you to my home, Cyrus and Sozar, and I hope that it gives you everything you could ever need."

The doors swung open silently. Vines retracted and stretched in response to the woman's touch. A hum filled the air instantly as he beheld the world before him. Energy seeped into his pores, alive and strong. Sozar rumbled in response, feeling it too.

Gemstones jutted from the rich dark soil, pink and vivid. Some crystals were as large as his head, others as small as his thumbs. A sweet smell wafted through the air—baked apple and cinnamon? Critters as small as his hand scrambled away, and a few took flight on wide, translucent wings. Cyrus made sure to watch his step, afraid he might hurt one. Light poured in from above through massive leaves that had holes in them. But with all the pink gemstones, it made him feel like he'd just stepped into some magical story from his childhood.

Zorya would have loved this. The woman broached his mind as quickly as the wind could change directions.

The homes were built into the wide bases of trees all around. Some trunks were wider than ships, and Cyrus watched countless people pour out of the interior, staring. A few descended the trees by stairs. Kids no older than five held tools for skinning animals. They were all dressed in simple garb that covered the bare minimum. What was left visible was covered in tribal marking done in white paint. A few of the men's faces were covered in red and white, and bones held their hair in place, while some women painted half theirs red. As he met the eyes of everyone he could, he realized they all had the same gray color as Chavi.

"My people. The Yavinks," Chavi introduced.

Cyrus felt the air ripped right out of his lungs. Evander's face shoved itself into the forefront of his mind, loud and obnoxious. The man's memory was not one he liked to revisit, but he couldn't help it. Evander had once said he believed in Yavinks. The name was so peculiar, he couldn't have forgotten.

"As in . . ." Cyrus stumbled for the right word. "What the stories say?"

Chavi chuckled as people started to approach. "Fairies. We all know what they say about us. We have much to share. My people wish to greet you." She motioned for those closest to come forward. Cyrus was gifted a few necklaces made of the gemstones he'd seen. Then a woman approached with a small wooden bowl. Her fingers dripped with white paint.

"Our traditional greeting," Chavi explained as the woman dragged two cold fingers across Cyrus's cheeks and over his chin. "Please consider it our highest honor."

Chanting began from behind, and he turned to see a dozen more of the Yavinks surrounding Sozar. They flicked the same white paint onto the dragon, decorating his scales in splatter. Sozar was eating it up, head held high, deviously proud. The people were speaking in a tongue lost to him, but the passion was enough to captivate him.

"Dragons are the bridge between realms," Chavi told him. "Honoring them means honoring the dead."

Simultaneously, those surrounding Sozar reached out and rested a hand on him. Their chanting grew in volume. Then they removed their hands, voices dropping, and circled him again before repeating the same behavior.

They smell different, the dragon mused. *Sweeter.*

Cyrus refrained from chuckling. The humming in the air intensified, and he watched Sozar's wings flutter as a result.

You think it's them? he asked.

This energy is not from them. There's something else here. The Yavinks did another full circle and chanted louder. *Perhaps what makes the place what it is.* Even as those words reached Cyrus's mind, Sozar sounded unconvinced.

"This way." Chavi was already moving through the dense crowd. Those closest stepped out of the way, but Sozar was still held captive by those praising him.

Enjoy.

The dragon snorted, blowing a small puff of smoke into the air. The Yavinks were delighted by it.

The Rider's Sword bounced on his leg as they walked, and he realized that with the weapon, he felt out of place. Nobody appeared to be carrying anything here—another strange case like Razan. "Am I being disrespectful with this?" he asked Chavi, and motioned to the sword.

She shook her head. "Just because we don't carry the same metal doesn't mean we aren't carrying weapons." They weaved through narrow tree-lined streets with houses built into the trunks. Children stared out of their makeshift windows, noses pressed against glass. Several parents swatted at their kids to pull their faces free, and he stifled a laugh.

Cyrus studied everything they passed. The hearts of trees were carved into homes and stores. The immaculate design would have made any woodworker drop to their knees in wonder. Doors opened and closed with ease, windows nestled perfectly into the wood, and the surrounding ground sprouted with vegetables. The wood wasn't like the rich browns and hazelnut colors he'd seen before. The bark had silver grains that, depending on how he looked, even appeared purple and blue.

They approached a small home carved from the base of a massive trunk. Wide, holed leaves reached low enough to scrape the ground. Cyrus touched one, unable to stop himself, and was alarmed to see one of those tiny creatures with translucent wings on the backside. He pulled his arm back, not sure if he should apologize. The creature gave an angry squeak.

"Are they Yavinks too?" The creature almost looked like a poor attempt at a fairy with the wings and stumpy body.

Chavi laughed with her entire being. "Oh, no. That's where people get mistaken. They think these are Yavinks." She shook the leaf, and the creature took off. "But they are just binters. So many stories get it wrong, but we prefer to let the world think they're the real deal. Keeps us protected."

Before he could reply, she knocked on the simple door. Cyrus cleared his throat, suddenly nervous. His tongue was dry, and he rolled on his feet. The reality was setting in. "Are we here?"

"Yes."

Cyrus looked at the house again. It was ordinary. "You live here?"

Now, she raised her brow. "Did you expect something else?"

"Well." Footsteps were approaching from the other side of the door. "I just thought it would be a bigger home, I guess." He wasn't sure what to say without sounding disrespectful.

The woman seemed to understand. "Here, royalty doesn't mean having a palace."

The door opened. A woman stood there with braided white hair. Her dark skin was complemented by fissures that stretched in various sizes across her face. Crinkles around her eyes and mouth told Cyrus that she was a woman with a lot of expressions. She grinned, revealing crooked teeth.

"You are the Dragon Rider!" She reached for him, pushing him inside. "Please, get comfortable. I wasn't sure when to expect you, but I was already making some food. Your boots, please take them off. Over here."

Cyrus did as he was told, placing the boots beside a hearth. The fire inside was raging, and over it hung a pot with a lid. He looked at her, waiting on his next orders. Chavi had disappeared into another room. The space was small but cozy. Furniture lined the walls, with some of the chairs positioned in front of the hearth. These were all made with aged leather. Simple, nothing elegant or royal about them. He'd seen better quality furniture at the orphanage he'd been raised in. The floor was laid with unpolished wood that groaned in spots. The walls were brown and plain—the wood from the tree. He watched the woman grab some cutlery and bowls from a shelf behind the hearth and then set them on the low table in the center. They would have to sit on the floor to eat. Different, but welcoming.

"Make yourself comfortable. Unshi will be here shortly. He will be so disappointed to know he wasn't here to greet you, but he was needed at Crescent for urgent matters. Chavi?"

"Yes, Ella?" She said the name thickly, and Cyrus wasn't even sure he'd heard it correctly. He settled himself into a cross-legged position at the table. The rug beneath was squishy and comfortable. The wood of the table was scratched up and old. He caught words and half-finished phrases poorly carved into it. It looked like children had gotten their hands on this.

The young woman exited the room she'd been in. No longer dressed in leather, she'd opted for a thin robe that left very little to the imagination. Her hair was down, braided in neat dreads that fell nearly to her buttocks. He blinked, averting his gaze. It felt rude to stare, although he couldn't say he was overly surprised. Ella was dressed similarly, and it was more than those who'd greeted him wore.

Chavi settled in next to Cyrus. Their knees touched, and she offered him a reassuring smile. "The others will be here any moment. You're going to experience a true Yavink meal."

Ella set six short metal glasses on the table. Each had a different animal carved into it. A wolf for Cyrus. Then she laid out flat stone plates. "The stew is just about done—"

"The Dragon Rider is here?" a man called. His gruff voice resonated in Cyrus's bones. "Can't miss a dragon. Ah." He came into view. He looked to be the same age as Ella, dressed in a few more leather pieces and holding a large walking stick. He shuffled inside and closed the door. Leaning the walking stick against the wall, he pulled off his shoes and approached Ella, then planted a gentle kiss on her lips and inhaled dramatically. "It smells wonderful."

Unshi turned his attention to him before he could ask. "It is our honor to have you here." Cyrus made to stand to give him a proper greeting, but he waved him off. "Don't. Our table is yours. Are you comfortable?" Unshi settled into a spot across from him and sighed.

"Yes . . ." He wasn't sure how to address the man. "Sir?"

Unshi laughed. The sound was raspy, deep. "No need. Here, our names are just fine."

As Ella laid out a few different plates piled with rice and bread, he said, "Ella?"

Chavi choked on laughter to his right, and he immediately regretted asking. Again, the door opened.

"Ella is our name for mother," Chavi explained. "In our culture, respected figures are given formal names. We use these over their real ones. It's how we're raised. Mother is Ella, and father is Kinsy."

"My birth name is Yu," the woman explained. "You don't need to speak to us in any formal matter. That's unnecessary."

"Kerí, this is our Dragon Rider," Unshi greeted. A young man approached, covered in the tribal paint Cyrus had seen earlier and wearing bone necklaces. His dark hair was loose and fell to his shoulders. Bracelets made of teeth decorated both wrists. He looked ready to kill or mentor him—Cyrus wasn't sure.

He wanted to show respect, but he'd already been dismissed for trying to stand. "It's a pleasure to meet you all."

Kerí sat next to his father, his skin a shade lighter. He looked at the cup and saw nothing in it. "Ella, do you need any help?"

"No, no." Yu took a wooden decanter and poured an orange-colored drink into each cup. When she was done, she grabbed the pot over the hearth and placed it on the stone center. She pulled the lid off, releasing steam and a delicious smell that made his mouth water. "Have you heard from Zanah?"

Her son shook his head. "Probably busy with her new prince charming. *Ikunsól.*"

Unshi clicked his tongue. "Your time will come. She is happy, and her decision will increase our resources. Besides, what are you complaining about? You are to take my place soon."

Kerí rolled his eyes as Yu settled in next to him. "I know, I know." His attention turned to Cyrus. Up until then, he'd felt partially like a bystander. "Your dragon is magnificent."

Cyrus kept himself from retching. He'd planned for the usual royal politics, not this family-style welcoming. It intensified his nerves. "He knows."

Everyone at the table laughed. Cyrus hadn't found his comment humorous, but he was glad for the reaction. With all the distractions, he was surprised to hear Sozar's snort from here. The dragon was pleased as well.

"Please, eat," Yu said. At once, everyone reached for food. Cyrus kept back, observing and waiting his turn. Bread was taken, rice was dumped onto plates, but the stew was eaten straight from the pot. A community bowl. Chunks of vegetables, meat, and beans were piled high and eaten. Cyrus accepted bread, unsure where he fit in with the meal dynamics. No clear hierarchy stood out to him. Children and parents alike ate freely. Words were shared, jabs among the siblings, and questions that were meaningless to Cyrus. He finally found the courage to take some of the stew after Chavi shoved the bowl of rice into his face. The rice, seared and crispy with a buttery flavor, he could have eaten for the rest of his life. He took a spoonful of the stew, following as the others did, and stuck some rice with it.

That was the best bite he'd ever had. Cyrus understood now, and quickly took more. The bread soaked up the leftover sauce, and he noticed the family using a combination of spoons and hands to eat. He did the same.

"Tonight, Rider, we celebrate you," Unshi finally said after the rest of the conversation died down. Cyrus had almost forgotten why he was here, so caught up in the feast. The stew was rich with foreign spices—sharp with heat that burned his nose—and paired with the butter and flaky bread, it was divine.

He washed the food down with the zesty tea. "That's unnecessary. Please, I don't want anything special."

"I'num," Yu mumbled. Cyrus didn't understand the meaning, but people shared glances across the table. He wanted to ask but knew it wasn't his place.

Are you okay? Sozar asked. The dragon's presence was a relief. He could almost hear the chants from here.

I'm fine. I'm eating with Chavi and her family. Are you still being worshipped? He said the last in play but sensed that Sozar was a bit reserved.

This was a first. The dragon was so often smug and proud—he loved attention—but this was different. *Sozar?*

These people . . . The dragon seemed to struggle for words. Again, it was unlike him. *They hum with a life I've never felt before. They look at me like I am more than just a spectacle.*

"Our people have waited for your return since the Great Fall," Unshi answered, dragging Cyrus back to the moment. "Preparations are already underway. We will celebrate tonight."

That made him squirm. He couldn't stand the attention. Feeling more courageous, he spoke up. "I came here because Hyle promised there would be information. I don't wish to be rude, but I want to ensure you understand my intentions." Cyrus looked at Chavi. She'd come to him with the invitation, encouraged by the very God he spoke of. The young woman gave a small nod, reading his mind.

"And you will," Unshi replied slowly. He grabbed more bread and tore at it with his callused hands. "Do not be mistaken, Silver Eyes. We know why you are here. We asked you here for that very reason, with Hyle's blessing, of course. The answers you seek lie here. Those who flew before you made sure of that. But to get to that, we must follow tradition."

Cyrus bit his tongue. It would do no good to question the man when they were all so set in their ways. This was how it would go, and there was no way around it.

He bowed his head in what he hoped would be taken as respect. "Thank you."

A celebration. They were already splattering Sozar's scales with white paint. *At this rate, you might be a different color before we leave.* He couldn't imagine what more they could do to the dragon.

In response, Sozar let loose a thunderous roar. The sound broke through the home and vibrated the plates and bowls before it traveled deep into Cyrus's bones. He hadn't heard this sound before. It was rawer, more primitive. Ancient, even. This was a call that resonated deep within the dragon's soul. For just a moment, Cyrus hardly recognized Sozar.

From across the table, Kerí beamed, wild. "Eei'on Rü."

That Violent Desire

Morei took a bite of the terone. He wasn't used to the strong, tangy taste—they were not available in Geral—but he loved it. He'd eaten his bread on the way to his study, but now that he was sitting across from Eli, he decided to eat the fruit as well. The young man wasn't talking. Not yet. He'd spent much of his time cursing and insulting everything, even the chair. Morei let him. Soldiers stood about, ready to protect if needed, and Edwin made a pathetic show of standing next to the king. Isla arrived, looking tired, dressed in a large blue cloak. Her white-blond hair was up, and she sat in the chair to Morei's left. They hadn't spoken since their heated exchange this morning. To his right, leaning against the massive desk like it was his own, was the chancellor. Stoic and smug as usual. No sign of his earlier behavior.

Morei took another bite, studying the young Energy Harvester. The Danshin was one of two that he wanted.

"Where's your brother?" he asked once he swallowed.

The young man didn't move.

The king took another bite. He hoped Eli would talk before he was done with this fruit. His temper was already out of hand, and his head pounded fiercely. Tonight, he felt like he was treading on thin ice. One wrong move and the ice would crack, engulfing him whole in a frigid lake of violence. Everything about this day was going wrong, tearing away at the control he'd so carefully put together since taking Caster's throne. His reputation proceeded him, but he hoped to prove the city wrong. Based on how tense he felt at the slightest inconvenience, he was worried his impulse might get the best of him. It was taking everything he had to sound and appear composed. The slightest gesture might trigger his temper.

"Grant," the king pressed. "You know, the older brother you shared a life with and likely fled with—"

"Dead." The answer came quickly, flat.

That was not what he wanted to hear. "You're certain?"

Eli was all Caster had. The other families he'd stumbled on were gone. Morei shot a look toward Rhys. This would pose a problem that would need addressing immediately. Perhaps they would need to put out an announcement in various cities calling for Harvesters. It was less than ideal, but Caster would never survive as the heart of an empire without layered defenses.

Eli's lips turned into a thin line. "I watched him drown."

Morei leaned back and ate the last bit of the fruit. Sympathy was not his strongest skill. Right now, the closest thing he could reach was agitation. It came easily given this man's blatant disregard for his title. "And you decided to return?"

The Harvester nodded.

"Why?"

"Why not?" Eli threw his hands up. "Come back, grab what's left, and leave. I was going to Diemon—"

"I hear their economy isn't doing too good after the battle against Geral," Morei interjected. His tone was cruel, and he saw Isla's hands tighten their grip on her arms.

"Better than here," Eli countered, annoyed. He kicked back and crossed his arms, looking like a thug ready to barter for a prized jewel, or someone's life. "I heard what you did with Ferguson. Children are being raised without their parents because of what you did." He scoffed. "There's nothing I want here, but now I'm sitting here with you lot *against my will*." He emphasized the last few words as if that would somehow change Morei's opinion.

"The only reason you're here against your will is because you fled in the first place," the king said, swallowing his urge to stuff a dagger down this man's throat. "You and I, we can benefit each other."

Eli scoffed. "No king wants anything to do with someone like me."

"And why is that?"

The young man glared. "I'm scum. I'm the peasant who works for next to nothing on the streets. You're a king. The most you do is bathe yourself, and I'm not even sure you do that."

Morei had to give it to him—the Harvester was a spitfire. That was good. He didn't like meek people, people who lacked initiative and stubbornness. Eli would do well if he could tame his tongue. On top of that, the man didn't seem to care about whatever wild rumor he'd heard about Morei. Heart eater, bathing in blood, Demon King—none of it fazed him.

"I like you," Morei said. The statement clearly caught not only Eli but the entire room off guard. Double takes everywhere, and he was certain he heard Rhys hum something. The chancellor had a bad habit of showing his agitation. He'd need to work on that.

"I know about your ability," he continued. "I also know that the previous king massacred our kind for the sake of proving a madman's point. You were afraid, rightfully so, and fled when you heard I was here. My reputation proceeds me, as I quickly learned on my travels." Morei wanted that drink now. The night was old, and if they didn't wrap this up soon, he'd either never sleep or someone would get hurt. His mind warred between listening to the screaming compulsion and staying right where he was. Half of him panicked, aware of how close he was to showing everyone just how cruel he was. It could cost him the little loyalty he'd gained. The other part, the part responsible for slaughtering Geral citizens and the death of Yaz and so many others, was elated to be heard. If he displayed his capabilities—his ruthlessness—then nobody would ever question him again. That was the growing logic.

If Eli wanted to walk out of this room, then he needed to bend to Morei's demands. The young man sitting across from him was not the only Harvester in the country. He was the easiest to learn of, but now Morei was starting to doubt his decision. Eli had two choices: obey or be killed. Morei wouldn't settle for anything else.

"I'm not here to imprison you, force you into something you don't want to do, whatever you wish to call it. What I want to do is give you a choice." The king raised two fingers and indicated to the first. "I offer you sanctuary and protection. No harm will come to any Energy Harvester while I reign. You will work alongside me and Edwin." He motioned behind him to the commander. "I will personally ensure you are trained to be the best you can be. Beyond that, I will grant you a lifetime supply of coin and ensure your family is comfortable." Morei shifted his focus to the second finger. "Or, you can leave. You refuse and want to travel to Diemon, I will not stop you, but you will be stripped of your Caster citizenship and will not be able to return."

Morei leaned forward in the ensuing silence. Eli didn't give much away with his expression. Everyone stood or sat motionless. If this man knew what was best for him, he'd accept training. They'd waited many moons for this moment, and Morei was desperate to grow the Energy Harvester ranks. The soldiers could only do so much, and Morei was not ignorant enough to believe that he wouldn't be faced with something supernatural again. He hadn't forgotten about the Inere, the Vore beast that had sought him out.

Finally, Eli shifted and leaned forward, resting his elbows on his legs. His eyes met the king's in a blatant show of confidence. "Fuck you."

The words sank into Morei's mind like fangs. They tore and shredded through the thin veil of composure he'd tried to keep. The world around him splintered, and he no longer could see the people in the room. He would not tolerate such disrespect. All he could see was Eli, and he lunged.

The young man never stood a chance. His arms flailed as he tried to move, but the king grabbed him by his throat and yanked him up. Shouts came from all around, and swords were drawn, but Morei had only one focus. Eli's fingers dug into his arm, a miserable attempt to pull the king off him.

His skin reddening, Eli's breaths came out in short gasps. Morei liked the sound of it—of the struggle. He smiled wider than he had in days. "You don't think much of me, do you?"

Eli tried to move but failed to, resorting to frantic jerks. "I'm sorry."

"Are you?" the king challenged. "Or are you telling me this because you think I'm a fool?"

"No . . ." Eli gasped, sharp and loud. "I didn't realize—"

"That I'm really what they say?" Morei drew up his free hand. In an instant, he summoned the fire. The cold sensation burned his hand, but he hardly noticed. The dancing flame before him was so proud and alive. The voices screamed in his head. They knew this was the moment he'd promised them.

"Listen—" Eli's voice cut off as Morei squeezed again. His bulging eyes jumped between the fire and the king, panicked. A tug on his arm forced energy outward. Dark Energy responded, casting a gust of wind laced with the unquestionable heat of fire. He couldn't hear anything, and it didn't matter. The Harvester's mouth was moving, likely pleading.

Morei listened to what the flames wanted. Gently, he raised his hand to the Harvester's face and watched as the young man squirmed from the hot kiss. His skin bubbled along his cheek, and he let out a gut-wrenching scream.

The flames took a life of their own, moving with intelligence, crawling off Morei's hand like a young animal curious about its surroundings. He watched, proud. The fire grabbed ahold of Eli's face as the man fought and screamed, mouth agape. The flames didn't even hesitate—they dove into the open cavity and down his throat, then burrowed themselves into the pit of his stomach and raged.

The king didn't let go of Eli. He watched as the Harvester's body thrashed, as steam rose from all possible openings, as the skin that was once so soft and lively shrank and cracked. He stared, thrilled to see the final moment, the moment Eli's life left him. The man might have been confident before, but he was terrified in the face of Death.

The king released his body. It slumped to the floor, his head hitting the table as it went. The sound was music to Morei's ears, and he sucked in a full breath of air. The king felt better—*relieved*. The earlier tension in his muscles dissipated, and his shoulders relaxed. The shake in his hands eased, and the headache settled, duller now, more manageable. Morei felt more like himself. The taste of bliss on his tongue was almost as satisfying as Kendell's

Milk. As he looked up, he saw a raven sitting on the terrace. It cawed. Eazon was here.

A stifled breath caught his attention, and he turned to see Isla with a hand over her mouth. Slowly, he swept his gaze over the entire room, noting similar expressions on everyone's faces. He'd lost control, let the compulsion win, and now he was faced with the consequences. As afraid as he'd been of that happening, standing here now, he realized he didn't care. The people had been afraid of him the moment he'd arrived. His reputation, no matter how hard he tried, had been twisted by the rumors and stories of his previous actions. Nothing about that would ever change. The only thing these people had now was confirmation that he was true to his word, and at least that made him an honest man.

"Get rid of him," he ordered. "If there are any more signs of an Energy Harvester in the city, I need to know. They have two options: join or leave."

"Or die," Rhys observed.

He said it in passing, but Morei shot him a glare. "Careful, Chancellor. I want to keep you around."

The bold threat made Rhys freeze.

"They don't understand people like us. They never will." He made sure the words were as frigid as the look he gave the chancellor. He wanted Rhys to acknowledge just how similar they really were.

"Yes, Your Majesty," he said with a slight bow to his head. He played his part as best he could, but the king saw how tense his shoulders were as he moved.

Nobody else spoke as they quickly got to work. The soldiers cautiously approached the body, likely afraid it would combust into flames, and took it out of the study. Edwin made himself busy by wiping off the seat, completely useless, before following his men out the door. Rhys didn't even look back as he left the room.

Morei turned to see Isla. Once more, the woman had made herself available when he didn't want her to.

"You're still here."

The princess slowly nodded. Her gaze said a hundred things: repulsed, disgusted, disappointed, sad, fearful. The king wasn't prepared for how ashamed he felt of her judgment. Isla didn't need to see this side of him, not when her loyalty to Caster already felt frayed. The woman didn't need a bigger reason to deny Morei the right to a queen. She was his key to an empire.

"Why?" he pressed when she didn't answer right away. Eazon was still sitting on the terrace, and he wanted to speak to the God.

Isla glanced to where Eli had been, arms still crossed. The sigh that broke free from her lips was too loud for his ears, stuffed full of frustration. "Is that what you wanted all along?"

"No. I wanted him to join Caster."

"Did you?" Isla's brow went up. She didn't believe him.

Morei snapped, "Are you here to give me a lesson on morality?"

"No." The answer came too quick. The slight shake of her hand as she gripped her arm—this woman was afraid. As she should be.

"Then why are you here?"

The princess pursed her lips and looked around. A long pause followed, during which Morei stared at the raven with the white tail feather. When she finally spoke, her words shook, hardly audible. "For a man so desperate for acceptance that he would steal a throne that isn't rightfully his, you have a terrible way of proving just how unlikeable you really are."

At that, she made her way to the door. She didn't understand, and she likely never would. What burned in him was an incurable need for violence, to hurt others. Acting on that was his only way of staying sane. Politically, if he wasn't feared, the people would see him as too soft to expand his territory. A risk to the Caster name. An insult to his Geral bloodline. "I want to do the right thing," he admitted. The words came out low, but she stopped just at the door. "All I've ever wanted was to be a fair king. To end all wars. Nobody can do that without getting their hands bloody."

Isla stood there, her back to him. Her head dropped, and she shook it. The princess left, and he didn't try to stop her. The lack of reply was more insulting than if she had turned around and cursed his name. That was what he'd wanted, not this silence.

The flutter of wings broke the quiet. Eazon was gone. He was finally alone.

No Smile Is Worth Dying For

Terror kept Syra on high alert. She stood in a wide chamber, full of a handful of bone-made chairs. No cushions, just the ground-down bones of victims from Elyas, where he sat comfortably now, just to her right. Behind, next to the door, stood a group of Gor-Geíons. Raid was not among the several Guardians who'd followed her here when Elyas ordered her taken from her dungeon. Raid's warning rang clear: some Guardians wanted her dead. Nobody here was trustworthy. She checked over her shoulder a dozen times, arms crossed, expecting a brutal end at any point. Elyas knew what he was doing. Ripping her out of the discomfort of all the chains and placing her here. He wanted to show her who was in charge, and it was working.

The chamber was plain. As the leader of the Geíons, she'd thought Elyas would have more to his name, but the chairs and a small table to the left, tucked up against the blackened stone wall, were it. No vines touched this room, and it was just as cold as her dungeon. It was impossible to worry about the decorations and climate when her attention was on what lay before her. A massive glass wall overlooked Ashýon. Endless leagues of ashen sand and cliffs lay ahead, full of beasts. Cer'hans dove, screeching, leathery wings wide, while creatures stuck to the ground scuttled to avoid being prey. They hid under rocks and in the shadows of looming peaks. Whenever they stepped out, they moved slowly, keeping a watch above them, and ran if the Cer'han saw them. Syra watched all sorts of beasts do this. Some were almost human-like on two legs, while others were covered in silver fur with four legs and a snout resembling a horse's. Demons.

Hooked, Syra watched, rooting for one of the humanoid demons. Its blackened skin was cracked, oozing yellow goop that broke off in globs. As the liquid struck the ground, steam rose. It ran as fast as it could as a Cer'han stretched its talons out in a steep dive. Syra tensed. The demon dove for a rock jutting out but never made it. The Cer'han snatched the creature right up, letting loose a victorious cry. She averted her gaze, not needing to see the re st.

"Entertaining, isn't it?" Elyas asked. No fear or worry. He kicked his boots up to the skull in front of him, large enough to hold a drink or two. It looked like a dragon's skull.

"Why am I here?" she asked.

Elyas didn't look her way, entranced by the bloody feast. "To observe."

She crossed her arms, sensing more. Elyas flashed those sharpened teeth at her. The expression sent a chill down her back. Haunting. His presence left a mark wherever he went. Elyas stood with the grace of a feline, and she took half a step back.

"Watch," he insisted, not addressing her behavior. He approached the window, and reluctantly, she turned to see. If she didn't, she was certain she'd be forced.

Before her, two Cer'hans were fighting over the corpse of a bloodied creature she didn't recognize. The heap was impossible to make out—matted fur, blood soaking into the sand, bones broken and torn free, scattered about. The Cer'hans lunged at one another, clawing. One's massive jaw latched on to the neck of the other. Panicked, the Cer'han tried to back up, but the first clamped down hard and snapped the spine. The creature went limp and was dropped without any regard. The victorious Cer'han turned its skeletal head to the prize on the ground.

"This is the heart of Cer'han territory," Elyas told her. His tone was blissful; he was watching a play only he could enjoy. "Those you see are prisoners. Well, most of them. Sometimes a lone beast wanders in, foolish. We take care of the Cer'hans here, and in return, they watch the surrounding land."

Syra's jaw went slack. She turned back to watch another demon bolt from a hiding spot, this one lucky as he narrowly missed the talons of a smaller Cer'han. "You sacrifice prisoners?"

A hollow feeling blossomed in her chest. She knew why she was here.

"Sacrifice is a terrible word," Elyas replied, shaking his head. "I prefer 'dispose of.' It has a better ring to it. Don't you think?"

Quietly, she fumbled for the right response. "You intend to put me there if I don't do what you want?"

"That would be a shame, wouldn't it?" Elyas took another step forward, and she took half a step back. Her wounds protested, her muscles groaned, but she kept her back straight and her legs ready to turn and run. This demon liked the way the power made him feel. "Last of your bloodline, and you end up there." He motioned to her. "A couple of fresh cuts with the Syckl Blade and you wouldn't be so tough out there, would you?"

She swallowed the putrid taste of dread. "You can't do that. I'm all this realm has."

"That's what they say. That's what they want to believe." Elyas faced the window again, sparing her, close enough that his arm brushed over her shoulder. Cold. No heat came from him. "When a drought occurs, the rains come. When it freezes, it warms up. There is always balance, even for the damned. I like to believe the same would happen here if you were fed to the Cer'han. Then again"—he shrugged—"I'm just a Gefon, so what do I know?"

Another Cer'han fight broke out, this time over a pile of bones that appeared freshly picked at. This fight didn't end as gruesomely. The smaller one couldn't hold their own and quickly flew off, while the larger, which sported a nasty scar down its neck that puckered pink against the gray, leathery skin, snatched up a bone.

"That's their favorite part," Elyas said. "They hunt but don't eat the meat. They horde the dead. Preferably, the skin decomposes, but they usually peel the skin and meat off and eat the bones. They were once scavengers, eating the leftovers of other kills. Over time, they've learned they have an abundance of resources. Makes them greedy."

Syra wanted to shrink away from it all. Her body hurt, her head pounded, and her stomach grumbled, starved. She didn't have the strength to deal with this. One wrong shift and tender scabs opened up, staining her torn sleeves and smearing across already dirty skin.

"Did you bring me here to scare me into agreeing to your terms?"

The door opened then, revealing a Guardian with a laceration down the side of his face. "We have a problem."

Elyas turned, pushing Syra out of the way. She stumbled, catching herself against the glass. He approached the Guardian, chin held high. The Geíons stepped aside, making choking sounds. Elyas raised his hand and they silenced.

"What kind of problem?"

"A scuffle in the main room. Your men are fighting over who's to have what weapons and valuables. It's a mess. There's not enough of us to split it up." The Guardian flicked his gaze toward Syra, cutting right through her composure. "I was told it was best to fetch you."

Elyas grumbled. "Wretched things. This is the second time today." He motioned at Syra. "Keep an eye on her. I'll be back."

This was normal behavior. Elyas seemed like a parent splitting up a fight between kids again. The Geíons watched him go before turning their attention to the Guardian. Paralyzed, Syra watched his hand stray to the pommel of Death's Sword. He was here for her. There were no weapons to defend herself with, and he blocked the only exit. Chaos was hesitant to come when summoned, exhausted.

"We don't—"

Her plea ended as the Guardian produced a dagger tucked up in his cloak and jammed it into the neck of the Geíon to his left. The demon reached for the hilt, gurgling, while the Guardian unsheathed Death's Sword and dragged it across the other Geíon's chest. Black blood oozed, staining the silver metal. In one clean sweep, the Guardian beheaded the second demon, sending his head across the chamber. It landed against the table with a thud. The remaining Geíon yanked the blade from its neck, its leathery skin glittering with fresh blood. It screeched, and the Guardian grabbed the dagger and shoved it back in. The demon struggled, but the Guardian was twice its size and easily overpowered it. After several heartbeats, the demon's head rolled off and dropped to the floor, splattering black blood.

He huffed and turned to her. "Either you stand there like a fool, or you run."

Syra opened her mouth, then shut it again, confused. Shouting and clashing metal rang from the hall. "What's happening?"

The Guardian pointed to the door with his bloodied sword. "Our attempt at regaining control. You need to go."

Syra moved, but her legs were sluggish and heavy. Sidestepping the body, she asked, "What about my things? What about Raid?" She couldn't leave Death's Sword behind. That was Dryl's.

"Too many questions," he snapped, leaning down to meet her at eye level. The blood dripping from his face didn't appear to bother him. "We orchestrated an attack around your arrival. Vaeke is in the weapons chamber. If he can, he'll retrieve your things. Guardians will be coming for you. They aren't on your side."

It was all a ploy. They'd lured Elyas out to give her a chance. Her mind worked faster than her body. Sekar needed her, and then they needed to get to the palace. "How do we get out of here?"

More shouting. Time was running out.

"Take a left and then another left. That'll take you back to the hall you came from. Sekar is there, in the same room where you found him. Take a right at the junction next time. That will lead you straight to the tunnels. Look out for a small stick jutting out of the dirt. When you see it, pull. That'll give you a head start. And whatever you do, don't light any fire down there. Geíons can smell smoke a league out. There's only so much time we can give you before Elyas figures out you've escaped. After that, you're on your own."

Syra nodded. Adrenaline surged through her, forcing her muscles awake and the pain of her wounds to numb. This was her only chance. She took one step before the Guardian grabbed her.

"Two more things," he said quickly. "The Geíons regenerate. So don't stab them in the chest and think you got them. Behead them, and make sure you kick that head as far as you can. I've seen vines come out of their skull just to crawl back to the body if it's close enough. Better yet, burn the head or feed it to something else. Safer that way." The Guardian peeked his head around the door as the sound of metal clashing neared. "The Starved Sands are the fastest way for you to get out of Ashýon. But avoid any areas with rippling sand. That means a Wurok is hiding underneath. Keep a lookout in the sky for the Cer'hans. They get hungry at night."

She raised her brow. As far as she'd seen, they were feasting already.

"You're wasting time," the Guardian said. He tapped her back with his bloody sword. "Don't make this for nothing."

Syra hesitated, not sold. "My sword. That was Dryl's. If I can help—"

"Syra." He placed a hand on her torn tunic, stilling her. "We will do everything we can to get you your belongings, but you need to go. There is only one chance at this. I've got men out there fighting for you." When she didn't move, he added firmly, "On Dryl's reputation, I promise."

This was what Raid had meant when he said they were waiting for the right time. A final look toward the endless landscape reminded her that she still wasn't close to rescuing Zarek, but this was a step in the right direction. Sekar needed her.

"Thank you." She didn't know if she would see him again, but she hoped so. Stepping out into the hall, she broke out into a run—the best one she could manage in her condition—avoiding the vines. This next part would either get her killed or be the greatest escape she'd ever made.

I'num

Cyrus's attire was apparently not acceptable. Chavi went and fetched him more traditional clothes for the celebration. This consisted of a long, tapered blue tunic covered in white beads and embroidered with a dragon curled up on the back. When he asked, they told him it was the original crest of the Rider Federation. They'd kept the design for centuries, remaking the shirt when the fabric frayed and grew too aged for use. He was dressed in dark leather breeches that had detailed dragons crawling up on either leg. The level of craftsmanship on the pieces was enough to cause Cyrus to pause. Shoved into a room to change, he'd stared at the paintings for a long while and only stopped when asked if he was okay.

The gemstone necklaces still hung around his neck. His face was still covered in paint, and he made sure not to rub it by accident when he swapped clothes. Cyrus slipped his boots back on and stepped outside with Kerí. Chavi seemed plenty excited to take charge when it was time to go.

The shadows were a bit longer now. They hadn't been in the home that long, but maybe he was wrong. The pinkish hue that filled the space was still surreal to take in. Some of the gemstones jutting out of the ground were as large as him, others even bigger. Children hung on a few of the largest pieces, using the crystals as steps to climb atop. Parents didn't stop them. If it was normal, he didn't know, because the parents were too busy staring at him when he walked by. In this attire, he stuck out even more.

"Couldn't you have put me in a similar leather outfit?" Cyrus asked when they passed a group of Yavinks.

Kerí snorted. "You are the center of attention, Rider." His accent was even thicker than Chavi's, and Cyrus hoped he understood everything correctly. "We will be speaking about you for centuries to come."

Ahead, Sozar came into view. Cyrus slowed, speechless at what he was witnessing. Men and women surrounded the dragon, buckets in hand, painting him. His horns were no longer white but red, and his black scales showcased a variety of colors, ranging from blue to orange and even purple. He looked like a mess.

"What is this?" he asked both Sozar and the man beside him. "Is this part of the celebration?"

They tell me that my ancestors were painted similarly. The dragon's tail twitched. *My brothers and sisters stood on these very grounds.* Kerí grinned. "A dragon embodies all aspects of life and death. We wish to uphold that tradition by representing this in color." He said some things in a different language, and Cyrus recognized a few Old Tongue terms. A woman straightened from one of the talons she was painting red and pointed at Cyrus. She replied in the same tongue.

Kerí grinned and laughed. When he didn't offer right away, Cyrus asked, "What is it?"

"She said you're next."

"What?" Cyrus looked between the two, horrified. As he did so, a vibrant orange and yellow butterfly with four wings flew by leisurely. It was as large as his hand, impossible to miss, and he watched it land on one of the paint buckets.

"Come." Kerí waved him along. "The celebration will start with dances. Food will come after. After that, well, it depends on how much you drink. We brew a mean wine here using the berries that grow in the nearby valley. They only mature once a summer, so we must pick them when we do. Else the animals get to them."

Cyrus checked the sky again, or what he could see through the hole-filled leaves. "When does the celebration begin?"

"Soon," Kerí said. "We have prepared for this day for centuries. Do not underestimate how little time we need to finally honor the Dragon Riders. Our ancestors dreamed of this day; so too do the children that you see. Each of us has been raised on stories of the Riders and what they did for our world."

This was all happening so fast. He'd just arrived this morning, and he halfway wondered if Hyle was at all involved with expediting this. Not that he would complain. The faster, the better. It meant he could get the information he came for.

Everywhere he looked, people were making preparations. Drums were carried by many at a time, too heavy to be held by one person. The dark, stained leather that stretched over the drumheads was covered in the same sigil. Two crescents sat opposite of one another with an infinity sign in the center, connecting the crescents, painted in gold. The drumsticks were intricately designed petrified wood, polished and stained dark red.

"What is that?" He pointed to the sigil.

"I'num." Kerí motioned to the Yavinks. "Those drums have been in our family for centuries. They were used to celebrate Dragon Riders every summer. You will find we've done everything in our power to honor our history. Tradition is something we take very seriously here."

Cyrus nodded, still watching the people work. Others carried large baskets full of various exotic fruits. He saw some with large green spikes, purple apple-sized ones, and orange berries. Loud chatter and laughs filled the gaps between the working. He watched several begin to carve into the ground, creating unknown designs.

"I'num means . . . ?"

Kerí laughed, loud enough to draw the attention of nearby Yavinks. Cyrus wanted to dissolve into dust and be swept away in the wind right then. "Never in my life did I think a Dragon Rider would ask what *their* sigil meant." He spread his hands wide. "But here we are. That sigil"—he pointed toward the drums—"is as integral to you as your dragon is. It represents everything you want to embody—courage, persistence, determination—and the Rider Federation used it as a symbol of promise wherever they went. Above all, it symbolizes loyalty."

Cyrus nodded, impressed. In just a couple of days, he'd learned more about what it meant to be a Dragon Rider than in all the time before. He felt humbled. This world that thrived before him was rich in culture, culture lost in the current day.

"Eei'on Rü," he whispered. Peace of the world. Strolling through Venkar, the rest of his problems felt leagues beyond his reach. Henry, Dameon, Razan, Geral—all of it felt like lifetimes ago. With that relinquishing came the loud thoughts of all the what-ifs. Had the Riders known that it would take centuries before he would arrive? A culture as proud as the Rider

Federation—it was impossible to consider that they would have ever believed it would come to an end.

They slowed at a small pond. The water was so clear that Cyrus could see the bottom without difficulty. Small creatures swam about. They looked like tiny fish with legs. The bushes next to the water were even greener than he remembered. Large flowers blossomed, white petals with purple centers. At least four butterflies with the same bright coloring as the one he'd seen before perched, fanning their wings. He didn't see the Dragon Blood flower, though.

Cyrus motioned to their surroundings. "Chavi spoke of the Dragon Blood flower, but I have yet to see it. Unless I've missed it?"

"You will see it soon, Sea Flyer." Kerí settled in a spot to overlook the water, lacing his hands in front of him. The commotion behind them didn't fade. Cheerful shouting resounded, and Sozar rumbled. He could practically taste the chunks of nameless meats the Yavinks were feeding him.

A long stretch of silence slipped between them. Cyrus enjoyed the peace, studying the small ecosystem in the pond. Next to him, Kerí inhaled deeply, and Cyrus took it as an opportunity to ask his next question. "The language you speak, it's unlike anything I've heard before, but if I'm correct, there's Old Tongue."

Kerí crossed his arms and nodded. "Your ears don't betray you. We have held on to the traditional Old Tongue. Much of what you hear in other parts of the world is choppy and incomplete. Rulers who thought they were doing the world a favor, or simply the curse of time, have changed our language. But here, we still speak the purest form." He chuckled. "If you ask the elders, it is not Old Tongue, but properly called Gýshin. Our word for *true tongue*."

Cyrus nodded, intrigued. He wanted to ask so many questions, but he finally settled on, "Why does everything look the way it does? This forest, the ground, the leaves—there's a pink hue to everything."

Kerí looked amused. He waved Cyrus over to the nearest gemstone protruding from the ground. The vibrant pink glowed in a bit of direct sunlight. The Yavink motioned for Cyrus to place his hand on it, so he did. Immediately he felt the deep hum reverberate through his entire body. His thoughts left him, the mere act of breathing became his sole focus, and the world around, once thriving with critters and people, disappeared. The energy that coursed through Cyrus was raw and strong, coming straight from the stone.

Kerí spoke, shattering the trance. "Crescent Lake is not just a body of water, but the closest this world has to Light Energy. It is the only place you will find the purest form of it. These surroundings"—he motioned to the land—"have all been heavily influenced by proximity. These gems are the result of the energy's reach. Think of them like roots and the lake the tree. In the passing centuries, we've watched more and more of these sprout as Crescent Lake grew more powerful. Only in the past few decades have we noticed the hum of her change." Kerí shook his head. "The world is changing too fast. There's an illness spreading across these lands. One of imbalance and hunger."

Cyrus pulled his hand free from the gemstone, feeling isolation engulf him. Sounds returned loud, and he moved to avoid a butterfly that flitted by without care. "You say the proximity has influenced everything. Do you also mean . . ."

"Yes." Kerí clasped his hands together. "We are not like the rest of the world. We've gained extended lives, accelerated healing, and other gifts. In return for this blessing, we protect this region. The world would crumble if anything happened to Crescent."

This would change the world. If others found out what the Yavinks really were, what they were capable of, it would change everything. Mad queens and power-hungry kings would move mountains to weaponize such capabilities. For so long, Cyrus had believed it was only him and Sozar against the world. Now, it was so much more than that.

"How have you done it?" he whispered in shock. Chavi's brother was not who he'd thought he was—nobody here was. Sozar rumbled, a soothing sound across their bond.

They understand us.

Kerí motioned to the butterfly that stayed close. "Nobody knows of our gifts, save for the animals that live among us. We've kept it that way. Only the Dragon Riders knew, and they did everything they could to uphold our secret."

A loud boom followed his words. Cyrus stiffened just as Kerí slapped him on the shoulder. "Ah! It is time, Rider. We honor you. Let us be off."

Abandon the Throne

Morei took a long drink of Kendell's Milk. It was still early in the day, but he didn't care. After last night, with the brutal killing of Eli and Isla's words, he wasn't entirely at rest. His mind raced, his thoughts scattered. The violent compulsions were stronger. That single act, no matter how satisfying, had broken him. The little control he'd sustained since murdering Drexis was gone. The man who woke up was not the same man who'd fallen asleep. But Morei was not worried—he was relieved. He could stop pretending to be someone else.

"The numbers." Edwin passed the parchment to him from across the desk. They were back in the king's study. Morei had insisted on it, wanting to make a point that the room wasn't cursed after what he'd done there. Edwin, while accommodating, appeared incredibly uncomfortable. It wasn't the dead that scared him—it was Morei.

The king reached for the parchment and studied what was written. The commander had worked overtime to get everything requested after the threat from the Red Queens. Right now, they were looking at hundreds fewer soldiers than Morei wanted to see, even with Ferguson. "What happened to our numbers from the last moon cycle?"

Edwin shrugged. "A bad case of luck. Men died, are sick, or left."

"Left?"

"Yes."

Morei forced a slow breath in. "Because of me?"

Edwin nodded, the faintest movement.

The king accepted this, though it irritated him. Caster was relatively okay with his title, but a strong opinion persisted that despite what Drexis had done, Morei was worse. Rhys had told him that Caster took immense pride in its bloodlines, and some people still thought that far more valuable than promises of lower taxes and peace. Taking Ferguson had helped bolster the people's faith in him, but it would only take him so far.

"Shame," he said. "And those in training?"

The commander motioned to a number on the parchment. "We've got a little over three hundred right now, but the majority of those hardly can swing a sword."

"I don't care," the king said. "Add them to the total."

"Yes, Your Majesty."

Morei took another drink. "And the defenses? How are they coming along?"

Edwin grimaced. "We're working as fast and hard as we can—"

"How are they coming along?" he repeated, slower.

"We've got men identified as archers, those who will hold the front line." The commander didn't expound. He clearly knew it wasn't enough, but he kept his chin up and shoulders squared.

Morei forced himself to remain calm. Now was not a good time to show his frustration. "That is far slower than what I believed you and your men were capable of. What about the stakes? Trenches? Ly'rün?"

The mention of the deadly chemical mixture forced Edwin's strong presence to falter. "We're working on it, Your Majesty, but there seems to be a problem. The containers of Ly'rün, for the most part, are missing."

"Excuse me?" That weapon was the best they had at defending themselves against an army of pirates. On land, they were restricted to protecting the coast with arrows and throwing whatever they could. He hoped to destabilize the Red Queens as much as possible before they could even make it to shore.

Edwin bared his hands. "We don't know. I have men down there right now looking. It could have been misplaced. It's been many summers since anyone has used the mixture. There's a good chance we've just overlooked something." His words came fast.

The king nodded. It wasn't what he wanted to hear, but it was the best they had. "If there is a problem with locating the Ly'rün, let me know. Continue with the rest of the preparations. I want cannons doubled along the coastline. Get creative, if needed. We can't risk the Red Queens landing on shore without a strong defense."

They'd estimated a full moon until their arrival, but he wouldn't risk it. He cleared his throat, wanting to keep the conversation going. "How is Ly'rün made? Perhaps we can make more?"

Edwin sighed. "The mixture requires a renuri. We do not have one."

"What is that?"

"An expert in poisonous explosives. They are hard to come by. The last one we had was wanted for treason in two cities. We gave her clemency in exchange for her service, which is how we managed to get Ly'rün made."

The king learned something new every day. "And this lady . . ."

"Died of old age."

"Can we find another? Or at least try?" Morei asked.

The commander pursed his lips. "I can try, but they are usually found in the underground markets and don't make it obvious what they are. It's a game of cat and mouse."

That was reasonable. Anyone who practiced a skill that dangerous would be unwanted in most cities. They could wipe out an entire population or even murder the royal family. "Very well. Identify someone for that. I hear Nighthunters are good resources for the underground market. I'd like to get another renuri—" He raised his hand to stop the commander from interrupting. "I understand the threats and fully accept them. Given the nature of our goals with Caster, I do believe the right renuri will see the benefits of working with us."

Edwin opened his mouth and then closed it. He nodded. "Yes, Your Majesty. I suppose there is good trade value with a renuri."

The king appreciated where his mind was at. "It will cause far less damage in the long run if we invest in our defenses."

Rhys delivered the financial report this morning. Caster's finances were in great shape, better even with the additional aid of Ferguson's if needed, and he was not worried about ensuring citizens were granted enough funding to leave the city. He'd instructed the chancellor to do a horse count, which Rhys had already done. The numbers were far less than what he wanted. Geral had twice the steeds, but nothing could be done now. He only hoped that most citizens wouldn't choose to flee, because then they would be short on horses.

The note from King Nerius was tucked away in the drawer to his left, along with the Lirallian Ring. He didn't want anything to do with it. Everything reminded him of Geral, including that relic he'd found on Boris's dead body. The relic he was too uncertain to wear after his close call with the dead woman. Geral was and would always be rightfully his, even if the citizens turned their backs on him. That was his bloodline, his right.

It was foolish, but he hadn't brought the discovery up. Rhys knew, but Edwin's lack of questions confirmed the chancellor hadn't said anything to anyone. He hoped this was an empty threat encouraged by Sekar, or perhaps from the God himself, meant to scare him. Morei didn't want to add fear without confirmation of the nature of the note. Caster would unravel if the city knew the threats that loomed just outside its reach.

A knock interrupted whatever Edwin was preparing to say. Isla stepped inside. She wasn't supposed to be here. She wore a blue halter dress with a gold collar around her neck. Her blond hair was atop her head, held together with a wolf clasp, and she wore gold bangles on either wrist. Today, she looked like royalty. Good.

"Your Majesty," she greeted respectfully. In her hand was a scroll. Her tone held no recognition of the previous night's exchange, and he couldn't tell how that made him feel. The princess stared at him like he was neither a king nor a man. "I was intercepted by a messenger." She held out the scroll.

Based on the wax seal, it had not been opened yet. "You didn't open it?"

Isla shrugged as he took the rolled parchment. Her hand retracted instantly to her side. Ah, so she was still afraid. "I didn't think it was appropriate."

"Glad to see you've learned something," he commented before he could stop himself, and let his fingers glide over the red wax seal. The lion glared back at him, proud and unbothered by his abandonment of the throne. This was a formal letter. His heart quickened, and he felt instantly flush. All thoughts of the Red Queens, Nerius, and Caster shattered, and he was faced with the biggest regret of his life: massacring the Geral citizens in his rage.

He knew they were waiting, and he didn't want to look weak or caught off guard, so he broke the seal. On many occasions, he'd used that very seal on agreements and letters. It was the only one used by royalty, which meant only one person could have written this.

Gently, he unrolled the scroll. The parchment felt so comfortable in his hands, and he realized how different Caster's parchment was from Geral's. Caster's was thinner and less textured. Geral's was thick, meant to survive the harsh and dry conditions of the desert. But as those thoughts filled his mind, mundane and unnecessary, he felt the serrated edge of his blade drive itself into his heart.

The king of Geral was missing.

This was a formal declaration that Ezra Geral had been taken, and that the chancellor had been appointed ruler. An investigation was ongoing, but as of the date of this letter being sent, there had been no active leads. Ezra had been abducted in the middle of the night. With no immediate family, Geral was asking for leniency with all costs and long-standing agreements as they navigated this troubling time. It was a standard letter, and every other royal family would have received this as well. Yet, to Morei, it was more than that. It was a challenge to his morals. Peter had written this letter—he recognized the handwriting.

"What's it say?" Edwin asked.

The words blurred. Morei blinked and stood. Snatching up his drink to distract himself, he blurted, "Geral's king is missing." The words tasted bitter on his tongue, and he stuffed more Kendell's Milk into his mouth.

"What?" Edwin reached forward for the letter and read the words out loud. Each one dug a little deeper, exploiting emotions that Morei had shoved so deep, he'd hoped he'd never have to face them.

He'd betrayed Ezra. He'd slaughtered his citizens, turned his back on the only thing that his family had left him, and fled like . . . like *a coward*. He was king, but he hadn't been prepared for the cost of that title. He'd destroyed Ezra's life by dragging the young man into his problems. Every day, he tried to be a better person, but it was impossible when the world constantly berated his patience and tolerance. The man he saw in the mirror was a stranger, but one he'd learned to accept. He had to. If he failed to embrace it, he risked losing everything he'd fought for.

Morei walked toward the terrace, observing the endless ocean. Right now, he hated it. He'd always loved the desert. It was where his heart belonged, and where he was happiest. When his boots sank into the sand, and the heat of the sun kissed his skin—that was where he felt most alive. Not here.

"Your Majesty?"

He looked. Rhys was standing there. Morei didn't know when the chancellor had arrived or how long he'd stood there. Isla and Edwin were behind Rhys. To some extent, he could say each one cared about him, but it was all obligated. All of this was a façade. Royal relationships were built on who could offer what and when. Rhys cared because he wanted power, Isla was afraid, and Edwin just wanted to stay alive.

"I'm fine," he answered. Everything about his response was stiff. "Just thinking."

"About?" Edwin pressed.

About how Geral failed Ezra. Soldiers should have been stationed outside his room. Unless the abductors snuck in through the terrace. If so, they would have had to pass the soldiers outside, just along the courtyard. Geral's palace was heavily guarded—it always had been. Whoever had done this knew what they were doing and what message they would send. Vulnerability. Power. Control. The abductors were exploiting Geral for either coin or more. Maybe to snatch the throne for themselves.

Geral was compromised, weakened with no strong leader. If the abductors intended on trying for the throne, they would do so soon. Peter was clever, but Morei would never trust an entire kingdom to him. The chancellor was too passive, more concerned about how he was perceived by others, and that would do more harm than good. Ezra had been a solid leader; the council would rip Peter apart before he ever got a chance to get a word in—if they hadn't already. It would be a frenzy, nothing would get done, and the city would crumble.

No. This was an opportunity. A chance for Morei to seize what has always rightfully been his. His bloodline lived in the walls of Geral's palace. An entire lineage of men like him who did the impossible.

He stopped himself. There were no men like him. There never would be, but the world would come to fear the Geral name for centuries. As much as he swallowed Caster and accepted the city and people, this would never be his home. Yet it would serve him well for decades to come. Caster had everything Geral lacked—a port, ships, access to the world. This was a chance to prove his bloodline, to prove himself the man he was destined to be.

"I want Geral to fall."

The three stared.

Attacking a city when the ruler was compromised was against royal code, but he didn't care. The Royal Treaty was void after his march to Ferguson. "I understand our numbers are spread thin," Morei said before the commander could tell him. "Whoever took the Geral king wants to send a message, no?"

Edwin nodded. Isla took a half step back. The woman wanted to leave. He didn't blame her, not after what she'd seen. The chancellor's brow went up faintly, acknowledging him.

"While Geral is at its weakest, we'll plan an assault. But we must wait until the threat of the Queens passes. There's too much at risk to split our men even further. Wouldn't you agree?"

The commander cleared his throat. "Yes, Your Majesty. That would be my advice. I have a question, though?"

When he didn't continue, Morei waved at him. "I'm waiting."

Edwin straightened and set his shoulders back. This was the ruthless leader of Caster's army that Morei knew so well. The one the lower-ranked soldiers whispered about and who would, without hesitation, send a man to the whipping post for saying the wrong thing. That was why he liked him so much. Edwin wasn't afraid to get his hands dirty.

"Geral's defensives will be on high alert with the taking of their king. All due respect, even if they find him before the next moon and the Queens' threat passes, I'm not sure our men could get past Gamer's Village without Geral knowing about it. We'd never make it to the city without losing men."

Morei regarded him, pleased. No questions of why, only how. Men like that made his life easy. "There is a way. A weakness. You will march into the Hazar Desert and circle Geral at night. The palace sits behind the city, unprotected, because no army is foolish enough to waste resources moving through that desert. But that will be to your advantage. You take the palace, and the city will be ours. When the time comes, that will be your best strategy for getting inside without drawing the attention of the army."

"Ah." That seemed to please the commander. His eyes glittered with the delight of a man who loved war, and he nodded. "I will pull together a report of my strongest men. There will be no movement until the current threat subsides. I will seek you out after the festival to go over more details regarding this attack. Until then?"

Morei took a drink. "Continue with the preparations. I'd also like a write-up of anything more you have on Diemon. We will have to act fast once we take Geral. In several moons, Geral will be ours."

Edwin bowed his head. "Anything else?"

"No." The king motioned to the others behind the commander. "You two remain."

As Edwin left the study, Rhys's shoulders relaxed. It was so subtle that Morei wouldn't have caught it if he wasn't staring at him. Isla kept her hands locked together, appearing smaller than he remembered her being. It occurred to him that she might have never seen a man die until last night. So innocent, but so naïve. The hardships of being a ruler would not suit her well if she couldn't learn to toughen up.

"What would you like, Your Majesty?" Rhys asked, opting for formalities. The behavior was unsettling, given how deceptive he was.

The festival was tomorrow. "Just ensure the staff does not need anything for the preparations." Rhys nodded but didn't move. "What is it?"

"I was here to fetch you for your hair appointment."

The news of Ezra's abduction haunted him. No matter how hard he tried to put the past behind him, he was constantly reminded of where he'd gone wrong. "Cancel that and all future appointments." It was time for a change.

"Are—" Rhys stopped when Morei shot him a challenging glare. A silent warning passed between them. Morei would not be questioned about his decisions, no matter how small. Rhys relented. "Of course."

Now his attention turned to the woman who was so willing to throw her bloodline aside to clean barns and knead bread. "You're upset about last night?"

Isla didn't move or make any response.

"Tell me," he insisted, so fiercely that Rhys flinched.

"Yes," she replied. Her tone was weak, pathetic.

She insulted the Caster name. He approached, each step causing her to sink further into herself. The chancellor didn't hide his emotions, stepping out of the way to avoid the king's wrath. Facing her, Morei spat, "You are so weak and pitiful. If you intend to be of any use, I advise you to learn that I will not lessen my actions because of your soft heart. Get used to the sight of blood, princess."

Isla didn't reply, but her expression shifted. Her jaw was set, her features plain.

"Do you understand?" He wanted to peel her fingernails off one at a time. Morei didn't care for weak people. They got in the way.

"Yes," she mumbled.

"Look at me when you say that," he ordered. "Have some pride in your blood, and act like your title."

They both seemed paralyzed by his demand. Morei thrived in these moments. He would stand here all day to prove who was in control. The woman was terrified of what it meant to be a ruler. That wouldn't do. He needed a queen who would stand by his side if he needed to slaughter hundreds, not cower when a man died. Politically, they needed to be aligned. If she couldn't accept this, Isla was of no use to him.

The silence grew darker, tenser. Rhys finally shifted, breaking the spell, and Isla slowly lifted her blue eyes to him. No kindness, only a need to get away. An injured bird, fleeing.

"Yes."

The king lifted his chin. "You are both dismissed."

Without hesitation, she turned and left. They hadn't confirmed the dance tomorrow, and after the last several days, he wondered if she would uphold her end of the agreement and even show up for the opening dance. If she didn't, the king would make an example out of her. He would not be embarrassed like that in front of so many citizens.

Rhys followed, slower, but with intent. The chancellor hovered at the door, nodding at Morei as the princess walked out. So Rhys approved. That didn't surprise him. The chancellor wanted to keep his head. He would agree to anything Morei had to say or do to keep his position, so that he could continue his illegal work. Morei also knew that the chancellor wanted to see Isla fail. It would seem he might get his wish after all.

As the door closed, Morei let his guard slip. He threw the drink against the wall, the glass obliterating the silence. Ezra was missing because of him. Because of the predicament he'd put the Geral king in. Grief surged in waves, nearly identical to the hot-red rage that turned his vision gray. He wanted to strangle the Geral councilmembers one at a time, let them watch each other die, and when he was down to Peter, he would string the man up and stuff those pastries he loved so much into his mouth until he choked to death.

That was who Morei was. Violent, unforgivable, merciless. Waiting for the Red Queens? Pathetic. He wanted to walk right into Geral and bring the city to its knees. Turn buildings into ash, scorch the sand, and let the fire do what she did best.

Revenge was bittersweet, though. Proper revenge took time. For Morei, it was all he wanted. Geral forced him out, stripped him of his rights as king, and made a mockery of his family. He held no sympathy for the people and their actions. Underneath all the anger, he needed Geral to be his, if only to prove to himself that he was worthy.

His compulsion, ugly and all-consuming, flared. Morei crossed the study, kicking the table and sending a book sprawling. It only worsened his temper. This was the side that made Death look peaceful. The side that would damn him if he wasn't careful. He grabbed another glass, filling it up to the brim with Kendall's Milk. Black veins glared at him, taunting. If he couldn't kill, then he would drink his impulses into submission.

Escaping the Tormented

Syra stepped carefully. Raid's warning about the bastards that lived in the thickest parts of the vines echoed through her mind. Waking a bunch of slimy creatures that wanted to eat her flesh while trying to escape would create an even bigger problem, one she wasn't sure she could handle. Barefoot, she wished she had her boots back. Not so much for the goop but for the warmth. Why her boots had been taken was unclear. Perhaps it was an attempt to demoralize her—a sick way of stripping her of anything that could prove resourceful. It didn't matter. If Syra had to travel across the Soul Realm barefoot, then so be it.

Her toes sank into a particularly wet spot, and she stole a look down. The vines were smashed. The contents were wet and clung to her skin, making the floor slippery. Syra continued, wiping her foot on a clean spot.

A noise made her pause, and she waited.

Distant, but she could hear shouts. Not close enough to be a concern, but that would change if they came this way. She instinctively reached for her weapon, only to remember that Death's Sword was not with her. She hoped Vaeke was true to his word and retrieved her things.

The hall she walked was one she'd already been in. The vines were everywhere, and the lighting was better but still not fantastic. She traced her steps back to Sekar, hoping her memory didn't betray her. Constantly, she stopped and listened. All around, she could hear the faint sounds of fighting and a tremor radiating down the hall. Nobody was down here, distracted by the call of battle, and she needed to move fast.

Doors came into view. She was getting close. The stench of rot no longer made her want to gag, but it was there, teasing her nose and reminding her that she was one wrong step away from getting herself killed. To her left, a thick layer of vines clung to the wall just underneath a chunk of ice, and she hesitated. This was what Raid had been talking about. Staring, she saw the vines shift slightly. A series of muffled clicks followed. That was the bastards.

She eased her way past, scared that even brushing a vine might cause the little creatures to come to life.

She looked back to double-check she was safe. Satisfied, she made a mental note to tell Sekar once they were out about everything that Raid told her.

Syra opened the door she remembered and found the God hanging there. At the sound of the metal grating against old hinges, Sekar raised his head. He looked horrible. A black-and-blue bruise stretched up the side of his face, a few more cuts were actively bleeding, and he had a fresh cut on his lip that stretched to his chin. He grinned.

"You continue to impress me."

Syra closed the door and rushed to him. "You're going to owe me for this one," she said. She placed her hands on the chains, fueled by adrenaline and the fear of getting caught. Chaos was already ready for her. The vast energy was everywhere at once, her chest burning from the sudden onslaught. As

Sekar had taught her, she redirected Mother toward the chains rather than letting the force fester for other uses. All objects had a threshold, and she just needed enough to break the metal. Managing Mother in her current condition was like wrangling a horse with just her hands. Her grasp on it slipped several times, and each time, she became more frantic. In a fit of frustration, she tightened her grip on the chains and mentally screamed for Chaos to obey. At once, energy burned her way down Syra's arms and into her fingers, burrowing into the metal. The chains grew hot, and she released them just as they shattered.

Sekar stumbled and started to fall. She instinctively tried to catch him, too stunned from what she'd done to do otherwise, but he weighed twice as much as her. Her knees nearly buckled, and she had to take several steps to right herself. Sekar didn't seem to even try to catch himself; he just let her do all the hard work. His face was smashed into her shoulder, and she swore she felt hot, sporadic breaths of laughter against her skin.

"Nice catch," he complimented, and slowly stood. That weird smile was still plastered on his face. "Chaos suits you well."

She nodded, not sure what was with him. "We got a little help from a Guardian. I know how to get out of here. Can you walk fine?"

"I think so." As if to prove his point, he stepped forward, but instead of remaining upright, he tipped sideways. Syra grabbed him, and he used her to hold himself up. "Yeah. That'll do."

"What?" Syra couldn't figure out what was wrong with him. "You can hardly walk. How does any of this work?" Her plan was in jeopardy if he couldn't stay upright. "I need you to put one foot in front of the other. Do you need me to demonstrate it or something?"

"Could you?"

He was toying with her. She'd have recognized that glimmer anywhere. "Are you being serious right now? You know what, never mind." Gesturing at him, she asked, "Is this the toxin working? Or are you generally giddy in life-threatening situations?"

He shrugged. "A bit of both. I feel a little like a drunk." A quick scan around, and he faced her again. "And our stuff?"

All she could do was hope some of that toxin started to wear off now. If they had to fight their way out of here, she feared he'd be rendered useless. "In the weapons room. As far as I know, Vaeke is retrieving those, but we don't have time to wait around. Raid and a few other Guardians orchestrated an attack against Elyas and Shevana's loyal members."

"And Raid is . . ."

"One of the Guardians helping us. Listen next time. I'm not repeating myself." Syra motioned to the door. "We move now or not at all. Let's go." She laid a hand on the cold handle and watched him approach. He had a limp, and he swayed slightly. "You're not making that up, are you?"

When he reached the door, he leaned a hand against it. The God was out of breath. "I'm trying to earn your sympathy. Is it working?"

"No." Syra opened the door. "If you fall, I'm leaving you." He opened his mouth to say something, but she stopped him. "One other thing—don't step on the vines. Turns out there are things that live inside them, guarding the halls, and we can't afford to try to fight off flesh-eating bastards when you can hardly walk straight. Unless you can harvest. If so, please let me know."

She didn't wait for a reply. They could talk later, when they got out of there. Looking left and right, the hall was empty. That was a relief, though she had no idea how long that would last, given the increasing commotion from behind. "Come on," she whispered, and stepped forward. She didn't look to see if he was following. This was Sekar—not even Death could slow him if he wanted something.

Voices echoed louder, and Syra ducked behind another corner. Sekar shoved himself too close, and he gave her a half shrug that she assumed was supposed to be an apology. This near, she could smell the sweat and copper from the beatings and blood. The voices grew louder, clicking and making all sorts of throaty sounds. They sounded frantic. Syra held her breath. She didn't want to fight now and risk an army showing up. If they came this way, Syra wasn't sure what use Sekar would be, and she had to trust she could fight them all off.

They waited as the voices grew louder until she was certain they were going to peak around the corner, but just as quickly, the demons continued onward. Syra sent out a quick prayer, only to realize how ironic that was. Alone, she yanked Sekar forward by his tattered tunic. "We're supposed to take a right."

They came to the junction that she'd been at several times already. Instead of left, they went right. Hopefully the Guardian hadn't betrayed them—they couldn't turn back now. The walls grew increasingly narrower, the vines sporadic. She walked more freely for a while, and when the walls became suffocatingly close, they stopped.

"Cozy," Sekar mumbled.

"Is that . . ."

They turned to see a Guardian with a hand on the hilt of Death's Sword, part of his cloak torn and blood smeared across the side of his face. He looked as stunned to see them as they were in return. Syra reeled. This could not get any worse. If he called out, their escape plan would be ruined.

Syra raised her hand, ready to summon Chaos, though to do what, she wasn't sure. Exhaustion reminded her that she was incapable of doing anything significant. "Listen—"

Raid came into view, punching the Guardian so hard in the temple that the man collapsed. He shook his hand out as he nudged the unconscious Guardian with his boot. "He's one of the fanatics." Raid glanced their way. "If you stand there any longer, I can't help you. Elyas knows you're missing."

Without thought, she nodded and shoved Sekar deeper into the tunnel system. The God didn't speak, which was uncharacteristic, but she didn't have time to ask questions. They needed to get out of this place as fast as possible.

The walls gave way to jagged rock, and Syra ducked to avoid hitting her head. Sekar was right behind, and she couldn't help but chuckle. He was twice her size and must have been squeezing through this passageway with increased difficulty. If he wasn't such an ass sometimes, she'd have felt a little bad. Well, she did. She just wouldn't tell him.

The footing became rockier and the air chillier. Syra stubbed her toes and stabbed her feet more times than she cared to admit. With no light, they were going by touch. Her hands grazed the stone around them, and they constantly stopped to check that they weren't heading to a dead end. When Sekar put a hand on her shoulder, she was about to make a snarky remark—until she heard his heavy breathing and felt how frigid his fingers were. They stopped. In the pitch black, she couldn't see anything, and the sounds were amplified.

"Are you okay?"

It took a moment for him to answer her. "I'm enjoying a leisurely stroll . . . through a tunnel. What more fun could I be having?"

Syra would have turned and faced him if not for the tight space. "Be honest."

Another pause. "I could use a sit to catch my breath. Chilly in here too, yeah?"

Despite the cooler climate, she was melting from the adrenaline. "Are you okay to continue?"

"I have to be. Someone said if I fall, they'd leave me behind. And I'm not dying in some dirty tunnel."

His sarcasm was great, but he sounded strained. He likely had a fever, and she was certain that if she saw him, his skin probably looked washed out. "What did they do to you?"

"Keep moving," he replied, ignoring the question. "I am a man of few fears, but tight tunnels are one of them."

No point in continuing the discussion. He needed strength, and she was wasting his breath. They crawled their way forward. The deeper they went, the more Sekar leveraged her shoulder as his personal weight-bearing tool. Her back muscles weren't happy about it, but she didn't say anything. Chaos granted her some reprieve from her injuries, but the additional weight of the deity reminded her of every muscle that hurt.

After what felt like an eternity, they came upon a junction. A faint light illuminated the stone—just enough for her to see four entrances. She looked around, trying to place the sudden light, but couldn't find anything. It was like the light was coming right out of the rock itself. Syra opened her mouth to ask Sekar about it, but when she finally turned to look at him, she saw he was well past looking washed out. The God had turned gray.

At her stare, he asked, "How do I look?"

"I've seen better," she said. Two of the tunnel entrances were wide, likely used more frequently with travelers. No sign of the stick that Raid had told her about, and she wondered if they'd taken the wrong turn. They couldn't backtrack; it was too risky. They would need to decide here and now where they went, so she swallowed the itch of anxiety that crept up the back of her throat. Now was not the time to think the worst, like how a Geíon or Guardian could arrive to strip them of their freedom.

The other two were a bit more wonky and uneven. She pointed at the one on the left. "What do you think?"

No response. Syra turned again and saw Sekar leaned up against the stone. Seeing the God who'd upended her entire life for his entertainment like this was not comforting. She'd grown used to the witty remarks, sarcasm, and harshness. To see him so vulnerable and struggling made her nervous. "Why don't I go ahead and look—"

"No," he answered. "I'm not being left here. If anyone shows up, I might as well roll over dead."

"My sympathy is running dry," she mumbled. "Come on."

They continued on their way. The narrow tunnel hardly gave any room to breathe. They constantly had to walk with their backs pressed to the wall, shoulder to shoulder, to squeeze by. Syra would have gone faster if not for the God behind her. He was slowing, and she was starting to bet on him passing out. If he did, she wasn't sure how she'd get him out of here. The tunnel wasn't even wide enough to drag anyone through. The thought crept into her mind, festering and growing larger. They might die in this tunnel without ever seeing the light again. The damp darkness was suffocating. Sekar's gasps didn't help. He sounded like he couldn't get air, but he didn't want her to ask anymore how he was doing, so she kept her mouth shut, though she couldn't stop staring every chance she had.

Her heart was in her throat. If they didn't find a way out soon, she was going to lose it. They were walking into the unknown, uncertain where they'd end up—

"Wait," she blurted out. The air had just shifted. Lighter. It smelled more of dirt than the stale, muggy rot she'd grown so used to. "Do you smell that?"

"I smell myself, and it's not good," he remarked quietly.

A low rumble ripped her reply right out of her mouth. It grew into a destructive roar as their world started to shake. The ground shifted. Syra's knees buckled from the violence of the mountain, and she dropped. Sekar dropped next to her, head buried under his arms. Chunks of rock broke free, scratching and cutting as they landed. The howl that ripped through the tunnel from the tremor deafened everything. An explosion followed, hot rotten air rushed them, and neither dared move as the surrounding world continued its outcry.

The howling quieted, the sound of rocks falling lessened, and she raised her head. The ground dug into her knees, and she was certain dust had made it into and onto every part of her. The smell clung to her nose, her throat burned, and she could taste dirt on her lips.

Sekar had fared no better. He looked like a reanimated corpse with all those wounds, dust, and grime. There were no snarky remarks. That last incident had pushed him over, and he was barely conscious.

Behind, where they'd just come from, the ceiling had collapsed. So much for trying to backtrack if they got lost, though it meant they might have a chance, after all. Nobody could come for them.

Her attention was turned to more important matters.

"Hey." Syra nudged Sekar, who leaned against the wall, wheezing again. "Are you okay?"

Hesitation. "I need to rest." The playfulness in his voice was gone.

She looked around in the dim glow from the rock. "We need to keep moving. There might be another—"

"Syra," Sekar interrupted, raspy. "I can't."

That should have been her. Raid had mentioned her bloodline may have something to do with why she wasn't responding like she should have been. If not for that, she'd still have been strung up and waiting for Elyas to return.

If Sekar couldn't reach Chaos, Syra felt like they were waiting to die.

The Blood of the Forgotten

T he sun hadn't fallen. Cyrus had been there for less than a day, and a celebration was underway. He felt out of sorts, disoriented, but trusted his legs to keep him up as he was led back to the center of Venkar. The streets all looked alike to him, but he was able to recognize the one they were on by the children piling out of the homes. They stood as tall as they could and crossed their arms over their chests. Adults did the same. More and more people did so, and Cyrus felt the cold tingle of anxiety ripple through him. They were all standing there for him. The street grew more crowded. He and Kerí were squeezed shoulder to shoulder until they finally reached the center. It wasn't much, but it was a large enough clearing that Sozar could stand in the middle, hardly recognizable with all his paint, with Yavinks dressed strictly in body paint, leaving little to the imagination beyond the small coverings around their groins. Sitting before them were the large drums with the I'num sigil. Multicolored beads and leather straps hung from the men and women, who played a tune he didn't recognize.

Boom, boom, boom. Faster and slower, the rhythm led Cyrus over to stand next to Sozar. Chavi greeted him with another woman who looked in similar age. They held bowls of white and blue paint.

"Your shirt," Kerí explained. "You now must remove it so that they can bless you."

"What?" The question slipped out before he could stop himself. The crowd staring at him was enough to make him feel smaller than an ant, and the drums continued, unperturbed by his hesitation.

Sozar reached down and blew hot air on his face. *A traditional Dragon Rider celebration.*

Cyrus looked back to Kerí, who must have sensed the conversation, because he gave the faintest nod of acknowledgment. "Um, okay." He carefully undid the buttons. The drumming didn't waver, but the people all started mumbling something in Old Tongue. His nerves were frayed, so he couldn't listen or begin to understand what it was. Between the growing sounds, overwhelming smells of spices, and the bold cultural presentation, he couldn't comprehend it all at once. The paint stank of crushed fruit, citrusy and sweet. As the last button was undone, Kerí reached out and slid the shirt off. He carefully folded it over his arm and stepped back.

Chavi and the other woman wasted no time. They took their fingers and dipped them into the bowls of paint. "Please, turn around," Chavi told him.

Every instinct in him wanted to refuse and run. This was well beyond his comfort, but he obeyed. Scars and all were visible, and he wondered what they all thought witnessing him standing there. Then the cold paint contacted his skin. Chills raced up his body, and he felt the hairs along his arms stand. Their fingers moved without stopping, sweeping up and down his back, side to side, before they began working along his arms. He felt like an animal being prepared for slaughter.

Settle yourself, Sozar told him. *You're making me anxious.*

Cyrus sucked in a deep breath of air, trying not to disrupt the painting. *This is the last thing I wanted.*

In the name of knowledge, the dragon pointed out.

He didn't see the humor.

The women turned him around so that he could face the crowd. That made it worse. He averted his gaze, instead focusing on the beads that dangled from Chavi's outfit. Or the lack thereof. Her skin was covered in oranges and pinks. Her bare breasts were painted with a large dragon in flight, its tail wrapping around her throat and down her backside. The other woman was painted similarly, but she'd chosen purple and yellow.

They finally stopped. Unshi and Yu stepped forward from the crowd. He hadn't even seen them originally when he took in the crowd. Each of them held a small silver chalice. They approached in unison, only stopping when they were right behind the painters. The drumming intensified.

This didn't feel like a celebration anymore. It felt like a sacrifice. If not for Sozar's persistent insistence that they were okay, he'd have abandoned everything then.

Chavi and the other woman moved aside, and Unshi and Yu came closer. They were dressed in leather and paint. White beads hung from their clothes, and detailed scales were painted across their arms. Atop their heads lay crowns of teeth. From a pocket that Cyrus hadn't seen, Kerí took a short dagger. The sheath was red with etched Old Tongue sigils, and the hilt and pommel were carved to look like a dragon talon. Unshi accepted it from his son, mumbling something.

The chalice in Unshi's hand was empty. Yu's was filled with a liquid that looked nearly black.

"Your name," the Venkar leader said quietly.

"Um, Cyrus," he answered.

"No, your full name."

His lips turned to stone. He should give his family name, Sacrow. It was the name he'd found when Alaric tasked Asher to gather more information on his mother. His father had abandoned him to rule the sea. The only other reference they could find to the Sacrow name was a ship, but it hadn't docked at the Delion Port in nearly a decade. That was Cyrus's heritage, and yet he couldn't bring himself to say it. The man he'd come to know so well was an orphan, given the name Wynter by the staff who raised him. Each child was given a different name pulled from a list of acceptable ones used specifically for orphans. It was for documentation for the city. It would do no good letting a boy run about without a proper last name. Everything Cyrus was came from those long and grueling summers.

"Wynter," he muttered. He refused to claim a name that meant nothing to him.

Unshi raised the dagger, and at once, the drumming stopped. The silence was deafening. "Cyrus Wynter, Rider of the sea and sky," the man boomed. "We ask that you take this gift without fear or question. We give you the truth in its purest, most complete form. We have carried this weight for centuries, burdening our children with promises of a future no one could guarantee, but here you are, in the flesh and scale. No gift is ever free, Rider, and so we ask that you gift us your truth in its purest form in return."

They wanted his blood. It was the only conclusion he could come to, what with the chalice and dagger. What could they possibly expect to gain from such an ancient practice?

His blood was . . . nothing. Declining the motion would disrespect them. The dark substance in the other chalice glared at him. Blood. It had to be, but it was unlike any he'd ever seen before. His stomach twisted violently at the thought, and he hoped he didn't look as nauseous as he felt at that prospect. *Sozar?*

Drink it, the dragon advised. *They would not poison you now. Remember, Hyle brought us here.*

Despite the dragon's reassurance, he felt hollow, uncertain, and his nerves worsened. He'd spent so much time running from people trying to harm him, and now he was going to willingly drink something that very well might be blood. It might even be tampered with. And if he refused, he would lose all opportunity to uncover the answers he sought.

Numbly, he nodded. Unshi unsheathed the dagger, the sound ear-splitting in the silence. The blade was dark gray, and the edges were serrated. That would make an even more painful cut, but he swallowed the trepidation and offered his wrist.

Unshi nodded and placed the chalice under his hand. "Hold still. I'll be quick," he whispered. Laying the sharpened edge of the blade down, he drove it across Cyrus's palm without warning. He hissed and tried to pull back out of instinct, but the man was quicker. He snatched his wrist while still holding the blade and directed the red river into the chalice. Cyrus grimaced at the fiery pain, but it could have been worse. This was no brutal whipping, at least.

They stood there for a long moment, watching the blood drip. When the cup was half full, Unshi let go, and another man stepped forward. He laid a warm, thick paste on Cyrus's hand to staunch the bleeding. It smelled faintly of mint and another vibrant leaf.

"In your blood runs the souls of both you and your dragon," Unshi said, and passed the blade back to Kerí, who took it and wiped the metal clean before sheathing it. "You were chosen because your dragon sees in you courage, strength, persistence, and the ability to do right when there is so much wrong with this world. You have taken on the burden to correct the damages our people have done, to be the messenger between man and God." Unshi took Yu's chalice then and poured Cyrus's blood into it. Now, he was certain he was going to be sick.

As Unshi handed the now-empty chalice to Yu, he said, "We ask that you accept our truth in its purest form." He handed the chalice to him.

He wanted Cyrus to drink it. That didn't need to be clarified. *I don't know if I can do this,* he confessed. *Why can't you drink it?*

You have both our lifeforces in your blood, Sozar reminded, his tone far too mocking for the seriousness of the moment. *Drink, before you make us look like fools.*

Gingerly, he took the chalice. It was heavier than he'd anticipated, and he gripped the cup with both hands, ruining the undried paste. Blood seeped through, staining the metal, and his hand stung. He swallowed the last bit of spit. Would it taste like sour meat? Metal? Inconspicuously, he sniffed. Nothing. That was bizarre. All blood had a stench to it, but not this. The proximity to Crescent Lake did strange things to the Yavinks and the land. It would make sense that it was blood from one of them. What else could it be?

The people were staring. He felt every single eye drill into his skull until a headache blossomed.

You don't think they've poisoned it?

The question remained unanswered. The passing heartbeats felt like an eternity. Then Sozar flared his nostrils and ruffled his wings, the only movement that broke the stillness of this city's small center. *These people come and speak with good intentions. We have nothing to fear.*

Cyrus had dragged this out as long as he dared without looking rude. The faster he drank, the sooner it would be over. His hands trembled slightly, sloshing the bloody mixture around. It was thicker than he'd realized, but he couldn't think about it. Pressing his lips against the metal, he drank.

The blood burned as it touched his tongue. The metallic taste bloomed, but with it came something else, a bitterness that caught him off guard. His mind battled between continuing and gagging, all while he shoved as much down his throat as he could before he lost this battle. The hot sensation turned his innards flush, and his stomach felt like it was on fire, like he'd just taken a long drink of the strongest liquor available.

Cyrus pulled the chalice away, but he gagged before he could stop himself. Hand to mouth with tears, he suppressed throwing everything up. The chalice was torn free from his hand, and all around, a roar erupted. Drums pounded, people screamed words he couldn't understand, and the rumble of stomping vibrated his legs. They were pleased.

Blinking, he pulled his hand away and saw the madness. People were dancing with each other, paint was thrown up and splattering all in sight; it felt like the forest shivered from the thrill of it all. Leaves rustled, critters jumped back and forth between branches, and the creatures that could speak did so in their native tongue. Even the dust in the air glittered.

Chavi was next to him, hand on his shoulder. "You have brought the Dragon Riders before and after you great honor, I'num."

His tongue moved as slow as thick mud. "Do you have water?"

She shook her head. "To ensure the success of this, you must not drink or eat anything until it is over."

Nobody had told him that. His thoughts were slowing. With Eazon's luck, he'd probably been poisoned after all. "What?"

"You should sit," Chavi said. Already, she was pushing him down. He felt drunk, and his legs obeyed, relieved to not be in use anymore. The people continued their celebration, oblivious to his reaction.

"What's happening to me?" The world around him swayed violently. Sozar wrapped a tail around him to secure his position. The dragon's presence tried to reassure him. Words passed across their bond, but he couldn't grasp them. The reverberation of the drums jolted his bones. Paint danced in the air with each beat. He watched, awestruck, as the paint rippled like a dragon with its head reared and roaring before it fell back onto the drum. As it bounced up again, the paint took on the shape of a bird with its wings outstretched.

Cyrus stared. Every muscle in his body failed to respond to him. He couldn't recall Chavi answering him, and now he couldn't even see her anymore. The Yavinks were lost in their dancing and shouts, leaving Sozar and him to die here.

His vision blurred. Heart lurching, he fought. He struck the hand of slumber as hard as he could, every muscle engulfed in fire, as he kept his gaze fixed on the drummers. His hand clutched one of the horns along Sozar's tail, keeping him upright, but even that was failing.

A dark and otherworldly presence entered his mind then, engulfing him whole. The last bit of Sozar was pushed out, isolating him. The presence moved with ancient grace, seeming certain with each step even in a place as foreign as Cyrus's head. Tentacles of thought wrapped around every thread of reality that he had left, squeezing until he couldn't grasp them any longer. Vision went first. A fog cascaded over what he saw now, erasing everything.

Chavi, Unshi, Kerí, and Yu dissipated like dust. The drummers continued their song as their bodies became mist.

Noise went next. A rumbling sound filled his head as the song and cheers and clarity of the drumming faded.

Visions bombarded him with no real order or length. He saw a dozen dragons in a courtyard, of varying colors and sizes. Large training rings where Riders exchanged swords, prestigious Riders dressed in some of the finest royal silk sitting at a massive, glossed table. A sword was released from a red sheath, showing a blade that looked to be made of a thousand gems, which glittered as the sun struck it. He was staring at a poorly done knot on his saddle, trying frantically to tighten it before he passed out, knowing he didn't have time.

He saw dead dragons, fallen warriors, and Riders killing each other. He saw chains and only darkness. People in cloaks humming a name repeatedly before driving a blade into the soft spot of the dragon's skin. He felt anger, betrayal, and desperation for freedom. As quickly as he saw this damaged world, a figure became clear in a new vision. Blond, with no scar. He screamed madly at those nestled around the table, words lost to Cyrus. Hyle was trying to tell them something, but they didn't care. Didn't want to listen.

The visions shattered, replaced with a wide-mouthed cave hidden by dense forestry. A chest sat at the front, easy for scouters to find. He saw a man writing a long and pleading letter, the skin aged but still firm. The lettering was crisp and legible, but he didn't have time to read it.

Cyrus's head rolled. The world around him was moving. He was being carried. Somewhere above him, a hundred voices chanted.

"Sozar . . ." He could hardly make the word work on his tongue. The sky was dark, and the only thing he saw was the dancing flames.

The dragon's voice shifted through the oppressive presence, confident and strong, bright against the darkness that filled his mind. *We have found the truth.*

No Dead Man Is Worth Saving

The wind was gentle tonight. Morei repositioned his boots on the chair beside him and reached for his glass of Kendell's Milk. The glossed stone table was cold, even after he'd been sitting here for so long. The king couldn't remember when he'd arrived at his personal terrace. It was some time after the news of Ezra's abduction. Night was upon him, the coast lit up with a beautiful storm. It wouldn't reach the city, but thunder still rolled across the coastline.

Morei's impulses became more manageable the more he drank. After the fifth person came looking for him, he threw a glass. That was enough to earn him some peace. He was supposed to see citizens, sign off on the final imports for the festival, and . . . well, he couldn't remember. And he didn't care. If it was important, he'd hear about it tomorrow. Rhys was sure to handle what needed to be done, and it would give the chancellor plenty of opportunity to work behind the king's back. The thought was bitter, but it was impossible to let go of. If he saw the chancellor tonight, he suspected things would end poorly for the man, but Rhys seemed to know that already. Morei hadn't seen him all afternoon and evening. He had good survival instincts.

Memories of Ezra filled his head with relentless force. He hated it, but he didn't push them away either. He didn't know much about the man's childhood, save for that he'd killed his father and felt great loyalty to his mother, but he knew Ezra was fierce and had been a survivor. He knew Morei better than anyone and was the first to challenge his morals, but also the first person to stand by his side. The loudest memory that came to mind was when they'd sat across from each other in his study. It was the first time Ezra had observed his ailment, but the Harvester had never judged Morei. Not like his citizens had.

Where could he be now? If the abductors were just after coin, they wouldn't touch the king, but if this was for the throne, Ezra would be beaten, whipped, stabbed—all of it. Morei was spiraling. His thoughts darkened, and he couldn't stop them. Without knowing the motive, he was left grappling for any thread of hope that the Harvester was okay. Alone, he was forced to wonder if Geral had let this happen because of Ezra's association with Morei. Politics made monsters out of people, and a chance existed that the council had orchestrated this just to finally get rid of the last thing Morei had done as king. They wouldn't ever accept Ezra.

Geral was his. It always had been. And the stronger Caster became, the more confident he was that planning the attack against Geral was the most strategic move. When they won, the citizens would have no choice but to accept him.

He finished off his third drink. He'd gotten comfortable a long time ago. Simple white tunic with the sleeves rolled up and loose-fitted pants. His boots were only still on because he'd been debating going to the galley later to get some food. He'd skipped supper again. The late-night staff would start having questions for him if he kept showing his face after everyone was asleep. Esme, the lead chef and baker, would be there. Her husband, Dan, cooked and prepped alongside her. He liked the two, but he didn't want them getting the wrong idea and asking questions.

Even that felt like far too much work, though. It had been a long time since he'd sat as he had today. The feeling was foreign but welcoming. If he'd seen the public today, he didn't know how many would have ended up dead. His compulsion was worsening. When the waves washed over him, they were harsher, harder to ignore, crippling. Eli had been a result of that.

Morei reached over to the decanter. He topped off his drink again, hoping to shut his thoughts up, but he saw movement out of the corner of his eye. A blue dress.

"I could have you hung for breaking in," he said, and took a drink. No point in asking how she'd gotten in. She'd been raised by servants and spent her life in this palace. The woman likely knew how to pick a lock.

Isla was bundled up in a fur cloak and carrying a small tray. She approached and set it on the table before him. An array of Caster's favorite fried fish stared back at him, unsatisfying, along with some bread.

"Why are you here?" She'd hardly been able to look at him earlier.

The woman didn't move. "I'm not afraid of you."

That made him chuckle. "That's not what I saw earlier." When she didn't reply, he motioned at the tray with his drink. "So is that what this is about? To prove how brave you are? That's almost worthy of my respect, but not quite. Are you done here?"

"You missed supper again."

The night was warm, but she was dressed for the cooler season. If he cared more, he would have asked. "I know."

Isla made herself comfortable across from him, ignorantly determined, staring at his hands. She'd never seen the ailment so publicly displayed before, and he didn't shy away. This was who he was.

"I brought you some stuff," she pressed.

Morei took another drink. "I know."

The princess pursed her lips and leaned back. She wasn't leaving—annoying. "Have you come to patronize me again, princess?"

"No," she said, sharp. "I came to make sure you were okay. The staff were asking about you."

"I'm flattered," he replied. She didn't speak. "I'm fine," he added.

Isla scoffed. "No, you're not."

Morei raised his brow. "Trying to be the hero will not earn my respect." He finished off the glass, then reached for the decanter, but she pulled it away. Agitation flared instantly. "Isla," he warned.

"Eat." She tucked the decanter in her lap. "Maybe you can have more after."

The food looked atrocious. "I'm not hungry, and I certainly don't need you mothering me."

She *laughed* as if she'd just heard the funniest thing. "Me being concerned about your well-being is mothering? Do you have any friends?"

"No. Now can I have a drink?"

Isla didn't miss a beat. "Eat."

If he'd been more clear-minded, he might have stabbed her, but the best he could do was pick up a piece of fish, give her a nasty glare, and stuff it into his mouth. The salt was overpowering, and while it tasted wonderful, he wouldn't let her know that. "Happy?"

The princess shook her head. The motion was stiff. When she didn't relent, he ate more, hardly tasting it. This was more to prove a point than to enjoy the meal.

After a few minutes, the tray wasn't empty, but he pushed it back. Any more and he might vomit. Morei leaned back, observing the distant storm. Nothing snarky came to mind anymore. It was as if eating had purged what little strength he had left. Now, all he could see was Ezra's face. The memories were trying to drown him again.

"You were close to him, weren't you?"

The king didn't look her way. "Who?"

It was a poor attempt to deflect, and he knew that Isla saw right through it. "Ezra."

"Yes." Nobody knew that here, and he'd hoped never to reveal it, but it felt useless to hide from that truth. Not after what she'd already seen.

Silence stretched between them. "I'm sorry," the princess finally said.

"Why apologize for something you have no control over?"

"Because I sympathize with you. I'm sorry that you have been dealt this awful news. I'm sorry because no matter who you want the world to think you are, you're still only you. And that version of you still wants what we all want: friendship, love, acceptance."

Her words cut right through him. Morei sat there, torn between telling her to leave and accepting her company. He should have been insulted at her for believing she knew him, but he couldn't even find the anger for that. Isla was right, and that made him wary of her. Few people could be so blunt with him.

"What do you want?" Morei asked. He looked at her fully now and saw she was surprised.

"I don't want anything."

He shook his head. "Don't lie to me, Isla. We all want something. We're all motivated by some goal. You came here tonight for something, so get it out."

"You think I came here in the depths of your misery because I wanted to get something out of you?" She sounded angry. "Do you think that little of me?"

Morei shrugged, unperturbed. "There's not a single person I've met who wasn't driven by some motive."

The princess snorted. "Then you've met the wrong people." She reached over and snatched his glass up and filled it with Kendell's Milk. Morei watched, shocked, when she took a drink and didn't offer it to him. "You want to know what I'm motivated by? Helping people. That's what gets me out of bed every morning. I constantly wonder who needs me and where I can help. If I can't do that, I feel lost."

The king opened his mouth, but she continued over him.

"When you found me yesterday, I'd just gotten done helping in the barn, because the barn hand who couldn't arrive? He wasn't just sick, he was dealing with the loss of his grandfather. That was the only family he had left. Who would I be or anyone be if they told him to work while he was struggling through that grief?"

Morei swallowed his sudden irritation. She was a riddle for him, and it drove him mad that he couldn't figure her out.

Isla motioned at him. "So who would I be if I expected anything of you while you sat here drinking your problems away?" She shook her head. "I am not that kind of person. I do not lack a heart like some." At that, she took another drink.

Morei didn't ask for the glass, but she handed it back to him anyway. He downed what remained. Her presence sobered him far more than he liked, and he was not in the mental state to befriend his thoughts. The king wanted them to be silent, or he might do something he would come to regret.

"What are you afraid of?" she asked. He raised his brow. "We're all afraid of something, Morei, even you."

The princess had come here to talk. Morei didn't mind her company, but he'd never been exposed in such a way. No, he realized, nobody had ever asked him these things. Nobody had ever taken the time to know the real Morei. But it wasn't like him to be honest with someone who could pose a threat, let alone someone who was almost a stranger. He and Isla hadn't been the best at making friends. They'd played by the rules for the most part—she upholding her duties as princess and he training her—but the line was drawn there. Now, she was in his personal space at his most vulnerable point, and that made him uncomfortable.

"I'd rather not," he answered. He handed the glass back to her, and she topped it off again.

"You're terrified of rejection," she said.

"No."

She tilted her head, looking amused. "Really? Then what person would travel across a country, steal a throne, and declare himself as king if he didn't want to be accepted? To want acceptance is to be afraid of rejection. You can't have one or the other."

"And you seemed to think I'm narrowminded," he shot back. "I did not come all this way for acceptance. I came here to have my revenge—"

"Revenge instilled by the rejection of your people."

The king held out his hand for the glass. He was too sober for this conversation. Isla relented and handed it over to him, but not without adding, "It's okay to feel these things."

"Isla," he said once he swallowed. He weighed the rest of the drink but decided to wait. "You don't know me. You don't know my childhood, my dreams, or even my pet peeves. But I'll tell you one of them. It's when people like you try to tell me how *I* should feel. Take that as a warning." Satisfied, he finished the glass and set it on the stone with a loud smack.

The princess poured more. Hardly anything was left in the decanter now. "And what if I want to get to know you? So that I can better understand you?"

Morei laughed. "You don't want to know me, Isla. I'm exactly as what you said: unlikeable. The only thing you haven't called me yet is a monster, but you will. Soon." Everyone did.

Isla took a drink, but he saw that she was more hesitant now. "Do you ever get tired of running from yourself?"

She was determined to sober him up, and no matter how much he drank, it was working. Ezra's face was clearer, and his mistakes glared at him with a mocking grin. The storm was heading farther out to sea, so he couldn't even focus on the lightning anymore. "I think it's time you left."

"Very well." Isla stood and walked around to pick up the tray. Even in the midst of this crummy conversation, she was trying to do good. It was annoying. Morei couldn't believe how shitty she was making him feel. As she reached over, he grabbed her wrist. He wanted to see what her hands looked like. Every servant had a story on their hands. If he knew more, maybe he could better understand her real motive. Helping people? A lie, and she was a fool if she thought he'd believe her.

The princess didn't pull away as he dragged his thumb over her palm, inspecting it. Her skin was callused from many summers of hard work, though still soft in some spots. A scar stretched from her middle finger to her wrist on her right hand. It looked old, based on the faded pale skin. He pushed the bangles up to see that scar stretched farther.

Reckless and stubborn. That was what her hands told him.

"How did you get this?"

"When I was twelve, I fell from the second floor and tried to catch myself. My hand went right into a meat hook. Not as charming as a battle story."

That made him snort. "But it makes for quite a scar." He let go, and she quickly picked up the tray. Isla was eager to leave now, and he was glad for that.

She stood there, fingers drumming the tray. "Why don't you tell me about one of yours?"

He looked at his hands then, covered in scars with similar stories from his childhood—foolish tales of bravery and half-assed courage. Scars from battle too, some seen and unseen. Isla represented everything he wished he could be. "You don't know my scars, and I beg you never have to." This was not a world she wanted to be a part of. "Isla," he said, still focused on his hands. "Do you ever get tired of giving people the benefit of the doubt?"

When she answered, she was farther away. "No."

He scoffed. "Even when the council tries to punish you for how and when you were born?" They hadn't discussed his theory that it was they who made her wary of her duties and potential, but he went with it anyway.

And it worked. A pause followed, long enough to tell him everything he needed to know. Even the kindest people knew the taste of dread on their tongues. "Try to get some sleep," she said at last. "Tomorrow is the festival."

These Long Nights

A nudge startled Syra awake. She blinked and looked around, finding nothing out of the ordinary. They'd made their way to the tunnel's entrance, but no farther. Out there lay the Starved Sands—the hunting grounds for the Cer'hans. The ground rippled when she first saw it, and sand was swallowed whole as a rumbling echoed. Originally, she'd hoped Sekar could open a portal and get them out of this mess, maybe even take them directly to Zarek, but he was hardly improving. Their choices were limited. Cross the Starved Sands without getting killed, or wait and hope they weren't discovered. Returning to the living realm without Zarek was not an option.

"Sorry," she told him, rubbing the slumber from her face. It felt like the middle of the night, but the sky looked the same as it had when they first arrived—purple. "I didn't mean to fall asleep."

"No worries," he said. They kept their voices low. "I've been awake for a bit, so I'm glad you got some rest."

That made her feel worse. "How long have I been out?"

He tried to shrug, but it was a weak attempt. "Time works differently here. Maybe less than half a day?"

"By the Gods, you should have awoken me," she said. "What if someone showed up?"

Sekar raised his brow. Nobody had come for them. The tunnel collapse was working in their favor. "I was willing to take the risk. Feel better?"

"Sure," she grumbled, not liking it one bit, but she did feel far more refreshed than when she'd left. Her muscles were stiff and sore, though, and when she moved her neck, she found it locked. She'd passed out against Sekar for warmth and slept wrong. "How do you feel?"

"The truth? Like shit. I can't reach Chaos." Sekar's dark gaze lingered toward the Starved Sands and then returned to her. "You have the same cuts, but you're not in the same condition. How?"

"Raid mentioned that it might be my bloodline," she told him. While they were both awake, neither had moved from the comfort of each other. It was cold out here, and the wounds didn't help. The lacerations across their forearms continued to bleed, staining pants and everything they encountered.

"Do you trust Raid?"

The question sat between them, burrowing into the small space. "I can't trust him, can I?" she asked, more to herself. "I can say he's done the right thing, but who knows if he's a good person. We could be walking right into another trap."

"You're learning." Sekar sounded pleased. He knew of Elyas and what Raid had told her. She'd told him earlier once they'd moved again. But that also meant they weren't safe, sandwiched between two threats and waiting like prey. The ground rumbled. This time, it was far less violent.

"We need to get back to Zarek."

The God scoffed. "He's nothing but dead weight."

She shot him a glare. "Don't be so harsh. He could be worse off than either of us."

"Or he could be enjoying some fresh wine with his old lover," Sekar said. He was trying to act normal, but Syra could see the sweat on his skin and hear the shakiness of his words.

"What do you think we have? A day? Two? I'm afraid of what Shevana will do to him."

Sekar leaned his head back and closed his eyes. "She will do horrible things to him." The sarcasm was gone. "She will find the worst memories and exploit them. She doesn't need to get her hands stained with blood. If she has her way with him, he'll be half the man you remembered."

That made her stomach twist with nausea. "We can't sit here another day." She sat up, ignoring the pangs of discomfort from her healing body. Her connection with Chaos was returning, but the energy only did so much. What she needed was a fortnight to rest, a hot bath, and fresh clothes. Boots would be nice too.

Sekar rubbed the back of his head, and a long silence filled the space between them. Something was weighing on him.

Syra was about to ask him about what was on his mind when he finally cleared his throat. "I may need your help." The words came out barely above a whisper.

"Me?" In all the moons they'd spent together, he'd never asked for help. "What could I possibly do for you?"

He snorted weakly. "I need to draw the toxin out. I am worthless if it sits in my body any longer. If we had days, I could let it work through, but we're lucky if we have one. If you want my help, I need you to do this for me."

Syra didn't like that. She could hardly predict Chaos when she used the energy; the idea of directing Mother onto him and hoping she didn't kill him in the process felt reckless. "This is a bad idea," she said. "I'm over here waiting for *you* to get us out of here. I don't know Chaos like you do. Can't she just heal you?" In a softer voice, she forced the bigger question. "Do you really think Zarek doesn't have much time?"

"Do you want the real answer?"

She nodded.

His Adam's apple rose and fell. "We'll be lucky if he's not dead when we get there, but we'll try. Only because you care about him." Sekar hummed, sounding more annoyed than content. "If I had days, I'd let the Dark Energy wear off, but we don't."

Syra played with the torn edge of her sleeve, recalling what he'd told her about corrupted Chaos. "This Syckl Blade. It's fatal for us, isn't it?"

Sekar nodded. "The Cer'han toxin kills Guardians. For a God, it is the Dark Energy in the blood of that beast that will kill us. A single drop could massacre a city of mortals." Hesitation, then, "I'm familiar with the blade."

Syra couldn't hide her surprise. "You've had a run-in with it before?"

A chuckle, shallow enough to make her tense. "I've used it before."

Syra bit her tongue, debating whether to question him further. By the tone of his voice, she knew however he'd used the Syckl Blade—and how he'd managed to get his hands on it—was nefarious. Sekar never did anything out of selfless compassion. If he helped, it was because he could get something in return, big or small.

"Do you understand the key differences between a God who harvests Chaos and an Energy Harvester who manipulates Light or Dark Energy?" The topic change was abrupt. If he sensed her curiosity about his experience, he clearly didn't want to talk about it.

She shrugged. "You're going to tell me regardless of what I say." Because he would, even if she couldn't have cared less about it right now. What mattered was how fast they could leave this place once and for all. Yet the deity loved to hear himself talk. He was stubborn, relentless, and persistent.

"This might save your life one day," Sekar remarked. "With Harvesters, they draw on the energy from outside of them. Occasionally their own lifeforce, but that's foolish. When they draw on the forces around them, those energies are never fully a part of them. Like collectors coming to pick up artifacts and relics—those are Harvesters. Once they are done looking at the piece, they set it aside. Do you understand?"

"Well, yeah, but Dark Energy—"

"Is a parasite. And if you toy with it, it will burrow itself into the deepest parts of your mind and corrupt you from the inside out. Nobody should touch that. An energy that can kill a God shouldn't be used." Sekar shook his head. "But Chaos? When she chooses you, she isn't just around"—he turned and placed a finger against her chest—"she's *in* you. The energy integrates into your literal being, your lifeforce. So even if I can't communicate with her, the essence of Mother is still here. That's the difference between a God and a Harvester."

Syra found the clarification helpful, but the timing couldn't have been worse. Now was not the time for an education. Sekar had no concept of time, but neither did a Guardian—they weren't rushed like she was. That was probably why he and Dryl got along so well. She bared her hands. "Are you ready for me to try this?"

He nodded and moved. Sekar positioned himself with his back up and propped his head on his arms. Syra shifted her weight so she was cross-legged next to him, scanning the scars that decorated his skin. Under the better lighting, she could see the layers of them; some were puckered, others flat. The questions bubbled up on her lips—she wanted to know his story. After everything, sitting here now, she realized she knew next to nothing about who Sekar really was or where he'd come from. This was a God who'd seen empires rise and fall. If she knew more about him, maybe she could understand him better.

"Right," she announced. "What do I do?"

He raised his brow. "You harvest Chaos. You are a Goddess, right?"

"Shut it." Her heart was racing, and she hoped he couldn't hear it. One wrong move and she could kill him. She kept glancing back at the tunnel's entrance, preparing for the worst but hoping for the best. A beast could meander in here, or something far worse, like Elyas. A Cer'han could stuff its ghastly snout in and rip her clean away with her back turned.

"Get out of your head," Sekar told her. "Remember what I once said to you?"

She let out a shaky laugh. "You've said a lot of things to me."

"I told you that you were Syra, and that meant you could do anything you wanted." His words were kind, a stark contrast to the cynical tone that had accompanied him out of the tunnel. "Trust your intuition."

Every now and then, Syra remembered the Sekar she'd known before everything changed. She nodded and placed her hand on his back. The skin was hot to the touch, no thanks to the fever that ravaged his body. He was right. She needed to trust her intuition. Chaos had not led her astray yet, and she was willing to bet that Mother wouldn't now. Not with Sekar's life on the line.

She closed her eyes and turned her attention to the man before her. Clearing her head as best she could, she focused on Chaos. Syra listened to the slight noises around them—a pebble that broke loose, creatures skittering about, and the low whistle of air escaping the tunnel that was too faint to hear otherwise. Syra could feel Chaos move within her as she sought the force out. Her intentions were clear, actions precise. This was not as spontaneous as it had been when she broke the chains. This was different, and she needed to ensure full control over the force.

To both Chaos and herself, she stated her intentions. The Dark Energy toxin needed to go. She focused back on Sekar. Her thoughts drifted farther and farther from her mind, and she listened to the blood rushing through his veins. The world around her vanished as the hum of Chaos filled her mind. The tingling sensation returned to her fingers, and she directed her attention to the foreign substance. Ailments such as this had their own aura, she'd learned. The toxin in Sekar's body was pungent, yellow, standing out against the bright white aura that Sekar naturally emanated. She directed Chaos that way. The energy devoured the toxin, and as it did, Syra felt her strength wane. The action took its toll on her, drawing on everything she had.

Syra watched as the yellow patches disappeared until nothing was left. She let Chaos wander through Sekar's body, easing the agony of his injuries. The muscles under her hand relaxed, and the God's breathing slowed immensely. Syra smiled. This was the meaning of having such a gift. As clearly as she could feel Mother worm her way through her body, she too could feel Sekar's connection with Chaos flourish. His aura brightened, and she retracted herself entirely.

Confined to her mind once more, Syra felt momentarily stifled. She blinked, and a wave of exhaustion pulled at her, caressing her into slumber. Her head swayed, and she kept her hand positioned on his back to hold herself up. When the wave passed, she took her hand away and waited for him to move.

He didn't.

"How are you feeling?" she asked.

"Thank you." The honest emotion in those words wormed its way right into her heart, and her shoulders slumped. It was done.

"How long do we wait?" Hopefully they could leave right away.

"I need just a little time."

Deflated, she leaned against the wall. A rock jabbed her back, but she didn't care. Sitting here felt like she was waiting to die. If she could open a portal like him, she could get them out of here, but she couldn't—not unless he could help her.

He scoffed, as if reading her mind. "Don't take Chaos for granted, Syra. Power like that comes with time and practice. Opening a portal stretches your mind between two places, and if you're not experienced enough—and you're not—you'll get yourself and everyone killed."

Syra paused. His words were harsh, and she wanted to say something in return, but nothing came to mind. Instead, she just stared at his back, thinking of all the ways waiting could be worse. Her fingers twitched, her mind was alive with worry, and all she could do was relive the moment when Zarek's throat was slashed.

Sekar didn't care about the details. Nothing she said would change his mind.

"We need food and water." The subject change felt safe and productive. Her lips were cracked, and her tongue was like parchment.

Sekar still didn't move. "We will address that once I rest."

"I'm going to leave you here." The threat left her lips before she could stop herself, and the God finally shifted his gaze to meet hers. She nearly choked on the immense disappointment radiating off him.

His next words were soft. "Careful, Syra. I might just start to think you're desperate." The insult itself was loud and clear, and Syra crossed her arms. Desperate people did desperate things, and that was why they wound up dead. Sekar was proud and calculating, and didn't take kindly to foolishness.

She was letting her emotions get ahead of her, wasn't thinking clearly, which went against everything she'd been taught.

The God's breathing slowed after a while. She should be sleeping too, but she couldn't shake her mind off all the possible ways Zarek might die. If it wasn't the Guardian's predicament—which she blamed herself for—it was Elyas's horrific features, and his offer. The realms were falling apart, the Infernol was most likely marching to battle, and here they were, nestled at the entrance of a tunnel in Ashýon, preparing to attempt a rescue on a man who had given his life for Syra. It was her time to be what they needed.

Immortal and Exhausted

Cyrus's throat was drier than the Hazar Desert, and his head pounded relentlessly. The cold stone pressing against his face was soothing, but his skin felt bruised when he tried to shift himself into a more comfortable position. Where the dagger cut flesh, his hand was tender. Moisture permeated the air—thick and hot—and he realized he was still without a shirt.

Slowly, the memories of last night came to him. Muddy at first, with no clear understanding, but then faster and fiercer. He blinked in the darkness, disoriented, as the visions of the Yavinks and Dragon Riders merged to create confusion. Head pounding harder, he closed his eyes and tried to focus on any one memory, but they all slipped from his fingers like sand. Past and present became one, different faces twisted and shifted into the same, and he could no longer determine what time or day it was, or if any of this was real.

Cyrus opened his eyes again. He'd been carried. That he remembered.

When he tried to reach Sozar, he found he couldn't, which only worsened his growing panic. Betrayed again. Cyrus couldn't fathom it, refused to believe it. Yet, as he lay here, damp and in the dark, he couldn't deny how much this place felt like a prison. This wasn't a vision like the ones he'd been having. He wiggled his toes, moved his fingers, and inhaled as large a breath as he could before releasing it softly. Wary, he shifted his arms. Nothing bound him. No cold metal to lock him away. He was free to move, but he wasn't sure where he was.

Something *moved* in his head. Cautious and curious, like a predator surveying its prey before launching an attack. Cyrus's breath caught in his throat, and adrenaline surged through his limbs with fiery intent. He scrambled, slamming his back into a jagged edge of rock. As he inhaled sharply, the pain blossomed to his shoulder and settled into a nice throb. He looked into the darkness, straining to see anything at all. Patting the ground around him, he found the same uneven stone. This was not a standard dungeon, he realized. The ground was damp in some areas, and when he sniffed his fingers, he found it could only be water.

A memory from last night entered his mind, summoned. The chest and the cave entrance hung there, like voices standing out from a crowd. Last night's vision had been a warning.

The presence in his head moved again. Cyrus nearly choked. Something was in his head, powerful and growing bolder.

If Eazon could give him a break, he'd appreciate it. Luck did not seem to be part of his life anymore.

A rumbling sound filled the darkness. Cyrus pressed himself into the stone, forgetting the rock that jabbed his back earlier, but he hardly felt the pain now. The noise was otherworldly, massive, like the entire mountain had just groaned. He frantically reached for energy to harvest, but the intent was severed. When he tried again, he found the same result. Terror gnawed a hole in his chest. This was real.

A deep voice split his head wide open, grating and enormous. *So many centuries alone. I've waited for you for a long time, Rider.*

"Uh." Cyrus's mind raced. He needed answers. The presence held a tone of familiarity, but it was still foreign and menacing. *Are you a dragon?*

The mountain rumbled again, and Cyrus tensed, ready to run. Although where, he had no idea. *Yes, but I am far from what you are familiar with.* The beast did not expand on the answer.

Then who are you? he pressed. The presence in his head grew, suffocating his own thoughts. The energy that emanated from this beast was dark, sinister.

I am the Forgotten. Üg'ahn. When the world changed, I sought peace and to fulfill a long and overdue promise. The dragon spoke slowly, as if time itself waited on him. Perhaps it did.

Cyrus repositioned himself so that the rock no longer gouged his back. *You've been alive all this time?* The idea was almost too much to comprehend.

Death does not even want me. The words were sorrowful. *When I realized that, I had to accept my fate. I hope to fulfill a promise with you, Rider. A promise I made to an old friend.*

An old friend? The question felt intrusive, but then again, this foreign beast that was so closely familiar to a dragon was already in his head. Üg'ahn knew everything he wanted to already.

A deep grating sound scraped at his ears. *A Rider who challenged the way the winds swept over the lands. It is because of him I am free.*

He swallowed bile. Üg'ahn was as old as the Great Fall, perhaps even older. That would put him over eight centuries old, during the Rider Federation's reign. Stories told of dragons living as long as time permitted, but never did he think he'd come to see it for himself. It was all starting to make sense, just not fast enough.

Last night, he started. *I was shown things.*

By my blood, Üg'ahn answered. *I am the result of man trying to play God. My blood was once sought after by those who wished to control Destiny.*

The chains, Cyrus replied, hoping he didn't overstep or make the wrong assumptions. *You were imprisoned, weren't you?* His heart softened, and the adrenaline was beginning to drain from his body.

Rock cracked too close, ear-piercing, and he grabbed at his head, certain the ceiling was about to give out. *I wanted to burn you all*, Üg'ahn told him, with so much anger that the emotion seeped into Cyrus's veins. *I saw no other escape.*

The sound continued, bone-chilling. As much as Cyrus wanted answers, he was terrified of what would happen if Üg'ahn grew even angrier. Not even the mountain could contain this dragon's emotions. Frantic, he grasped at the only thing he could think of, but the urgency in his tone betrayed his fear. *What promise?*

To ensure the knowledge of the Rider Federation is passed on when the time was right. The answer was so simple, but its gravity struck Cyrus like a galloping stallion. He swallowed, struggling to find words, but Üg'ahn continued. *No matter how starved man gets for power, there will always be dragons. We were here long before the empires made this land their home, and we will be here long after the last falls. The pairing with your kind was done by accident, or so the stories once said. We were never bound to each other, and the ancient Dalamyns wished for it to remain that way. Some embraced this. Bonding to your kind has changed everything for the dragons. To thrive, we need each other.*

He couldn't tell if Üg'ahn was insulted by this or just in a constant state of dissatisfaction. But he held his tongue, sensing more was coming. One never rushed a dragon. Sozar had taught him that much.

You grow as restless as the wind, Üg'ahn observed. *An oath is what I seek from you, Rider.*

Cyrus slid to the right, unsure where he was going but needing to move. *What could I possibly promise you that you couldn't do yourself?* Üg'ahn was centuries older, and knew so much, and Cyrus was hardly what he would call a respectable Dragon Rider.

The mountain rumbled, and for the first time, he caught movement in the darkness. If Cyrus could have melted into the rock right then and there, he would have. Üg'ahn, whatever portion he'd just seen, was massive. *An oath to the Rider Federation. You are to bring honor to the dragons, restore Eei'on Rü, and train the new era of Dragon Riders.*

Cyrus was growing lightheaded. "What?" The last dragon eggs he'd found ended up in Henry's hands, no doubt tarnished by dark rituals and Dameon's influence if they'd hatched.

Vikter saw potential in everything, Üg'ahn continued. *He saw it in me, and I owe it to him to see that in you. I've judged your soul, Rider. You are the one.*

The ceremony with the Yavinks, the blood . . . Cyrus had been presented and tested without ever knowing it. A chill raced through his body, otherworldly. He'd been watched, observed, and judged. *How long have you known about me?*

Üg'ahn chuckled, a raspy sound. *I knew of you and Sozar long before you left Eiyrăl. The world does not keep secrets. I have ears everywhere. You spoke to one of my creations once. Raveth. Now, tell me, Rider, do you accept this oath?*

Cyrus stared into the darkness of the cave, cornered. The memory was so distant that he halfway thought he'd hallucinated the entire encounter, but now, as clear as if it had just happened yesterday, he recalled the strange fox that had approached him in the Releuthian Mountains. The creature had warned him of the dangers ahead, and even controlled the wind. All this time, he'd been led to this moment. Every decision he'd made found him here. That was profound. As much as he thought he was in control, he wasn't. Cyrus was so caught up in trying to stay alive that he never considered that Destiny had gotten what she wanted all along.

The visions bombarded him. A world well beyond his reach had greeted him last night, full of majestic dragons and Riders who feared nothing. He saw the massive city that was home to the Dragon Riders, a large training ring where men and women laughed and placed bets. The warm wind that ruffled his clothes from the back of a dragon, and the cold pelt of rain that struck his face as he and his dragon dove toward the sea. These were men and women who lived their whole lives being someone. Born and raised for the greatest purpose this world would ever see—to bring peace. Kings and queens bowed before Dragon Riders, fully aware that any altercation could cost them their kingdom. Cyrus felt proud, confident, capable of taking on the world in those visions. Those Riders had heart. They were fearless, and their emotions bled into his own. But now, sober, he didn't feel any of that.

He licked his lips, finding them dry. "I am not like the Dragon Riders of before. Not even close to those like Vikter and Hyle. I was never given a proper upbringing or gifted knowledge at a young age. I took off on the run because I was scared of what the people would do to Sozar if they learned the truth. I've made massive mistakes, Üg'ahn. You're asking me to make a promise I'm certain I'll fail to keep. Not because I don't want to let you or anyone of the past down, but because I don't know what I'm doing."

His words were raw, desperate. Cyrus was sitting in the dark in a cave, being told he was to resurrect the Dragon Riders. That responsibility alone made him feel like he was suffocating. Cyrus wasn't anyone special. Alaric had told him otherwise, and Hyle seemed to believe he was a prodigy, but deep down, Cyrus was a nobody. A child raised in an orphanage, mining for an ungrateful queen, and forced into life-or-death circumstances. He was lucky to be alive.

Movement in the darkness forced his attention back. The silhouette of Üg'ahn grew closer, eating up his vision until all he could see was a dark gray presence. The dragon shifted his head, and he caught sight of horns and bony features. A milky eye found him, protruding from the crushing darkness, giant and unsettling.

Dragon Riders are not born of royal blood or titles; they are chosen because the dragon sees in them the potential to make a change. Sozar chose you for a reason. Do not prevent him from his right to fulfill his purpose. Üg'ahn's tone shifted, growing quieter. *I did not wait centuries for you to deny your destiny.*

Cyrus nodded, even before he'd come to a conclusion. Üg'ahn was right. At the very least, the dragon would refuse to hear otherwise. He might not have all the answers now, but he would. The world was falling apart, and the more he ran, the worse it became. He wanted to do something good. He wanted to bring honor to the Dragon Riders. Sozar was owed a chance to embrace a long-lost heritage. If he continued to run from himself, chances were the dragon would never know a life of peace. Cyrus couldn't live with t hat.

To your left, Rider. What you seek has always been within reach.

Numbly, he crawled in that direction, not trusting his legs and too stunned to feel the pain in his hand. The slick stone was cool against his hands and knees, rugged too. He moved at the pace of a snail, uncertain where his head was, hoping he wouldn't knock himself out. Üg'ahn would undoubtedly take back everything he said.

From behind, he knew the dragon watched. Cyrus wasn't sure how far he crawled before he felt a slight dip in the slope and paused. It was still pitch-black, and he wasn't sure what he was supposed to see or do.

Keep moving forward, Üg'ahn instructed. The dragon's presence was so intertwined with his thoughts that he felt Üg'ahn raise his head and summon the raging fire within his chest. A panicked thought made Cyrus lean left, and he hit his head. The howling sound of flames escaping the dragon's massive maw filled his ears, and the world around him lit up in white heat.

A dozen or more dragon eggs lay before him, nestled with straw, silver and gold. To his right, fire clung to the rock, lighting the entire interior. The warmth that radiated from the white flames was nearly unbearable, and sweat sprouted from his brow. Cyrus wiped at it, paralyzed in awe. Hope unlike anything he'd ever felt before consumed him. There *was* a chance. Cyrus was confident now. The Dragon Riders would reign again. And he wouldn't be alone.

Vikter and Asif brought these here, Üg'ahn explained proudly. *The Yavinks are aware of them, and have done everything in their power to ensure this region of the land remains untouched by man.*

"Unbelievable," he breathed. "Hyle knows?" The answer was obvious, but he still needed validation.

Of course. If allowed, he wishes to be a part of the rebuilding.

That shook Cyrus out of his spell. *Why wouldn't he?* Now, he faced the dragon. Üg'ahn was indeed massive, five times the size of Sozar, but he looked skeletal—Death's dragon. Bones jutted outward at odd angles, his dark gray skin wasn't covered in normal scales, and horns and cartilage decorated his face, back, and tail. His snout, long, was complemented by rows of nightmarish incisors, and covered in raised gray scars. Üg'ahn was ghastly looking. A mix of monster and dragon, a beast caught between realms.

That is his story to tell, Üg'ahn said. He blinked, one milky eye locked on Cyrus. *Sozar awaits you outside. May the wind be with you. If Destiny permits, I may join you.* The dragon flared his nostrils, which looked to be the size of him. *Take what you can. It is time to reclaim what was once ours.*

PART 2

"There is no greater mockery of man than the dragon."
~ The Vorelian Scrolls

Howl for the Divine

The weather was perfect. The smells of roasts, pastries, fried fish, and spices filled the air as Morei wandered through the massive celebration hall attached to the palace. This was where the heart of the Festival of Seasons would be held tonight, though the streets would be full of partying citizens. Here, he would showcase his title as king by sharing the first dance with Isla Caster. Tonight, he would do his best to forget about Geral and the unforgivable abduction of Ezra. It was also the first time he'd come out of his study since his drinking binge. Faced with the people, he swallowed his dark thoughts, hoping his spiraling impulses remained quiet enough to manage.

Shouts from staff members crossed the room. They were setting up the already-prepared food—fruits and cheeses, specifically. The rest would come later, once the festival was close to starting. Morei stepped out of the way of a young woman carrying a large sack of flour. He opened his mouth to offer to help, but she shook her head fiercely before disappearing into the crowd. His reaction was too slow, sluggish from the lack of sleep. Hopefully that would change as the excitement of the day bubbled up.

The king took in the extensive blue banners with the silver wolf. Long tables stretched through the hall, decorated with the same color scheme, along with small wolf statues. Those looked carved out of silver stone, which he could not place, and garnished with gold gems. The tables themselves were as thick as his arms and made with multicolored wood, dark and silver. He'd never seen wood like that before and made a note to ask about it later. Beyond the iconic wolf emblem on the marble floor, this had to be the most grandiose preparation he'd ever seen. It made Geral's celebratory feast in honor of his title look laughable.

He was impressed, but he couldn't help but wonder what this would all mean if the Red Queens showed up and destroyed everything. Or if Nerius sent his army to them. The bodies had been disposed of, though the pungent smell of decay from the fires still lingered in his nose, and nobody had challenged his statement about the shipwreck. While he was grateful, he worried the lie would come back and haunt him. Morei couldn't believe how much he lied now. As a man who hated dishonesty, he was becoming a master at it. The people needed tradition, though, and he couldn't shy away from a festival that represented everything this city wanted to be. Proud, prosperous, happy. If he denied them this, he was certain the ramifications would far outweigh the Red Queens and King Nerius. Caster took their culture seriously.

A resounding growl caught his attention, and the king made his way toward it. Ahead, he could see a handful of guards and staff members helping with something hidden from view. Morei earned himself a few glances and acknowledgments as he neared. People shuffled out of the way once he insisted on seeing what the scuffle was about.

What he saw was an Onye. It was caged, red-eyed, and massive. The beast was snarling and slamming itself against the thick iron bars. At the sight of it, his stomach twisted. "What's that here for?" he asked, loud enough for everyone to hear.

"For tonight," the nearest soldier answered. "Part of the show."

"Why wasn't I made aware of it?" he pressed, too harshly. The Onye stopped snarling and turned its giant head toward him. The black fur along its jaw was stained red, and he felt a cold sweat start on the back of his neck. Onyes were well known to be the selected familiars of Sekar.

An awkward beat of silence passed. "Well," the same soldier answered, "no king, especially Drexis, ever wanted to be involved with the preparations."

That was not the point. "The beast, soldier. Why wasn't I made aware we would bring *that* here?"

He earned several stares. Were they ignorant? These wolves were far too dangerous to be in the city. Sekar was too close with that thing here. Between yesterday's note and now this, he was almost shocked the God himself didn't appear in the crowd. Morei thought he was brave enough to see Sekar, but now faced with this creature, he realized he couldn't. Not yet.

The man rubbed his face, obviously uncomfortable. "Um, because that's what we've always done?" Quickly, he added, "Your Majesty."

Morei gestured at the beast. "Get rid of it. I don't want a single Onye in this city by tonight. They're nothing but bad luck. Do I make myself clear?"

The soldiers all rushed to agree.

"Are there more beasts?" he asked.

The first shrugged. "Yes, Your Majesty. We have about four others that are brought in for the festival. None like—" He motioned at the Onye, which was eerily quiet now. It made Morei's skin crawl. Like it knew. Like *Sekar* knew.

"Show me," he ordered. "I don't care if it's a rabbit, I want to see what we've brought for tonight."

He pulled the first soldier aside, and they made their way through a staff hall. The others were left behind, tasked with ridding Caster of the Onye. The king didn't like to consider himself superstitious. He was the first to admit he'd outright denied the Gods were real for many summers, but now he knew Sekar's sick gleam, knew just how powerful a God could be.

"I apologize, Your Majesty," the man said once they were alone.

Morei tried to dismiss it with a laugh, but it came out forced. "Not a problem, soldier. I'm not sure what stories you grew up with around here, but those beasts were highly frowned upon in Geral. A terrible omen." Partially the truth, though exaggerated to justify his actions.

"Ah."

"Your name?" He wanted to change the subject.

"Leo, Your Majesty."

A good and strong name. The soldier carried himself confidently too, which was refreshing. Caster held a reputation for having some of the most ruthless soldiers in the world. He hoped to confirm that when the time came for battle. "How much farther, Leo?"

"Right here." The soldier stopped and unlatched a hook from a metal door. They were completely separate from the main halls and rooms. He led him into a small chamber with cages. The stench of manure, piss, and livestock struck him hard. Chirps, rumbles, and all sorts of noises met his ears at once. It was dimly lit, and straw covered the floor.

"Nothing quite as serious as the wolf," Leo observed with a hint of humor. The soldier was loosening up. "These are more for the performers." He motioned to the large, pink-feathered bird with a black beak and eyes. It cawed. "That is for Hanna. She's been performing at the festival for over twelve summers now. Saw this lad when he was barely hatched. Crazy to see him all grown up." Leo pointed at a four-legged creature with spiraling horns covering its jaw and head. It had tan fur, hooves, and four eyes. "This is from the Dark Forest. Stories call it a trembar, but I like to call it a bastard. Always manages to eat through leather and anything that isn't made of iron. This one's been around for a while. Lord Bastard here knows me, and I know him."

Morei followed him deeper through the aisle of cages, amused.

"This lady here has a bigger bite than the Firóle that struck Raveer," Leo said as he pointed at a large feline. The creature had paws as large as Morei's head, incisors that extended past the jaw, and white fur speckled with orange stripes. The beast looked their way, revealing glacier-blue eyes with slit pupils. "Don't look at me like that, Princess. I've got food coming shortly." He tossed his hand dramatically. "I'm the only one who can feed her. I worry about the day anyone else tries to get close to her. Stories say she can snap a hand clean off."

Morei raised his brow. "How long will she live?"

"She's a regule. They're from the Beutóne Mountains up north and can live up to three hundred summers. Last I heard, Princess here is only twenty-one. She was obtained as a cub and raised by a handler in Razan." Leo motioned ahead. "Let's keep it moving. Princess has a terrible way of guilting me into feeding her too much."

The king laughed. It felt good, too. Leo's excitement was infectious, chipping away at the tension in his shoulders and neck. "I appreciate your work, Leo."

The soldier shrugged, meek. "Just doing my job, Your Majesty. Now, beyond the horses, which we'll have some big ones tonight, we've got one more that is our pride and joy." Leo raised a finger. "Nothing like an Onye, but a bit of a hybrid between an ancient Vore beast and something unseen. Tonight, we'll be showing him off for the first time. He's been raised in captivity, worked with by handlers, even myself, and we're all quite proud of him."

They walked toward the back of the chamber. Chains were nailed into the stone there, old, though the nails looked brand new. "Just a personal marker for us down here. Nothing to worry about," the soldier explained, more upbeat now. "He's a docile one. A bit too smart for his own good, but he's an observer. Knows we're not his enemy."

Morei nodded. He wasn't sure how he felt about that. They stopped before a floor-to-ceiling cage. The iron was newer and marked with Old Tongue sigils, and on the floor inside lay a bundle of fresh straw. Metal bars crossed it at different heights, and there was a little hut in the upper left corner. Morei paused next to the cage, curious. "What's inside?"

Leo couldn't contain his excitement. "Your Majesty, we are the only city in the world with this creation. We paid a large amount of coin while Drexis was in power to bring in a specialized Energy Harvester. He didn't do the dancing and all that like you're going to do, so he invested a lot into creating the most unique shows."

"Which meant . . ."

"This." The soldier tapped the iron, but not randomly. He played a tune on the hollow bars that Morei didn't recognize.

A little winged creature crawled out of the hut. It was small, could fit in Morei's hands, and had leathery wings. By the Gods, it was a miniature dragon, but with an incredibly long tail and no horns. It—*he*—had teeth and talons, but even his skin, which should have been covered in scales, looked like soft leather.

"He is the only of his kind," Leo said, proud. He whistled a tune, and the tiny creature jumped out onto the nearest metal bar. Another whistle, and the winged beast hopped to the one closest to them. Now, knowing he was being observed by them, he sat on his haunches with his tail hanging and kept his head high. "We call him Savage. I know, moronic name, but he's devious and can kill a buffalo. Don't let his size fool you, Your Majesty."

Purple eyes with slit pupils stared at him. An unnatural color. A chill rushed through him, and he recognized the feeling instantly. Dark Energy.

"Who was the Harvester who helped create this?" Morei asked.

Leo shook his head. "Private information. We're just the handlers. Drexis was particular about who could access stuff like that. I don't even know if more could be made. All I know is that the handlers were brought into this room a few seasons ago and told to do something with him." He shook his head. "Bit the head off a mouse on his first day. That's why we call him Savage."

This was unbelievable. "And you don't know how the Harvester made him?"

Leo sighed. "I tried to get information. We all wanted to know, but—"

"Drexis withheld that," he finished.

"Yeah."

No answers. That drove him mad. The Dark Energy was palpable—could anyone else sense it like he did? Or was it only possible because of his familiarity with the volatile force? He would find Rhys and see if the chancellor had any information on the matter. Surely there had to be documentation somewhere, even a basic agreement with a name that he could go off of. Morei wanted the name of the Harvester responsible. Whoever had made Savage was powerful, and that made the king determined to find him.

Morei looked between the soldier and the creature. "Is he capable of being handled?"

Leo opened his mouth and then closed it again. His expression twisted. "Well, uh, he's a bit grumpy with who he lets hold him. He bit a finger off Sheri." The soldier let loose a nervous laugh. "Only a couple of us can handle him."

"Us?" Morei pressed. "You can?"

Slowly, the soldier nodded.

The king took a step back to show he wanted to be respectful. "Show me." Curiosity had him by the neck. The closest he'd ever gotten to anything like this was Cyrus's dragon. This beast looked so close to a tiny version of one—it was the most interesting thing he'd ever stumbled on. Even the Onye felt leagues away now.

Leo nodded, although Morei could tell he was nervous. A slight shake of the hand betrayed that as he unlocked the iron door. "Savage is a bit temperamental. I told you he's smart, so we let him decide. If he's not having it, then we don't push him."

"Well, what about tonight?"

Another nervous chuckle. "Well, that's why we didn't say much of anything. We aren't even sure he's going to let us show him off tonight. Don't want to get anyone's hopes up, you know?"

Morei nodded. "I understand."

Behind, the commotion of the creatures faded. Savage studied the out-reached hand. If he wanted, he could lash out and do some serious damage. "Come on, my winged bastard. You know you want to show off a little, eh?" Leo's tone was calm, low. "You know me. Don't act all shy now. We just chatted a bit earlier," the soldier insisted.

The dragon—for that was what Morei wanted to call him—gave a snort and hopped off the bar and onto the man's wrist. His talons dug into the fabric, but the skin didn't break. He must have been heavy, because Leo's arm dipped before he recovered and slowly pulled Savage out of the cage. Savage's tail hung to the man's knees and moved with an intelligence of its own. The dragon reached forward and placed his weight on Leo's hand. Talons pressed into the skin, and he watched the soldier grimace.

"Easy now, Savage." The soldier raised the beast and grinned. "You happy?"

Savage made a deep sound from his chest. Morei realized that he was staring so hard, he probably looked like a boy given his first sword. "This is incredible," he breathed. The king didn't know what else to say. Watching Leo work with Savage was intriguing, and a sliver of him wanted to reach out and touch the beast's snout, but he refrained. It would be neither appropriate nor smart.

"We're proud of him," Leo said. "We've worked tirelessly to make sure he's comfortable and has everything he needs. Been a learning curve, that's for sure. No books on Wynzers."

"Wynzers?"

"What we're calling his kind," the soldier answered. "We kind of made it up."

Morei nodded. The name was atrocious—it sounded more fitting to a sleazy gouger on the side of the street than this impressive beast before him. He wasn't even sure he could properly pronounce it. The way Leo said it sounded like an extra syllable was tucked in there. But he didn't want to take away the man's moment. As king, it was his job to acknowledge the hard work.

"Does he fly?" Morei asked. At his voice, Savage glanced his way again. That same icy chill raced over him.

The soldier laughed. "Of course he can! Those wings aren't big for no reason. He's chosen to stay with us. You know, when we first saw that he could fly, we got uncomfortable at the idea that we would keep him locked away. That's not something I can easily rest with every night. So a couple of us snuck out one night and tried to let him go. Set him right on the coast and gave him plenty of space. And you know what Savage did? He flew right to us." His expression softened. "He might be a bit nasty at times, but we're all he's got, and I think he knows that."

Morei believed it. Those purple eyes looked more like a person's than a beast's. Even the Inere, despite being so foreign and clever, could not come close to the gaze that met his now.

Commotion echoed from the main chamber. A roar and grumble, followed by some cawing. Leo shook his head, but in that endearing way only a parent could do. "Ah, there they go. Last time they got rowdy like that, it was over some rudine. Give me a moment." He turned his attention back to Savage. "I'm putting you back. The Gods know how the others feel about you. Last thing I need is to deal with that plus whatever that feces-eating rodent wants."

He raised his hand back to the interior of the cage, and Savage plopped right on the metal bar. He gave a quick roar, which Morei couldn't help but note the high pitch of, before Leo closed the door and nodded to the king. "It will be just a moment."

Morei raised his hand. "Take all the time you need." When Leo scurried off, calling out all sorts of names and reminding them this was the third time in two days, the king looked back to the Wynzer. Savage was staring at him.

He didn't want to get too close and disrespect whatever personal bound-aries Savage had, but with the iron bars, he felt a bit bolder. The king hovered as close as he dared, studying him. The beast flicked a forked tongue out, then made a series of grumbling noises. He sounded annoyed, at least to Morei.

"I don't like Wynzer," he confessed quietly. "I'm going to call you a drag-on."

Starved Sands

Hope kept Syra going, but she had none now. When Sekar had woken, she'd believed he would be fully healed, at least enough to get them to the palace. And he was better, capable of harnessing Chaos, but not strong enough yet to tear a portal through the realms. Instead, they stared at the Starved Sands, figuring out the best way to cross and not get eaten alive. Cer'hans swarmed the sky, waiting for their next victim. Earlier, she'd heard a bloodcurdling scream that made her toes curl. Another prisoner fed to the flying beasts.

Time couldn't be measured the same here, but she knew it had to have been at least half a day since she'd removed the toxin from his body. That was too long for Zarek, and she insisted they needed to figure out a way across. It was possible. They just needed the right plan. "Foolish" and "reckless" were his words, but she pressed the matter enough that he was willing to sit here and watch the land with her. Who knew how long they had before one of Elyas's grotesque undead soldiers stumbled upon them—or a Guardian.

Another tremor. This one was farther away, and the ground faintly shook, but they tensed. When it didn't get any worse, Sekar said, "That isn't natural behavior."

"Do you think it's because of the realm fracture?" Her theory was becoming more valid. The Soul Realm was suffering from the ramifications of Chaos drawing life from the living realm.

"Yes. These will get worse if the fracture isn't dealt with." He pointed to an area along the horizon, to their right. "Did you see that?"

Syra squinted. "No. What was it?"

"A ripple. Slight, but I think there's something over there."

"We could cut left, avoid that altogether," she offered, but he was already shaking his head.

"These things move fast, Syra. Your Guardian friend is trying to get you killed."

She dipped her head. "He's not a friend. We've established that, but this is the fastest way. It'll take too long to go around. What is this? Two, three leagues across?"

The God scratched near the healing scab on his lip. "Maybe five."

"What else?" She hoped for something good.

"A league at its widest. These sands weren't here a few centuries ago." To make his point, he reached forward to where solid ground met sand and picked up a handful. The pebbles fell through his fingers. "It's cold. This used to be a lake before it turned to solid ice, but even weirder was when that ice became what you see now. The realms are in a dangerous situation."

She stared at the vast region, trying to imagine this world as it once had been, but it was becoming increasingly difficult. The illusion Sekar had conjured up felt like an eternity ago.

"Past these sands, we'll be able to find water and food," he said. His face was still beaten, but his eyes were bright, and some of the bruising was yellowing. They were healing quickly with their link to Chaos, but not quickly enough.

A small creature came into view. A bird with long, scaly legs and a large body with a white beak and dark orbs for eyes. The wings were black with purple tips. Syra and Sekar jumped back, startled, but the bird gave no mind. It shuffled its wings and kept meandering around, plucking at the ground for food. After what she'd seen, it didn't look to belong here.

"Haven't seen one of those in a while," Sekar said.

The bird was large, at least the size of a baby foal. Syra was impressed that it could stand upright on its twig for legs. "What is it?"

"A Xaxer. They've struggled to survive in these new conditions, so their numbers dwindled quite a bit. I thought they were extinct."

"Huh." Syra watched as the Xaxer crossed the Starved Sands with no concern. "Look."

The bird moved differently on the sand. Two steps, stop. Two steps, stop again, and then pecking the ground. It continued, waiting a bit longer every now and then before moving. It was hunting for food, unbothered by the threat of the Wurok.

"Do you think that's—" she began.

"No," he finished. "Weight plays a huge part. Xaxers are incredibly light, with hollow bones. They could walk on water if needed." He shrugged. "That's an exaggeration. But unless you're an expert in wrangling beasts, I can't see how this will go our way."

"I was told this was the best option," she insisted. "There must be some way we could get across."

"There is." Now, he sounded irritated. "Harvest Chaos, slay the beast, and run. Hope you don't attract the attention of a Cer'han either, because they love the smell energy emits. And once there's one, there's a hundred."

"Are you trying to be helpful or not?"

He shrugged, unbothered by her accusative tone. "I'm trying to keep us alive. Another half day, I can get us out of here, but not now. And trying to cross is the worst idea I've ever heard. We wouldn't make it five steps. Elyas is probably waiting for us to be slaughtered."

Frustration couldn't even begin to describe how she felt about this whole situation. Zarek was going to die before they made it to the palace. A vast landscape lay between them and saving the Guardian—hunting grounds. The logic of waiting was obvious, but she struggled to accept it. Syra rolled over and stared at the rocky ceiling, holding her tongue. Now was not the time to start a fight. Stuck in a cave with a God who was a master at screwing her life was not entirely ideal, but he hadn't led her astray yet. He just had a complicated way of showing his loyalty.

"If Zarek dies, I will never forgive you," she mumbled. Dryl wouldn't either. That she knew. The people in her life, while few, had given everything for her. The least she could do was return the favor. If she couldn't do that, then she deserved no title or recognition. She'd never be able to look Dryl in the face again if his brother died because of her.

Sekar didn't answer. She'd hoped for something to stir him up, but he gave her no such satisfaction, and that only made her hate what she'd said.

"Listen—"

Another tremor started, different. A small rock broke free from the ceiling, hitting her head. She rolled over, narrowly missing another rock. It fractured where she had lain only moments prior. Sekar was already moving, shoving her forward into the Starved Sands.

A howl started, deafening. She stumbled, losing her footing in the frigid sand. Sekar was next to her, but when she glanced his way, a horrifying image greeted her.

Rock bled from the mountain in waves, revealing the intricate tunnels they'd moved between. Vines retracted, and hundreds of tiny creatures scattered before being swallowed whole by the ground opening up beneath them. A large cavity revealed a torrent of dust and stone. The mountain was collapsing.

Her legs couldn't move fast enough. The sand sucked in her feet, deep enough in some parts to reach her knees. But she didn't slow, and when Sekar almost tripped, she latched on to his arm and dragged him until he could get his footing.

Behind, the tremors sounded like screams. Chunks of rock as large as palaces broke free and tumbled below. Creatures took flight, frazzled, while the ripples in the sand intensified all around. But they couldn't stop now. If they stopped, they would be crushed.

To her left, the sand broke free, revealing a hideous creature. Hundreds of incisors, a glistening black exterior, and a long body. Antennas as long as Syra's body moved, and the Wurok screamed in frustration. The high-pitched sound dug a blade right into her ears. Just as quickly as it showed itself, the beast dove into the sands, burrowing deep.

They kept running as hard and fast as they could. Pain burned Syra's side, but she didn't slow. The wind stung. Beneath, the sand grew shallower, giving her better footing. Neither dared slow, not when they were so exposed.

She looked over her shoulder. The mountain was gone. What lay in its place was a vast chasm. Cer'hans flew low, curious, but claws reached up and plucked the creatures right from the sky. Syra tripped, too stunned to pay attention to her feet, and landed hard in the sand.

In between gasps, she asked, "What is that?"

The God shook his head, covered in sweat. "I . . . don't know."

Syra scrambled to her feet but couldn't look away. Hordes of Wuroks and Cer'hans closed in on the chasm, either mad or curious. Those that got too close were yanked from their place, lost to whatever lived below.

All around, the sand started to ripple. Syra and Sekar stepped back, and she opened her mind to Chaos, finding the force was right within reach. But a small head appeared next to her toes. Then another, and another. Hundreds of tiny mouse-like creatures popped out of the ground and fled from the scene. They chirped and squeaked. Large incisors gave them an awful appearance. Their gray fur was long, their claws curved, and they moved with immense speed. They didn't stop to look at Syra and Sekar. They were trying to get out of here.

But when she looked to the God, he remained still. His gaze was focused on the chasm and the disaster unfurling. Screeches and roars echoed, some so hideously loud that Syra felt like they were right beneath the beasts. The sky's rich purple hue pulsed, but now, a streak of red appeared.

Sekar dropped to his knees and pressed his hands into the sand. "What are you doing?" she demanded. "We need to go."

He shook his head but didn't reply. Syra stared, watching as more beasts were swallowed whole by whatever lay inside the chasm. Another clawlike hand reached for a Cer'han, so large that it could have swept a city up. Panic molded into cold fear.

Sekar sat back, unmoving. His expression, usually so stoic and hard, was baffled, in awe. A single tear rolled down his face, one of horror or amazement, Syra couldn't tell. In the softest of voices, he said, "It's Chaos. She's here."

An Era Forged in Sacrifice

The sun burned. Cyrus kept his gaze low as he exited the cave, blinking rapidly to adjust to the daylight. It had to be midafternoon based on the intensity of the sun, but he didn't bother looking right away to confirm his suspicions. Without a shirt, exposed now, he could see that the paint had chipped and rubbed away on his chest. His pants were dirty, and he felt more akin to a drunk waking up from a long binge than a Dragon Rider who'd just found the answers to the future. His tongue was parched, sour, and his back was bruised where he'd slammed it when first meeting Üg'ahn. The cut along his hand throbbed with vengeance.

A strange sense of loneliness followed him out. Without the large presence of the dragon, his thoughts felt isolated. Üg'ahn's mind was vast, overwhelming, beyond any power he'd encountered. He didn't know how the dragon went to and from the mountain, or even if Üg'ahn left at all.

Tucked in his arm was a single silver egg. The scaly texture was cool to the touch, but he knew without a doubt that a dragon lived inside. Cyrus could feel the creature's lifeforce. Faint—concealed mostly by the shell of the egg—but there. Out here, away from Üg'ahn, he questioned his decision to take just one. Doubt was the reason, of course. Cyrus feared letting the eggs fall into the wrong hands, and they were far safer with the dragon than him. In time, he would return to the cave for more. This egg was a promise for the future.

When the time was right, she would choose her Rider and fully awaken to leave the comfort of her egg once and for all. The responsibility weighed heavily on his shoulders. Cyrus would rather cut a limb off than let another dragon down. He owed it to Sozar, Hyle, Üg'ahn, and everyone to prove that, but most of all, he owed it to himself.

The surrounding landscape was thick with tropical forest. He'd been told this place was called Pynsole Forest, named after the jagged mountains that hugged the trees. Wide leaves, moss, white bark, and strange critters that he'd never seen before. The air was thick with moisture, hotter than the cooler climate in Delion, and a pinkish hue covered everything. Slight compared to that of Venkar, but still there.

A branch groaned to his right. Cyrus looked to see a green-furred animal hanging upside down by its legs. A tail moved lazily around, plucking at berries. In the same breath, the creature reached for different leaves, inspecting them closely with thickly padded, clawlike hands. Cyrus stared, momentarily dumbfounded. A bright blue gaze met his own, intelligent and without fear. A chill raced through him. That was no ordinary animal.

Cyrus gripped the egg tighter. He'd been so distracted that he hadn't even reached Sozar, who was supposed to be waiting for him out here somewhere. Their bond was always there, and without Üg'ahn's control, he easily reconnected. The dragon embraced him warmly but prodded his mind. Sozar was looking for something, even if he tried to be inconspicuous about it.

How are you? Sozar asked, strained.

Everything else was forgotten. *What is it?*

Heartbeats of silence slipped by them, and he felt the dragon poke around a few more times. *Your mind feels different. Tampered with. Stained. Like mold.*

I appreciate that, Cyrus remarked, not hiding the cynicism. *I've spent the last, what, day locked in a cave with a dragon that's exploited every piece of my mind, and you treat me like I've come back a different person.*

You don't see it, do you? Sozar asked, gentle. He was close, Cyrus could tell by the strength in his presence, but he wasn't sure how to navigate this forest yet. *The dragon you spoke to bleeds Dark Energy. His lifeforce, dark and wild, left a mark on yours. I can feel it. You can't?*

He couldn't. Or maybe he didn't want to. Cyrus stood there for a long time, stuck between moving and sitting. When he searched his head, he felt fine. Tired, but fine. Sozar sifted through his memories, gentle but intrusive. He didn't stop the dragon from experiencing and seeing everything that Üg'ahn had shared, but he also learned that Üg'ahn had already spoken to Sozar. This ghastly dragon knew everything without ever having to ask.

The future is in our hands, Cyrus finally said, studying the silver shell. *It was a promise made centuries ago.*

I wait for you, my friend. Follow the path.

That forced life into him. He started to walk, following the small path through the trees ahead. No obvious signs about which direction to take or whether he was going the right way; he just followed his gut. Sozar and him shared words about the future, about what it would be like to live among others like them. To see a world where Dragon Riders weren't weapons but peacemakers. Sozar would not be alone and could help raise the young dragons, share experiences, be what he was destined to be. Cyrus would help where he could, but even as he walked, he became more determined that they needed Hyle by their side. The God knew the Rider Federation better than anyone, understood its downfall, and had knowledge that no book could ever give.

The canopy of trees above grew thicker as the path became more clear. Sozar's bond strengthened too. The dragon's presence enveloped him like an old friend, and he picked up the pace. All around, the forest came to life. Birds of various colors and sizes squawked and screeched. Odd animals hung from branches with long tails or arms. Butterflies as big as his head flitted by, oblivious to him, their wings as vivid as the sun or as dark as midnight. He sidestepped a few times when a snake scurried past, startling him nearly to death. The dragon chuckled, amused, but Cyrus couldn't find the humor. The second time, the snake looked big enough to strangle him, its scales a blue and black ombre.

The air held moisture, which was common, especially since the soil was constantly wet and mushy. The leaves closest to him were covered in a light sheen of dew that was warm to the touch. As he grew closer, the pinkish hue intensified, and the trunks of the trees grew wider.

Then he broke free. The clearing revealed a small city carved out of the mountainside. The rose-pink rock was designed to look like the front of a palace, three floors tall. No polishing was needed to capture the magnificence of this display. Linework as small as his fingers perfectly captured the regal presentation of sharp angles and sigils that decorated the palace face. Pillars as wide as two of him held the palace up, providing a wide path for exploring the underside. The mountainside was wide, at least a half league, and hundreds of wide-leaved trees stretched beyond the palace. Birds in various colors flew about, excited.

Sozar waited before him. Handsome and majestic in this setting. Magnificent, if he was to use Alaric's word. Wings tucked, Sozar regarded Cyrus from where he stood. His slit pupil dilated once, twice, and Cyrus got the impression the dragon was trying to find the right thing to say. Instead, Sozar's talons sunk into the soil as he approached. Under the weight of the dragon's gaze, he was paralyzed.

He stopped, Rider and dragon face-to-face, and Sozar dipped his head until the crest was before Cyrus. Without thought, he leaned his forehead against the dragon's, scales hot but welcomed after the last day. They'd been through so much together, and in this moment, it all faded. Cyrus could only hear the breath that flowed through Sozar's nostrils as air washed over him. Affection and appreciation poured out from them both. Cyrus ran his free hand over the hardened scales of Sozar's neck, remembering a time when he could hold this dragon in his arms. Now, he could barely get a hold around his neck.

Life moves fast, Cyrus finally said.

One day, we'll appreciate the madness. Sozar leaned into him a bit more, breaking the moment. Cyrus laughed and gave him a good pat.

"You will crush me," he said aloud, and pulled away. The dragon snorted, unamused, and rested his snout against the top of the dragon egg.

She does not know her path yet.

Cyrus regarded the dragon, grateful to have him. *But she will.* Their attention was turned to the palace standing before them. "What do you think it is?"

Home to the Dragon Blood flower, Sozar answered. *Come. It is within these walls.*

Quietly, they walked to the wide-mouthed entrance. The looming mountain sucked in the light, casting long shadows that consumed them and the heat. A chill raced over Cyrus, reminiscent of the cave's touch. He'd left his fur cloak at Venkar. He kept close to Sozar, hoping to absorb some of his warmth, but not even that did the trick.

They passed the large pillars, and instantly, the world went quiet except for their steps. Lanterns hung evenly spaced, casting an orange glow. The interior was mundane, contrasting the grand face, but he still had a sense of awe. The hard-packed ground was devoid of dust, rugged, and the walls fared no better. No paintings or carvings, no furniture or thrones. It was as if the interior had been dug out and cleaned. Still, Cyrus checked over his shoulder. It felt as if the walls had eyes, watching them move deeper.

Ahead, a single chamber. Cyrus clutched the egg tighter, curious but wary. He'd experienced his fair share of traps. This could be another one.

Reaching the entrance, they both paused. It was dark, but the little light from the lanterns reflected glistening leaves and petals. He scanned the area, trying to locate an unlit lantern, but saw nothing. He was ready to grab one off a hook when writing on the rock caught his attention. Squinting, he read:

"Grant me eternal light, and I will see forever." Cyrus read it again, not understanding. "What's that mean?"

Sozar poked his head into the chamber. In the dark, with his coloring, he almost disappeared.

"What is it?" Cyrus could sense hesitation.

And then he heard the howl of flames as air was sucked in and spit back out from Sozar's maw. Heat coated Cyrus's skin, and he stumbled back, too close. The hairs on his arms felt singed, and he watched in awe as the flames took hold of the giant flower in the center. They didn't dry out and dissolve from the dragon's fire but rather became a conduit. The flames leaped high, revealing crystals that reflected dozens of different colors. The Dragon Blood flower looked black under all the fire, and if it was possible, it shuddered with life.

Sozar tilted his head. *I wasn't sure that would work.*

The chamber grew warm, inviting, and Cyrus stepped in to survey the flower. Not too close, though, because the heat was strong enough to blister skin. The crystals above, on closer inspection, glittered. The ceiling looked to go on forever, more akin to a night sky than the heart of a mountain.

Cyrus would have stood there forever, awestruck, but he knew he couldn't. *They said the Dragon Blood flower bloomed, but how, when Üg'ahn has lived all this time?*

Sozar flared his nostrils. *He is not as true a dragon as he wishes he was.* The answer was somber. *His lifeforce is tampered with, violent, a poor result of man's interference with our kind.*

How damning, Cyrus realized, to be imprisoned in a body not rightfully his own. Turning his attention to the burning flower, he knew they would be due back to Venkar, but he wanted to savor this moment longer. Here, beyond the reach of the Yavinks, he didn't have to shuffle through the complex emotions rushing him. They'd handed him over like an offering with no warning. He repositioned the egg to the other arm and ran his fingers over the gem-filled walls. The crystals jutted out of the rock, some smooth and others rough. In his mining days, this would have been the biggest discovery of the kingdom. But now, he saw that these crystals were exactly where they needed to be. Man's involvement damaged the natural beauty of things. While he wouldn't take his summers back, he appreciated the current state of letting things just be.

The air was drenched in the scent of blood, metallic and pungent. Smoke rose upward, granting them reprieve. The Dragon Blood flower earned its name for a variety of reasons, including the stench it gave when shuddering in the flames. Cyrus wondered how long this fire would last, or if it would continue until Sozar no longer walked this realm.

Let us go, the dragon urged. *We have given what was required.*

He was right, and Cyrus wandered back to the entrance, running his hands over the words carved in the rock. Out there, the world waited for them. Where he'd have to face the crushing reality of who the Yavinks were and what they'd done to him. They pretended to be kind, generous, and whimsical, but underneath all that, they were ruthless and disregarded morals. They'd drugged him and left him to a mad dragon for judgment.

What do you think Üg'ahn wants out of this? The dragon tilted his head, curious. *He must have some motive.* Cyrus was certain the dragon wasn't doing this out of compassion. Üg'ahn was after something. Everyone was.

A dragon as ancient as him might only be after freedom.

Cyrus raised his brow, unconvinced.

He's protected these eggs for centuries, Sozar rumbled. *If his nature is true to the dragon, he wishes to stretch his wings.*

Cyrus didn't like the answer. Something was odd about Üg'ahn. Perhaps it was his connection with Dark Energy or his vast mind, but he found it difficult to believe a dragon as powerful as him would want nothing but freedom. Üg'ahn's presence alone could destroy kingdoms and bring kings to their knees. Maybe even stir the dead. No. He would be careful with Üg'ahn.

Do you believe we can do it?

Sozar nudged the arm with the egg. *Do what?*

Lead them. Cyrus fell into step alongside the dragon. *Lead them all.*

Daylight awaited them ahead, the vast forest vivid after their encounter. It seemed Sozar wasn't going to reply, and he was content with that. Some answers were better left unsaid. But the dragon finally spoke, slow.

I believe I hatched for you for a reason. Among all the eggs still intact, why is it that it was me who found you?

Cyrus didn't know what to say.

Destiny can be cruel, but I believe that underneath the tricks is kindness—and a cry for help.

The sun bathed them, momentarily blinding Cyrus. He followed the dragon's lead, trusting their way back to Venkar. He chewed on those words, knowing exactly what they meant but unable to respond out loud.

The Festival of Seasons

The music was a combination of sea shanties and orchestrated masterpieces. Morei didn't know any of the songs, and he loved that. He listened with a drink in hand. The musicians laughed, jabbed at one another, and drank heartily, and that was all before they started playing. He was impressed they could remain upright, because he was certain that a barrel of mead had already been finished between the five of them. The singer—a short and wide man with a braided beard nearly as tall as he was—possessed the richest baritone voice Morei had ever heard. Kizer was his name, and the king made a note to compliment him later.

He was stuck in a room with royalty—Destiny's cruelest joke of the day. Councilmembers, extended family members, and a list of people he was unfamiliar with but who were quite comfortable. They were mingling before the event, drinking and snacking on the small items provided, like cheese, cured meats, and bread. Royalty was kept separate until the dance, which would happen at sundown. That was when the Festival of Seasons truly began. Until then, they chatted, wandered, and waited.

Morei was antsy for the festival to begin. Being locked in a room with these people was maddening. The wealthiest people in the world, and raised as such, given lavish gifts before the age of five, waited on by servants of the palace. Childhoods spent racing through halls and dressing up in ostentatious jewels. These were the people Morei knew so well—not the citizens who traded work for food, or the nomads. Yet he knew they thought of him as something else entirely. Royal families might come from the same bones of wealth and power, but they didn't come as prisoners of political war, as he had.

Still, they needed each other. In time, they would learn that he was the greatest thing to ever happen to Caster.

The entire city was shut down. Streets were covered in colorful lanterns, drums beat from the city center, and citizens' celebrations were already well under way. Some of the staff members not required to serve were already enjoying their party in the courtyard. The king had seen them earlier when walking from his chamber. Esme and Dan were relieved after all the cooking and baking and were hosting the courtyard event. Nobody was dressed in fine silks, all just enjoying each other's company with lanterns hung about. He envied them.

Morei should have talked with the people around him, who were all dressed in costly custom attire, but he didn't. He watched Lord Cayden and Lady Genesa lean in close, then laugh, watched Lord Eli take down his fourth drink, and observed Rose exchanging promiscuous glances with Lord Varun. Certain staff members like her had been cordially invited at his request, and he was satisfied to see she was doing so well for herself. The woman had practically dressed every royal member here.

Several other decorated soldiers, like Edwin, were present as well. Seeing the men trade their armor for fine fitted suits was strange for Morei. He hadn't ever seen them dressed in anything but plain tunics.

Morei kept to the back and hoped they opened the doors soon. It was getting hot in here with all the bodies. Staff members squeezed among the crowd, refilling drinks and handing out snacks. He declined the food.

Everyone was on their best behavior. Even Rhys laughed with a few ladies he didn't recognize.

Morei's thoughts were still on the Wynzer and the events of the previous day. Everything felt like it was on thin ice. He hadn't stopped drinking since Geral's declaration about Ezra's abduction. The less he drank, the more he saw the man's face, and that was not something he could afford. Isla's sobering conversation still clung to him like mold. The woman had a way of getting under his skin. He was glad the staff didn't ask twice when he requested more Kendell's Milk this morning.

"You look like you're having fun." The voice came from his left, and he turned to see Isla there. She was dressed beautifully. Rose had fitted her in a blue and silver dress with a cinched waist. The body was embroidered with silver wolves chasing each other in play. Her back was exposed in a deep V, and the thin straps were embellished with silver gems that reflected light in a dazzling display. A wolf clasp was fastened to her white-blonde hair, which hung in loose waves past her shoulders.

"As fun as one can get." He made no effort to act excited. Her goal was unclear to him. Last night, she'd wanted to prove she wasn't afraid. Isla seemed determined to shove herself into his life as of late, and no matter how many times he tried to push her away, she kept coming back, like a persistent fly

She shrugged, and he noticed how tense she was. The princess was nervous. "I've never been to anything like this before."

He swallowed his mood. Now was not the time. Them being friendly would serve his reputation if he chose to make her queen. As much as he wanted to avoid her, he knew he couldn't, not tonight. "No?" It made sense, given she was a servant and not one of the overly dressed officials, though he'd thought she'd be a part of the service that kept an event like this going.

Isla shook her head. "It's strange, seeing everyone come together like this. Like Lady Yara and Lord Malachi? I've never seen them even look at each other in all my summers here. I swore they hated each other."

That made him chuckle. "In the council meetings, they always look at each other. Haven't you noticed?"

"No." She took a half step closer. She was getting brave, playing her role as the king's dance partner. He appreciated the effort. "I was too busy trying to listen."

"Fair enough." Morei took a drink, studying how the councilmembers meandered with their families. Charming, warm, no sign of the callous, rude behavior he knew them capable of. Nobody understood how complex carrying a royal title was—men and women took on different personas to appease the needs of the citizens, no matter how feared or loved that made them. "The next meeting, look around. You can tell a lot about these people based on their behavior."

She nodded, and he watched her fingers drum the glass she was holding. An anxious habit—something was on her mind. "What is it?" he asked.

Her grip tightened. "I've never been in front of so many people like this." The princess motioned to the chamber of councilmembers. "I'm already worried, and I know there's an even bigger crowd out there."

Morei stared, realizing that while this was all normal for him—the political show of grand attire and being the center of attention—this was outside her comfort zone. Glancing at her again, it dawned on him that this was probably the first time she'd ever dressed this nicely. Isla was far more comfortable in loose-fitted clothes, cleaning grime off the bottom of a ship.

"Hey." Morei faced her fully. Whatever they disagreed on could wait. He wanted her to have a good time. Not only was it important for her, but how she carried herself would leave a lasting impression. This was the first time she would present herself formally, and it was his job to ensure she was comfortable. "Just don't look at them, yeah?"

Her shoulders slacked, but only slightly. "Kind of easy for you to say."

Morei gave her a stern look. "If it makes you feel better, I used to count my steps. It distracted me, gave me a place to put my nerves."

A loud symphony of drums started, drowning out whatever the princess was going to say. Morei hooked his arm through hers and waited for the council to pair up as well. He, as king, would enter last with Isla by his side.

They stood behind Lady Yara and Lord Malachi, who passed them a quick glance. Rhys was not required to be among them when they entered, and Morei knew the chancellor preferred it that way. He would be out with the crowd, several drinks in and probably wagering a bet on something obscure or illegal.

The drums intensified. The sound was so loud that it made his teeth chatter and bones vibrate. Isla was as stiff as a corpse next to him, and he tried to catch her eye, but it was no use. The princess was panicking. He only hoped she would gather herself for the dance.

The large doors swung open, and even as the drums continued, applause deafened the hall. Morei couldn't hear anything as they entered. Councilmembers took their places in a wide circle in the middle of the massive chamber, and Isla and he stopped in the center, their steps matching the drums. The king took his time studying the people. Many he couldn't identify, but he did recognize a few from routine appointments and trades. Bennett, Edwin's second-in-command, was paired with a woman with black hair, and he spotted several other higher-ranked soldiers with their partners.

The drums ceased, but the applause continued. This moment was significant, and he soaked it all in. The people were witnessing him for the first time. Not just as a king giving orders but as a strong believer in the Caster culture. That meant more to them than any promises he'd made. With a Caster-born to his left, he hoped to gain all their loyalty. This night would change everything, and standing here now, he knew he'd made the necessary impression.

Instruments started up again. Morei turned to Isla, and he offered his hand to her. The dance was iconic in Sorréleian culture, carried over from Diyră. He knew it in his sleep; every royal family member was raised to live and breathe the same steps.

Those raised outside royal tradition were unfamiliar, of course, like the princess. Beyond the practices, she'd never danced before. The royal dance reflected the delicate balance of ruling. A king was to never act without his queen, but the king was also expected to lead. It was Isla's job to take his hand, confirming she trusted his rule.

The king dipped his head and waited. His heart was steady, the chamber was deathly silent, and he could hear Isla's breathing. He would have said something, but their voices would have carried.

Gently, she rested her hand over his. Her skin was hot to the touch, and he raised his head to acknowledge her. Isla faintly nodded. From somewhere in the crowd, a mumble rose.

The king cupped her waist with his other hand, and together, they moved. The steps came flawlessly, the instruments lost in the heat of the moment. It had been a long time since Morei had shared a dance with a woman. Last night's encounter melted into a heated exchange of steps. She was bold, confident, all signs of her nerves absent from her movements. He questioned that she'd never danced before. If that was true, she'd practiced relentlessly to master these steps. Not a single misstep—which would have been devastating for his aims, as it would've reflected on his ability to rule. She had come through for him.

As the music shifted, the king slowed and, with Isla's hand still in his own, dropped to one knee, head bowed. The final gesture to honor the queen. Customarily, it would be romantic, because there would be a marriage. Tonight, it was both formal and Morei's attempt to uphold a Caster tradition.

The people erupted in cheers. They approved.

Councilmembers joined the floor, falling into similar steps in unison. Morei led Isla away, hand clasped around her waist, and people continued to clap with praise. As they neared the crowd, Rhys stepped forward. He was dressed in silver with blue accents and the same wolf embroidered on his tail-shaped tunic. The chancellor looked like he'd been born to rule, but Morei would never tell the man that. Rhys didn't need help being an egotistical maniac.

"No woman?" Morei asked. He tugged at the collar of his shirt. It was stifling in here.

Rhys shrugged. "I'm not fond of partners. They tend to get in the way of whatever I want to do." He glanced at Isla. "You look marvelous tonight. It's impressive to see what Rose and her ladies can do in such a short time."

The princess bowed her head. "Thank you. I feel a bit out of place, but I'll get used to it."

Morei liked that answer. Maybe she was serious about her position after all. He was pleased to see the two holding a normal conversation too. Rhys had struggled to show respect for Isla, even with her bloodline. After their discussion, though, Morei understood it was in part due to his envy.

"Well, you're doing a fantastic job at it," the chancellor observed, and then he raised a finger at the king. "And who knew a man like you could dance. You're a complicated one, that's for sure."

That forced a chuckle out of Morei. At times, he couldn't stand Rhys's arrogance. At other times, he felt a kinship to his sarcasm and ill-mannered statements. The chancellor didn't care who he offended, and the king could relate. He appreciated Rhys, even if he wanted to cut his tongue out. A man with great potential, and Morei intended to utilize that as the empire grew—if Rhys didn't ruin his chances.

"Enjoy your evening," Morei told him. He would not spend the rest of it tied to the chancellor. Rhys had extensive work to do to prove he was worth any time to Morei outside of business.

The chancellor's smile was strained. The façade between them slipped, and Morei saw the thief and conceited man he couldn't stand. "You too."

He guided Isla away from the crowd. "Tell me," he said, hoping to get to more interesting matters, "why did you show tonight?"

Isla regarded him, keeping her expression pleasant for all the guests. "I don't understand."

"I was expecting you not to dance," he admitted. They stopped for some drinks. Morei opted for a dessert wine, while Isla gravitated to a berry ale. The alcohol was making his head buzz. He'd been drinking for the last day already, of course. He should have requested water or tea, but he couldn't bring

himself to sober up quite yet. Maybe tomorrow. They walked until they were far enough from the crowd that nobody could listen but still visible. It would be impolite if they disappeared. "After your recent behavior, I was betting on i
t."

A group of performers stepped onto the floor, blue silk ribbons tied to their bodies. The song shifted, taking on a more tribal feel, as the dancers moved in unison. The crowd watched, thrilled by the show, and he couldn't blame them. They wore gold masks, each designed to look like a different emotion—anger, fear, excitement, and so on—and only had small holes to see with. They were barefoot, and bangles clattered as they moved with precise intent.

The princess took a drink. "What would I gain by abandoning our promise?"

He shrugged. "You tell me, Isla. You're the one who continues to disregard my orders. I'm starting to wonder if you care for your bloodline or not."

That petite face betrayed irritation. Her cheeks, already flush from the night, reddened. "Did you pull me aside to berate me?"

"You were fine criticizing me last night."

"Your dress is gorgeous, Your Majesty," a woman called as she walked too close by. She raised her drink, and Isla nodded in appreciation. When she was out of earshot, the princess turned her attention back to him.

Morei leaned in and lowered his voice, emboldened. He was pleased to have the upper hand with her for once. She couldn't walk away without drawing too much attention. "You never answered my question last night."

The music grew louder, and people cheered and encouraged the song, leaving Morei and Isla in privacy. The princess took another drink. "What question? I thought I answered everything."

"The council," he reminded her, but she already knew that.

Isla, deflated, slumped against the wall. She averted her gaze, drumming her fingers on the mug. The scar was obvious on her hand now that he knew it was there. He let her stand there with her thoughts, bearing his weight against the wall too, hoping they at least looked the part of a royal pairing.

"I've heard it all, Morei, and I don't know if it's a good choice for me to be a part of something nobody else wants me to be a part of."

Alarmed, he shifted his weight, eying a few stragglers who walked by with drinks in each hand. The city would be hungover tomorrow. "Then prove them wrong." Her brow went up, surprised by his support. "Do you want them to talk about how you couldn't stand on your own, or do you want them to curse your name because you defied everything they wanted you to be?" Morei spoke from experience, but he hoped the point was clear. "Do you believe them? What they say about you?"

Isla shook her head, fumbling with her words. "No, I—I just didn't know if it was a smart move politically."

Clever answer, but it didn't work on him. Isla's blood was as rich as the next royal member's, and it troubled him that she didn't grasp what that meant. Royalty gave people like him a right to do the impossible, a chance for the finer things life offered, and her disregard for those privileges enraged him. The royal families who ruled did so because they'd fought with everything they had to earn their territories. And here she was, tossing that pride aside because it was easier than standing up for herself.

A horn blew. The music ceased, and a hushed whisper passed through the crowd as people gathered toward the center of the massive chamber. The king exchanged a look with Isla, and they both agreed to approach. The princess practically launched herself off the wall, relieved to be done with that conversation. Morei took his time, satisfied to have gotten the answers he wanted.

Most people were pressed against the walls. A few ventured forward, and Morei recognized one as Leo from earlier. He was dressed in simple leather to protect his limbs while he wore a white tunic. No point in expensive attire if one of the creatures lashed out.

When Leo saw the king, he gestured for them to step forward a bit. "Front and center," he called. "A proud representation of the power and control that Caster has over the land they call their own."

The king liked that, and once they were all in position—ten paces in front of the rest of the crowd—Leo nodded. This was his moment, that was clear, and Morei was curious to see what would transpire.

From the back of the hall, a door opened. A flap of pink feathers came in, followed by a woman dressed in hardly any clothes. She was covered in beads and ink, her brown hair braided and positioned atop her head. She looked like she belonged out at sea or with an extreme group of people who lived in the mountains, not here. When she looked in the king's direction, he was stunned to see that her eyes were violet. This was Hanna.

"How?" Morei mumbled.

Isla leaned over and whispered, "An occultist." She had his attention. "There are rumors that people go to the Dark Forest for rituals and certain deals. They never come back the same."

Morei didn't reply as the woman stopped at the hall's center. Without even a word, the bird came to her and landed on her outstretched arm.

Leo announced, "Hanna and Kyro. They have been with us for over a decade now, and it would not be a proper festival without them. They need no formal introduction." He glanced at Morei and Isla. "Enjoy."

Kyro launched into the air, and streaks of mist followed. It almost looked like fire, save for the fact that no flame was pink. Morei watched Kyro perform a series of intricate moves that no normal bird could have followed before swooping low and passing Hanna with a whistle. The bird was fast, and while most attention was tuned to Kyro's impressive performance and strange appearance, the king watched Hanna.

The woman's face was taut. He continued to watch until the bird swooped back down, and as it did, Morei caught a glimpse of her slit pupils before they shifted back into normal orbs. It was quick, and if not for him staring, he'd never have seen them change.

Strange. He leaned over to Isla again. "Does she live in the city?"

She offered the smallest of shrugs. "I think she lives on the outskirts. A bit of a recluse."

The large trembar entered. Lord Bastard, Leo called him, and Morei could see why. The beast growled, unlike any sound he'd heard before. The noise reverberated into his bones, and some people covered their ears. Rhys looked visibly uncomfortable in the crowd.

"We all know who you are," Leo said in introduction. "From the Dark Forest and known for the incisors that are too big for their mouth." He took the chain leash that the other soldier was carrying, a man dressed in similar attire. "That sound you hear is how they debilitate prey. But notice how some of you can't stand it and others manage?" Leo gestured around the room, not at all bothered by the proximity of the beast. A single lunge would kill the man. "In the old lore of the Vorelians, that single differentiator decided who was weak and who was the strongest. Men and women alike would march into the Dark Forest in search of a trembar to prove their worth."

That was how the performances went. Morei watched, impressed, as Leo worked with ease around Lord Bastard and the feline that came next. The man constantly looked back for the king's approval, which he gave with slight nods. It was odd, given how little he knew Leo and how short of a time he'd been here, but he appreciated the gesture. Leo obviously had immense respect for rulers and didn't want to offend Morei by saying the wrong thing. More importantly, he wanted to know Morei was enjoying his time here, not growing bored.

As the last creature was escorted out of the large hall, a long silence followed. Leo's expression was serious, his hands clasped tightly. The man was nervous. Savage, the Wynzer, would dictate if this would happen or not.

"You're probably curious as to why I haven't ended the show," Leo announced. "Assuming everything is a go, you will see something that nobody else in the Vore World has. This was a creation that took many long nights to train and understand. We still don't fully grasp his capabilities or what he wants to do. We tried to let him go, but he refused to leave." He shrugged. "I'm not sure if that's a compliment or not."

A few people chuckled. Isla looked at Morei, hoping for an answer. He gave none.

This was the part of the performance he was most excited about. He was honored to know Caster was the only city in the world with his kind. Curious, too. The Wynzer was not ordinary. He'd been forged with Dark Energy, and that made him fascinating.

A growl echoed from behind the door, and that caused the few talkers in the crowd to fall quiet. For such a little creature, it was an impressive sound. Morei straightened, and Leo passed him a quick glance. A thrill glittered in those brown eyes—the soldier was confident they were about to get a show.

A loud thud followed. The king knew the sound of a body striking the floor just as well as a musician knew the strings of their instrument. Someone had died. The soldier seemed to sense it too, though that manic grin was still painted across his face. He started to approach the door, though he was quite a bit of distance away when the metal swung open and a bloodied soldier stepped out with Savage on his wrist. The dragon—Wynzer, Morei reminded himself—was gnawing on . . . Morei squinted.

A hand. Savage was eating a hand. Likely from the body he'd just heard hit the floor behind the door of this chamber. He wasn't alarmed, rather enthralled. Isla placed a questioning hand on the king's arm but said nothing.

Leo didn't miss a beat. "There he is!" His voice shook with thrill, and he gestured wildly at the approaching creature. The soldier who held Savage had a slight limp but walked confidently. Blood smeared his face, and Morei wondered whether that was even his own.

People started talking in hushed whispers. They didn't seem to care about the blood.

"Dragon."

"The tail is unnatural."

"What is it eating?"

They were afraid. Morei should have been too. He should have felt the familiar pangs of uncertainty and anxiety at such a wild and untamed creation, but he didn't. Before him was a creature of immense potential and intelligence. It reflected Caster's superiority—which he intended to leverage.

"Are you okay?" Leo finally asked.

The soldier nodded, arm never wavering. "Bit of a scuffle back there. The prisoner tried to flee and, well, Savage got a little too excited by the commotion." Those words came out in an uncomfortable laugh that reached the entire hall.

"Ah." Leo's gaze passed over the crowd. "This is a Wynzer. You may not recognize the name, and that's because he does not exist anywhere in the world. Under funding from the previous rulership, Savage was born. We have cared for him since, but I know what you're thinking." He wagged his finger like a parent scolding a child. "He is not dangerous unless provoked. Savage is clever, perhaps too much for his own good, but if you respect him, he respects you. Don't let the blood scare you."

As if to make a point, Savage let go of the hand he was chewing on. The bloody heap landed with a light thud on the ground. Blood splattered and stained the pants of both men. In the deafening silence, the sound was jarring.

Then, without hesitation, Savage took flight. The beast let out a piercing shriek that sounded more like that of a large bird as he flapped and climbed above everyone. His abnormally long tail trailed behind him. He stayed up there, circling, and everyone watched.

Morei took the opportunity to approach Leo and the other soldier. The viewers were too caught up in watching Savage to pay much attention to him, even Isla. When he got close, Leo beamed. He looked like a proud father.

"Impressive, isn't he?" Leo asked.

"Aye." Morei motioned at the other man. "You sure you're okay?"

Unbelievably, the soldier chuckled. "I'll be fine. It's the dead prisoner who isn't."

"You feed Savage . . . people?" He knew the dragon ate meat, but he'd suspected cattle, or even fish.

Leo cleared his throat and lowered his voice. "Not always, Your Majesty. We were going to display his skills to you and the viewers. The prisoner wasn't supposed to die—not tonight, at least—but Savage got carried away when the man ran. Hunting instincts kicked in."

"But you still feed him people sometimes?"

Leo gave a sheepish shrug, looking guilty. "Well, just the real bad ones. You know, the type who aren't ever getting out or are already dying."

"Why didn't I know?" Withholding information from the king was disrespectful, a blatant display of disloyalty.

"Your Majesty, it was not done intentionally. Started as an accident one day, really, when Drexis was still in charge, and"—he looked pale—"we kind of just kept doing it. A bit of a rogue group of men we are, yeah?" When the king didn't laugh at the nervous joke, he added, "Your Majesty, it will never happen again."

The other soldier nodded in agreement. The two resembled children caught red-handed. Morei let the silence speak for him. This was not behavior he needed to be dealing with when he was worried about war and expanding Caster's reach.

"Men, I'm not opposed to the idea. It's clever when we have an abundance of prisoners, or a nasty one who is too dangerous to release, but please make me aware of it moving forward. I won't tolerate dishonesty. Understood?"

"Yes, Your Majesty," they said in unison.

The soldiers here were far different than those in Geral. The men he was used to leading were far more respectful of rules. Caster soldiers were troublemakers. They bent the rules, and that could be a risk if he didn't have their loyalty. "Well, if anything is needed, let me know. The work you've done is incredible. You're changing the world, no?" Morei meant that.

The men looked at him as if they'd never heard a compliment in their life. Maybe they hadn't. Either way, he wanted them to know he supported their endeavors, despite their actions. "Consider anything you want to do funded. If you have ideas, let me know. Caster will be the heart of the greatest empire the world has ever seen, and that starts with people like you."

They nodded, stumbling over their words like drunks. The king knew he had their loyalty. Word would spread, and more citizens would come to support him. He didn't need to be sober to know that. His next step was determining how Savage was born, and if he could determine that, maybe he could replicate it into full-sized dragons.

An Empire of Chaos

Syra told Sekar her working theory about the relationship between realms. He listened without question, only offering a word here and there to encourage her to continue. Chaos's arrival in the Soul Realm was abrupt, which meant they had far less time than they wanted. If the Soul Realm was the bridge, then a chasm was due to open in the living realm—the Gods' Realm. Everything came back to the Soul Realm. Its behavior and condition impacted the other realms. Chaos's presence here indicated the delicate balance needed to sustain all three realms no longer existed.

They didn't fear any beast would come for them now—the chasm created an allure like a moth attracted to a flame. Those closest were affected first. That didn't stop Syra and Sekar from checking over their shoulders and stopping to listen every so often to ensure they weren't being tracked. In time, Sekar believed Chaos's reach would continue to expand.

The realm fracture needed to be addressed. Zarek had spent so long investigating through old text and half-restored books, but they were no closer to resolving the issue. Sekar seemed to think that while a fracture origin point could be in the Gray Realm, the odds of it sustaining were unlikely. The volatility and purity of such a force would make it unstable. Syra disagreed.

Mother was intelligent. If a realm fracture was unsustainable, then perhaps Chaos had learned to draw in energy from the other realms through other methods. A realm fracture could be a side effect between the Soul Realm and the living realm. That would mean what they were dealing with was far larger than anyone imagined.

They'd walked for a while, crossing the Starved Sands where its reach was shortest, and now were on the outskirts of the dead woods. Sekar called it the dead lands, where most life in this realm didn't roam. However, that didn't protect them completely. Beasts roamed these lands, and they hoped not to attract the attention of any nearby.

Syra wandered about, feet crunching into brittle branches and mush. Boots would have come in handy right about now, but she'd stepped on worse. The truth was that she had no idea what she was looking for. He'd told her they could find food and water here, but everything looked lifeless and the same.

She pushed aside some blackened branches and found absolutely nothing. Just more soggy dirt. Ice the color of midnight stared up at her. While she was hungry, she was admittedly unwilling to eat dirty ice quite yet. Raid had been holding some root, but these trees were well past their prime summers. And unless they melted the grungy ice, she couldn't figure out how they would get water. She'd never seen a river in all her time in the Soul Realm.

Frustrated, she shoved more branches. This was foolish. What they needed was to figure out how they were going to save Zarek. Nothing could happen until the Guardian was rescued. Without that peace, and with the disaster with Chaos, she hardly had an appetite.

Syra made her way back to the small space they'd claimed. It wasn't much, more of an uneven section where nothing grew. Arms crossed, she stood there and waited. It didn't take long for Sekar to return with a few things in his hands. He raised his brow at her empty haul.

"I don't know what I'm looking for," she confessed. "I'm stuck in the middle of a realm I know nothing about and have no idea what food to find or where we can even get water." She motioned at their bare feet. "And we didn't even get Death's Sword or our stuff. That was Dryl's, you know. He's going to be pissed once he realizes it was lost." The words tasted as sour as they sounded, but they were all she had.

The God slowly nodded and stepped forward. His shirt was hanging on by threads, but he didn't seem to care. Syra didn't look better herself, she knew. They both looked like they'd seen Death. "Well," he said, "why don't we take this one step at a time?" Sekar offered one of the items in his hand. It appeared nearly identical to what Raid had had. "Food, water, then talk."

"About Zarek?" She took the root. It was heavier than she'd expected. "We need a plan."

"Eat," he insisted. "And follow me."

Begrudgingly, she did so. The root snapped like a carrot. It was sweet and quite good. The root wasn't a plate of fish or a rich hearty stew, but it would do. Sekar walked up to a dead tree and knelt. She followed. There, she saw that he'd been digging.

"I thought these were dead," she said after she swallowed. "You're telling me these are alive?"

"More or less," Sekar answered, and peeled away more soggy soil. "When the Soul Realm became sick, we had to quickly find means to eat." *We.* He always spoke like he was still impersonating a Guardian of Death. It made it harder for her to differentiate between the man she thought she knew and the God before her. "Most of the food resources have died, given the current state of this realm. But as the trees shriveled up, their roots thrived. All the nutrients one could ever need packed into the roots. They don't replace a good meal, but with resources growing more slim, these have become a must." Sekar latched a hand over one of the roots and pulled. It snapped. "They are a good source of water too."

He handed it to her, and she took it. Fresh out of the ground, it was coated in dirt. "So, this is our food and water?"

"No." Sekar stood and motioned for her to follow. "Water still runs, but it's a bit trickier to find. Streams and rivers now flow underground, sometimes through layers of ice, and we have to find an opening."

Syra wiped the dirt off as best as she could, but even with some on the root, she ate anyway. The soil was a bit bitter, but it paled in comparison to the satisfaction she felt at finally eating something.

"See this?" Sekar pointed to the ground. At first, Syra didn't see anything, but after a few moments, she started to see a slope. Faint, but there. "This is the sign of erosion. Water runs underneath us."

They walked a short ways, then turned back and walked some more, and then he finally stopped over a small hole. With all the leaves and branches on the ground, Syra never would have seen it. Kneeling next to the hole, Sekar pulled away branches and pushed his hand through. She watched, intrigued, as the God pulled his hand out. His skin was soaked.

"Help me." He started to pull more soil away, and she followed. The rushing current of water underneath stared back up at her, oblivious of the world they'd just exposed it to. The sound met her ears, and she couldn't help but grin. Here they were, sitting in the middle of some not-so-dead forest, digging in the dirt, in a realm beyond the living.

Once they could both stick their hands in, Syra stopped. She plunged hers in and relished the ice-cold sensation. It felt incredible, and she splashed her face. Only days had gone by, but after being locked up and escaping, the sensation of water against her skin felt like a fresh start. She washed her face as best as she could, drank some, and carefully rinsed the dried blood off her arms, hoping not to reopen any wounds.

Sekar did the same, and when they were both done, they sat back and looked at each other. "Let's talk," Syra said.

The God shook his head and propped himself up against a tree to lean on. "You really care that much for him?"

She didn't move from her spot next to the hole. "He has been there for me when you weren't." The words were harsh, but they were the truth. "After the Demon Killer—"

"I haven't forgotten."

"Zarek helped me. He came because of Dryl, and he taught me a lot. He risked his life to help me. What more do you want from him?"

Sekar's jaw muscle ticced. "I want his word that he won't ever betray you."

Syra couldn't believe her ears. "I should say the same about you."

His dark gaze flashed over her before returning to the root in his hand. After everything they'd witnessed, it was unbelievable that they were sitting here now and talking about this, but Syra couldn't say she was surprised. Their friendship was complex, even a bit wild and untamed.

"They will be expecting us," Sekar finally said, relenting. "Shevana will be with Zarek, keeping him as bait. The Guardians who remain loyal to her will be on guard, along with Elyas and his familiars. They know we're coming. If Zarek isn't dead, he will be if we screw this up."

Syra nodded.

"When we're closer, we can determine the best way of getting in. Without knowing what the situation is, how many are waiting for us, or if we can even get into the palace, there's little we can discuss."

That was not what she wanted to hear. "Well, what if there's a dozen Geíons? Guardians? What do we do?"

He took a bite and chewed slowly. When he swallowed, he said, "Kill them."

"That's hardly a plan," she countered.

"It's the only one I have."

"Shouldn't we discuss what happens if we get to Shevana?"

He raised his brow. "If I get to her first, I'll kill her. If you do, kill her."

Syra was becoming increasingly irritated. "I need you to try and work with me." She tried to keep her tone level, but it was failing. "I don't know how to kill Shevana. I don't know what to expect when I get there, and I can't constantly rely on you to save me when there's trouble."

The reality was setting in: they would charge Shevana's palace and try to rescue Zarek, but in doing so, they would be faced with many enemies. They were in the Soul Realm, a place once foreign to her, home to Ashýon, the Starved Sands, and so much she still didn't understand. Syra wanted to hope they could remain together, but reasoning said otherwise. If need be, she would go straight for Zarek, but she kept visualizing everything that could g o wrong.

"Don't think," Sekar observed. "Thinking will get you killed in battle. It's all about instinct and intuition."

She dug her fingers into the dirt before her, trying to keep herself busy. "It's a lot easier said than done."

Leaves crunched, and Sekar sat straight. They looked around. Syra's heart was already racing. Another enemy, another problem. They would never make it to Zarek.

Then his lips tweaked upward. "I can't believe it's you." His tone shifted, sounding more paternal. Syra looked around and couldn't believe what she was seeing. An Onye with white fur and red eyes was approaching at a leisurely stroll. She tensed. The last time she'd been in the presence of such a beast was on a ship in the Beritisian Gulf. That Onye had murdered countless people.

"Don't be afraid," Sekar said.

"How . . ." She couldn't finish the question. This Onye was a bit larger than the other. It passed her, fur brushing over her shoulders, and nuzzled Sekar. He smiled and scratched its ears. He appeared innocent, unresponsible for the crimes he'd committed or would soon execute.

"This is their home," he explained. "Where they were originally from. They've moved into the living over the centuries for resources, but when this realm was at its best, this was all they ever needed." The Onye raised its head. They were so close that the God rested his head against the beast's. "They are everything to me."

She gawked, watching this beast receive affection. The stories she knew of these creatures called them bloodthirsty and violent. But as she watched the God scratch the Onye's neck and ears, his words sank further into her.

"You created them," she whispered. "Didn't you?"

He looked at her. The Onye settled next to him, laying a head on one of its large paws. The beast watched her, and she bundled her hands into her lap. After everything, this felt mundane, but she couldn't shake the uncertainty bubbling up in the back of her throat. They'd always said the Onyes were familiars of Sekar, but now she knew why.

"I was lonely," Sekar told her. He looked at the root in his hand and offered it to the beast. The Onye pinned the root between its paws and started to eat. "I was learning my capabilities, testing what I could and couldn't do. About a decade after my rebirth, I stumbled on an abandoned pup in the Releuthian Mountains." His fingers grazed through the Onye's fur. "I didn't know what I was making then, but when I realized what I had done, I brought her here. The Guardians gave the pup sanctuary, a place to roam without the brutal hand of man to interfere. In time, she grew, and I brought more, wanting to give her company." His expression darkened. "Little did I realize what I was creating then."

"This is her, isn't it?"

He nodded. "Few remain as old as her. Many have since been killed, no thanks to man." Those words came out cold. "But they have learned to self-sustain their population. If this realm is saved, I hope for them to return to their peaceful selves."

Syra wanted to shove her head in the hole and drown out her shame. Like all the Vorelians, she believed these creatures to be the heart of nightmares. They slaughtered villages. Those were the stories she was raised on, but what she saw now was an Onye that had no quarrel with the world around her.

They didn't speak for a long while. Syra watched the Onye doze off. The world was getting stranger, but she was relieved to be with someone who knew so much more than her. Sekar leaned against a tree, comfortable. Sitting here slouched over a hole with running water was no longer as thrilling as it had been.

Soon, this would all be over. Whatever happened in the palace would come to pass, and she would have to accept the fate that lay ahead. But she couldn't help but wonder what would happen to the man across from her. She still wanted answers.

"Your deal with Henry," Syra whispered. Sekar looked up at her. "What happens?"

A cold but lifeless smile touched the God's lips. "I take the consequences as they come."

So much went unsaid in that response. He'd told her about the blood bond between him and Henry. Sitting here now, she realized that the God, like anyone, made mistakes. It didn't matter how old he was, where he came from, or what he could do, he was still capable of having regrets like anyone else.

"Can I ask a question?"

Sekar's hand wrapped around the Onye protectively. "You know you don't need to ask permission for that. We've been over this."

She squeezed her hands together. "I don't know your story. How you became a God."

In an instant, Sekar's entire demeanor shifted. He went from this overwhelming and obnoxious hothead to a statue. Few times, if ever, had she seen him so uncomfortably quiet. Not even being chained and beaten could dampen his stubborn attitude, but her question seemed to rip the life right out of him.

She shifted, uneasy, wanting to apologize, but he broke the awkward silence. "In another life, I was the victim." One hand slowly tugged aside the tunic to reveal more of the same scars across his shoulders and upper arms. Then he let the fabric fall back into its pitiful, torn place. "These scars are from the day I died."

A man as horrifyingly cold as Sekar didn't easily win the hearts of many. In their travels and encounters, though, he'd managed to gain Syra's sympathy and proven to be a valuable friend. She knew so little about Sekar's life before he was a deity, and barely more after. The Onye made no movement, fast asleep.

"The family I came from was well off. We were considered wealthy, even royal. During the Vorelian Empire, massive festivals were held, festivals that could last days. Many came to the Dionson family to have special leather outfits made, among other things. We were one of the most sought-after leatherworkers in the entire empire. For many decades, it was tradition to wear prestigious, even raunchy, leather pieces during these festivals, especially during that empire's reign. The more expensive, the better, and that's what we were known for."

Sekar looked away, and his tone grew softer. "With power came illegal trades and business. We worked with the worst of the worst, struck deals to increase our profits, and killed those who found out the truth about how we worked. I was the second-born and was raised in that business. It was all I knew, so when I was asked to retrieve some material from an illegal trader, I didn't think twice about it."

He scoffed, as if hearing something she didn't. "I was ambushed, tied up, whipped, tortured, strangled until I passed out, and then they would wake me and do it all over again. They stuffed my head into buckets full of feces or water, whichever they felt like. They hung me upside down, pissed on me, the list goes on." Sekar's fingers dug into the Onye's fur. "You see, my father broke some promises with the wrong people, and they wanted blood. Without my knowledge, I was the solution. I was sacrificed to keep the family's name."

He fell quiet. Syra stared, bewildered. What a horrific and tragic way to die, no less to be betrayed by the ones he loved. It was easy to think her life had been unfair and to be crippled by the memory of how she'd *died* at his hands. But hearing his story humbled her. "I'm sorry," she said quietly. "I can't even imagine what that must have been like."

"Don't apologize. Your sympathy is not what I want. I tell you this so that you know where I came from."

Numbly, she nodded. "What happened after that? After Chaos intervened?"

A glimmer returned, dark and wild. "I tormented my family, screwed with their dreams, and picked them off one by one. I killed them all, Syra, and then I hunted those who took my life. I told you we all earn our scars. Those early days, when I was a new God, that was when I earned mine. I extended myself too far without the knowledge to harness such a force. I lost a large piece of myself and spent centuries wandering the world, chasing the man I once knew."

Syra wanted to apologize for the actions of those who wronged him, but she couldn't even say that. It was so easy to say sorry when it meant nothing. Sekar didn't want accolades for his revenge or sympathy. He just wanted her to listen.

Sekar was everything but the victim. He was a nightmare, an ass, cruel, corrupt. He spent more time causing trouble than resolving it. Underneath all that was a man who'd gotten so twisted with the taste of revenge that he tarnished everything he was.

When he didn't share more, she dipped her hands into the water, washing them clean again. "What's next?"

A vicious grin crossed his face. "We go to the palace."

No Secret is Safe

The egg never left Cyrus's sight. When they made it back to Venkar, the Yavinks exploded in cheer. They threw paint, passed drinks, and stuffed every plate they could in Cyrus's face. He was grateful for the food, but he was wary around them. They'd acted recklessly by drugging him, they possessed world-changing secrets, and instead of addressing any of that, now they just shoved a drink in his hand and celebrated once more. Everything about this was wrong.

Trust was a currency he was running low on, especially after what had happened to him with King Raj, and he debated speaking with Unshi on the matter. He didn't want to offend anyone, but it was impossible to swallow what had happened.

Sozar was presented chunks of raw meat from a jhigar, a large beast that roamed the Pynsole Mountains. The Yavinks hunted the creature for what it could offer: coats, leather, tools, and food. Yu, Unshi, and others came to him to honor his name and to state their loyalty to him and Eei'on Rü, displaying no sign of malice after what they'd done. Not that he expected it. They thought they'd granted a Rider entry to a secret they'd kept hidden for centuries. He gave his thanks to each, just happy to be wearing a shirt and not stuck in a cave, possessing no need to celebrate. He let them have their party, and he remained cautious.

With the people distracted by drinks and food, he sought Unshi out. The leader was hardly dressed, covered in bone necklaces and pink and black paint. White lines dressed his face, making up Old Tongue sigils. When he saw Cyrus, he lifted a wooden mug, and cheers followed. They were mad.

"Can I speak to you privately?" he whispered.

Unshi nodded, breaking away from the men and following Cyrus. He wasn't sure where he was going, but they stopped on the outskirts of the festivities where no one was around. Confirming they were alone, he inhaled the courage needed. This wasn't something he normally did, but it needed to be done.

"Why did you do it?" At Unshi's raised brow, he added, "Drug me."

Unshi looked back to the celebration, his earlier bright demeanor shifting instantly. "It was the only way to get you to Üg'ahn."

"Was it?" he pressed. "You could have told me—"

"No. These were Üg'ahn's terms. It was his blood you drank. We couldn't tell you the truth. Not when Üg'ahn still needed to see if you were worthy of what he protects."

Cyrus stared. Sozar remained as still as a statue from where he sat, tuned in to their conversation. So it was blood. He'd been repulsed to think so, but now it was confirmed. His stomach knotted and protested, threatening to empty right here. "Do you serve Üg'ahn?"

"We serve Destiny and her best interests," Unshi replied. His previous kindness was gone. "You were brought to us because of Hyle, who's given us protection from a world that would destroy these sacred lands, providing us the chance to fulfill the promise to the Dragon Riders that soared these skies well before you were born."

"Then what of Üg'ahn?"

Unshi took his drink and poured the remaining liquid onto the ground. The leader was not amused by the festivities anymore. His face revealed the true nature of his character—hardened and cold. "He arrived several summers after the eggs were brought here. He has remained here since. Cursed blood, but he has fulfilled his oath as we have. Does that satisfy you?"

Cyrus dragged a hand over his face. More cheers. For what, he didn't know and didn't care. "Can I trust Üg'ahn?" Asking the very people who'd drugged him seemed pointless, but he needed confirmation he wasn't walking into a trap. A sign.

Unshi's mouth twisted into a half-smile, both pitying and amused. "Would you trust a starved beast if you were locked in a room with him?"

Cyrus didn't answer. The answer was obvious.

Unshi squeezed his shoulder, a miserable attempt to ease the awkwardness that bubbled up around them. "Remember, Cyrus, Destiny will always have her way. And if you don't give her what she wants, she'll steal it." He let go of Cyrus. "Enjoy your evening. We waited centuries for this."

He walked away, disappearing into the crowd. Cyrus stared, unsure if he wanted to pack up and leave now or hide out until the morning. Nothing about that encounter had put his mind at ease. The Yavinks wouldn't apologize.

Finding a tree trunk away from them all, he sat down. The last bit of strength he had to look the Dragon Rider part evaporated. All he wanted was silence and solitude. Only a few approached to lift their mugs and cheer in his name.

By the time the celebration quieted and people started curling up on the ground to sleep, he was still wide awake and eager to get away. The day was still bleeding off him. Üg'ahn's overwhelming presence was everywhere, reminding him of his oath to the Rider Federation. He stepped carefully over a few people, not wishing to disturb them. He tried to ask a couple of them why they slept on the ground and not in their own homes, but he only got a mumbled giggle and half answer. Chavi said it had something to do with the lights. He had no idea what that meant.

Dragon egg tucked in his arm, he met Sozar on the outskirts of the people. The dragon kept his tail up to avoid hitting anyone, though that didn't stop him from knocking over an empty bucket. Cyrus froze. He looked back as the bucket rolled several steps away. Some of the Yavinks shifted, but nobody looked. Relieved, he motioned for Sozar to come.

They headed out of the city.

There wasn't a plan, but Cyrus couldn't sit there any longer. The egg in his hand hummed with life, a constant reminder of his duty. His muscles were tired, his mouth dry, but his mind raced. Sozar gladly accepted the offer to take a stroll through the forest, and once everyone was fast asleep, they took their leave.

In the night, the trees glowed blue. The air was still thick, and Cyrus wiped perspiration off the back of his neck. When he looked over at Sozar, the dragon's scales glistened with a light sheen of dew. It was humid tonight, and he decided here and now that he was not fond of it. In Creitón, even the chilliest nights were drenched in sweat. His clothes stuck to skin, and it felt like he couldn't get enough water. Cyrus missed the dryer climate of Diemon, but not the nightmares that came with a place he once called home.

They came to several different paths. Under the full moon, he could see the more worn-out path to the left. It was wide enough for Sozar to fit through without causing a ruckus. Without a word, they took it. They walked side by side, enjoying the crunch of the soil and the noises from all around. Crickets and critters made all sorts of sounds. They went silent when Sozar passed—he didn't blame them—and started up again once they were out of range.

Cyrus hoped the dragon bundled up in the egg appreciated the travel. He brought this up to Sozar, who snorted in amusement.

We can hear everything, sense intentions, and feel our surroundings. She knows she's in safe hands.

That made him pause. *How much can you feel of her?*

Enough to know that she is at peace with us, the dragon replied. *I cannot reach her as clearly as you or those around us. It is our hearts that speak when we are in the egg, not our minds.*

Cyrus didn't entirely understand what that meant. He could sense the young female, but only enough to confirm she was alive.

Dragons are connected. I can feel Ashtir's own wings beat when we are close enough. This close with an egg, I can sense her emotions, needs, and worries. And she knows that I am here.

"We will have to introduce her to people, see who she likes," he whispered. Dragons were extraordinary. That thought sobered him. He didn't want another Dameon and Ashtir pairing—not that he could control who this dragon was destined to become. The two were too much alike, driven by similar needs and wants. It was likely why the dragon had hatched for the Rider, both survivalist spirits with a penchant for violence. A small hope filled Cyrus's heart that the two would change their ways, but they were with Henry. If anyone could encourage the birth of a monster, it was that man. still, he would not give up.

She will be brave, Sozar observed. The dragon dipped his head under a low-hanging branch, but his wings still scraped it. They were coming to a clearing.

"I hope," he replied. Carefully, he prodded the consciousness of the dragon in the egg. He couldn't quite reach her, but he pressed to her the importance of her existence. *Have courage, little one. There is a Rider who awaits you.* He hoped she heard.

The trees gave way to a serene view that caused them both to stop. A pink lake stretched ahead. No waves rippled, and if not for the soft movements against the shore, he would have thought the landscape were made of glass. The lake's other side was at least a league away, a gem nestled between thick trees and jagged mountains. The water's glow gave him the chance to see their surroundings clearly. Everything was painted in variations of pink. The trees closest stood the tallest. No critters, no sound to betray this lake that sat in the heart of a forest. It was like the entire world stopped here.

Slowly, he approached and knelt on the shore.

He ran his fingers through the sand, not quite bold enough to submerge his hand into the water. The fine pebbles were dry and frigid to the touch—a stark contrast to the humidity—but they were nearly weightless. He scooped up more, finding no resistance. The stories of the Yavinks protecting Crescent Lake skewed his thoughts. Curiously, he lowered his fingers toward the water. As he did, he became acutely aware of a buzzing in his head that deafened his other thoughts.

This place kept getting stranger. The Dragon Blood flower sang in his thoughts, the burning flower still as clear to him as if he were standing before it now. Faced with the lake he'd heard so much about, he couldn't get enough. This was one of the hidden secrets of the Vore World.

Sozar . . . He wanted the dragon to tell him to stop. He didn't want to be reckless, but he found Sozar just as captivated, urging him.

Light Energy, the dragon rumbled. *Massive amounts of it.*

That was all he needed. When his skin made contact with the water, his strength evaporated. Cyrus slumped onto his butt, the egg still nestled in the crook of his arm, but it took everything in him to keep that hold. His thoughts moved with countless others. He heard a hundred wants, felt a thousand needs, hardly able to decipher which were his own. Food, sleep, hunt, shelter. Those were some of the major things he heard. His body was everywhere and nowhere at once.

"Unbelievable," he mumbled. He felt and heard the world around him. Crescent Lake was made up of countless networks that spanned leagues beyond its reach. The frigid touch of the water was akin to a winter snowstorm, and he let his hand wander to the bottom, where he pressed his palm into the wet sand. No, it couldn't be. Cyrus dragged his fingers against the bottom before scooping up the contents. When he broke free from the water, his connection with the world fractured, but in his hand was dry sand.

It defied all sense. Cyrus presented it to Sozar. "Look," he insisted. The dragon sniffed his hand and blinked.

There is so much energy here, he replied. Sozar lowered his snout to the still lake, then pushed his front legs into the water and froze.

Cyrus watched, transfixed, as a wave of white light shimmered across the dragon's scales before disappearing. His eyes, usually the color of fire, shifted into a deep blue but only for a moment. The dragon's mind, usually so vast and accessible, was beyond his reach—a wild wind against the fragile leaves of Cyrus's.

They stayed there. Cyrus sensed the building thrill from the dragon next to him, and he was eager to hear Sozar's opinion. True magic lived here, and he didn't want to interrupt this. He turned his attention back to the egg. Shifting his weight, he sat cross-legged and held it over the water.

Cyrus lowered her to the surface and hesitated. It felt foolish, but he couldn't deny the bubbling energy, this energy that turned his blood hot. The air here was charged. Every breath he took made him feel stronger, more daring, like he could do anything. It was a high he couldn't shake himself of. Crescent Lake was *alive*.

His fingers brushed the surface of the cold water, connecting him back to the vast world around him. He could feel lifeforces as small as the insects scattering across bark, their thoughts and needs as loud as the rest. Another breath and Cyrus let the water brush over the egg's shell. Just like with Sozar, a white light shimmered across the exterior. Extraordinary. Cyrus scooted forward until his legs were submerged, and he rested the egg there.

Sozar's thoughts merged into his own. They listened to everything, caught up in the spell. Time no longer mattered. He could feel the young dragon's lifeforce strengthen. She was enjoying this. As she grew more confident, she prodded his mind. Still faint, and not bold like Sozar, but unique. It was hard to miss her, even amid the organized madness of this world.

Above, another spectacle began. The sky, once dark and scattered with stars and the moon, now danced. Vivid pinks, greens, and reds moved to a tune only they could hear. The movements were fast, sporadic, and the intensity of the colors changed in response. Entranced, Cyrus watched. These were the lights Chavi had mentioned. Never had he seen something so wonderful. If ever a time existed where he longed for Zorya's company, now w as it.

The crunch of sand met Cyrus's ears. Drunk off the magic of this place, he held no fear when he looked to his left to see a large feline sitting on its haunches, fur slick and black. The creature looked at him, nose twitching, and grunted. Cyrus blinked, unsure if he was supposed to understand. The cat approached, sniffing, and he remained still. A part of him knew this was dangerous. He'd been raised with the same stories as anyone else—be careful with wildlife. But another part of him, the part connected with Crescent Lake, knew he didn't need to worry. The creature was curious, and so he let it sniff about. It stuck its nose into his lap, fascinated by the egg. Whiskers tickled his exposed skin. Paws as large as his hands sank into the water and s and.

Then the cat raised its head, displaying emerald gems. The creature regarded him as if it recognized him. Or perhaps knew of him. Nothing came close to these *real* moments, the ones reserved for once in a lifetime. Cyrus knew that through his travels, and as he sat here now, he recalled the fox—Raveth—that had stumbled in his path in the Releuthian Mountains. Perhaps this was another one of Üg'ahn's creations.

He focused his thoughts, dragging them reluctantly away from the countless connections, and directed them to the creature. *Your eyes tell me you know more than your forest companions.*

An ear twitched, and the feline cocked its head. A slight shift in the green gaze with a pupil dilation confirmed his words were heard.

You are the one who will bring peace. The words came back slow, deep like rolling thunder, and old. Indeed, this was Üg'ahn at work. The feline dropped its head back to the egg and pressed its nose against the shell. Blinking, the feline stood there for a long moment. Cyrus let it, not finding the right words to reply with. He was learning quickly that sometimes the best response was nothing at all.

The cat's tail flicked. Without hurry, it walked away from Cyrus, leaving prints in the sand. Cyrus was fascinated. He knew the world was special, but this was different. Magical. Humbling. It gave him hope that the future wasn't as bleak as others feared it would be. He turned his attention back to the night sky's show.

Good Deeds Make Bad Stories

S yra had never seen the Soul Realm's palace from the outside. Gloomy architecture, black stone, three wings, and an extensive courtyard now covered in vines and crumbling. The fountains were long dried up or frozen, but she could see old paintings along the stone floor that must have once been grand. The paint was long faded and chipped. Networks of grimy marble cut through the stone, and statues of ravens decorated intricate iron bars that garnished the top of stone walls along the courtyard and entrance. Several Guardians walked about, along with a few Gor-Geſons.

Syra and Sekar were crouched behind a cluster of fallen trees, their hot breaths turning to mist. They'd finally made it. The blackened branches were brittle, and so they had to be careful with where they placed their weight. A broken branch was pressed against her calf, and she did her best to shift without snapping the thing in half. It worked, and she looked at Sekar.

"What's the plan?"

He spun around, back against bark. "I've got something in mind."

The Onye sat behind, quiet. She couldn't believe how clever they were. Sekar's features shifted, the air around him rippled, and before her was Kar, the man she'd once trusted with her life. No injuries or signs of the last few days showed. She tensed, not liking the memories that washed over her. It had been them against the world for so long, and now the Guardian illusion was only a weapon.

His fiery red gaze met hers. "Stay here."

He stood and brushed off some of the leaves. Death's Sword was strapped to his hip, and the iconic Guardian cloak looked untouched by the terror of their past few days. She grabbed his leg, and he looked down at her.

"Are you telling me that sword is real?"

Sekar laid a hand on the prestigious hilt. "As real as I want it to be." With that, he started his walk toward the palace with a confident stride, head high. Syra watched, the branch uncomfortably digging into her leg. Next to her, the Onye appeared.

They were too close, but she was trying to remind herself that this creature was nearly as old as the God. Zari was what Sekar called her. It was endearing when she removed the stories that inspired nightmares. The Onye looked at her, blinked, and returned to watching Sekar.

The God-turned-Guardian approached the palace and nodded toward the other Guardians. They didn't react, not until he got closer. Then they took a double take, stopped, and opened their mouths to say something. In quick succession, Sekar unsheathed Death's Sword and drove it into the closest one. Madness erupted, but the God had a blade across the second Guardian's throat in a heartbeat. Gor-Geíons flooded the area, coming up from behind in clunky fashion. Unperturbed, Sekar swung Death's Sword around in a clean beheading, killing two instantly. Demon heads rolled, and he turned to the next Geíon as it lunged for him.

The Onye launched from her place and started a run toward the palace. Syra followed, knowing hesitation would get her killed. Her toes dug into hard-packed dirt, and she didn't even stop to help Sekar. This was his plan. Draw the attention to himself and let her get inside.

Zari didn't stop at Sekar like she'd expected. Instead, the Onye kept going. Syra followed, trusting the beast's instincts. Passing the courtyard, they cut through a narrow path overgrown with vines and dead trees. Arches overhead were cracked, and chunks were missing. The ravens that stood watch over the small path were massive. Chips in the stone gave away their age, but even that could not take away from their majestic air. Writing was etched at the base of each, but she didn't stop to read it. The overgrowth of dying branches scratched her, and she squeezed between two oversized trunks that had obliterated the stone ground. Ahead, a wide wooden door stood, covered in iron. Zari sat, waiting. Syra glanced behind to make sure she wasn't being followed. Sekar's mad plan was working. She yanked the latch back and entered the palace.

Must and metal met her nose. She closed the door behind her, studying her surroundings. This was a weapons room. Chains, daggers, swords, half-finished hilts, and an assortment of other things hung about. Leather sheaths and belts accompanied the metal. On the table in front of her was a sheath in the process of being engraved. Oil sat next to the leather, along with a small carving tool and stool. Syra wanted to study the work more—the Old Tongue sigils were partly complete, and done with incredible precision. Instead, she reached up and grabbed a sword that looked somewhat manageable, although nowhere near as heavy as Death's Sword, and ran for the door.

She had no idea where she was going. The hall was plain, lifeless; the only character was the fissures running along the marble walls. She strained her ears, hoping to hear anything that might sound like Zarek.

The hall was uncomfortably hot, and a sheen of sticky sweat coated her skin already. Zari trotted ahead, as light as a feather, but stayed close. The muggy stench of pungent spice made her wrinkle her nose. The air was charged with something otherworldly, and the hairs along her neck stood on end. She gripped the sword tighter, wary. This place was sinister. Whether it was the presence of demons or energy, she couldn't tell yet.

Syra took precautions as she moved through the lower floor of the place. This area was reserved for training, armory, weapons, and even several dusty study rooms that hadn't been used in what appeared to be decades. Deep scratches cut through the flooring and walls—a giant beast—and she studied them long enough to conclude that they couldn't be fresh. That didn't give her any sort of relief. This was the Soul Realm. Anything was possible.

Ahead, a set of spiral stairs in a narrow stone hall. Zari bolted up them, taking two at a time, and disappeared. She waited, hearing a commotion at the top. Snarls, shouts, and a thud as a body struck the floor, hard. Syra followed, muscles tense and sword ready, in case anyone came rushing for her. The closer she got to the next floor, the more commotion she heard. Her heart was in her throat now. No training or assurances could take away the fear trickling down her back and into the pit of her stomach. If she wasn't thinking straight, she'd end up with a sword jutting from her chest.

At the landing, she paused. She could see a hall ahead, this one a bit more decorative, but only from gashes that ran the length of the walls and blood that splattered the floor. Zari's jaw was locked around a Geíon's throat, black blood oozing from her lips and onto the floor. A Guardian was nursing a wound to his shoulder with a hand that was a bloody mess. He took one look at her and tried to stand, then stopped.

She didn't get the chance to harvest Chaos. The Guardian snuck up from her right and lunged, and she bolted from the safety of the stairwell. Syra turned in time to deflect a blow. The impact sent a jolt up her arm, and she quickly shifted her feet to offset the Guardian's strength. All those days of practicing with Zarek suddenly clicked—to fight without mercy was the Death Seeker's motto.

He kicked out, but she saw it coming and jumped, then swung at him. The Guardian stepped back and defended himself but threw a punch with his free hand. Startled, Syra narrowly missed his fist and dragged the edge of her sword across his leg. The opportunity lasted only an instant, and she felt his elbow dig itself into her back where her healing stab wound was. She hissed and kicked out, striking his knee. The Guardian cursed and stumbled back, but her small victory was short-lived as she felt the cold kiss of metal across her arm.

Syra spun around to deflect another swing. This Guardian didn't hesitate, swinging harder and faster. A claw of panic grabbed at her—this was more than she could handle. She had training, but she wasn't a master swordswoman, especially against two Guardians. Already, the muscles along her back and arms were protesting from the nerves and stress of the fight, while these men looked like they could go until the new dawn. Her only goal was to find Zarek, and that meant she needed to get out of this mess.

Mind racing, she ducked to avoid the starved metal of a sword, only to see a boot come her way. Syra dropped to the floor and rolled left. As she did, she stopped just before a Guardian lashed out. The metal dug into his leg, catching him off guard. The opening gave her a chance to jump up and run.

She didn't make it five steps before she was hauled backward. For a fleeting moment, Syra was airborne; then she landed on her ass and slid. The impact ripped the air right out of her and momentarily dazed her. With a huff, she pulled herself back up, flinched at the twang across her body, and raised her sword to defend herself.

As she did, the Guardian in front of her was shoved out of the way by another. Syra never even had a chance to greet Raid before he drove Death's Sword right into the heart of the man beneath him and twisted sharply. The body spasmed and fell quiet. Behind, the other stared. The injured hadn't attempted to attack, only stood there.

A lot of things crossed her mind at once. The uprising that had started in Ashýon was still happening. Guardians were fighting each other, and demons were running rampant. Their screeches could have been heard a league out. Raid and his men's timing couldn't have been more perfect. "How?" she gasped.

The Guardian took a step back just as several more ran toward them. "Portals, My Lady. We knew you'd make it." With that, he turned to face the oncoming assault.

She wanted to thank Raid for showing up, ask how he managed to squeeze his way back into her life, and wanted to beg these Guardians that she was on their side, but all she could do was turn and run. Zari was nowhere to be found now, either feasting on a demon's skull or aiding Sekar.

The sound of clashing metal reached her ears, but she didn't look back. Syra was frazzled. Time was driving a wedge between her and getting Zarek out of here alive. She shoved every door open, saw a handful of Gor-Geíons in one room, and ignored them when they turned her way. If they followed, she only hoped they couldn't keep up.

It was hotter, the air thicker, harder to breathe. Syra traversed to the third floor, shoving a demon over the railing as she went. Elyas was right—the Gor-Geíons were mindless. They slashed without direction, gurgled and clicked, stared with a constant state of hunger. Spineless rule followers. She saw no Ka-Geíons, and she wondered if Elyas didn't work well with others or if Ka-Geíons ruled their own territories, much how kings and queens did. Regardless, she was relieved. Running into two would be a problem. Elyas was enough on his own.

As she reached the top, she stopped and stared.

Double doors. Of course, she should have known. Zarek was in there. In the throne chamber. Shevana wouldn't want it any other way for the grand meeting.

As best as she could, she slowed her breathing and collected herself. A humming filled her ears, but she couldn't place where it was coming from. Commotion continued behind her, but she didn't look back. Syra wasn't sure what to expect, but she knew it would be a fight.

The doors opened without a sound. Before her lay a mangled room. Stone had long since chipped away, tapestries had shredded, and the floor was covered in cracks. The podium didn't have a throne, but Zarek was on his knees there, bloodied and unresponsive. The gash across his neck seeped onto the floor.

Next to him stood Shevana, and in her hand was the Syckl Blade. Skin an ashen gray, eyes and hair solid black—she looked otherworldly. Black lace clung to her thin frame, exposing her bony features. At the sight of Syra, she lit up with maddened glee.

"I was expecting you."

She drove the blade right into Zarek's heart.

The Guardian hardly reacted. His body stiffened, but he was in such poor shape that he simply slumped over and didn't move again. Shevana let him take the blade with him, and it clattered as the hilt banged against the floor. The sound was deafening.

Red Is the Color of Death

Morei's head pounded. The beat was persistent, and he groaned into the armchair he'd passed out in. The festival was supposed to last three days, but he'd already drunk himself sick on the first night, which was not a usual behavior of his. Generally, the king could handle his alcohol—far better than many—but he'd pushed his luck last night. After the heavy drinking on his terrace . . . Actually, he couldn't remember much of what happened after he saw Savage. The evening had gotten away from them all. The introduction of the Wynzer made people wild. He'd never seen so much celebration, even when Geral had won the battle against Diemon.

Someone shifted next to him. Morei blinked, trying to find the strength to move but failing to do so. The day was young, his body sluggish and his tongue parched. Exhaustion threatened to drag him back into slumber, which he welcomed, but the pounding in his head was making it impossible. It was chipping away at the dense fog that lay over his mind with a sharp knife. The body next to him moved again, and he realized they were sharing a seat together. The king couldn't even remember getting here. That was concerning.

The thought sobered him just enough to sit up. His head swam, and he blinked rapidly. When he finally looked to his right, he saw Isla, half her body lying over the arm of the chair. The position looked terribly uncomfortable, and he grimaced. She would feel that when she finally woke.

Why they were sharing a chair was still in question, but he was willing to bet she didn't know either. The king scanned the room. He didn't recognize it. A bed and the normal amenities for royalty were here—large closet, bathroom, terrace, and more decorations than necessary. Across from them, sprawled out on the table, was a soldier he didn't recognize—no, wait. That was Leo.

Passed out on the floor was the chancellor. Rhys was snoring, and Morei kicked out with his boot to hit the man in the shoulder. The impact startled the chancellor, and he grumbled and woke, but he barely looked in Morei's direction before he rolled over once more.

The bloodied soldier from the night before stirred awake on the chair across from him. It looked like someone had attempted to clean the grime off his tunic but failed miserably. Dried, bloodied cloths lay on the floor.

That pounding was constant, and it echoed with a high pitch that was increasing in urgency. Morei rubbed his head and tried to stand, but a jarring thought shattered his hazy reality. The pounding wasn't coming from his head.

Those were bells. Caster's bells were ringing.

"Shit!" Rhys scrambled, and nearly knocked himself unconscious against the low table. The king watched as the chancellor caught himself just in time and looked around. "Is that—"

"Yes," Morei said. He stood and swayed, rubbing his face fiercely. The timing of this could not be worse. Every city followed a strong code, regardless of culture, religion, or ethics: continuous bells meant danger. "We need to move." He turned around and saw Isla still lying over the chair arm. He kicked her legs, and she startled awake.

"Good morning, princess," he said. "It appears we've got an issue."

She blinked, dazed, and he reached down and hauled her up by the arm. It was time to move. Morei didn't care about the soldiers—they would find their way. He needed Edwin. Nothing sobered a man up faster than the imminent threat of war.

"Ouch." Isla yanked her arm free and shot him a glare. He didn't care. If they lived through the day, maybe he'd apologize.

The chancellor was already on his way out. Just as he was reaching for the door, it swung open.

"Just the man I wanted to see," the king lied. It was Bennett. The second-in-command looked frazzled—not good. Behind him, soldiers were shifting and stumbling, muttering and asking questions that went ignored. "What do you have?"

Bennett took a massive breath, like he'd been running and needed air. His dark hair was untamed. "The scouters never even saw them coming, Your Majesty. They came overnight, no lights, not a sound or warning—"

"Get to the point." Though he already knew, and his muscles tensed. They were supposed to have almost a moon cycle to prepare, but between the warning and their arrival, it had only been a few days. They would be lucky if half the men could stand after last night. That didn't even include all the citizens who were probably passed out in the streets.

For the first time since Morei had met him, Bennett looked completely defeated, and the battle hadn't even started. "The Red Queens are here."

Morei made his way to the door, past everyone. The orders came out instinctively. They would reach Edwin's ears. "Bennett, I'm confident you'll get this to Edwin. Get men on the wall, towers, and coast. Light the fire pits, drench arrows, pull the cannons out and get those set up as fast as possible." He stopped in the hall. "How far are they from the coast?"

"A half league, but approaching fast."

"That gives us just enough time to scare them a little," Morei said, continuing on. Footsteps followed, but he didn't stop to turn and see who it was. "Were there any updates on the Ly'rün?"

Bennett was to his left now. He looked more put together already, which was a relief. The king knew a nasty man thrived underneath the title, and he needed him to come out and take charge. Edwin wouldn't have chosen him for his compassion and thoughtfulness. The commander was brutal—Bennett had to be similar. "A few bottles were recovered, Your Majesty."

Morei's response came fast and cold. "We can hold off on the proper titles right now, Bennett. I'm more worried about the Red Queens than how I'm addressed."

"Okay."

They turned down another hall, and Morei got a good look at the Merrél Sea. He stopped, stunned. Ten ships were approaching, flags raised, led by the largest, clearly the captain's ship. They were covered in red and different imagery that was hard to decipher, and he wasn't sure he wanted to. The flags showed skulls wearing crowns on a crimson background—simple but strong.

And behind those ten were another dozen. Those remained unmoving, waiting. The Red Queens were preparing to assault the city in waves. He didn't need to be an expert in pirates to see the strategy.

"By the Gods," Rhys mumbled next to him.

"You told me a full moon," Morei said. He couldn't hide his anger. "*A full moon.*"

Rhys gestured at the sea. "This isn't normal behavior. Never have I seen so many Queens in one place. My apologies if my usual knowledge failed." The last bit came out thick with icy sarcasm.

"It did," the king snapped. "And if we live through this, I expect this mistake never to happen again, or I'm going to think you lied to me about your expertise. I'll have your body displayed for the world to see."

The muscle in the chancellor's jaw ticced. Morei saw the snarky comment coming a league away. "Hold your response, Rhys. I'm not in the mood to hear why you're the greatest. I might give you to the Queens." He turned back to Bennett. The man's clothes, up close, looked covered in stains. An inhale confirmed it had to be ale. They probably all smelled like shit.

"Go. I don't know why you're still standing here." Bennett nodded, coming to life. As he ran, Morei yelled, "The Ly'rün! I want the coast visible from Diyră." The flames would keep the pirates at bay . . . if the potent mixture proved effective.

The king surveyed the sea again. The Red Queens were racing to the shore. Smaller ships appeared as well, coming out of nowhere. The palace was too close to the sea, a nightmare for warfare. The others were covering the half league with impressive speed. They'd be on land before he made it to the battle. Already, he could see figures moving on the main deck with fierce precision. He patted himself—the sword. Morei needed his sword, but it was on the other side of the palace. He had a dagger in his boot, and he leaned over and yanked it free. When he stood, Isla and Rhys were staring.

He motioned at the hall with his dagger. "We need weapons and armor. There's a good chance these Queens will make land."

"There's a staff hall just over here," the princess said. Her voice didn't tremble like he'd thought it would. The boldness looked good on her—that was how a queen should act. "We can take it. It will save us time."

Morei saw Rhys's face twist in absolute horror before he felt the impact. Stone and glass fractured, and the force tore the king right off the ground. His head and shoulders hit the wall, and pieces of debris struck his body at random. Morei rolled and covered his head. He felt more rubble land around him. The sound was deafening, like a crack of thunder, but he didn't hear anyone scream.

When the floor stopped shaking and no more rubble or glass fell, he slowly raised his head. The hall was in ruins. The gaping hole to his right, where they'd been standing, was extensive. Half the floor was missing, and the chilly morning breeze shoved dust aside. The king could barely make sense of it before he heard the moans from his left.

Rhys shoved pieces of rubble off him. The chancellor was covered in dust, scratches covered his face and hands, and he looked visibly disoriented. Isla was on him instantly, helping Rhys to stand. A piece of her dress remained pinned underneath a large chunk of the wall that had narrowly missed her legs. A laceration across her calf bled profusely, but she didn't seem to notice it—or didn't feel the pain yet. Adrenaline was a powerful motivator in the face of Death.

Morei stood, legs weak from the jarring assault, and leaned against the wall to his left. His right hand was covered in blood, but he couldn't place the pain. He patted himself, confused, only to find that the cut was along his forearm. The tunic, so precisely fitted to him, was now ruined. He flexed his hand. At least it would work just fine.

"We need to move," Isla insisted. "Get to lower ground."

Shouts followed, but his mind was scattered. The explosion had rattled him to the bones. He'd seen death, fought in battle, and ripped the life right out of a man, but he'd never experienced anything like that. The feeling he felt underneath all the adrenaline and frustration was fear, and he hated that.

The bells ceased, and another thunderous boom echoed. Two bell towers had just been destroyed, debris from them tumbling to the ground. He looked at the shore to see a measly fire—a poor attempt at the Ly'rün—and many soldiers already in combat with the Red Queens. More ships were anchoring, with pirates dashing through the shallow water and into the city. He watched fire arrows fly, but their aim was frenzied, and he couldn't blame them. It seemed almost comical that Morei would wish for his Geral men now, but he did. Those men knew how to act under stress. These Caster soldiers were like scattering rats. If the city didn't fall from the explosives that the Red Queens were using, it would be from their piss-poor training.

This wasn't what he'd envisioned—the lack of control and the grotesque appearances of these pirates. He'd hoped for rusted swords, no armor, clumsy fighting. What he saw instead were men and women covered in red and black paint, including their faces, their hair braided with bones. They wore simple leather for protection, and some didn't even have that. Their weapons were serrated, their fighting animalistic—quick, assertive, and brutal. Soldiers fell all around, while very few Red Queens met the hand of Death.

Morei could see the end already. Not even Geral could have held up against this kind of fight. He could see the devastation of this city as clearly as he saw the destruction of the Geral citizens when he took their lives. This was a losing battle. The Red Queens had sent their warning strategically so that the council didn't react immediately. They knew Rhys would promise a full moon; they knew the Festival of Seasons was days away. This was their plan all along, and he couldn't help but admire the tenacity. Underneath all the anger, he respected whoever had made that decision.

But then his attention turned to Rhys. The chancellor had failed to give him any sort of valuable information. He'd known the Red Queens were dangerous, but he hadn't predicted this. Plants were dangerous. Some animals, too. Even the occasional madman. But the Red Queens were malicious barbarians.

He needed to be on the field with those men. Stuck up here, he was no better than the cowards who ran. The king itched to get there, and his boots were already carrying him away from Isla and Rhys. The Red Queens wanted a battle? He would give them war.

A hand latched on to him, forcing Morei to turn and face the princess. "Where are you going?"

Rhys was already leaving, halfway down the other side of the hall where they'd originally come from. Of course he was. Thieves never had backbones. The chancellor didn't even look back, focusing on the sea and any more possible cannons.

Morei tugged himself free from Isla's iron grip. There she was again, forcing herself into his matters like she cared. If she wasn't careful, she would be on the receiving end of his compulsion, inflamed by the battle. Morei almost laughed, thrilled to finally submit to his darkest needs, but instead, he gestured to the gaping hole in the palace and hissed, "To end this."

Forsaken Sunsets

Disbelief was the first emotion Syra felt. For what felt like an eternity, she just stared at Zarek, waiting for him to move. The Syckl Blade jutted out, ugly and final. Words left her mouth, but they were without sound. It felt like only yesterday they were walking the forest path, sparring and talking about the realms. When she'd awoken in Ashýon, her only concern had been reaching Zarek. He was owed rescuing after everything he'd done for her. Friends. That made them loyal to each other. They'd traveled across Diyră, trained her, and stood by her side when the waves of this sea grew too violent. She'd acted without thought, never once imagining she'd be too late. No matter what happened, they would make it to the palace in time to save Zarek.

And now, it was over. The reality before her was so overwhelming that she felt nothing. Time stood still, the sounds of the fight beyond this chamber deafened by her heartbeat. No matter how hard she tried to process what was happening, she couldn't.

Shevana didn't even react. The woman seemed just as surprised as Syra, hunched over the body of a man she'd spent centuries with.

Noises returned. Metal clashing and shouts. The air remained still, stuck, unwilling to stir. Syra's fingers tingled as her mind was bombarded with a hundred emotions, exasperation being the first to greet her.

The humming from earlier returned with a vengeance, becoming a deafening ring. Shevana shifted and said something, but Syra couldn't hear. What followed next was rage. So raw and unmanageable that the hot emotion engulfed her immediately. Her hands shook, but she couldn't move. Instead, her knees buckled, and she let loose a scream.

Everything was released. Her grief, disappointment, fear, all of it. Syra felt Chaos rupture all around her, coming to life without warning. The ground shook, chunks of the walls fell, and wide gaps tore open across the floor. Shevana stumbled, struck by rubble.

When she finally stopped, she blinked, smothered in sorrow. It had all been for nothing. No world existed without Zarek. He'd been her rock, her mentor, her friend. To walk out of here without him felt impossible. More blood was on her hands, another person who got too close and was killed for it, and now she was left to pick up the pieces. The Guardians had nicknamed her the Goddess of Death. Now she knew why.

The leader straightened and tugged at the torn fabric of her sleeve from where the rubble had torn it. "I know what he did," Shevana whispered, never looking away from Zarek's body. "I know he guided Nala's soul to the Afterlife. He betrayed me." She pulled harder on her sleeve. Lace broke free, but she didn't seem to care. "He did it all behind my back. Everything we built together, he walked away from. And all for what?" She laughed, a sound akin to glass shattering. "Nothing. It brought him nothing."

This woman had taken everything from her. Enraged, Syra lunged for Shevana, crossing the distance in just a few short strides. The queen sidestepped, and Syra swung her sword, reckless but desperate to land a cut. Shevana sidestepped again, avoiding the weapon, so Syra swung faster, following her every step. The woman before her showed no fear. Syra kicked out, striking Shevana in the knee and sending her stumbling. Emboldened, she drove the blade down, but the sword halted in Shevana's hand.

Metal failed to slice skin. The force of the impact jarred Syra's bones, and she froze, surprised by the sudden turn. The queen straightened and closed her hand around the blade. In one snap, metal shattered, decorating the floor in silver crystals. Shevana tilted her head, a predator studying her prey, and raised a hand. As she did, Syra lashed out with the broken end of her sword, jamming it into flesh. In one quick sweep, Shevana ripped the hilt from her grip and tossed it to the side. Syra didn't have a chance to recalculate her plan before the queen raised her hand again and the air was sucked right out of her

Syra buckled, knees striking marble and sword fragments. Black tendrils of smoke emerged from the ground, slipping around her hands, icy. As they contacted her skin, her mind felt like it was being torn in two. The tighter they squeezed, the harsher her mind felt. Muscles protested, as if her limbs were being ripped apart, and her bones screamed, bending at unnatural a ngles.

Chaos blossomed, burning her from the inside out. She grappled for it, wheezing, her vision turning gray. Just as she latched on to the force, she was tossed back. Her body slid across the floor, and as she came to a stop, Shevana raised her hand again.

"I wouldn't if I were you," she said. Her flesh was untouched from where Syra jammed the end of the blade. It was impossible. She'd known the woman to be capable of a lot, but she hadn't planned for this. The sinister touch of the black tendrils left a stomach-turning mark on her thoughts—Ön'grusah. Different from Dark Energy's countless voices that hummed with contact, this was menacing and devoid of the many dead who screamed to be heard. Shevana's features weren't a result of anything else.

Syra opened her mouth, but Shevana shot her a deathly glare. The pit of those black orbs was endless. Any closer, and she feared she would get lost in whatever madness called that place home. "You're just like Nala. Always running from your problems. While you avoided this realm, I kept it safe. While your mother bedded mortal men and lied about who she really was, I protected this realm. And now you come here, thinking you have any place?"

Shevana took a single step forward, then stopped. Syra's throat was scratchy, her eyes blurred, and her body was fighting tooth and nail to stay upright. Anger kept her alert, listening for any sound of approaching boots. She needed Sekar now more than ever.

"You have done nothing but ruin this realm," Syra hissed, buying time. "Your men aren't even loyal to—"

"Yes, they are," Shevana snapped. "They are the children of my hard work. Intentionally chosen to carry the Guardian name forward. I would have not kept them alive otherwise."

Raid's words burned a hole in her head. If they spoke out, she would have killed them. They'd spent all this time living a lie to stay alive. Waiting for her. Shevana was too deranged to see otherwise.

"Elyas is going to betray you," Syra said. It was a pathetic attempt to get a reaction, and it failed.

"That's lovely," the woman replied, tilting her head. "Demons say a lot of things. Did he also tell you he wanted you by his side?" She took another step forward, then paused again. Syra's heart was in her throat. Chaos crept back into her fingers like she was sifting through thick mud. "Demons are power-hungry, always seeking a way to better position themselves. They'll say anything if it means they get the upper hand."

Zarek was dead because of her. A result of this madness. "Did you have to kill him?"

The woman tensed. "Yes, I did have to kill him. I don't tolerate insubordinate behavior."

It was more than that, though. Shevana hated him for what he'd done to her, but she wouldn't share that with Syra. Words failed her. This was the woman she'd run from for so long, and now here with her, with Zarek dead, she felt nothing. All of her was wrapped up in the harrowing grief that simmered just below the surface.

"What will you do when you get what you want?" she asked. Shevana raised her brow. "This is it, isn't it? End me, keep your control, and what, a happy ending?" Before the woman could speak, she motioned to her surroundings and continued. "There is nothing after this. The realms are falling apart, and you don't care."

"I do care." Shevana faced her fully, hideous. "You have no idea what I've done to keep this realm alive. All this was happening before I dragged Elyas into this. I have been trying to stop it."

What was she talking about?

"Fools. All of you," Shevana spat. "This mess you've made will ruin everything." She pointed one long finger at Syra. "The realm was sick centuries ago, but we didn't know why. One day, the sky wasn't as blue as it should have been, and the leaves died. Nothing in our texts warned us of this or how to counter it. Some of the youngest Guardians were killed overnight by Honuyál." She tossed her hands up. "Beasts became violent, demons crossed into our territory, defying our treaties, and we had no way of knowing how far this sickness would stretch. Do you think I wanted this? Do you truly believe that I wanted this realm to be what it is now?"

She waited for an answer. Slowly, Syra shook her head. Everything she knew of this woman made her out to be the villain, and now Shevana was telling her otherwise. The queen spoke with so much passion. Had the truth gotten lost? Or was this just a wild lie to earn Syra's sympathy, so that she could slit her throat when her back was turned?

"My father ruled this realm for six centuries before I took over," Shevana continued. "This family has reigned for as long as the Gods have lived. Why would I throw that all away?"

Syra was dumbfounded, struggling to find the words. Under Shevana's intense glare, her mind moved like sludge. "Control," she finally said. "You haven't tried—"

"*I have tried!*" Shevana yelled. Syra flinched, sinking further into herself. "I am doing everything I can to keep this realm standing. Has it ever occurred to you that I might be trying to get the answers we need to secure this realm? I've sacrificed everything I am for that."

None of this was adding up. Shevana was delusional. She'd poisoned Nala, Syra's mother; she'd burned Guardian material and killed Zarek. "But you want me dead."

Behind, Elyas approached Shevana from around a pillar. Syra reeled. Now was not the time to deal with the demon. He didn't slow in his walk, his eyes locked on the queen, who shook her head and scoffed at what Syra had said. Only once did they meet Syra's, just as he unsheathed a long, serrated black dagger and drove it right through Shevana's back and straight through her heart.

The tip of the weapon broke free from the front, tearing fabric. Elyas twisted, and Shevana gasped, fumbling for the man behind her. The demon yanked the blade free and drove the bloodied metal across her neck, then did so again several more times until he was able to rip her head off.

When he was done, he looked right at Syra. "I never liked her."

Centuries for the Blade

I t had only been a few days since Cyrus had left Delion and flown into the forest depths. So many stories about the Pynsole Mountains filled the pages of the books he read. Lakes as deep as the sea, black soil broken up by the bright green landscape, and fjords that overlooked a horizon that no man had ever crossed. The world was big, and many had set sail long ago to explore the primary countries everyone knew today. But on the southern side of Creitón, where land met sea—no man had ever set sail from there and returned. Storytellers called it the end of the world. Some said that ancient beasts long driven from their homes lived in hordes there. A few even said a portal lay in those dark waters that led straight to the Soul Realm. Cyrus didn't believe the last. Too many questions. He believed in the impossible, but with boundaries. A portal at the bottom of the sea was too much.

Still, he did let his thoughts wander. If people got sucked into a different realm, would they appear on the surface of another lake? Cyrus had never given the Soul Realm much thought. Properly, he'd been raised to reference it as the realm of the dead. It was a far-fetched idea that some realm out there hosted the dead. Many believed in it, though he teetered on uncertainty. It was hard to believe in something he'd never seen before. He made a note to ask Hyle the next time they spoke. The God would know more about the matter.

"Are you ready?"

"Hm?" Cyrus wiped his mouth with the cloth. Sleep did wonders. Mind alert, his body felt stronger, and his hand didn't hurt as it had. Perhaps Crescent Lake had done something to him. He was dressed in his normal attire but with a small bag to carry the egg in. Made of leather and with leaves for strings, it sat over his shoulder. He continued to try and prod the dragon whenever he could, reassuring her that everything would be all right. She seemed to acknowledge him, but he was never entirely sure. The night before, at Crescent Lake, was the closest he'd gotten to her, but after they'd pulled themselves free from the spell, she'd closed off again. Sozar told him not to worry—Cyrus was not her Rider.

It was easier said than done.

"Yes," he finally answered, and stood from his place on the ground. The table was cleaned, save for his small plate of cheese, bread, and tea. Yu and Unshi had insisted on providing him with a meal before he left, but he'd refused another feast. After some back and forth, they'd finally settled on the bread. He was still troubled about their conversation last night, though Unshi had showed no problems in the morning. The people of Venkar were strange, and he was glad to leave. Sozar awaited him, already saddled.

Chavi gave him a good look over. She patted his arms, tugged at the tunic he was wearing, and even examined the fur of his cloak. The warmth in this house made it uncomfortable, but he knew once he got back in the air, it would be chilly. His gloves were on, the Rider's Sword on his hip. He was ready.

"You are a proper Dragon Rider," she told him. If she was aware of any tension, she didn't show it.

Cyrus stared, unsure what that meant.

"Underprepared for everything," she mused, and gestured at the food. "Didn't eat all of it or drink your tea. What if you get stranded? What if you aren't in a warm bed tonight?"

"That's the reputation? I flew across the world with hardly anything. Ate more fish than I could ever admit to, and slept on pieces of a shipwreck when I was desperate. I can manage a day's flight back to Delion."

The woman raised an eyebrow, clearly unsatisfied. "You are our future, our chance at a new era. Don't mess it up because of foolishness." She smacked his arm like a sister would to a brother and motioned for him to follow. "Come, my father awaits you."

Cyrus took one last look around the small home. It was cozy, perfect for him. Life would be simple here, and he wouldn't want for much. Something even smaller than this would do just fine, so long as he could have a fire, a bed, and a place to store his belongings. Here, in Venkar, all his problems felt leagues out of reach. The charm of the hidden city made his heart beat a little faster and a genuine smile tug at his lips. Here, the world couldn't touch him. But once he stepped out and back into the saddle, Henry, war, the pressing needs of the people, the eggs, Üg'ahn—all of it came back with crushing force.

You have me. Sozar's warmth smothered the frigid reality awaiting them. He looked away from Chavi long enough to collect himself, messing with the clasp of his sheath. No matter how much everyone believed in him, he was still struggling to do the same.

Thank you, he replied. With a deep breath, he raised his head again to Chavi. "After you."

She nodded. If the woman had any idea how nervous he was about what lay ahead, she didn't show it. They walked to the front door, and she slipped on her plain shoes, which looped over one toe. Cyrus already had his boots on. Stepping out into the morning sun, he found long shadows still stretching across their surroundings. Dew clung to the leaves, and he was happy to have the cloak after all. It was cooler this morning than it had been when he arrived.

The small city slept, with only a few already about their business. They waved and showed their respects but did not approach. It was nice to simply walk without the world breathing down his neck.

Ahead, toward the city's entrance, he could see Sozar with a small crowd. Not many, but Yu, Unshi, Kerí, and another woman he didn't recognize were all there. In Unshi's hand was something wrapped in red cloth. Another gift, Cyrus assumed. He had been given more gifts in the last season than his entire life before.

The dragon still had some flecks of paint left over on his scales. The people had taken time to wash him this morning before his departure, which was thoughtful. Cyrus enjoyed the festivities but didn't want Sozar flying around covered in different colors. Alaric would never let that die. The king already wanted a statue. Best to not give him any other ideas.

Venkar held a secret that the world would start a war for. Üg'ahn lay nestled away in the mountains, protecting a clutch of dragon eggs that would change everything. If anyone found out, he feared the consequences. This pristine and peaceful city would become the scene of a massacre. He trusted Üg'ahn could fight—no dragon could live this long otherwise—but it shouldn't come to that.

Alaric would need to know. The king was faithful, but Cyrus hesitated with how much to tell. Alaric had pledged the city to Cyrus's cause, whatever that may be, and he knew the king stood by those words. But to what end? If Cyrus showed up with a dozen dragon eggs, would Alaric change his tone? Any city that housed that many eggs would become the most powerful place in the world. Razan housed a mere two eggs and thought themselves the keepers of life itself.

Yet the Yavinks had these and did not seek power, more land, resources, nothing. They enjoyed what they had, did not start wars; they kept the peace. There wasn't a single battle in history that spoke of them. To the rest of the world, they were ghosts, a purposeful move to secure their place in this new e ra.

"Chavi," he said as they walked. They were closing in on the small crowd, and Sozar was eager to stretch his wings, but he needed confirmation. "You have protected this secret for hundreds of summers. I understand that, but I struggle to grasp why you have no concerns that this could all change. What if someone exposed the truth? There would be a war."

She sighed. "I imagine to the outside world, it is strange to see us. We have kept Üg'ahn a secret for centuries, along with what he protects. But you miss why we do it in the first place. Do you know what that is?"

They were too close, and he didn't want to waste time. He wanted to know how similar her answer would be to her father's. "Tell me."

"Trust. We are a city built on a culture of trust. We do not seek war, because what would that do? It would break trust. We don't tell others what we know, because it would go against our entire culture. We are a proud people, Rider, and that means we take our values seriously."

The explanation left a hollow feeling in his stomach. He needed more, like an oath, or guards, or anything. Cyrus had once believed in trust too, and it had nearly gotten him killed twice already. He also doubted these people trusted Üg'ahn.

"I know you don't believe me," Chavi observed. "I don't expect you to. But I do ask that you trust me and my people."

At this point, Cyrus would have handed all his values over for a sliver of certainty, not that that was much. Chavi might have been ignorant enough to call it trust, but he knew better. Hospitality wrapped up in the underlying goal of protection and survival. The Yavinks would stop at nothing to keep their secrets, and he knew that included him.

Unshi stepped forward as they arrived. "Do you have everything you need, Cyrus?"

He nodded. "I do."

The man's gray eyes swept across the small group, a shade brighter than they'd been last night, landing finally on Sozar. The dragon was becoming more and more of an observer every day. It was shocking to Cyrus to see how much he'd changed. Sozar was mature, thoughtful when needed, and chose to listen rather than interject. He could take a lesson like that.

"We have spent many generations wondering when we would meet another Dragon Rider. I admit I didn't believe it would be my lifetime," Unshi said. "To have brought you and Sozar here is an honor I will never forget. Your story will be shared for generations. Our promise to you is to ensure everyone remembers Cyrus Wynter and Sozar, who changed the world."

Cyrus wanted to disappear. The pressure was already mounting, and they hadn't even left yet. "Your people have given me everything I could ever need." He couldn't get to the saddle fast enough.

The man nodded. "Hyle chose wisely."

The God's name sat between them. Once upon a time, Cyrus had hardly paid the Gods attention. His prayers were inconsistent at best, and he spent more time trying to prove to himself that the deities could be real rather than believing. Yet now, he spoke of them freely, knew one by name, and couldn't wait to see Hyle again.

"You say you have everything you need," Unshi continued, unperturbed by the silence. If he sensed Cyrus's anxiousness to depart, he made no show of it. He raised the item in his hand and slowly unfolded the cloth. "But you do not have a Crescent Blade."

He unveiled a dagger the length of his forearm. The hilt was narrow, made of dark leather and braided leaves, and the pommel was flat. The blade stood out, vivid. It was pink, translucent, and wavy, narrow with a sharp tip. Cyrus could see the red cloth reflected through the blade.

"These do not come by often," Unshi continued. "Once a decade, perhaps. It is dependent on the growth of the Crescent stone. We have scouters who dive into Crescent Lake in search of a crystal long enough to work. When we do, we take it and begin a rigorous process to cure it for wielding." He raised it to Cyrus. "This is our gift to you."

Cyrus opened his mouth to speak but failed to produce words. He couldn't accept this. He already had a Rider's Sword. Accepting such a heartfelt gift when one of the Yavinks could use it gave him pause. "I wouldn't wish to take this if you say it takes so long to make," he started, but Unshi shook his head.

"We wouldn't want it any other way. The land gives to us when she is ready, and we are patient. To us, a decade is necessary. A gift made in a matter of days does not possess the same value as one forged for summers. A Crescent Blade is not made simply for entertainment. If there is no one set to receive, we do not dive into Crescent Lake. Each crystal is taken with the intent to give to the right recipient. We made this blade knowing one day it would be given to the Rider who stepped into this city."

Any argument that Cyrus was ready to give shriveled up and died on his tongue. He nodded numbly, knowing well enough that he would never win this. Unshi motioned, and his son produced a sheath for the blade. Kerí offered it to Cyrus. The sheath was as plain as the hilt.

"A Crescent Blade never breaks," the father explained. "You will find the blade can also store massive amounts of Light Energy. Perfect for any situation when you find yourself exhausted or without the ability to draw from your own lifeforce. It is not intended for battle. In our culture, a Crescent Blade should never touch blood, but that does not mean we expect you to uphold this tradition. The world is different out there, and if you find yourself in a situation where this blade is all you have, we hope it is enough to keep you alive."

Gently, Cyrus reached for the weapon. The surrounding world had gone completely still. His breath was loud in his ears, and he was certain everyone in the vicinity could hear his heartbeat. Cyrus knew he couldn't let these people down. They respected him so much, and he owed it to them all to prove their dedication meant something. The egg, the sword, the Crescent Blade, and Üg'ahn were all pieces to an identity that Cyrus wanted to embrace.

The weapon fit perfectly in his hand, as if they'd sized it intentionally for him. The hum of the energy already stored in the stone met his ears and turned his blood icy with anticipation. He'd never felt such power from a weapon. Not even the Rider's Sword made him feel this way, It was incredibly light, and when he dragged his other fingers across the blade itself, his hand tingled.

"Thank you," he mustered. These people were complex but passionate. "This means a lot to me."

Those words were exactly what everyone wanted to hear. Subtly, he watched those around Unshi relax. Unshi's shoulders slumped as well—he looked visibly relieved. "You always have a home here. We will continue to protect the eggs until Üg'ahn or you say otherwise."

He nodded, although he couldn't quite figure out how he and Üg'ahn wound up in the same sentence concerning the eggs. "I trust Üg'ahn's judgment." The words sounded hollow to his ears. He wanted to. Every part of him wanted to believe the ancient dragon knew best, but he knew better. Everyone had a motive, a reason they did what they did, and he worried the ancient dragon's was contorted by madness and desperation. "When the time is right, I will return for the others. For now, I need to have a strategy—and a place these dragons can call home."

Unshi squeezed his shoulder. "That is what the Rider Federation is for." He let go then and stepped aside. "Safe flying, Sea Flyer. We will see you and Sozar soon."

The Yavinks filed away with slight bows to their heads. Cyrus stared, baffled. He'd assumed there would be a bigger goodbye, maybe even a word from Chavi.

Sozar nudged his arm. *Let us be off.*

The dragon's insistence forced his attention back to their situation. *I thought you liked it here.*

Sozar sank his talons into the soil. *What dragon enjoys not being able to see the sky fully?* He said it in jest, but Cyrus scoffed. He sheathed the weapon and looked at the belt.

"Ah." A spot stood out to him where he could tie the sheath to. The new belt he'd been given had more holes for tying pouches to. The heavier weapons, like the Rider's Sword, were attached with a combination of metal and leather to hold the weight. But this lightweight dagger only had leaf-made strings. He hoped they held, and he made a mental note about having the leather master test them back in Delion.

Cyrus quickly tied the sheath on, nestled between his coin and snack pouch. Content, he ascended Sozar, then looked back one last time. Chavi was standing with a small crowd of children and mothers, waving. The small gesture made his heart swell. He waved back.

Master of Fire

Morei's heart was in his throat. He could practically taste the thrill, sweet and as smooth as Kendell's Milk. This was where he thrived, where no one questioned how many were killed by his hands. The last time he'd stepped onto the battlefield, he'd been shunned and ostracized. The rejection drove him over the edge. But he couldn't stand by and watch this city fall because of mistakes he never had control over or the opportunity to correct. Drexis had made horrible decisions, and he would not lose everything he had worked so hard for because of that reckless king.

These soldiers needed him. Caster was giving it their all to defend themselves, but none of it would matter if something drastic wasn't done. The Red Queens made sure of it.

Morei had fetched a weapon and grabbed some gauntlets and bracers, along with basic leather armor found in the weapons chamber. It was snug but would work for the occasion. Black and silver, scuffed up, it looked like it was in for repairs, but he didn't see any major damage that would cause him to pause. The priority was to deflect a sword, not fashion. As he ran, he strapped the leather gauntlets on. The wound on his forearm hissed, mad, as he tightened the bracer. He even grabbed a random sword because he didn't want to waste time getting to his chamber on the other side of the palace.

When he reached the bottom, he ran into a soldier. The man was coming back in, his skin slick with grime and blood. He had a slight limp. Morei stopped him, and the man gawked, clearly not expecting to see the king.

"Sir— Your Majesty?"

"Your men. What's the numbers?"

The soldier stared and shook his head. "I, um, I don't know."

"Why are you here and not out there?" His temper already had the better of him.

The soldier raised his broken sword, as if that was an answer. Young and foolish. This must have been one of the untrained ones Edwin had spoken of.

Morei scoffed. "Grab a dead man's next time. You're wasting time up here."

He exited the palace, keeping a steady pace as he left the courtyard and ran down the main street. This close to the coast, he could smell the metallic tinge of blood and salt from the sea. Shouts, the clash of metal, and the boom of cannons assaulted him from either side. A lot of people ran the opposite direction, but he saw quite a few citizens grabbing whatever weapon they had and running to the fight. Broken pieces of homes, chairs, iron pots, and more. No armor, and people of all ages. A few glanced his way, and he met their gaze, proud. This was the Caster he knew. Merciless, stubborn, and resourceful. Not the frenzied soldiers he'd seen before the palace hall was st ruck.

A whistle met his ears. Morei looked up in time to see an oncoming boulder. He cut left and was shoved into the wall by a soldier. Rubble met his back painfully, and the wind tore through the narrow alley. When he looked back, a large hole in the street greeted him. People peeked out from the other side through a door barely on its hinges.

Morei met the eyes of two soldiers. They were young, barely men, and based on their frantic and abrupt movements, they probably didn't even know how to handle a sword. More of the untrained. Their armor was coated in blood, and one was nursing a laceration across his neck. Lucky miss, he realized. This soldier should have been dead. Instead, he'd acted to save the king's life.

"You're injured," he said. The young man flinched as Morei got closer. His reputation preceded him, and he hadn't even made it to the field yet. "How does it look down there?"

The less wounded soldier cleared his throat and wiped sweat from his brow. "It's bad. Like, really bad. We're outnumbered four to one. Whenever we kill one, two more show up. Bennett's dead, my brother was killed—it's just a slaughter. We don't know what to do."

The man with the bleeding neck motioned to the street, keeping one hand on the wound. His pressure was poor. Blood seeped freely from between his fingers, dripping down his armor and arm, and he looked pale. "We never had a chance to get to the shore before they were there."

Fury as hot as the Hazar Desert blistered his veins. This cruel trick from the Red Queens had already gone too far. They'd acted out of line, betrayed this city's trust, and ruptured whatever deal they'd originally possessed with Caster. They knew Drexis was dead—the message had been sent loud and clear—but they'd chosen to attack rather than make peace. Morei would do everything in his power to make sure they feared this city for the rest of time.

Shouts, and another boom. A new structure was collapsing. Screams followed. Morei continued toward the coast. His boots crunched on gravel, debris, and cobblestone. Where cannons struck, the dead lay in wait to be taken. He passed a cluster of men and women hardly recognizable by the way their skulls had been caved in.

The Ly'rün was out. He found shattered pieces of jars as his boots met blood-soaked sand. The putrid scent of rot clung to the air, and he saw black smoke billowing upward from where he had originally seen the toxic bomb released, staining the sky. The grip on his sword tightened. The metal was curved and wide, not his usual serrated family weapon, but this would do.

He made his way to the heart of the battle, where the forces were locked. Morei took his time, surveying the situation and preparing himself. Adrenaline raced through him, fueled by the part of him reserved only for these moments. This was where he thrived. Here, on the battlefield, nobody questioned Death or her methods.

The ships loomed as close as they dared. Morei had seen them from the palace, but they were menacing from here, where they dwarfed all men. Several were parallel with the coast, and he could see the paint-colored pirates loading their cannons. On the other side, in Caster towers that had yet to be destroyed, men fired flaming arrows and launched their own cannons back.

This was *his* city. Morei hadn't traveled all this way and killed the king for pirates to take it all away. He was born to rule, and that wouldn't end today. He refused. Drexis's decisions were haunting him, even now, and he was determined not to meet his end at the hand of some dead man's mistakes.

The nearest Red Queen met *her* end instantly. She was looting a soldier for his weapons, and Morei drove his blade right through her back. Up close, it was more than just being drenched in red and black paint. Designs covered these pirates. Culturally significant, he assumed; he would have to ask Rhys later if he didn't kill the chancellor first.

A shout came from behind, and Morei turned to deflect another serrated sword. The strength of the swing made his bones rattle. The king slid his weapon to the hilt of the enemy's sword and, in one quick sweep, disarmed the pirate. It was a classless move, but Morei didn't care about the code of fighting. Looting the dead was as low as one got on the field. These pirates didn't have a code, only a desire to see Caster fall, no matter what. He shoved the bloodied blade right into the enemy's exposed chest. So much for armor.

Two dead, but the swarm of these Queens mounted. Morei saw Caster soldiers fighting as hard as they could, but from afar, he could see the shifting tone. They knew they were losing. The goal of keeping the enemy on the coastline was failing miserably, and he watched as a handful of Red Queens broke off and ran across the port and into the city. He saw a soldier cornered by three pirates. He ran over, shoving a Queen to the ground as she raised her blade with the soldier preoccupied. Morei kicked her and drove the blade straight through her neck. As he did so, he felt his leg sear with the icy kiss of metal.

More shouts. Another boom. The madness was deafening, but here, in the heart of battle, it all faded. Morei yanked his weapon free and turned to see a bulky Queen covered in blood. Not red paint, but blood. The glisten was unmistakable. He didn't hesitate to lunge for the king with both swords.

Morei moved in time to miss the right sword and deflected the left. He ducked and swung but the pirate jumped. As he landed, he kicked but the king rolled and lashed out. The metal met flesh, but only barely. When he stood, he saw another Queen join the first.

He did a quick sweep of the coast. More pirates were pouring onto land, doubling, even tripling their original numbers. The next wave of ships had arrived. His goal of wanting Geral to fall felt like insanity now. Lose this battle, and he'd never lay eyes on the desert again. A choice needed to be made. And he knew what that was, what needed to be done, but it would come at a cost that he wasn't sure he could pay.

The reality was sinking in as these vicious pirates stared at him. They were in a standoff, testing who would strike first. Another explosion came from somewhere in the city, but nobody flinched.

One of the Queens lashed out, and Morei deflected it with ease. They were toying with him; the strategy was obvious, but they were ignorant as to whom they were targeting. They wanted to scare him and see to it that he begged for their mercy. With so many pirates, they would try to do that to every soldier—isolate them until nothing was left but to bend the knee.

Morei wouldn't have that. It was now or never.

The strong scent of blood met his nose, and he wrinkled it. Geral's battle with Diemon was vivid in his head, but instead of the hot and relentless Hazar Desert, he was standing on the sandy beach of Caster's coastline. The decision he'd made then was strictly for the people—he had always wanted to protect his citizens, then and now. But today, the choice was also for him.

The surrounding world ceased. His thoughts drifted to the embrace of the power that always remained in the back of his head. The voices were there, waiting, just like always. Dark Energy came far too easily for him now, but that was because they'd come to an agreement. Stay with him long enough, and he would always give that energy a soul.

He burrowed himself into the volatile force, submerging himself like he'd never done before. Morei didn't want to be cautious, didn't want to submit—he wanted absolute *domination*. In one hand, the fire came to life, cold against his skin. The pirates immediately stumbled with their footing, and someone cursed their God as he laid the flames across his sword. The Dark

Energy took to the metal, engulfing the sword without damaging it. Morei lunged.

Even as the pirates jumped back, the flames leaped with intelligence. Fire took to their clothes and hair with starved intent, and the men panicked. The fire would consume them whole, as Dark Energy always did, and Morei took the opportunity to kneel.

He pressed his hand onto the blood-soaked sand. The voices were screeching, ecstatic, and he was thrilled to appease both his and their appetite. Today, they would feast. For so long, he'd avoided hearing what the voices had to say, but not anymore. He let them have their way with his mind, clawing, digging, settling into the farthest corners. They wanted the space for themselves, and in doing so, they would give him what he wanted. Control.

The first tiny flame popped up from the sand, wickedly close to his thumb. The next was by his palm. Morei willed the flames to grow, demanding they obey, and they did. He stood just as the wall of fire ravaged the Red Queens who had been before him. Their screams pierced his head but only served to intensify his lust for the violence. A flick of his wrist, and the flames shifted left. His veins were icy, his heart raced, and he felt the overwhelming elation of a predator feasting after a long stretch of famine.

This city was his. Over and over, that thought chanted in his mind. He drove the flames higher and higher until they danced with one another in an unstable vortex. The monstrous fire took over the coastline, and he watched as pirates and soldiers alike scrambled. The firestorm took lives, regardless of sides. The voices were working as one, driven by a common goal, and taken souls brushed over his consciousness with a morbid chill. He loved it.

As the Red Queens bolted into the shallow waters, he drove the vortex toward them. Men and women were massacred. As they dropped, Morei turned his attention to the ships. He wanted to send a message.

His desire was heard, and the fire evaporated at once over the burning pirates. At the captain's ship, Morei raised his hand, summoning the Dark Energy for one final bidding. The black veins were stark, but he was proud of them. For the first time ever, he wasn't ashamed of what they represented. Power like this would have consumed his lifeforce if not for the dreadful night all those moons ago, the night that had changed his life forever.

Flames sprouted off the main deck of the captain's ship. He watched as the Queens scrambled, shouted, and then jumped overboard. The flames burned nearly white as more of the ship was engulfed and more souls were stolen. His body started to burn, as if he too were standing in the fire.

Morei's knees buckled, and he met the ground. He watched in awe as the ship was destroyed. The other Red Queen ships were quickly retreating. Shouts were too far to be understood. Morei didn't care, anyway. What he was witnessing was victory. The king's name would be spoken across the world for what happened here, and he challenged anyone mad enough to step foot on his territory again.

A hand clapped his shoulder, and he looked up to see a soldier he didn't recognize. The wide, manic expression was made nightmarish by the blood across his face. "You did it!"

A thunderous cheer followed. Men surrounded him, taking their fists and pounding their chests in a slow-building unison. Some wore armor, so the sound reverberated. With their tunics, others created a thud that rippled through the coast. A handful of Caster men easily took possession of the Queens who hadn't yet reached the sea.

The king was momentarily stunned. He let go of the Dark Energy. As he did so, he felt a massive wave of fatigue tear through him, but he forced himself to stand. The first time he'd harnessed such power, he'd collapsed. Not today. His thoughts were unreachable, though, and a tremble ravaged his hands, which he clenched into fists to hide the reaction. These men couldn't see this.

"Your Majesty." A voice came through the commotion. Edwin. "The pirates. What do you want us to do with them?"

The men didn't question him, didn't shy away from the danger that he was. The total destruction didn't even make them flinch. They embraced him. After so much time hiding who he really was, it felt good to finally be appreciated. This was the monster the world had created, and he loved it, and Caster did too.

Morei's eyes drifted over to the dozen Queens, each with a blade to their throat. Caster soldiers had lined them up, and the king saw several pirates struggling to break free. One soldier kneed a Queen in the back to still her.

He should keep them as prisoners. Morei knew that if Rhys were here, he'd suggest it. It was the proper thing to do. These pirates could have answers to the attack and the potential strategy of the Red Queens who had fled. They could answer if they were working under Junok. The thought was fleeting, but he latched on to it.

Approaching the closest Queen, Morei grabbed his jaw with bone-breaking force. "Who sent you?"

The pirate spit, but it never made it farther than Morei's hand. The warm saliva trailed across his hand with repulsive slowness, leaving a trail as it went. The king squeezed harder, tempted to break the man's jaw for that.

"We don't work for anyone but the sea," the pirate hissed.

"Hm." The king squeezed harder. The man tried to push away, but the soldier kept him in place. The bone fractured under Morei's grip, and the pirate screamed in agony. Morei let him go then, shoving his mangled face away and stepping back. They would not give him an answer. Honorable . . . but foolish.

"Kill them all."

Deals Are for War

Hot tears streamed down Syra's face, finally released from their prison. Her vision blurred, but she couldn't tear her eyes away from the blond-headed Ka-Geíon, who stared for a long while at the headless body of Shevana. Her words still hung between them, harsh and jarring. All her troubles had come from that woman; her entire life was built on the leader and her merciless ways. She'd taken the throne for herself, Nala had fled, and it was through this that Syra was born. Shevana was the root cause of her entire life, and now, just like that, she was dead.

And next to her body was the man Syra had risked her life for. It was anticlimactic to see him this way, lifeless. Somehow, she'd expected so much more after everything she'd been through to get here.

Another piece of stone fell, delayed, and the impact of it against the floor startled her back to reality. She blinked, taking in her surroundings, realizing what she'd done. Chaos escaped her like steam from a hot kettle, and the destruction numbed her to her core.

"Gods exist to destroy," Elyas said softly. He sounded leagues from where he stood. "But in their destruction, life finds a way. Even the dead must adapt."

Syra slowly shook her head. She could hardly look away from Zarek. "No," she mumbled. "How did you do it?"

The demon stretched his arms wide. "Finally, an interesting question." He stuck his boot out and nudged Shevana's head. It rolled off the podium, sending splatters of blood across the floor, before dropping through one of the wide cracks. "Shevana wanted me dead, thought I was too much of a risk in the long run." Elyas shook his head. "She and I had our differences, and unfortunately, they just got in the way of any real progress. She was going to have one of her Guardians kill me after she was done with you. You could say I spared us both." He scoffed and walked toward Syra, blade still in hand. He twirled it, appearing more like a warrior than the result of tampered energy. He stopped five paces from her. "Have you thought more about our deal, Syra?"

"No. Go back to whatever forsaken hole you crawled out of."

He knelt and regarded her. "Careful what you wish for, little redhead. The dead bite back." Elyas let his fingers trail over the metal of the dagger. "You should probably hear more of what I have to say. I don't want to see this place destroyed, much like you. In the past, my kind have been shoved into the shadows, shunned and exiled. We were killed for walking in the wrong place, gutted for looking the wrong way. Our time has come to change that."

When he didn't add more, Syra finally tore her eyes free of Zarek and met his gaze fully. Frantic, her mind had to do the only thing possible: deal with the next problem. "How can you ask me this after what you just did?"

"Because you're the rightful heir." His reply came out deliberately slow, and Raid's words crumbled around her. "Your place was destined here before you were born. I've heard what the Guardians said about you well before Shevana slaughtered them for their beliefs."

More tears decorated her cheeks, fresh and angry. "Accept my place so you can spare my life while you destroy this place? I don't care what they said about me. I don't want this." She motioned at the crumbling palace. "I want to go home, live a peaceful life. But not here."

"Syra," he whispered. He sounded almost like family—kind. "This is your home. It's always been your home." Elyas dropped his dagger to his side. "I can't do it without your bloodline. Well, I could try, but is it really worth that risk? We want a home just like you. The only reason we are what we are is because of what this place has forced us to become."

She shook her head. Her mind was all over the place, and she was trying her best to pick up all the pieces. Emotions were out of reach, thoughts were like mud, and she grasped anything she could get her hands on. "I can't trust you. You just killed Shevana. You'll do the same to me."

"And why would I do that? What would I gain from killing the last of the Gods' Death Keepers?"

Syra hadn't heard that term before, and she chose to ignore it for now. "Power. What better way to get everything you wanted than by killing any-one standing in your way."

The dagger rose again, and he flipped the weapon in the air, easily catching it. "You know nothing of your heritage or why your blood runs the way it does. Shame." He walked back to the podium, stepping over Zarek. "The Guardians have failed you more than one way, I'm afraid."

She shook her head, which was pounding now. "What do you want? Don't give me some bullshit answer anymore."

That made him snort, but he didn't move. "Eventually, the problems you face now will be resolved, and you'll be left with one little thing: me. If you could think clearly, you'd know I'm trying to spare your life. Give you a future you can learn to enjoy. I would hate to keep the final Death Keeper locked away for eternity. Sounds terrible." He stopped next to Shevana, nudging her headless body with his boot. Whether it was morbid curiosity or a fascination with the dead, she didn't know. "As much as I'd love for us to arrange something today, I'm afraid I don't have the time. I've got a realm to explore—I hear the heat is marvelous. Your little soul has been through so much already, and I imagine you've got bigger issues to deal with."

Syra tensed. He knew about the realm fracture and the chasm, everything. Of course, he did. Elyas was in control.

"But the next time we see each other," he said, "I will not ask again."

The threat grazed over her skin like broken glass. Agree for him to spare her life, letting him rule the realm, or risk a war they couldn't afford. He was unreliable, volatile, and couldn't be trusted. A blind man would have seen that all just fine, yet in her compromised state, she couldn't stop thinking about the possibility that accepting *might* resolve so many problems, especially for this realm. They couldn't afford war with these beings. No army could defend against the Geíons.

Elyas slipped through the side door, and Syra started her crawl toward the Guardian. Thoughts of his words dissipated as she grew closer. She worked on her hands and knees, not quite strong enough to stand on her feet. The only thing she wanted to do was get to Zarek. The realms could wait. She just needed a moment to grieve.

He looked so content, despite the blood and beatings. Still, she pressed a finger under his jaw, hoping for some heartbeat. The blade jutted out from his chest, and she pried that out and set it aside. His blood stained her hands as she surveyed his wounds, and she carefully propped his head up in her lap, certain that might make him more comfortable. It was unfair, life, and now faced with the harsh reality of her decisions, the tears came without mercy.

Syra wanted to take it all back, to save him. This was not how any of this was supposed to go. They were supposed to get everyone out alive, but not even that could be granted. Destiny spared no one, not even her. If she could have traded places with him, she would have. Zarek had fought to regain order in his life, fought for something he could stand for, and all it had done was kill him. That was unfair.

Desperation tore apart her grief. She could do it. She *could* save him. With Erun, it had just happened without thought. Yet here, no matter how much she touched and even slapped his cheek, nothing happened.

Footsteps came from above, and she looked up to see Sekar enter, scanning the condition of the room before landing on her. That proud expression faltered, and his mouth twisted when he saw the Guardian.

Before he could say anything, she said, "I can bring him back."

Sekar shook his head and made his way over to her. "No, Syra, you can't—"

"*Why?*" Every single emotion was stuffed into that single word.

"Mortals are different. To resurrect someone like him, a man who has lived beyond the reach of Death for so long, is not the same."

She held Zarek tighter. "I don't understand."

Sekar's moved his hand through his hair. "I don't know the consequences. Guardians are bound to a Gor-Geíon during the Commitment Ceremony. Their heart doesn't beat like a mortal's. Resurrecting someone like that could have devastating impacts on both you and him." He bared his hands to her. The hard expression she'd come to know so well softened, revealing a man who once wept and grieved like the rest of the world. "I don't know, Syra. No God in history has possessed the gift you do. There is nothing that can predict what will happen."

"We have to try," she replied, quieter. "I can't go back to Dryl like this. I can't walk away without trying."

The God knelt next to her and placed a hand on her shoulder. He squeezed it. "I know you want to do the right thing, but I don't know the burden you may be left to carry after this. We both saw what happened with that boy."

She did, and she also knew the ramifications of it after what Raid told her. Syra wasn't making this decision foolishly. Her head was in the right place, and her purpose was clear. "If I was given this gift, then what good is it if I can't use it?"

He smiled at that, but it was somber. "Gods can't save everyone, and no matter how hard we try, we are still monsters to the world."

She shook her head, unwilling to hear him. "I have to try."

His hand cupped her jaw then, gentle despite the urgency of his actions. "Okay."

Support. That was all she needed. Sekar didn't need to tell her that for her to know. Regardless of their journey, his loyalty and honor to her well-being outweighed everything. Each day, she saw more and more of Kar, the man she'd once considered a friend. She was grateful to have him by her side.

Turning her attention back to Zarek, she forced in several breaths. The ground rumbled then, a distant call to the destruction caused by Chaos. More debris fell, and in the doorway, a handful of Guardians appeared. Her body went rigid with anticipation, only to relax when she saw Raid among them. Sekar nodded. He knew.

This was it. No turning back. Syra reached for Chaos, feeling the hot force stir with eagerness at her summon. Mother hadn't denied her yet, and she wouldn't now. Syra wouldn't allow it.

The motions came easily for her. Syra stated her intent, hands placed on Zarek, and felt the familiar tingling in her fingers begin as the energy moved her way into the body. Slow at first, but as the intensity of her request increased, so too did the force with which Chaos ravaged the Guardian. The sensations clawing at the corners of her mind were different, and strange, the experience unlike Erun's, and she panicked. Something wasn't right, and when she tried to release the energy, she found she couldn't. Her entire body was frozen in place, a conduit to a force much larger than her.

The clawing sensation worsened, tearing apart the last barriers before the energy poured into her mind. As it did, her body was consumed by ice, sweat broke loose across her skin, and her heart felt like it was going to beat itself into the grave. Memories, visions, sounds, and smells engulfed her senses.

She smelled the fire. The kind lit on a chilly night with stew and a good drink. Laughter followed, and she saw the drunk grins of mortal men as they handed a flask around. As quickly as she saw it, the stench of metal filled her nose, and she saw the flames grow higher before revealing a horrific scene of death. Bodies lay strewn about, and Syra felt her hand grip the hilt of Death's Sword tighter, dissatisfied but relieved to have the job done.

A whisper caught the memory's attention, and now she clinked glasses with Shevana, who looked more like a young woman. Cheerful, laughing, with a pinkish birthmark along her left cheek. Her hair was tied up, and they were overlooking a small river in the middle of the woods. They'd snuck off in celebration before the Commitment Ceremony was to begin.

Then the memory crumbled, and Syra was exposed to countless more at once. She saw and felt the agony of the ceremony—the days of writhing and near-death experiences—followed by the harsh fights and executions done in the name of Shevana. Zarek acted without mercy, never doubted her, even when the victim was an innocent child. A girl. And she wasn't the only one. Syra saw it all. Young girls were slaughtered for decades. Orders to find Nala's daughter, to end the bloodline.

Horror as cold as Death's fingers grabbed Syra's spine as the bloodshed continued. Zarek's centuries of life were anything but innocent, even complemented by the tender moments of love he shared with Shevana. But as the memories continued, the tearing sensation got stronger and stronger, digging past her mind and right into her heart. She could feel the very essence of the memories burn through her body, and along with it came the emotions that the Guardian so often felt: rage and shame.

And then, without warning, it all ceased. Syra swayed, her body released, and her head swam. Her stomach twisted violently, and she swallowed bile down. Her body was soaked in sweat, her mind hardly recognizable but growing more familiar, and she wiped her eyes when they burned, only to find that blood stained her skin. Her hands shook, and she blinked rapidly, trying to regain some composure, but her vision went in and out of focus. The world around her was gray, and she thought she saw a hand reach for her, maybe even boots, but she couldn't stay awake long enough to find out.

Granted the Right to Fight

Alaric was in a meeting with the council when Cyrus arrived back. Late in the day for such a thing, but Cyrus didn't protest. He was relieved for the chance to settle back in, bathe, and get comfortable. Well, as comfortable as one could get when carrying a dragon egg. He even bathed with the egg sitting in front of him, not trusting it out of his sight. When he was done, he slipped it back into the bag that he'd been given and put that behind his pillows.

"Sorry," he told her. "The Yavinks say to trust, but I'm not quite there yet." He patted the top of the egg before closing the bag. He'd sent word advising Alaric to come directly to Cyrus once his meeting was done, so he sat in his chamber and waited. He was hungry, but he was wary about leaving until he spoke with the king.

He paced the large room. The bed was done up in new colored silks—green now—and staff had come in here and cleaned everything. He could tell because all his clothes were arranged in a new order in his walk-in closet. Shirts on one side, organized by formality, pants on the other. Travel gear was placed into its own section. Cyrus wouldn't call himself organized. He put things wherever he saw fit. In all his life, he'd never had so many clothes, and at times, it was overwhelming, so he tried to keep to a handful of things that he liked to wear. Apparently, based on the organization, that was noticeable, because he saw new shirts and pants that he didn't remember own ing.

Cyrus had drunk all the water that was left for him. His tongue was still parched, though, which made him more anxious about the conversation to be had. He knew what needed to be done, but it still unsettled him. Who knew what Alaric would say? Sozar had told him the king was on their side, always had been, but that still didn't silence the nervous screams in his head. He retreated to the bed and pulled the egg out from the spot behind the pillows.

"It's me again," he said, although Cyrus assumed she might know that. He pulled her from the bag and held the egg in both hands in his lap. Walking wasn't helping, so he wanted to talk to the dragon. It felt fitting to make sure she understood why everything was happening. Sozar had never had a choice, and he knew, to some extent, this dragon didn't either. The world she was going to hatch into was cruel, and he wanted her to be prepared. He didn't know how to tell her, though, and he sat there for a bit, running his thumbs over the textured, scale-like exterior. When the words finally came, he realized the only way to tell her was by telling her about him. "I want to tell you my story."

And he did. Cyrus told her everything, from his childhood to the moment he found Sozar's egg in the mines. He spoke about the fear, and the constant running. About being taken by Morei and breaking out through sheer luck. "Not the nicest man you'll meet," he advised her. Then he told her about Evander, finding the sword, and Razan. He spoke in depth about watching Sozar grow and the guilt he felt for forcing a dragon on the run. That was no way to live, especially for a majestic beast like that, but it was the only choice they had for a long time.

He told her of Dameon and Ashtir, the prince of Saveen, and about Henry Junok. The words came easy, and he didn't hold back anything, not even about Zorya. The now-queen of Razan was always within reach of his thoughts. She'd have loved Venkar City and all its history. Zorya always appreciated that kind of thing. Cyrus didn't want to shy away from the truth. He'd made mistakes—big ones—but he and Sozar were alive, and that was all that mattered.

He told her about Hyle. That hadn't originally been the intention, but he couldn't stop himself. Everything that was on his mind came out in one massive storm of words. The God's elusive past, his time as a Dragon Rider, and his willingness to help all came to the surface. It helped pass the time, and when he finally finished, he felt empty.

"You're coming into a world that wants to destroy you," he admitted. "My biggest fear is that you'll be forced to become something you don't want. Whatever you do, little one, I hope you hatch for the right person, whoever that is."

"She will."

Cyrus jumped. Next to the doors to the terrace stood Hyle. The God looked tired today. A dark cloud hovered over him, and the scar looked more hideous than it had in the past. It was obvious that he was troubled.

"A knock would be nice," Cyrus grumbled. His stomach twisted, starved, but he ignored it. "You knew about the eggs, didn't you?"

"Of course." He stepped forward until he was next to Cyrus, never looking away from the egg. "But only the Rider Üg'ahn deems fit can enter. He and I knew each other, but he had a promise to keep, and I was not here to argue with him. We both wanted the same thing, and it was not my place to challenge."

Cyrus swallowed. "Because of Vikter?"

The smallest, most strained smiles revealed itself then, catching him off guard. Behind that action was agony, so raw and unchecked that his chest tightened. "Yes," Hyle answered, "because of him."

The God sat next to Cyrus, the bed groaning from the added weight. "May I?"

It was not Cyrus's right to grant permission or deny the man's ability to hold an egg. It was likely the first one he'd touched since the Great Fall. Cyrus handed it over and watched Hyle's face twist into a hundred emotions as he held her.

"Why did you take a female?" the God asked sharply.

"I—" The harshness caught him off guard. "I thought because she was female . . ." The words didn't come as easy as he hoped. "Rebuilding the dragons will take time, but I'd hoped we could have a female to pair for Sozar." If Dameon weren't so unreliable, he'd have considered Ashtir too.

Hyle ran his thumbs over the egg. "When I lost Kelise, I tried to get another egg. I thought I could beat Destiny and have a second chance. I didn't even want a female, because it would remind me too much of her, so I tried to get a male."

Cyrus bit his tongue, trying to figure out what to say. He'd thought Hyle would be impressed, but he was disappointed.

"Riders only ever get one chance, Cyrus," he said, hardly audible. "There is only one dragon that chooses them. It is a bond that should never be taken for granted because it is not replaceable. You can't pay your way into another dragon or force-hatch one. If you tried that, as some have in the past, you would have an incomplete bond. More harm than good would come out of that relationship for both you and the dragon. I've watched Riders consumed by grief try to force themselves into a new bond, only to take their own lives because the hollowness is too much to bear."

"And the dragons?" Cyrus whispered.

"They stop eating. They starve themselves to death usually. Even as young hatchlings, they struggled to cope. It's a violent way to live. The Rider Federation tried to minimize this by placing the eggs in a chamber only few could enter." His face pinched, flashing with something hideous. "The federation once stood for beautiful things, but it grew corrupt."

He handed the egg back to Cyrus then, who took it gratefully. It was nice to hold her again. Even with the God, he felt overly protective of her. She embodied everything he needed to do right this time around. "You watched the city change?"

Hyle stood and walked over to the empty decanter of water. With his back to him, he said, "I was raised in it. Dragon Riders live a long time, and because of that, things move slower. There's no rush for anarchy or political wars when one has centuries. But because of that, when there is an uprise, things happen far more carefully. Those who acted planned their moves for decades. Ever so slowly, I watched a once-peaceful culture turn into a bloodthirsty battlefield." The final words came out hardly audible.

Cyrus opened his mouth to ask more, but the God turned around and spoke first. "What will you do with her?"

That was Hyle's way of changing the subject. He should have been grateful that he got that much information, but instead, he felt bitter to be teased once more about Hyle's past.

The door opened. Alaric stood there, staring at the God and dragon egg before finally meeting Cyrus's gaze. The king closed the door. "I was told to come after the meeting. If this was an urgent issue, let me know next time."

"It's not urgent," Cyrus said.

Alaric raised his brow. He was dressed in fine blue silk with a shirt that was tapered to a point and embroidered sleeves. On his hand was a large ring with a red ruby. "This isn't urgent?"

"No." Cyrus hoped he sounded as calm as he was trying to be.

"I walk in and see a Dragon Rider, a—is that a dragon egg?—and a God, and you're telling me this isn't urgent." Alaric walked over to the decanter and checked. "Not even a drink." He sounded annoyed.

Cyrus looked between the two men, still shocked that this was his new normal. "Venkar has dragon eggs," he announced, and motioned to the one in his hand. "I brought this one back as proof, but also because we don't have much time." On his flight back, he and Sozar had decided what to share and what to keep to themselves. Üg'ahn was not information that should be shared freely. When the ancient dragon was ready to reveal himself to the world, he would.

"How many?" Alaric asked. Hyle shot him a glare, and the king raised his hands. "Okay, don't answer that."

"Alaric, I trust that you know people who know people," Cyrus continued. Trust. It felt like it was everywhere now. The king nodded. "I want you to choose from that group the most trusted individuals. Women and men, no children if we can help it. We don't have time to train for a decade or however long until the child is old enough to stand on their own. If they are young and strong, that's preferred. Easier to work with and more willing to change their lives for what is to come." Just like him.

"I want to get them together, and each one is to swear to an oath not to speak on the matter. Anyone who does will be punished severely. Death, even. We cannot afford word getting out that we are trying to bond a dragon to a Rider. If that happens, Delion will become a place of war." He couldn't believe what he was saying, but he knew no other choice existed. "Each one will be tested with the egg. If they are the one, the dragon will hatch. If not, we move on. If none of those people work, we get more. We do this until there's a bond. I don't care if we have to sort through the entire country—someone is bound to be here who is meant for this dragon."

Hyle nodded, obviously satisfied with Cyrus and Sozar's plan, but Alaric looked a little shaken. "We're really doing it, aren't we?"

Cyrus knew what he meant. The age of dragons was here. The people in this room would have a firsthand encounter with the new era, and it would only be possible with their help. "Yes. And when she hatches, we must determine a place to host the new Dragon Riders."

The king scratched his chin. "You know you always have a place here."

"No." The answer came from Hyle, abrupt. "Delion is a safe place, but it is not and should not be home to the dragons. You do not have enough space."

Alaric tugged at his sleeve. "What kind of space do you need? We have the Warón Sea and Hil Islands."

"And a massive amount of people who have spent their lives without dragons," the God countered. "It is a thoughtful offer, but the dragons belong somewhere designed specifically for them."

Cyrus stared. "Nowhere in the world has there been a city constructed for the dragons, not since the federation. I mean, Razan maybe—"

"No," Hyle said again. His tone left no room for dispute, and Cyrus wasn't bold enough to argue with a God anyway. "Razan was constructed in mind to host a handful of dragons at best. But it was never made to be a home. Razan and Kalic were the closest cities to the Rider Federation at its prime, and they were required by treaty to have dragon holds for traveling Riders."

Cyrus could see where he was going with this, even if it wasn't said outright. "The Rider Federation?" That was in ruins. Hyle had said so himself. They didn't have time to rebuild a *city*.

"And who do you have in mind?" Hyle turned his fury on Cyrus. "What place will offer the sanctuary dragons need to thrive?"

Alaric was visibly irritated, but he thankfully held his tongue. Cyrus swallowed. "Do you really think all those dragons will hatch in our lifetime?" At best, he suspected a handful.

Hyle approached. The only thing that separated them was the egg. The God knelt so that he was at eye level and whispered, "Doubt is the enemy of a Dragon Rider. You would do good to remember that." He straightened and looked to the king. "Your word is what I seek. Do not let me down. Ensure everyone is checked. Soldiers will triple-check those who enter, and Energy Harvesters are forbidden."

That was ridiculous. "Hyle—"

The God turned to Cyrus, who regretted speaking up.

"Unless you have a Harvester who is attuned to both the dragon and person being tested, no Energy Harvesters. We cannot risk someone causing harm or trying to force-hatch an egg while you all stand there, unaware of what's happening." He turned his attention back to the king. "I have entrusted you for a reason. Don't make me regret that."

Cyrus didn't doubt those words. "Could you be present?" he risked asking.

"No." He dripped with irritation. "I would be an entertainment piece. I trust you and Alaric can run the show, and if not, Sozar can burn them."

That pleased the dragon. Cyrus couldn't understand Hyle's agitation, but he knew better than to press anymore. "Okay."

Hyle walked to the door that led to the terrace. He opened and stepped through without turning back. Cyrus wanted to say goodbye, but he failed to speak. It was obvious the God would leave the very way he came—with Chaos. When it was clear Alaric and Cyrus were alone, the king cleared his throat.

"I've heard of nastier Gods." The comment was said in humor, and Cyrus shook his head. Alaric tapped the egg with his fingers. "Strange to see one in person. You hear stories growing up and expect them to be all sorts of things, but not this. So simple."

Cyrus nodded. "We need to move fast," he reminded the king. It was the only thing he knew how to say after that tense discussion.

Alaric looked relieved to be moving on as well. "How fast?"

"How about tomorrow?"

Graced by Luck

The destruction from the battle would take at least a season to fix.

Sixty-some Caster soldiers had died, plus a dozen or more citizens, and holes lay scattered across the city from the explosive cannons used by the Queens. The Festival of Seasons was cut short days early, so that the people could begin cleaning up from the aftermath and say their piece to the dead. Two large burning ceremonies had already taken place in the last two days, but Morei hadn't gone to either. His attention was on ensuring the army was well-equipped for any future attack by the Red Queens. The Queens' fleet was extensive, spanning across the Vore World, and word would soon reach them that Caster hadn't fallen. His name would be carried across the sea.

Rhys avoided him, but Morei didn't care. The chancellor thought himself so bold, but he was a slippery criminal with too much power. Rhys had spent many summers working right under Drexis's nose, and now, faced with a king who wouldn't have it, the chancellor was panicking. He didn't have to tell Morei anything for the king to know that. He had Rhys under his thumb, which was what he'd wanted all along. One wrong move and the chancellor would be dead. Rhys knew that.

The king had known people would talk about what happened on the shore, and he'd expected that people would turn their backs on him, just like Geral had. In fact, he was betting on it. He'd tasked a dozen soldiers with attending popular pubs so that they could report to him about what was being said.

They were *grateful*.

Not everyone, of course, but the vast majority. And anyone who opposed him would be killed without question. He made that clear once the soldiers reported back. Morei wanted the respect of his citizens—that was what made a true king—but he was not afraid to impose fear to obtain his long-term goal. The council had requested a meeting yesterday, but he'd pushed it off, more worried about speaking with the soldiers and the recovery process. Political squabbles were the least of his concerns. If any of the councilmembers were truly concerned, they'd have sought him out privately, but nobody had.

Isla looked at him differently. He wasn't surprised. What he'd accomplished on the coast hadn't only saved the city but had been a blatant display of power. He knew what this country thought when it came to Dark Energy. No one doubted him anymore.

Morei opened and closed his hand. The tremor, while only slight, was still there. He hoped it would go away in time. The king didn't like to look weak, and he was careful not to let anyone see it. The ailment, however, was a different story. With each use of Dark Energy, it seemed the black veins took more of his skin as their personal playground. Before, he could hide the majority of the ailment with a high-collared shirt. Now, a handful of veins stretched to his jaw and behind his ears. His hands looked pale, a network of black veins covering his fingers.

The choice had consequences. The power significantly progressed his ailment—a price he wasn't sure he could keep affording.

"You've been standing there for an eternity," Eazon said from behind him.

Morei didn't flinch at the God's arrival. His voice rang with an accent that didn't belong to this country, and carried a tone of smugness.

"I was beginning to think you were dead. Actually, I was hoping for that," Morei replied. He was standing on the shore where the battle had taken place. Where water hadn't reached, the sand was still stained red, but the bodies had all been burned and disposed of in a respectful manner.

A part of him still anticipated the Red Queens' arrival at any moment.

A chuckle. "Why? Because I wasn't here to entertain you every day?"

"Because for a while, I was certain you were just here to fuck with me." Morei stole a glance at the God of Luck. "Still dressed like you're in the wrong era, I see."

A silence fell between them. It made Morei uncomfortable. He was the one who usually imposed the silent treatment—a way to test those in the room with him. Now, however, he was getting a taste of his own weapon from a God who was an apparent expert at it.

He swallowed and tried to remain still. Morei was happy to oblige if they were going to play this game. Keeping his head high, he waited, listening to the lapping waves.

Eazon inhaled sharply, stepping up next to him. "I want to tell you a story. At the end, I will ask you a question."

"Is this where you finally tell me about Sekar or Syra? About what's going on between them and what could they possibly want with me?" Morei had asked the God countless times, but Eazon had never budged. Useless.

The God was silent, and Morei glanced his way, finding that the man's expression didn't falter. This would not be about Sekar and Syra, of course.

"Go on," he said with a sigh. Morei wasn't in the mood for stories and higher callings, but he knew better than to tell the God to leave. He wouldn't until he got what he wanted. Morei had learned that the night Eazon sat across from him in Gamer's Village. The sooner the king submitted to this little game, the sooner Eazon would go.

Despite the undertone of sarcasm in Morei's voice, the God hardly glanced his way. He was serious. "There were two sons, born from two royal families. The sons had everything they could ever want—coin, weapons, books, the finest foods, you name it. Above all else, they were being raised to take the throne when the time came. The only difference was that neither knew the other existed, because they were from separate kingdoms."

Morei could see where this was going.

"One son, despite having the world literally handed to him, never was satisfied. His overexuberance with life made him greedy for it, and he felt he was owed something at every slightest inconvenience. The other son grew to appreciate the simplest things, visited the city, and even helped staff in the galley. Can I ask you a question, Morei?"

The king looked at him fully now. "You've already gotten this far, so get it over with." A drink was starting to sound nice.

"Which one is you?"

The question surprised him. He had assumed it would be a tale about overcoming hardships. "I'm not going to entertain you."

"Why?"

"Because what right do you have to come into my life when you please and then challenge who I am, like you know me so well? You don't know anything about me."

Eazon crossed his arms. He didn't look swayed. "Answer my question."

The anger came fast, but Morei stuffed it back down before it flared into something unmanageable. He didn't like being told what to do, especially by a God. He felt trapped; accommodate Eazon and hope he leaves, or pick a fight with a deity that had centuries to wait this out. In the end, he finally spat out, "The second son. There. Happy?"

Eazon raised his brow. "What makes you say that?"

"You said one question."

The God stared at him. Hard.

Morei, relented, still wanting him gone. "I was exactly that boy. I helped the staff, worked the stables, even went into the city and offered assistance where I could before I was told I couldn't do so anymore. My favorite place in the Geral palace was the windows, where I could sit and watch the sky all night." Even as the words left his mouth, he regretted them. That was too much information. Nobody needed to know that.

"So why is it that you emulate the first son?" Eazon asked.

The God's tone was curious, innocent even, but the words burrowed themselves into Morei's chest. "I'm not. I'm trying to stay alive and do the right thing." He motioned to the sea. "We were attacked. Am I supposed to roll over and play dead?"

"That's not what I mean, and you know that."

"I will not do this. I will not be toyed with like some floundering worm while you peck at me like this is comical to you. Go." He shooed at the God with his hands. "Fly away."

Eazon laughed, but the sound came out loud and cold. It was the first time Morei had heard such a noise from the usually mischievous God, and he didn't like it. "You are all the future has, Morei. You can either burn a path there or walk it—the choice is yours. But let me tell you one little thing."

Before the king could react, Eazon grabbed his hand and twisted it so that the palm was facing upward. In the night, the veins looked like trenches across a pale landscape. "There are greater things in the world than Geral. Even bigger than this country. When you decide to be a real king, I can tell you. But not now." His face twisted in disgust as he looked away from the hand. "You are on the path to be just like your father, and I cannot intervene."

He let go and stepped away. Morei stumbled over his words. "What are you trying to tell me? Just say it." Why was his father being brought into this? "Eazon," he warned. "Tell me."

"You won't be seeing me for a long while," the God said. He sounded sad, defeated even. "Be careful with what you decide to do next. Every decision you make is forging a destiny you cannot change."

Gods were annoyingly philosophical. The king stepped forward and reached out, but his hand went right through a mist. Eazon's body disintegrated like dust before disappearing altogether. The king stood there, staring at where the God had been moments prior, enraged.

He was tired of constantly being told who he should be, and even more pissed that a God would so recklessly inject themselves into his life without clear reasoning. Morei had faced Sekar, tampered with dreams in an encounter too close for comfort, and even spoken to Syra, the girl the world wanted. He'd tried to put that all behind him in a crazed attempt for some normalcy, yet no matter how hard he tried, Destiny had a twisted way of mocking him. If it wasn't ancient beasts, it was a God who couldn't decide if he wanted to turn into a raven or mist.

The comment about his father angered him. Eazon didn't know the previous king of Geral like he did. Morei was ashamed of his actions because he knew his father would disapprove. His father had been the most compassionate man he knew, someone he'd idolized, but the God had sounded on the verge of repulsed. No, he decided, he refused to acknowledge those words. They were meant to harm him, and he would not give Eazon that gratification.

Morei was supposed to be raising an empire, not worrying about who he was becoming. He was ready to embrace what the world wanted him to be. It all started with Geral, taking out his revenge on a city that failed not only him, but Ezra too. Geral was the economic powerhouse of Sorréle, next to Caster. Take both cities, and Diemon would have no choice but to bend the knee or be taken by force. The strategy and justification were clear now.

At the same time, he was unsure how long he had until Nerius would send another threat or a fleet of ships to Caster's shore, and he needed to consider that moving forward. Resources would be split thin in the coming moons. Yet if Caster moved fast and ruthlessly, the enemy would never stand a chance.

Soldiers were stationed to rotate in the surviving towers overlooking the sea, but he could hardly place his trust in them. Frustrated by Eazon's words, Morei walked toward the waves and stopped just where the water brushed over his boots. Tomorrow was the city speech, a tradition after battles, an event he always looked forward to. He would update the citizens on anything important, speak of the battle, and then declare any special funding for the rebuilding of homes, businesses, and so forth.

After that, he intended to pull Rhys aside and hope he didn't stab the chancellor before meeting the council. For now, maybe he would pay Esme and Dan a visit for a late-night drink.

A Truth Too Hideous

Syra's head hurt. Her muscles ached like a bad fever was ravaging her body, and she lay there for a long while. The ceiling was cracked, the bedsheets smelled sour, and the room was packed full of various items. She saw hanging swords with different designs—older versions of Death's Sword, she assumed—and paintings. Based on the uniqueness of each one, this had once been a Guardian's room. She saw green landscapes, creatures with four antlers and others with three eyes, and even detailed depictions of the steeds they rode. She hadn't seen Zarek's steed in a long while, now that she thought about it. She'd grown fond of the undead horse.

The memories resurfaced, and she looked at the cracked door. The wood was carved in intricate detail, displaying a raven in flight. A Rü'shane. Carefully, she peeled herself off the bed, still dirty and dressed in her torn attire. Syra's hair had long since given up being tamed, and she made a silent promise to herself to put the locks back in a braid that she could manage.

For now, she took one look at the blood-stained red strands and grimaced. Not her finest moment.

Next to her, leaned up against the wall, was the weapon she'd never thought she'd see again. Death's Sword. Syra reached for it and unsheathed the blade, finding the inscription along the base. It was Dryl's. They'd managed to take it when the Guardians fled the crumbling mountain. The belt was a bit scuffed up from improper use, but nothing a good oil couldn't fix. Tears burned in her eyes. This weapon meant more to her than she would ever admit to. It represented her journey, sacrifices, growth—everything she needed to be and wanted to let go of. Sheathing it, she stood and latched the belt on, glad to feel the familiar weight.

Walking to the door proved easier than she anticipated. Once the first few steps were out of the way and her legs worked again, she moved quickly. It was cooler down here, akin to the climate on her travels. She needed to find out what had happened. Elyas had been here, and she was chained to Zarek's consciousness and unable to break free. Were they still in danger? Her life had been one disaster after the next, and now she couldn't recall anything between then and this moment. That frightened her. Nobody could rely on her if she was incapacitated.

When she opened the door, she saw a hallway lit well with hanging lanterns on either side. No windows. There wasn't much to look at outside, yet she felt confined without being able to at least see. A chill crept up her back, and she crossed her arms and started to walk. The cold stone felt good against the bruised soles of her feet.

She reached the end of the hall, having passed several more doors with identical carvings, and stopped. Looking left and right, she wasn't sure which direction to go. They both looked similar. She decided on the left.

"Wrong way," a voice called.

Syra jumped, alarmed, and looked back. Raid raised his hands. "Sorry." The Guardian approached her, looking cleaned up and dressed in fresh clothes. He looked more like Zane, and the thought of her missing friend made her cringe. "I was heading to check on you. I see you found my gift." The Guardian motioned to the sword. "How are you feeling?"

"Where is everyone?" she asked, then shook her head. "After everything, Vaeke held his word." Her fingers easily found the pommel of Death's Sword. "Thank you."

Raid didn't miss a beat. "Upstairs."

"And Sekar?"

"Quite the character," he commented, and motioned for Syra to follow. She did. "He's been hanging out down here since you passed out. He finally just stepped away a bit ago to pay Zarek a visit. Not sure if I like him or not, to be honest."

"He's a hard one to like," she mumbled, but her attention was on one person only. "Zarek's alive?"

The Guardian nodded, but his expression squirmed, seeming torn between content and concern. "He's moving slow, was a tad confused for a bit, but he's there in the flesh. Knows his name, so I guess that's a start. We were trying to make sure he came back and not some demented demon that took possession of his body. It happens. Anyway, we were asking questions, and he seems to be himself, just . . ." He trailed off and shook his head. "Different. Can't quite figure it out."

Syra wasn't sure how to feel about that. Guilt wiggled its way into her chest first. She glanced at her discolored hand. Maybe her gift wasn't so special. Perhaps it was a curse—a selfish need to defy Destiny and have her way. Gods couldn't save everyone, and they shouldn't. Sekar had said so himself.

"I'm supposed to tell you an Onye is running about this palace." Raid snorted. "Sekar said you know of her?"

"Zari," Syra clarified. Relief flooded her. Strange or not, she was starting to feel a little affection for the white beast.

"What you did," Raid said, more measured now, "the men can't stop talking about it. There was no guarantee it would work on him, but you did it. We've never seen or heard anything like it before."

That made Syra uncomfortable. "Save for Erun." The words sounded hollow to her ears—he'd been refused the life he deserved. She didn't like praise or anything close to it. Her skin crawled, and she would have rather been stuck at the bottom of a ship, scraping off barnacles in the hot sun, than to hear a compliment. "Where are the Geíons? They were here."

Raid gestured for Syra to take the lead up the stairs. She did, hugging herself tighter. The chill wouldn't let go. "They retreated. Left without a fight. We've got men surveying the area. Shevana was their way in, and now that that's gone, we suspect there might be war."

Elyas would stop at nothing to get what he wanted, with or without her agreement. The Guardian numbers were hardly impressive; there was only so much the few of them could handle without destroying the Soul Realm. Then again, maybe the realm was already destroyed. The chasm was sure to cause widespread destruction.

Panic replaced the guilt she'd been chewing on, and she couldn't swallow it, no matter how hard she tried. They were out of time.

"Zarek's in here." They stepped off the stairs, and just to the right, she saw a door cracked open. Up here, the hall looked to have slightly better décor, although that didn't stop the fissures running across all the walls and the floor. Some of the marble was gravely scratched, and a few of the white chunks of stone were decorated in red splatter. Dried blood.

"Where were we?" she asked.

"That was the dungeons." Raid seemed a bit hesitant with his answer. "Many of us started sleeping there to avoid Shevana's wrath. Far more peaceful." He pushed open the door and revealed a much nicer chamber. The walls were plain. Several rooms split off from the large living area, and a tall window overlooked the purple landscape. A lounge area made up the center, near the window, and she saw Zarek sitting there, back to them. It looked like a royal chamber, made for visitors to use. "We didn't know what would happen to you after you passed out. Thought it might be best you were kept separate while we worked to clean things up."

She shot Raid a glare. "What? Like I would explode?"

He shrugged.

Sekar appeared around the corner, dressed in better clothes and cleaned up. It seemed Syra was the only one who hadn't gotten the invite. His visible wounds were scabbed over, but the bruising looked menacing across his jaw. Chaos was doing the best she could, and Syra was sure she looked quite similar. "You're awake." He stopped right in front of her, then inspected her. "How are you feeling?"

"I've definitely been better," she said. "When can I get a bath?"

"Whenever you want," Sekar replied. "There's food in here too. We got some for Zarek when he woke."

That made her brow go up. "So now you're friends with the man you wanted me to leave for dead?"

Sekar straightened as a low chuckle came from the chair in the living area. Zarek didn't turn around, though, which she found odd. Quickly, Sekar ushered her out of the room and dropped his voice. The façade fell. This was not in play, she realized. Something was off.

"Remember when I said we didn't know the consequences?" the God said, hardly audible. He spoke fast, and stole several glances back to the entrance. His urgency made her anxious. This was not like him. "Something did happen. Zarek's there. We've confirmed that, but he's not the same man. What happened when you brought him back?"

"Is he okay?" she asked. "You're making this sound—"

"What happened when you brought him back?" he repeated, harsher now.

She swallowed. "When I, um . . . When I connected with him, I couldn't let go. I started to feel strange, like I wasn't entirely alone in my head, and I tried to release the energy, but then I couldn't. It was like I was stuck. I saw everything." The memories flashed—both violent and tender—and she blinked. "I felt consumed, violated, and then it just stopped. And then I woke up in some dungeon-turned-sleeping-arrangement."

Sekar stared at her. "And how do you feel now?"

"I feel fine," she rushed to say. She felt like she was taking some kind of test. "I mean, besides the aches and all that. What's this about?"

Sekar ran his hand over his face and stole another look inside. Raid nodded in return, an unspoken conversation between them. "You need to tell me if anything starts to feel odd, okay? I know we talked about the energy imbalance caused by the realm fracture, and how that can disrupt how one harvests energy, even Chaos. Our dreams are more vivid, the energies more volatile—"

"Sekar," she pleaded. "Is he all right?"

"I don't know. I think the imbalance did something. There's too much Chaos in this realm—if you pay attention, you can feel it. Something changed while you were in that room, and I think when you harvested Chaos to bring him back . . . Well, that was the final push."

Syra reflected on her running theory and the chasm. She shook her head. "When I saw Shevana do what she did, I collapsed and—"

"I know," he replied with a snort. "I saw the destruction."

Syra didn't find it so humorous. "I did it. I'm the reason this is all happening."

"Don't do that to yourself," he snapped. "I didn't come all this way to watch you pity yourself. I won't sympathize."

"I wasn't asking for your sympathy," she said, and crossed her arms. "Are we done here?"

A muscle in his jaw ticced. "Think with your head," he warned, voice low. "If he poses a danger, I'll kill him myself." He turned and walked down the hall without even glancing back. Syra watched him go, startled by his words. Zarek wasn't threatening. She refused to hear that. The only person here who was any threat was Sekar. And even that was hard to admit after everything he'd done for her.

She entered the chamber again. "I'll be right outside," Raid told her. The Guardian stepped out but kept the door cracked. Syra was finally alone, but she couldn't move. Zarek still hadn't turned her way, and that made her fidgety. He was intentionally not doing so, and she feared he was angry with her. Perhaps he just had nothing to say.

"I can't eat all this," he announced. Zarek sounded almost normal—an attempt to break the awkwardness—and that gave her the courage to finally approach. Her heart pounded against her ribs, practically bruising them, and she hardly breathed until she sat in the chair to his left. Then she looked at him.

The pale blue skin was the first thing she saw, followed by his ruffled black hair. But it was his eyes that startled her. The red coloring was there, but it was garnished with patches of white. They were a stark contrast to his usual stoic look. His Marking peeked out along his neck and forearms where the sleeves stopped. His wounds were nearly gone, a relief after the state she'd seen him in on the podium—though that too was the result of what she'd done.

Nervously, she prodded his lifeforce, and her body went rigid. Zarek's was chaotic, unsettled, full of different souls that didn't belong. Each fought for a chance to be in control, shoving and pushing the others out of the way, all while Zarek's lifeforce remained brightest. His soul was condemned.

Syra didn't know how to fix this. Nausea stormed her senses. When she'd brought Erun back, she never had a chance to meet him and see the consequences of her actions. Now, with Zarek, it was clear that her decision to keep him alive might be a fate worse than death. Old stories of the possessed were passed down through every generation. Soul Speakers warned to keep the restless souls at arm's length. If one got in and tampered a lifeforce, it was torment. If more arrived, it was an ugly descent into madness. Sekar must have known.

In Zarek's hands was a cup. He raised it to his lips and drank slowly, not speaking until he set the cup down. "You came for me."

"It was the right thing to do." The answer felt shallow on her tongue, and by the looks of it, Zarek thought so too.

"That and risking your life are two different things." He motioned at the array of basic cheeses and breads. "You should eat." Tension as thick as sludge seeped its way into every crevice around them.

Syra wasn't hungry, but she reached for the bread anyway. It was stale and dried out, flavorless, but she ate it. "How are you feeling?" she asked once she swallowed.

"Like I've got a hundred voices trying to tell me what to do."

He knew. Syra thought she might throw up. "We can try and fix it."

He laughed, but it was short, hollow. "You have no idea what you did to me, do you?"

Syra kept quiet. At the time, all she'd wanted was to keep him alive.

"You bound my soul to countless others with Chaos. You see it, don't you?" Faintly, she nodded. "Sekar did too. No man can withstand a sentence as damning as this. When I close my eyes, they get louder. When I stay awake, my thoughts drift and aren't my own."

Syra could taste his desperation—sour—or maybe it was her own. "We could try and find a Soul Speaker."

"And do what?" He scoffed. "You've done this with Chaos."

She wanted to insist that a path existed, but nothing came to mind. This was her doing, and unless she could manage to figure out a way to split souls and still keep him alive, she was at a loss. Guilt crushed her in her seat. This was not the life she wanted for Zarek. He was tough, but few stories existed of men living long when they were bound to a soul.

"You shouldn't have come for me."

The words were a blow to her already fragile mindset about the entire encounter. She nearly choked on the bread but managed to get another bite down. Her mouth was drier than the desert. "What do you mean? What was I supposed to do?"

"Anything but that," Zarek said. He stared at the tea in his hands. "You could have gotten yourself killed."

Instead, she'd condemned Zarek to a life that would spiral out of control. He was a Guardian, a friend, and her mentor, but no mind was built to withstand the prison she'd sentenced him to. She'd wanted to hope it would be different because of what he was, but the volatility of his lifeforce confirmed he was already at war with the countless who wanted him.

Still, that didn't change how she needed him. How she couldn't imagine a life without his poor-timed sarcasm and unwavering support for her.

"I would have rather gotten myself killed doing that than living my life wondering if I should have done something different."

"And now look at you," Zarek replied coolly. "The hero."

Syra gawked. "Was I supposed to let you die? What would I have told Dryl?"

The Guardian was a statue. "You would have told him you did the best you could, but it wasn't enough. Don't bring him into this."

The warning was clear. "Zarek, I don't know what you want from me." Emotions made her cheeks flush. The chill was gone from her bones. His temper was always short, but this was unrecognizable behavior.

"I want you to do the right thing," he told her, his grip tightening on the cup. "But you can't even do that."

Bread still in hand, she waved at him as she spoke. "*Saving your life was the wrong thing to do?*" She emphasized each word, getting louder. She didn't care if Raid heard. Let the whole palace hear her. There would be no shame in what she'd done.

"Yes." Zarek's response cut right through her, tearing apart the rising frustration. He looked at her now, heated. "Yes, it was. That was my destiny, and you couldn't even grant me that. Instead, you've given me a life that will undoubtedly end in the hands of madness."

Syra stared, unsure if she was speaking to the real Zarek or if someone had taken his place—one of the countless souls she felt shifting inside him. Her hands fell into her lap, and all the fight left her instantly. The Guardian shook his head, set his tea down sharply, and dragged his hands over his face. The silence spanning between them lasted centuries, but the tension remained, bubbling over like a hot kettle.

"Everything I ever was came from that woman." His words were drenched in spite. "I spent centuries doing her bidding, molding to her needs and desires. The man in the mirror was who she wanted, not who I was. And when I left it all behind, I . . . didn't know who I was anymore."

"That's not true," she whispered.

"It was—and still is." He left no room to argue. "I thought time would give me a chance to heal and collect myself, but it only made the separation more agonizing. Every decision I ever made became more real." Zarek scoffed. "I couldn't believe my luck when we were ambushed. It was finally my chance to be free."

Syra opened her mouth to speak, but he shot her a glare. "I was *relieved* when she plunged that blade into my heart. Finally, I could be free of her torment once and for all." His voice shook, and Syra shrank into her chair. "And then you come along and rip me from my peace, only to bring me back and remind me why I ran in the first place."

A tear broke free, carving a fissure on her cheek until it dropped from her chin and landed on her hand. This was not the man she thought she knew. Zarek was strong-willed, stubborn; he could piss off Death herself. That was the Guardian Syra had come to know so well, but underneath that tough exterior was someone else. Someone who hated himself for what he'd done and loathed the world. He'd been trying to manage the winds of a storm he couldn't dare dream of controlling.

"At the Infernol," she whispered, "you were so distant at times." It was not a question. It was a fact. Zarek's behavior made sense now. Sure, they'd had their good moments, but when he thought no one was looking, the confident and overbearing attitude dulled.

The Guardian didn't answer and instead grabbed his tea. His silence was worse than if he'd insulted her.

Syra hauled the bread at him. It was childish, but she didn't care. It got his attention, and that was all that mattered. He startled, and the bread fell to the ground. She partially rose from her seat, letting the words escape without wondering how they sounded. "How could you?" The door opened, but nobody came in. Let them have their show. "How could you dare think about that? You gave me a chance at life that nobody else has done. You left everything behind to help me. Risked your life for me, and what do I get in return?" Fury trickled from every part of her, and she lashed out, knocking the cup from his hands. Tea went all over the bread and cheese, and the cup bounced off the table and onto the rug. He never flinched. "I get a man who can't even face his own reflection. Who wanted to *die*."

"Syra—"

"No," she snapped. "I don't care what you have to say to justify yourself. When I was chained and bleeding, you were my priority. When I marched into this palace, the only thing I cared about was you. And this is how you repay me? This is how you repay Dryl? Everyone?"

"Was I supposed to ask permission for how I should feel?" The question cut right through her. Zarek's tone was hot, the words hardly audible. He might as well have screamed. "Was I so desperate for Syra's approval that I needed to tell you my deepest secrets? I have a duty. That was why I did what I did. I didn't do it to earn your friendship or gain your approval. I did it because I was upholding the Order's promise to protect this realm. What I feel is none of your business."

Syra wanted to disappear. No. She needed to leave. Zarek was a lifeline, a friend, someone she'd relied on for many moons. But he hadn't felt the same in return. Being chained and wounded hurt far less than his words.

Nodding, she mumbled, "Okay." When she could look at him again, they would speak about the realm fracture, but not now. Right now, she wanted to run.

Syra made her way to the open door. Raid didn't make it obvious he'd been listening, but she knew he was on the other side. Humiliation washed over her, and she was ready to bolt out of the room when Zarek spoke up again, and she stopped.

"What you did to me. I don't even recognize myself."

She dabbed at the rogue tears, vision blurring.

"I hope you're happy, Syra." He still hadn't raised his voice. "Granted the ability to bring the dead back? There is no crueler gift than that."

She didn't wait to see if he said more.

The Royal Code

The chamber they stood in had once been a study. It had been dusted, furniture rearranged, and guards set up next to the door. Cyrus stood by the podium, which now held the silver dragon egg. Alaric was on the other side, and next to the king was the chancellor, Asher. Asher constantly returned to the dragon egg, and Cyrus had already caught him once holding it. He didn't blame the man—to the rest of the world, this was divine intervention. To Cyrus, it was a task that needed to be checked off his list.

They'd stayed up most of the night identifying potential individuals. Alaric insisted he could go to bed, but Cyrus refused. Sitting in the king's large study, they handpicked each person who would be requested to arrive throughout the day.

A total of seven—three women and four men, of various ages, all from high-standing families. He'd told Alaric that he wanted to see normal citizens, but the king explained that it would take another full moon to identify the right citizens to be approached. They wanted secrecy, not a public show.

The respected families selected would keep their mouths shut, as Alaric promised, but Cyrus wasn't satisfied, reminding him of his own upbringing. The king swayed, and they decided to compromise. Today would be the respected families, handpicked for their loyalty, resources, and reputation. If this failed, they would expand their search.

The youngest today was sixteen, which Cyrus had also argued over. He appreciated the young spirit, but to him, that was still a child, and he would not be responsible for a child's death if something happened. After some debate, though, he relented. If the girl knew what she was getting into, then that was on her.

They'd slept in his study. Cyrus never made it out of the chair, not until dawn crested the horizon and spilled into the room. Alaric had quickly signed off on the names then, wiping the sleep from his face, and handed them to Asher.

As they waited for soldiers to find those they'd chosen, Cyrus ate roasted vegetables and bread, then got dressed. Sozar paced the courtyard, restless, and for once, Cyrus shared the sentiment. He could hardly sit still. It felt like their entire existence was now being weighed. If today failed, they were back to the start, identifying names and hoping they were as reliable as Alaric said. He would do that, over and over, until the right person came along for the dragon. Cyrus just hoped it was sooner than later.

Standing here now, he resorted to drumming his fingers against the top of his hand. He'd listened to Alaric's pleading and worn something that fit the "royal" perception of Dragon Riders—the king's words, not his. The fine shirt's collar hugged his neck, the cuffs were tight, and he couldn't wait to get out of it when this was over. He was far more comfortable in commoner's clothes.

Alaric cleared his throat, and Cyrus looked over. "I feel like I'm courting a wife."

Asher chuckled, and even the soldiers joined, but it was marked by a stifling heaviness.

Sozar was just outside now. They'd purposely chosen this study because it had a window facing the courtyard, so the dragon sat there now, a bold challenge to any potential Rider who dared step out of bounds. The window was open, allowing direct access. Everyone who stood here or had helped make this happen was sworn to secrecy.

The door cracked open, and another soldier poked his head in. "Your Majesty, it is time."

"Has the first arrived?" Alaric asked.

The soldier nodded.

Alaric pulled a small piece of parchment from his jacket. He unfolded it and peered at the scribbled writing. "Vince, son of Lord Gregory?"

"Yes, Your Majesty."

"Good." Alaric folded the parchment but didn't put it away. "At least they are on time." They had spaced each arrival intentionally so that there would be no line. The less obvious they could make the event, the better. Sozar's presence at the window hid the event from any curious onlookers in the courtyard, while still giving the dragon a chance to observe. Staff members had been instructed not to come near this area of the palace for the afternoon.

The door opened again, and a young man stepped in. He was dressed in a dark red coat that looked uncomfortable, and white pants. His hair was pushed back, shiny, but Cyrus could see by the look in his dark gaze that this was an outfit of his father's choice, not his. This boy wanted to run, not be stuffed in royal attire.

"Your Majesty," Vince said in greeting, and bowed. He had no weapon at his side, but Cyrus still eyed the boots. He assumed the soldiers had searched there too. "Is that . . ." The young man's accent was thick with the southern tongue that Cyrus had grown so used to hearing here.

"It is," said Alaric. "You've been sworn to secrecy—do not forget." A warning. Cyrus shot him a quick glance. He hoped the king could maintain his composure.

"Um, yes, Your Majesty," Vince hastily replied. "I, um—" His put-together demeanor faltered instantly. "Is there something you need from me?" That dark gaze shifted back and forth between the king, the egg, Sozar, and Cyrus a dozen times in a matter of a few heartbeats.

Alaric showed no concern. "Step forward, Vince." When the young man hesitated, the king said, "Do so now. We're on a schedule." That snapped Lord Gregory's son back to reality, and he did as instructed. Cyrus wanted to call him a young man, but the untouched skin and polished hands made him grimace. This was a boy—he didn't have a single scar on his hand. His nails looked trimmed, hair precisely placed, and his arms were thinner than those of most warriors. This was not a fighter. This boy would spend his days sitting at a council table before he ever raised a sword. He halfway wondered if that was Lord Gregory's intent—the man didn't have a place on the council, but things could always change with the right persuasion.

"Place your hand on the dragon egg," Alaric continued. He sounded bored, devoid of emotion. Like this was another day of managing appointments rather than trying to find the next Dragon Rider. Vince hovered his hand over the egg but did not lower it. "It's not going to explode." When Vince still didn't do anything, the king reached over and pushed the boy's hand onto the egg. "That's what I meant. Now, hold it there."

Cyrus was happy to just stand by. Alaric was more than thrilled to take control of the situation. Vince would have never made it to the egg if Cyrus had been in charge. One look made it obvious this was not a Rider.

"Right, take it off." Vince pulled his hand back like the egg burned him to the touch. He looked at his hand, then at the king.

"Now what? What was that for?"

"Just a little test," Alaric replied. "Go on now. You've done your duty. Remember what you swore to, Vince. I don't want to have a chat with your father about a loose tongue."

"That's it?" Now that the moment was over, Vince didn't want to leave. Cyrus chewed on a reply, knowing the king wouldn't let this last. "You invited me here to touch an egg? Is it even real?"

Cyrus snorted, drawing attention to him. Vince's brave arrogance shattered instantly. "It is real," he said, "and you're wasting our time. The king spoke. You are dismissed."

Sozar rumbled his agreement. *You have come a long way*, the dragon observed. Cyrus wasn't sure what to say, so he didn't reply. The only thing he did was share a small look over his shoulder with the dragon.

"Apologies, Your Majesty." Vince bowed his head at Cyrus. "Master Rider." He turned and immediately left without a single glance back. When the door closed, Alaric let out a long sigh.

"His father will have his head for that behavior."

Cyrus raised his brow. "You're going to tell him?"

"And why wouldn't I?" The king raised his chin, proud. "He is the son of a lord. There are standards to be upheld, acceptable behaviors, and a bloodline to honor. Gregory will hear from me. I have no tolerance for disrespect. He was chosen because of the family's reputation, but his son behaves like a wild boar. Unacceptable." Alaric looked at his parchment again. "Ah, we should be expecting Malari next. Our youngest."

"Let's hope she's got a bit more between the ears," Cyrus commented. He was happy to do this with the king, but they were already one down, with no luck. That left six, and if the rest were anything like Vince, they might as well pack up now. Alaric could have pulled from more respected families, but Cyrus had refused. More people meant more risks.

Don't be so hard on yourself, Sozar said. *This is a lifetime commitment. I would be surprised if we found anyone today. This first list is a bit . . . political. Dragons don't care about riches or family names.*

We don't have time, Cyrus countered. He knew the dragon was right, but this was part of the compromise.

Sozar was not amused. *You've made that clear. I waited centuries for you, and I would do it again. She feels the same.*

Cyrus held his words. The point was clear. They might be rushed, but the dragon in the egg wasn't. If she had to wait another century for the right bond, she would, even if it damned them.

Time slipped by. The anxiousness of the day burrowed itself into everyone's stiff stances and small talk. Asher removed a small book from his coat pocket and began to read. A soldier asked what he was reading.

"Pirates," the chancellor replied. "Old stories about their greatest explorations."

Cyrus shifted his weight a dozen times, impatient. When he got bored, he counted his heartbeats, which only reiterated how long they stood there for the next appointment. The soldiers hardly shifted—they were trained for this—but he was losing his mind. Seven prospects split up over the course of the morning and early afternoon. It was a long wait, and now he regretted not bringing something to keep busy, like a book or a gem that needed polishing.

Not that he'd worked with gems in a long time, but he was sure the motions would come back with ease.

The door opened again, and Cyrus nearly jumped from excitement. Finally. "Your Majesty. It is Malari, daughter of Captain Eugene Philips."

"Early," Alaric stated dryly. "Let her in."

A petite girl stepped in, two heads shorter than Cyrus. She wasn't dressed in royal attire but rather seaman clothes. A tunic was tucked into a sash tied around her waist, and her loose pants were swallowed whole by tall boots. Dark, curly hair framed her face, and she bore green eyes akin to the very gems Cyrus had been thinking of. "Your Majesty. Master Rider." She spoke with assertiveness and respect.

Cyrus appreciated her authenticity, but she smelled of the sea. What lover of the water wanted to be stuck in the air? He held his reservations, though. Perhaps he could be wrong. He'd been a miner once, after all, and now look where he'd come.

"Malari," Alaric said, "it's good to see you. Is your father well? The last I heard, he'd caught the seaman's fever."

She nodded, not quite breaking her attention away from the egg. "He returns to work tomorrow, Your Majesty."

"Good. He always knows how to keep the men going. Tell him I wish him well." Alaric didn't miss a beat as he jumped into the next portion. "Malari, what you see before you is a dragon egg. I ask that you step forward and lay your hand on it."

She didn't need to be told twice. The girl laid her hand against the shell. "Whoa," Malari mumbled. "It's so warm to the touch." She looked at Cyrus, who nodded.

"That's good," he acknowledged. "Anything else?" Cyrus sensed a slight shift in the energy around them but nothing worth noting. Still, he stared hard, hoping—praying—that perhaps this was it.

It is not, Sozar informed him. *She finds Malari charming, but that is all.*

Cyrus gawked at the dragon. *You can communicate with her about this?*

Sozar blinked. *Her words aren't clear, but her feelings are. She knows what's happening.*

He nodded and met Alaric's curious gaze. The girl was too focused on the egg to see the look, and as subtly as possible, he shook his head. The king nodded.

"Thank you, Malari, that will be all."

The girl looked between them and then back to the egg. The realization of what this all meant must have dawned on her. "Whoever this dragon hatches for will be so lucky. Thank you for having me." She bowed and left.

When the door shut, the king asked, "How'd you know?"

Cyrus pointed at Sozar. "He can sense her. Just enough to give us some guidance."

The king grinned like a madman. "The magnificent Sozar constantly surprises me. Well done. This will make our job so much easier. I haven't forgotten about our statue, either. I've got men sketching out a design as we speak." Alaric looked at his parchment before Cyrus could beg that Sozar not be referenced as such. "Igran, son of Resere. A good man. He has served the family for as long as I can remember, as head cook. His son is set to take his place."

"And what if his son is chosen?" Cyrus teased. "Who will make your supper then?"

"Asher here will do it," the king said, and patted the chancellor on the shoulder. "I hear you can pour a strong drink. After everything, that's all I need to be a happy man."

Igran wasn't chosen. Neither were Ivy, Serena, Kinsler, or Tule. The frustration mounted, and Cyrus didn't bother hiding it. He paced, rubbed his face, and asked too many questions that were probably unnecessary. Kinsler had had so much potential. The moment the man walked in, Cyrus thought he was perfect. He had the build of a warrior, so little training would be needed for sword fighting. Bright and inquisitive, he carried himself with a humble air. Kinsler asked a lot of the right questions, and he even showed an interest in Sozar. The young man spoke clearly, and most importantly, treated the egg respectfully. Yet, nothing happened. Sozar informed Cyrus that she was not settled on him being the one.

By the time Tule showed up, their last attempt at sealing the future today, Cyrus's head hurt, and his feet were sore. Asher finished his small book, proudly tucking it away as the last arrived. Ivy had been good, and so too Serena. Both women were excellent options in his opinion, and a gnawing fear grew that maybe he should have brought more eggs back. If he had, maybe they would be celebrating rather than trying to keep their tempers in check. If it had been up to him, he would have chosen one of the women, but it wasn't. It was the dragon's final say. She was the one who would pair with a Rider for the rest of her life.

Cyrus was not one to lose his composure, but as Tule left the room, he grumbled and slunk down to the ground. "Tomorrow, we need to do the same thing." He looked up at Alaric. "Can we do ten tomorrow?"

The king nodded at the chancellor, who left them alone. Soldiers stood at the door, unmoving, but Cyrus didn't care. After all this time at the palace, he'd grown used to their presence wherever he went. Them not being there unsettled him now.

"I can try, but I am due for several trading appointments," Alaric said. "You can use this room, though. We can do the same setup— Sozar here is our key to making this seamless."

Cyrus dreaded the idea of leading the process but knew this was the best option. "Fine. We'll start early tonight, so that we can finish and get some rest."

"Fair enough." Alaric tapped the egg like a child would a rock. "How do you feel about stuffed fish?"

"Are you asking me or her?"

The king shrugged. "Whoever wants to answer."

For once, Cyrus needed something to take the crippling anxiety. "Why don't we get something to drink?" he said, standing. "And then we can worry about names."

The king grinned and motioned for the door. "You're speaking my language. I'll ask Jarmen to bring extra liquor."

To Be Worshipped

Sunny flicked his ears in annoyance. The shire had been munching away at some hay when Morei reached him. The steed was grumpy this morning, unsurprisingly. He was on edge too. Everywhere was thick with tension. Morei glanced up. No storms, so why was it so hard to breathe? The air was crisp, the heat manageable, but he was still sweaty. He opened and closed his hands over Sunny's reins several times, and a jolt of unrecognizable anxiety shot down his spine.

Morei was terrified.

He didn't want to admit it, but the feelings were there. He'd tossed and turned all night, and when slumber didn't find him, he drank. Truth be told, it was either that or killing, and he knew he couldn't act violently without staining his reputation even further.

The king replayed his actions on the coast over and over, wondering if he could have done anything else—or *should* have. The last time he'd harvested fire, he'd become the scapegoat. Geral had rejected him, after everything he'd done for them. Morei swore he'd be more careful moving forward, especially with a kingdom that he'd forcefully conquered, but in the moment, the only thing that had mattered to him was protecting the city.

The soldiers who witnessed it respected him, but he couldn't decipher if it was out of fear or awe. The king knew the benefit of fear and the control he could elicit, but he didn't want to be known as an authoritarian ruler either. There was a delicate balance between power and respect.

Prior to this morning, he'd told himself he'd done the right thing. He reaffirmed this even after Eazon left. The encounter with the God was nothing but a nuance, but he was mildly annoyed that he'd said he wouldn't be back. Not that the deity had offered anything beneficial to begin with. Morei was tired of Gods—and people who thought they knew him better than he did.

Sunny laid his ears back. "Hey," Morei said, placing his hand against the shire's neck. "Behave yourself. It'll be over soon." If the steed could have responded, he knew Sunny would have scolded him for his piss-poor attitude.

He looked over to where Isla and Rhys were on their steeds, along with a handful of soldiers, including Edwin and Lord Varun. They were going to make the speech in the city center, and it was important to have at least one member of the council present to show support. Lord Varun had offered without hesitation. They'd had words in the past, but the lord's tough exterior had softened for Morei. They shared commonalities, and while neither spoke on the matter, they now shared a mutual respect.

Soon, Morei would be face-to-face with the citizens, and they would either reject or accept him. He didn't know what he would do if they denied him like Geral had.

No. Morei knew what he would do, but he hoped it didn't come to that.

The king stole a look at the princess. She looked away, which irritated him. It felt like she wanted something from him, but what? To tell her she was right and that he did want to be accepted? Morei would never admit that.

When he met the chancellor's eyes, Rhys held them. For someone so close to seeing Death, he was sitting tall and comfortably.

"You and I need to talk," Morei told him.

The chancellor nodded. "I know." No disdain or anger, not even sarcasm. He sounded resolved.

"Don't do that," Morei snapped.

Rhys raised his brow. "Do what?"

Morei gestured at him. "Sound normal. It doesn't fit you."

That earned the faintest smile—the most genuine one he'd seen from him—and Morei straightened in his saddle. "Let's get this over with," he said. He urged Sunny forward with his boots, and the shire obeyed. The king needed to replace his leather soon. His gloves and boots were the same he'd left Geral in.

Hooves clapped against the cobblestone street as the group made their way to the city center. The stench of ash still hung in the air, but it was easing up with the new day. Up ahead, the people were waiting. At the sight of the crowd, Morei swallowed. He'd never been this uncertain in his life when facing the citizens he was supposed to lead. The tremor in his hand was no longer from the aftereffects of harvesting the Dark Energy, and he squeezed the reins tighter.

When he'd dressed this morning, he was requested by the council to wear the Caster crown, but Morei refused. He didn't want to separate himself even further from the citizens by wearing a piece that reminded everyone of his title. The people didn't need that. What they needed was reassurance that a greater plan for Caster existed.

"Try not to kill anyone," Rhys whispered from behind. It was clearly in jest. Even if he despised the man, Morei liked that he offered some predictability.

As they neared, people of all ages stared, even children. Some citizens had bandages on various parts of their bodies, others had open scrapes, but many were unharmed. Some of these people had picked up weapons without hesitation to defend their city, and that told him a lot about how they felt.

They stopped. People encircled them, with soldiers taking protective positions. Still, the entire setup felt informal. When Morei looked over at Isla, she returned his gaze. Things had been awkward between them, but he'd realized something this morning. If he didn't take her as queen, he risked losing the people's trust. The day he'd reinstated her title was the day he'd made the decision to have her as Caster's queen, even if he hadn't known it then. Seeing her here, dressed formally and by his side, he knew he didn't want anyone else.

People stood, smashed together, filling the streets. He was surprised nobody was on the roofs of the buildings, but perhaps that was against the law. Anyone could sneak up on a roof and let loose an arrow; it would be harder to charge the king directly.

He cleared his throat. The last of the crowd's mumbles died.

"We are alive." Those first words came out with ease, despite the raging storm of anxiety that tore through his insides. No matter what, he was still a king, and he intended on staying that way. "But it came at the cost of people you knew. Family, friends, comrades. It was their lives that were taken to secure this city, and that will not be forgotten." He motioned to Rhys. "With the chancellor's help, we will construct a statue to honor those who gave their lives. It will be placed on the port and will list all the names of the fallen.

So, if you know someone who passed, please set a time with the chancellor to confirm the name they were known by."

He saw some nods. Good. "Isla will see to it that those directly impacted by the attack are taken care of. Funds and resources will be provided to help you rebuild your lives as quickly and easily as possible. So, if you are one of those individuals, please set up time with her." That earned a quick wave of murmurs. The people needed to be acknowledged.

"As for me," he started. What he would say next would be the first time he'd made this announcement publicly, and he hoped the citizens approved. "My goal is simple: I want Caster to become the heart of an empire. It will become the greatest city the Vore World has ever seen, but I can't do that with just the council's support. It is not a secret that we've expanded our territory"—a politically correct phrase for seizing Ferguson—"and that's possible because of you all. What Caster displayed against the Red Queens was courageous, and if not for the quick action by those who weren't even soldiers, I don't believe we'd be having this conversation."

Morei wasn't here to take the credit. He needed these citizens to feel like they were the most important part of this victory. As he prepared to say more, he watched people exchange looks. The words died on his lips as the first row dropped to their knees. The soldiers looked startled, and some even reached for the hilt of their swords. Then people started to pound on their chests, just like the soldiers had done on the coast, and more fell to their knees behind.

A chant followed, low and barely audible, but it grew as more joined in. "Master of fire. Ender of wars." The words repeated over and over and soon became so loud that Morei could hardly hear himself think.

He remained motionless. The people weren't rejecting him or throwing insults, they were praising him. He, the ex-king of Geral, who had murdered their ruler, was being worshipped by the very citizens who should have demanded his head. He let the words sink deeper into his mind, turning his blood hot with bliss.

"Master of fire! Ender of wars!"

They believed in him. They wanted him. Morei had spent so long floundering for the acceptance of Geral, even well before he'd taken the throne. His sole purpose had always been to protect the citizens, and here he'd done it. He'd forged a path between tradition and progressive thinking, lowered crime, and reestablished Caster to be known for more than just violence. He'd poured his all into this city. Damn the risks, he'd done it. And he would do it again.

A grin stretched across his face. He couldn't remember the last time he'd smiled this euphorically. Slowly, he slid off the saddle and approached the people. Soldiers stepped out of the way. If they said something, he did not hear. The nearest people provided him with a path through the crowd. The king did not hesitate, walking deeper into the sea of bodies. Those he passed dipped their head in respect as they continued their chanting.

He was completely separated from his soldiers. If the citizens wanted to do something now, they could, but they didn't. Instead, he was handed gifts. One older lady gave him a rose, another a bracelet. People grabbed his hands and squeezed them. Nobody displayed fear at the visible black veins, and a few even pressed their lips against the top of his hand. That stunned him, but he couldn't react fast enough to tell them to stop. The warm lips against his skin were unpleasant—worship and praise were separated by a very fine line, and it was blurring. But Morei couldn't stop them, and he didn't want to. He deserved this. After all that he'd done, he deserved to be acknowledged.

An older man stepped in front of him. Scarring covered his leathery skin, and his white hair was braided down his back. Faded ink decorated the exposed skin. This was a retired seaman. Morei had been here long enough to recognize one.

The seaman dug into the pocket of his old tunic. He wasn't chanting like the others, but the respectful dip of his head assured Morei he wouldn't do anything malicious. Slowly, he reached forward and unveiled the gift in his hand.

A gold medallion. Imprinted on it was the Caster wolf, and along the edges of the metal were three words in the Old Tongue. The king recognized "resilience" and "luck" but could not decipher the last one. The lettering was worn out, and he would need to study it more closely. The medallion was old, maybe an heirloom.

"Take it," the man insisted. "You have our men's respect."

Our men. He wanted to ask more, but he didn't. Morei took the gift and nodded. It was a bit larger than the Krye coin, but still small enough to easily conceal. The grooves in the metal were worn down from countless summers of touch.

"Carry it with you," the man added. "It will bring you luck."

The king nearly laughed. A word he wasn't fond of. People wanted to pray or wish their way into success or good fortune. Morei didn't see it that way. Power brought good fortune. Not the Gods or some medallion.

"Thank you," he told the man.

The seaman stepped back into the crowd. Morei continued on. He didn't want to rush it. If this took all day, so be it.

The king greeted everyone he could. Gifts came, and he finally had to start turning them away. He simply couldn't carry any more. A rose was tucked behind his ear, another in his belt, and he even started putting pieces of jewelry in a pouch, including the medallion. A woman saw him begin to refuse gifts and presented a woven basket. Morei tried to refuse that too, but she insisted. They revered him.

When he finally made his way back to Lord Varun and the others, he was relieved to see that nobody had moved. The soldiers greeted him with a bow, and the king handed the basket to the closest one. "To my study," he ordered.

Morei ascended Sunny, then unsheathed his sword and raised it above his head. "Citizens, this is the start of a new era," he cried out. Immediately, the crowd jumped to their feet and roared. The king continued over them, drunk from their approval. "Long live Caster!"

People called the phrase back. It carried, and soon everyone was shouting, "Long live Caster!" as loud as they could. They pumped their fists in the air, some holding their weapons to replicate Morei. Even the soldiers joined. He watched them in awe. This was what being a king meant. No greater feeling was possible.

He spun Sunny around and motioned for the group to follow. They rode in silence back to the palace, listening to the praise continue. The citizens were going wild now.

After they handed their steeds over in the privacy of their stables, Morei looked to the group.

"How was that?"

The chancellor limped from the injury he'd earned but was the first to speak. "You've done something that hasn't been seen since my grandfather was a boy."

They walked through the courtyard, earning the looks of staff members and other soldiers alike. "What is that?"

"Bring the people together," Edwin answered, as if it was obvious. "Nothing is more terrifying than Caster citizens getting along."

Morei looked over at Isla. Her shoulders were squared, her chin up. She looked like the queen she was born to be. Morei knew what the next step was politically. He needed to leverage the people's acceptance. They saw him as a hero, and they would see him as reliable and stable if he took a wife. Isla was his key. Proud or not, she needed to accept her bloodline if he was to get the empire he wanted. When they were alone, he would ask her, but not here. It might be just a formal arrangement, but she was still owed the respect of deciding for herself without an audience.

Not that she had a choice.

"Your thoughts?" he asked her once the group started to disperse. She was walking behind everyone, so he fell back to meet her.

The princess blinked. "What can I say? I've never seen anything like it."

The king stared at her, unsure if she was being cynical or not. He hated to admit it, but he needed to know her opinion on the matter. If they were going to rule together, they would need to act as one. A fractured ruling wouldn't last a season, not in a city like this.

"What?" she asked. He didn't like the way she was looking at him.

Morei took a deep breath as he stopped her at the base of the grand staircase. Staff and soldiers made their way around them, stealing looks their way. At him. He tried to ignore it. The spell would wear off with time, or so he told himself. After Geral, he knew what they said about him. They were talking about Dark Energy, his black veins, his actions.

"What's wrong with you?" he challenged. "We just secured Caster, and you're acting like we lost. What is it?"

"I'm glad we won," Isla replied, and crossed her arms.

"Are you?" He lowered his voice, keeping his expression devoid of the anger he felt. "Because you don't act like it. Isla, I can't figure you out. One moment, you're breaking into my room to prove you're not afraid, the next you won't even look my way. What is it? Are you unhappy with your position?"

The princess ran her fingers through her hair as if trying her best to look unbothered by his harsh words. It didn't work. A blind man could have seen how uncomfortable she was. "Tell me," he insisted. "You think poorly of me for my actions?"

"Yes, I do." Now she sounded furious. "You walked out there and slaughtered countless people. And when they were trying to leave, you continued to kill. I understand defending Caster, but not the rest. Is that really who you are?"

It was. "You don't know the first thing about war, Isla. You've spent your summers scrubbing stone and cleaning clothes." He leaned in, hoping to assert control over this conversation. "When your enemy is at their weakest, you end them. I didn't just win the battle, I won the war. The Red Queens won't think twice about storming our port again. A critical win when we are expanding west. Would you prefer it otherwise?"

"I would prefer that we didn't have to worry about war." Her hard exterior cracked, and he saw a woman drowning in compassion. "I know what the soldiers are saying about you, about what they saw." She looked at his hands, studying him as if seeing him for the first time. "You have no reason to do what you do. You're desperate and cruel when there is no need."

This woman had no idea what he would sacrifice to have what was rightfully his—what he'd already sacrificed. If she feared war, he would give her more than just that to worry about. "I'll give you war." He lowered his voice, dragging out every piece of disgust he had for her empathy. "I'll give you a reason to hate me."

She leaned back, flinching. "You already have."

Isla might as well have stabbed him, twisted the blade, and left him for dead. She was the most important piece in all this. If he failed to secure a queen, he would never make it. No matter what he said, he couldn't deny that. The cold truth was that he'd given her a second chance, but he'd been willing and ready to take it all away if she didn't prove she wanted this. Now, faced with that opportunity, he couldn't.

Morei swallowed the hard lump of pure frustration, unable to find anything to say in return. Empowered, Isla raised her chin. Even with their height difference, she might as well have been taller than him at this moment, as her next words slashed him at the knees.

"You don't know what you want, Morei. You never have."

The Dead Spare No One

Ten Guardians, including Raid, stood in the tight space. Syra was squeezed up against Sekar and a Guardian she didn't know the name of. Raid stood before them all, arms crossed and face scrunched into a scowl. She'd barely gotten a bath in and wiped the sour taste from her mouth with day-old stew full of unidentified meat when she was fetched for the meeting. Dressed in oversized clothes, she'd cinched the waist with a belt and stuffed the pants in some worn-out boots. It was either this or one of Shevana's dresses. Death's Sword hung at her hip. The one good thing to come out of this day.

The chamber was windowless, devoid of color, and made up of dark stone. It was cool, and she wished for a cloak. Several fissures breached the ceiling and walls, casting shadows from where the lanterns' light struck. One piece drew her attention—a massive raven carved into the stone behind Raid. Its wings were spread wide, the feathers done in precise detail, all in various shades of black. The raven was the only polished piece in the room.

Everyone knew what was wrong, but if they had concerns, they didn't say anything. Not here, anyway. Zarek's arms were crossed, and he was leaning up against the wall. He hadn't even looked her way when he arrived, which hurt more than she could describe. She'd overstepped and made a decision with a price too high to pay. Those crimson-and-white-flecked eyes were locked on no one in particular, his lips pinched into a thin line.

The air was thick, and between the pungent tension and being pinned between two men twice her size, she felt like she was going to suffocate before this was all over. She was relieved when Raid finally opened his mouth.

"This is it." He gestured at everyone. "This is all the Soul Realm has left. Those who still remained loyal to Shevana no longer serve us." An elegant way of saying they'd been killed. "Centuries ago, there was an army of us. Now . . ." Raid shook his head, then turned to see the raven behind him. "Stay curious, stay bold. That was our life's work, and I know for everyone in here, it still is."

Raid looked back at the small crowd, meeting Syra's gaze fully. "We owe it to you to keep going. We owe it to the souls awaiting passage to the Afterlife, and we owe it to the living realm—a place we all once called home—to keep moving forward." His chest rose and fell, and he shook his head. In an instant, the tone shifted. "The realm fracture has widened, and the demons have started to cross. They intend to wage war against the living, but that means war against us. Does anyone remember our oaths?"

A beat of silence, then slowly, men spoke.

"Protect the defenseless," Razer muttered.

"Honor for the those who have yet to cross," Meril said.

"Ve'hem," Vaeke added.

Several others spoke, lost to Syra, but when everyone grew quiet, Raid nodded fiercely, ready for battle. "We must close that realm fracture. The chasm changes everything. We can't wage a battle across two realms with just us. But what we can do is cut them off at their knees, then pick them off one by one here. Does anyone have any objections to that?"

Syra could hardly believe what she was hearing. Elyas would rage a war against the remaining people in this room if she didn't consider his offer, but worrying about the Ka-Geíon felt petty. Everyone knew what was at stake. They would have nothing if they didn't prioritize the fracture.

"We've been here," she announced. Men waited, expecting her to continue, so she stood a little taller. "The Infernol. They've had the same discussion about closing the realm fracture. Zarek . . ." She immediately regretted bringing him into this. "He was looking into ways of addressing the fracture."

"And?"

Everyone's attention was on the Guardian. He softly chuckled at a joke no one heard. When he looked their way, he finally acknowledged Syra. It was like looking at fifty men, all with different motives, and she couldn't tell which one she trusted or feared.

"We need an immense amount of energy to close it, and there's no guarantee that even that works." Zarek's words came out deliberately slow, and he didn't move. "Historical records are slim to none. Most of the text we could have used was either buried with the fall of the Rider Federation or burned by Shevana."

"So we go to the ruins of the Rider Federation," Jerun said.

Sekar scoffed. "You can't. With the fall, a curse was placed. Perhaps more like protection. Only the one chosen can enter and see what has been hidden all these summers."

"So, what?" the Guardian next to her said. She thought his name might be Sazi, but she wasn't sure. "We go door to door and see if someone is chosen?"

"Can we even confirm the records are in these ruins?" Raid asked. He scratched his face. "I mean, it makes sense. They were the guardians of the living. They had all the ancient text they could get their hands on. Tombs from the Vorelian Empire only existed in their library." Sekar nodded. Of course, he would know that. "So much of our documented communication was lost when Shevana did what she did. There's very little we can confirm."

"I can," Sekar announced. When everyone looked his way, he laughed. The sound was haunting. "Don't act so thrilled."

"You are the God Killer," Raid added distastefully. "Your name is on the dead's tongue."

"I'm flattered," Sekar bit back. Syra tensed. The vision of their linked memory flashed before her. She couldn't forget his brewing rage while he stormed the Liral palace. "I have walked those halls. I saw things none of you will ever have the chance to see. Indeed, some texts date back to before I was born. What you seek is in those ruins."

She nudged him in the arm. This close, she was able to do it without hardly moving. He looked at her, and she gave him a small nod. In the motion, she hoped he understood that she appreciated him here.

"It won't be just anyone," Zarek said from behind. "The rise of the Dragon Riders has begun. One of them will be chosen."

"How can we even confirm that?" Syra asked. Hunting a Dragon Rider felt like an impossible feat, especially when they weren't even in the same realm.

"It will be Cyrus." The answer came from her left. The God spoke quietly but without hesitation or doubt. "Dameon is with Henry."

"Well, that sounds great in theory, but how are you certain?" Raid challenged. "A Dragon Rider is a Dragon Rider."

"Because Hyle is making the decision."

Another God. Another risk. Sekar was the only deity she'd ever met, but he'd proven to be complicated, and she couldn't fathom dealing with another God with the same mentality. These were the people the Vorelians worshipped, herself included at one point. She wanted to ask so many things, but she settled on, "How can you trust him?"

"Cyrus? Or Hyle?" Sekar asked.

"Hyle."

A small smile touched the God's lips, appearing more disappointed than satisfied. "Hyle is probably the only God you should trust."

They stared at each other for several heartbeats. She wanted to push, shove, slap him, anything to shake Sekar out of this perpetual need to say all the wrong things. He had saved her life, protected her, and yes, he'd done horrible things, but he'd never done her malicious harm. In retrospect, he'd been the only one ever willing to tell her the truth. And while it had been a bitter reality, she was grateful. She was stronger, braver, and more capable because of what he'd done.

"So, what now?" Vaeke asked, finally breaking the silence.

"We wait," Sekar answered. A groan swept through the room, and he raised his hand. "One never rushes a Dragon Rider."

That annoyed her. "Who are you to have patience?" When he faced her, she added, "You ripped me out of the living realm and threw me into the Eternal Flame. What patience do you have?"

He didn't flinch. "Let me rephrase that for you, Princess. You can't rush him. The Dragon Rider who is chosen must willingly choose his destiny. You cannot go to him, demand he storm the ruins of the Rider Federation, and think all your answers are granted that way. The Rider must accept all consequences and outcomes, even before he sits on the back of his dragon and takes flight. It was to protect the chosen one from fools like you who believe they can get anything they want by raising their voice high enough."

Syra was in no mood for the passive-aggressiveness. She'd had enough from Zarek already. "Now I know why so many people don't like you. You can't ever figure out who you want to be." She turned to Raid, who looked more like a young boy caught red-handed with stolen food than a centuries-old Guardian. "So, we wait. But we need to watch him, right? Is there any way we can track this Cyrus to ensure he makes it to the ruins? Isn't that in Eiyrăl somewhere?"

"Northern Eiyrăl," Zarek confirmed.

"And does anyone have any idea where he is now?" Syra pressed.

"No."

She looked to Sekar, expecting him to have the answer, but he kept his mouth shut. The way he looked at her, like he couldn't decide if he wanted to stab her or yell at her, made the hairs on the back of her neck stand on end. She'd struck a nerve. Good.

"We are in a terrible situation," Raid continued, breaking the tense spell. "We can't act until this Cyrus pulls his head out of his ass, but we can't stand by and let the demons have their way with the living realm. What do we do?"

"We need men scouting the fracture," Zarek proposed. "We don't even know how many are crossing right now."

Syra chewed on her bottom lip, eyeing him. He spoke like normal, like he was unbothered by his current circumstances. She knew it was for show. Guardians didn't betray vulnerabilities, raised to be callous, but she wondered what he was thinking after their discussion. Nobody looked at him differently, not like how she was, waiting for him to drop dead or succumb to an unforeseen illness. Not that either of those should happen, but she was thinking the worst.

"There's another idea too," she added. "Elyas—"

"No," Sekar answered sharply.

"I wasn't going to propose marriage," she shot back. "Who do you think I am? I was thinking that when the time came, we could leverage that offer. Lure him out. Use me as bait." Syra shrugged, trying to act calm even though she was a nervous wreck about the idea. "My bloodline must rule, but now Shevana is dead, and we have a chasm the size of a city in Ashýon. We need to start prioritizing."

"That cannot last forever," Zarek replied, softer now. "The Soul Realm can't sustain without your bloodline. Eventually, even you need to choose a side."

She couldn't fathom staying here. Not now. Not with everything going on and the realms on the verge of war. She couldn't turn her back on everyone—Dryl, Zane, her promises—so that she could fulfill some family duty. Syra swallowed her bitter anger, needing to stay composed, but underneath all that, she was panicking. They expected her to pick up where Shevana had left off, to take her place and accept this new path without doubt, but she couldn't.

"Destiny is impatient, though," she mumbled, mostly to herself. "I cannot take that throne in good faith now. We need to inform Dryl, resolve this realm fracture, and stop this war before we lose everything. I can't do that from here." The living realm was falling apart, and this one would be next. By the Gods, she hoped Dryl was doing okay—it had been days since they were taken. So much could have happened.

Syra wrinkled her nose, not satisfied. "There has to be a way."

"There is," the Guardian continued. "We take measures to rebuild our forces and wait for Cyrus to reach the Rider Federation. He will. I have no doubt. Until then, we defend our territory, guide souls, and monitor the activity in the living realm."

"With the ten of us?" Raid countered.

"Do you see anyone else?" Zarek challenged. "We need to begin rebuilding immediately. Choose older boys. Find them. Young men, if need. But we cannot stop making progress. If we have to do it all, then so be it."

"How . . ." The question stuck to her lips, and the men watched, waiting for her to finish. They were talking about taking young boys from the living realm and raising them as warriors. Zarek had once told her his story when he and Dryl were boys. Their parents were killed, their village destroyed, after the White Horns raided the coast. Abandoned boys were the Guardians' target, but that still didn't explain how they would train in a realm falling apart.

All empires started somewhere. Syra had heard that once before in her early summers. Perhaps in a story or by a drunken man, but she'd never forgotten it. Small steps were necessary to get anywhere, and even if that meant taking it one day at a time, then that was what had to happen. The men around her all nodded slowly. They were tough, ruthless—she had no doubt they would give this their all. She trusted Raid and Zarek. They had this realm's best interest at heart. And she did too. They would act fast, work hard, and try to keep the Soul Realm from crumbling. In the process, they needed to lessen the blow of the demons bombarding the living realm. That would undoubtedly cause massive energy fluctuations—instabilities that neither realm could afford with this fracture.

"Get your last meals, baths, whatever," Raid ordered, not addressing her unfinished question. She still didn't know if he was their commander or not. "I want to see you men in my study as soon as possible. We'll break up duties then."

Guardians shuffled out. Syra was glad to get some space, but as she followed the last man out, she stopped and closed the door. She turned to face Sekar, who hadn't moved. They'd been through thick and thin, but every time she thought she knew him, she was reminded of just how wrong she was

.

"Why did you say that?" she whispered.

Sekar didn't show one bit of emotion. "Say what?"

It was a challenge. They both knew what this was about. "About Hyle," she told him. "Why would you say that after everything we've been through?"

The way he carried himself, nobody would have ever guessed that two days ago, he was strung up and dying if not for the healing wounds. "I do not lie, Syra."

She swallowed the frustrations, feeling the tone shift. He wasn't speaking out of anger or some need to be cruel. "I don't understand."

"Everything I've ever done, I've done because it was the right thing," Sekar said, closing the gap between them and forcing her eyes up. "Before you or Henry, it was me keeping order. I was the ender of Gods and the bringer of peace. I kept the realms from collapsing, because it was my duty alone to oversee everything. When my brothers and sisters were killed, it was not by anyone else's hand but my own. Chaos wouldn't have it any other way." He plucked her wrist up, twisting it so that the Zyulë Bond glared at them. His grip wasn't as tender as she remembered. "This is my promise to you that no matter what happens, nothing I do was ever meant to intentionally hurt y ou."

Syra didn't try to pull her wrist free, and he made no motion to let go. "I still don't understand. Why this? Why now? What are you trying to tell me?" Sekar was acting odd.

"I've made mistakes," Sekar continued, letting his thumb graze the raised scar. "I've walked a hundred of your lives, and will walk a hundred more so long as Mother permits. Yet, between the thousands I've encountered, you remain the only woman I will ever regret."

Tears burned, and she blinked rapidly. "You're not going anywhere," she pleaded. Something was different about his words, something that tore free any feeling of certainty. They were so *final*. "Why are you telling me this?"

He smiled, and for the first time in a long while, he looked free. "I'm not going anywhere, Syra. Not for a long while." He wrapped his other hand around her neck and brought her in, pressing his lips against her forehead. Everything they'd been through—from the day he met her at Gamer's Village to when she hauled him out of Ashýon—was summed up in that single act. When he pulled away, he whispered, "I can't ever be what you need me to be, and I'm okay with that. I have to be. But I hope that our journey remains as it is—wild and unpredictable. You've given me life, and I will forever be indebted to you for that."

He broke free and approached the door. A chill clung to her, and she swallowed a sob. "Where are you going?" she choked out.

Sekar studied her, looking more untamed now, more like the man she'd come to know so well. "For a walk."

Nobody Lives Forever

Shouting met Cyrus's ears as he stumbled out into the hall. Dawn had hardly arrived, and the night's shadows clung to the surrounding walls and floor with a haunting chill. He closed the door, dressed in a plain tunic and pants. He'd grabbed his belt, afraid he was running into a threat, and was still fumbling with the clasp when a soldier barreled into him.

"Greve's graces," the soldier blurted out, patting Cyrus like he was a fragile ceramic piece. "I'm sorry, Master Rider. Apologies—"

"Don't," Cyrus cut in with a wave of his hand. "What's happening?"

The man's lines deepened across his face. They started down the hall, and the soldier answered, "The chancellor and king." He grabbed leather gloves from a pouch on his belt and put them on midstride. "An assassination attempt."

His heart spasmed. Cyrus gulped in air, trying to understand what he was hearing. This couldn't be happening. They'd just been speaking last night over drinks. Yesterday was the presentation of the dragon egg. Things had gone well, despite not having any serious leads. But Cyrus and Alaric had felt good after going over more names.

Back less than a day, and already a disaster was unfolding. Ever since Hyle showed up on the shore, his life had turned into one catastrophe after the next.

A sharp turn right, and they slammed into a crowd of people, the backs of countless heads, some with armored helmets, others plain. An abundance of soldiers were shouting. Anxiety bubbled up in the back of his throat—he needed answers. The desire to know if Alaric was all right outweighed all other concerns. He tried to ask but got no direct answer. No one was saying anything informational, just spitting more questions and confusion. A cluster of bees making too much noise and not doing anything. When he tried to push his way through, no one budged, distracted by whatever was in front of them, which only worsened his nerves.

Sozar roared. The sound shattered the madness instantly, shook the walls. Some even dropped to their knees for fear the ceiling was caving in. Cyrus ducked out of instinct, only to be met with the dragon's disgusted words. *Rats. Scattered and lost like rats.*

In the newfound silence, people turned to him, wary and in awe, and he shrugged, then pushed forward. This time, the people parted, staff and soldiers alike, until Cyrus was able to wiggle his way up to the front. As he neared, the anxiety blossomed into something akin to cold fear. He couldn't bear the thought that Alaric was dead. They'd formed a brotherly friendship in the unlikeliest of circumstances, weathered each other's quirks, and he admittedly trusted the man with his life. Alaric might have been cruel, but he was loyal.

Relief was the first thing he shamefully felt, but it was short-lived. Before him lay the body of the chancellor. Asher's throat was slashed, allowing the blood to escape. The death was still young, as the red liquid had yet to set, freely roaming the floor. His gaping mouth stretched in a frozen scream, but that was not what unsettled Cyrus. Asher's eyes had been gouged out, leaving dark, gory pits, and in the blood that covered the marble, a single word had been written.

I'num.

The violent mockery of the Old Tongue made his mouth dry. Questions ceased, save for the single one on everyone's mind: Why? The intent was clear—the crime was for Cyrus. Dragon Rider, Sea Flyer, Mountain Flyer, Silver Eyes. Whatever it was they wanted to call him, whoever had done this had carved those letters out in Asher's blood for him.

Sozar. He needed the dragon's opinion. All around, the whispers grew to a frenzy. The people all wanted the same thing: resolve.

The dragon was as concerned as he was. *Perhaps Henry?* Sozar sounded unconvinced. *An act for the king?*

Alaric. Cyrus straightened. He scanned the horde of people, knowing that he wouldn't be among them but needing to be sure. Then he looked beyond Asher and into the chancellor's chamber, a few paces away, the door wide open. Cyrus stepped forward, ignoring the hushed interest of the others. He took care not to get near Asher or the haunting message. At the door, he peered in. The place was untouched, save for the messy sheets and a drink that was half full on a small table next to a chair. Asher had been enjoying some silence, maybe up early due to restlessness, when he'd been attacked.

Commotion ripped his attention away. Voices carried, angry ones, but one in particular drew his attention. Cyrus watched Alaric round the corner with several soldiers, talking fiercely about locks and guards. He was still dressed in his night attire—green silk bottoms—and a cut was partially bandaged along his shoulder. Blood still seeped from it, and the king took a cloth in his hand and dabbed it against his skin. Some old scars that Cyrus had never seen before garnished his chest—gifts from his dead father. Some were burn marks, only a few imprinted by a sword. Alaric slowed to a stop as he beheld the crowd and chancellor's body.

Tension compounded, and he fidgeted with the hilt of his sword nervously. Cyrus knew that look all too well. It was the same look Raj had given him when he refused fealty. Animalistic, a lack of control, rage.

"Who was Asher's next in line? I can't recall," the king asked, devoid of emotion.

The soldier closest to him cleared his throat. "There was no next in line, Your Majesty. We never had that opportunity. Not after what your . . ." He hesitated, beady eyes looking around at the crowd, opening and closing his mouth like a fish out of water. "Father did."

"Hm." Alaric approached the body of his chancellor, showing no disgust. He looked curious. The king knelt before the message. "I'num," he breathed. His gaze flashed to Cyrus, who leaned into the door more, wanting to disappear behind it.

Alaric stood. "Markus, pull the council and get names. I need a chancellor by the end of the day. If I don't like who the council chooses, it's your head." Alaric turned to the crowd and started to give orders. "Priscilla, get you and your ladies to clean this mess. I'm honestly surprised we're still staring at it. I don't want the marble stained, so make sure you scrub good. Repolish it, too. It's looking a little rough." To make his point, he rubbed the sole of his boot. "See how it catches? Good opportunity. Vern, I want you to head the investigation. Two men came in here last night and attempted an assassination—well, one was successful. Based on what I see here, they were not acting together." He waved his hand that held the cloth. "Ah, apologies.

There's a dead man in my chamber. Priscella, I'll need that cleaned too. Have some of the men help carry the bodies."

Nobody answered right away. Cyrus was as shocked as he was sure everyone felt. The king hardly paid any mind that his chancellor was dead. He was treating Asher's death like he would dirt on the bottom of his boots. Cyrus swallowed, trying to regain his composure. It would do no good to look like an imbecile.

Alaric motioned. "Well, go on. Let's get moving. I've still got appointments." A handful of people started moving, bumping into each other. Their anxiousness bled into Cyrus. He understood why they were so eager to get out of the king's way. His tone left no room for argument, and his crassness confirmed that he was not afraid to add to the body count.

He approached Cyrus, cloth still in hand, though he'd failed to dab at the blood that now dripped freely from his poorly patched wound. "Cyrus," he started, voice low, "what's your thoughts on all this?"

"Are you all right?" Cyrus asked.

Alaric raised his brow. "Why wouldn't I be?"

"The assassination attempt—"

"Was unsuccessful. The price of power comes at a cost some aren't willing to pay. I am, and I have paid that toll for many summers. A blade does not scare me, but a lack of answers does. Tell me, what do you think of all this?"

In that moment, Cyrus envied the king. His lack of fear of Death was something to be revered. In that recklessness, true power blossomed. A willingness to do the impossible, no matter what that might be. Cyrus, deep down, was afraid to die, and now, faced with a man who showed no affection or disdain for Death, he realized he still knew so little.

Sozar urged him to think differently. *We all share a different relationship with Death, my friend.*

Cyrus cleared his throat. "You mention the assassins weren't working together. That seems impossible. Not even the Gods could be that accurate. Unless it was the same buyer." Glad to leave the gruesome scene behind, he pointed into the chamber. "There's blood on the ground here." They walked in, approaching the chair with the drink and revealing more blood that Cyrus hadn't seen earlier. Where Asher's head would have been, blood stained the leather. A bloody handprint smeared the arm of the chair, and the ground was decorated like a mismatched painting. The rug was stained crimson as well. "He was attacked here, killed likely, then carried to the hall. The assassin, whoever they were, wanted Asher's body found."

"Nighthunter," Alaric commented, hands planted on his hips. "That's my guess."

Cyrus looked at him. "How? They're in Diyră, right? You think someone hired them?" He wasn't entirely familiar with the hired assassins, but he knew they were feared. They never failed, and if any of their men were killed, they kept a grudge until revenge was paid.

The king nodded. "Look at this." He started to circle the chair. "Asher was sitting here, drinking by the looks of it. No book, so he wasn't distracted. No fire. Nothing. That would mean that whoever came in here would have been in the chamber the entire time, maybe even snuck in last night and waited. But why wait? If Asher came in here and fell asleep, this assassin could have ambushed then. Clean kill, and the usual Nighthunter method. But instead, they waited. Asher got up for whatever reason—a lot on his mind if he was pouring a drink before dawn, I suppose—and sat here. That's when they attacked. Hardly a fight either by the looks of it. Asher probably panicked, tried to get up, but collapsed. The cut was deep enough that he bled out here. Never had a chance."

"And then they picked him up and put him in the hall," Cyrus echoed. "They took time to draw I'num out, to make a display of the body."

"Interesting." Alaric knelt before the blood-soaked rug and grazed his fingers over it. The fabric was still wet, and his fingers came back red. "It's an unusual method, but I do still think this is a Nighthunter. But why? What's the difference?"

Cyrus's tongue failed to work as his thoughts started racing. "This was meant for me," he whispered. The words tasted putrid.

"But why now?" Alaric didn't seem to care who it was meant for.

Cyrus stared at him. "What about you? How can you be certain the other assassin wasn't working for the same person and was just a ploy to scare you?"

The king was taken aback. "You think the same bidder hired two different assassins, knowing one would be killed?"

He nodded numbly. "If I wanted to send a message, I would do that." A single name continued to pop up in his head. Henry Junok. "I failed to keep my promise, abandoned those eggs to him. This was meant for me." As he said those words, he felt more certain of them. I'num was not used freely, and the odds that it would be the message following his visit with Venkar was too wild to ignore. No. This was all intentional, like he was being watched.

"The coincidence that there would be two assassination attempts from two different buyers on the same night is too hard to believe," Alaric said. He picked up the drink and sniffed its contents. Wrinkling his nose, he set it down. "Always poor taste." The king circled the chair again. "There's one thing I can't figure out. If the buyer purposely hired two different types of assassins, why would they push for the same night? Why not spread it out?"

Cyrus didn't have an answer for that, but Sozar did.

A distraction.

"Oh no." Cyrus turned without thought, nearly falling over the rug. "The egg." If he failed again, he would never forgive himself, but as the revelation sank deeper into his bones, he realized one thing: nobody was thinking about the egg, which had been stored underground in the dungeons overnight. Cyrus needed to get down there and see for himself. Maybe it was Henry waiting for him, or Sekar. The idea of facing the God scared him more. Sekar had nothing to lose, while the Lirallian leader had everything.

Sozar spoke in his mind, drenched in urgency, driving a serrated blade right through his chest. If not for the wall, he'd have collapsed. *They're here.*

He didn't need to ask. The ground shook, sending him to his knees. Shouts echoed from the hall, but his mind went blank, consumed by another presence that he'd hoped he'd not have to face anytime soon.

It's good to see an old friend, Dameon said. His mind was darker than Cyrus remembered.

Sozar's anger ripped into his head with bone-breaking force. He stumbled to his feet as another wave rocked the ground. "What's going on?" he asked aloud. Alaric's hand was on his arm, keeping him up.

"Fire!" someone screamed from the hall. "Pull the water reserves!"

The king was shoving Cyrus out of the chamber. "Those appointments will have to wait," he muttered, stressed. "We'll check the egg—"

A searing agony tore through Cyrus's mind. The world around him grayed, and the only thing he could see was Dameon on the back of Ashtir, tossing bundles over the saddle.

"You can't hide from me, little Rider," Dameon said aloud. Cyrus could almost taste the sea. Everything was as clear as if he were the one sitting on Ashtir's back.

Below, fires exploded, sending black smoke billowing into the sky in angry protest. With their link, he could hear the bloodcurdling screams of terror and agony. Countless were already injured, many would die or were already dead, and Dameon sat smug, daring. He was the main event all along. All this for Cyrus's attention.

He wanted to plead with the Rider to stop. If Dameon wanted a conversation, they would have it, but not at the cost of innocent lives. He tried to relay this, frantic for the man to hear him, but Dameon shoved him out of his head for good.

The world returned. Cyrus pulled on his training, barricading his mind as quickly as possible. Dameon was far stronger than he remembered. Alaric was still yanking him down the hall. This time, the sound of an explosion echoed, and the king was yelling at someone.

"Alaric," Cyrus said, stopping in his tracks. The reality of the situation crashed into him with suffocating force. He didn't think it would ever come to this, not now. He hardly considered himself prepared, but the words still left his tongue. "Dameon and Ashtir are here. I need to go."

The king stopped yelling and looked at him, shocked. "The Dragon Rider?"

He nodded.

"What are you going to do?"

Sozar was already preparing. The dragon dug his talons into stone, cracking it, and flared his wings, letting loose the rawest roar Cyrus had ever heard. Angry, untamed, and bloodthirsty. He hardly recognized Sozar, but he knew this was the way of the dragon.

"I'm going to end this."

Liars Make Bad Thieves

The library was Morei's sanctuary. Geral's had been small and cozy, holding hundreds of books. Caster's library was a royal palace. Cathedral style, two stories, and with a small galley and private room attached. The galley was manned by a single woman who was always here when Morei showed up. She looked close to sixty, with gray hair that was constantly in a bun and soft skin that said she'd lived most of her life out of the sun's reach. Every time he asked for her name, she simply called herself the Book Master.

She was gone now. When Morei had arrived a bit ago, she'd fetched him a glass of water and then grabbed a book before disappearing behind a narrow door. The king didn't know where it led, though he assumed it was somewhere specifically for her. A private chamber, perhaps.

Morei was sorting through a dozen books, hoping to find more information about pirates. The tremble remained in his hand, and he made an effort to use his other hand while working. He'd relied heavily on Rhys to tell him about the sea masters, but that had to change. Morei was more confident in his role now. After today, he was certain he'd made the right choice abandoning Geral and taking Caster. The people here were far more accepting of his behavior. They associated ruthlessness with success.

The more knowledge he had, the better off he was. Morei's reliance on others was needed for the time, but seeing what the chancellor was willing to do behind his back confirmed that he couldn't rely on anyone. Once he had enough information on the pirates and their culture, he could get rid of Rhys.

The Book Master had pointed him to a selection of the most prized volumes. It turned out a dozen different types of pirates existed, ranging from the Crowns to an obscure group called the U'cans, named after a small mouse found in the Releuthian Mountains. The Red Queens were the masters of the sea, considered the top of the food chain. Whatever problems different pirates had, they reported to the Queens. If a law specific to how these ships sailed was established, it was the Queens. Nothing got by them. Arrogant and power-hungry, that was what Morei read. He couldn't blame them when they'd been the masters of the sea for centuries now. But that was where they stayed—the sea.

With their tails tucked, he intended on hunting them out once more and striking a deal. The king was certain they'd accept. If they didn't, it would be suicide, and he knew they knew that. Their pride in their heritage and bloodline far outweighed their ignorance, or at least so he'd gathered from these texts. If he had the Red Queens, he would have all the pirates.

The soft thud of the door ripped him out of his thoughts. "You didn't have to rush," the king observed.

A scoff followed. "The day I learn to be at two places at once, I'll let you know." Rhys stopped across from him. "What are you doing?"

Morei flicked to another page. "Research."

The chancellor picked up a book and made a poor attempt at flipping through before placing it back where it was. "Pirates? Any particular reason?"

"The Red Queens are keeping me up at night." It was partially the truth. Morei pointed to one of the open books. "They've ruled for centuries. Impressive, don't you think?"

"Tre'lang ungahr." The words rolled off the chancellor's tongue like he'd said them hundreds of times. "It means Destiny herself loves the sea. A perfect marriage of death and rebirth. The Queens created that when they established order. Anyone who denies Destiny what she wants has no right on the sea."

Morei nodded. "I didn't see that in here."

"Information that detailed will only be found by speaking to one directly. Pirates aren't fond of documenting their lives like the rest of the world is."

"And you've managed to wiggle your way into their more private information," Morei noted, not at all surprised. The pieces were coming together. "How?"

Rhys fumbled with the pages of the book closest to him. "Time and dedication," he replied, smug. "You think I deal with scum when I work in the underground market?"

Morei laughed, unable to stop himself. "Was this all planned, Rhys?"

The chancellor shook his head. "A miscommunication. I deal with members of the Queens. That does not make me responsible for their actions. I trade in coin and information, not war."

"And do you expect me to trust you when you've done nothing but lie to me?" Morei tugged a parchment out from underneath one of the books. He'd kept it there until the right moment. Ink noted the date and the transaction, and it was signed by Rhys. "What's this?"

The chancellor reached across and picked it up. The rustling of the parchment was loud, cutting through the thick tension. The king had hired a few soldiers to work behind the scenes. They've been keeping tabs on the chancellor, seeing what he was up to, following him when necessary. This transaction had been brought to him by one who'd snuck into Rhys's study the night before after some suspicion.

"Who is Gonsín?" Morei asked.

"It's Old Tongue—"

"I know what it translates to," the king interjected coolly. "I want to know who you're making deals with that you refer to as leader. That's a lot of coin you've asked for a small chest full of wine, don't you think?" Caster was well known for its control on imports and exports for Sorréle, but the city was also renowned for its wine-making. Morei had seen enough transactions to recognize what was normal and what wasn't.

Rhys cleared his throat and laid the parchment back on the table. "That was the name given to me. I'm not sure what you want to know."

Morei raised his brow. "And the price?"

"Fast shipment," Rhys answered calmly. "This Gonsín wanted the wine for a special occasion. I told them that I could make it happen but would need to shift some exports around and the ship departure dates. They were willing to pay more. Happy?"

"No." Morei snatched the record up. "I have a hard time believing this when I haven't seen anything close to it before. How many shipments of wine have we had in the last season?"

"Forty."

He'd already known that answer but wanted to see if Rhys would lie about something so mundane. "And why would this ship depart on the day of the festival? I reviewed reports from the past, and no ship has ever left on the day or during the Festival of Seasons."

"Like I said, this Gonsín wanted the shipment immediately. I made accommodations for them." Rhys played with the ring around his finger. The chunk of blue stone had an ivory rose engraved in the center. Probably a part of the underground trading Rhys has been a part of.

The king set the transaction atop the open books. "You understand that anything out of the ordinary with you causes me questions, right?"

Rhys nodded.

"And you also understand that the only reason you're still alive is because you've proven worthwhile to me, but even then, I'm starting to wonder if you're no longer of value."

"Do you believe me to be a mind reader?" Rhys's question came out forcefully meek. It repulsed Morei, and the chancellor knew it based on the look he gave.

"The Red Queens attacked during the festival," Morei told him. "You told us a full moon. How do I know you didn't lie?"

The chancellor laughed. "You are delusional, do you know that?" Leaning forward, he pressed a finger into the table. "What would I gain by orchestrating this?"

"The throne. Isn't that what you think you deserve?"

Rhys's face darkened. "A crown and thousands of dead citizens. Sounds perfect. I can rule the dead."

Agitation flared, turning his blood hot. Morei wanted to kill the man where he stood. Start with his tongue, then move to his ugly eyes. It wasn't clear where Rhys's loyalties lay, but he also hadn't proven invaluable either. He was wild and untamed, and Morei couldn't figure him out.

"I have information on Syra Castello," Rhys announced. "That was where I was before this."

Morei bit his tongue. Between wanting to rip this man's heart out and serve it to the pigs and hear about Syra, he decided the latter was more valuable. "Go on."

"She has sought refuge in the Infernol."

The answer was so abrupt that Morei felt slapped. "That place is a myth."

Rhys beamed, proud. "It's real."

"How do you know?"

"My source is inside the Infernol."

An organization of misfits that spent more time causing trouble than accepting their places in the cities they were born in. A nuisance. Morei had a hundred questions. "When were you going to tell me you had a source *inside* the Infernol?"

"When it was appropriate," the chancellor replied. "I haven't received word from them in nearly six moons. I didn't want to tell you about them unless I knew they were reliable and still alive."

His tone was defensive, but the king only saw one justifiable reason. "You didn't trust me. I'm wondering if you even do now." Rhys had no reaction to the accusation. "I'm willing to bet Drexis didn't know, did he?" Morei closed the book he'd been eyeing. "What were you planning, Chancellor? I doubt you stumbled on this by accident."

Silence. Not a sound came from the grand library, and the king was grateful. Now was not the time for the Book Master to show back up. He'd always known Rhys had a motive. What he'd not prepared for was the powerful connections the chancellor had. The Infernol, if the stories were real, was an organization that no one could track. Members of the Infernol came and went, destroyed cities overnight, and were notorious for infiltrating anywhere.

The chancellor wasn't responding. "What aren't you telling me, Rhys?"

"It was a debt," he said at last, arms crossed. "About a decade ago, I helped him escape Sorréle. He had a bounty on his head from Diemon. Drexis contained him and his family, and I got them out. I didn't realize then that he was a member of the Infernol." Now he looked back at the king. "He occasionally sends me information that I inquire about."

Morei didn't believe him. "So, this source tells you about Syra in a nice letter," he stated, and scanned the other titles. Nothing stood out to him, but he was trying to keep himself busy to avoid doing something he might regret. "What else?"

"That was it."

"Ah." Morei picked up a thin book and flipped through the pages. "Well, that was nice of him. Really, it was. Feels like he's going above and beyond to prove his loyalty to you after you helped him and his family. Honestly, what a good man."

The chancellor nodded. "He is."

Morei swallowed his rising temper. Now was not the time. He needed to decipher more about Syra. "Did he mention anything about Syra?"

"No," Rhys answered. "Just that she was there and had been for a while."

"Hm. Can we get someone inside the Infernol?"

He shook his head. "It's secluded. The entrance is only known by those who are part of the organization."

"Did your trusted ally tell you this?" Sarcasm dripped from those words.

Rhys didn't look amused by the tone. "Yes."

"So how can I trust these letters are real? How could this man possibly send you letters if the location and entrance are so secretive?"

Rhys regarded the king as though he pitied him. Morei wanted to punch the look right off his face. The chancellor had an incredible gift at being an asshole. "Hawks."

"What?" Morei wasn't sure he'd heard right.

"The Infernol has trained hawks to be their messengers. They tie letters to them and send them off."

Morei raised a hand. An old practice. Syra's face was in his head, loud and proud. There she was, walking alongside him on a forest path and sitting on the coast. Possessing her felt wrong, but he couldn't stop himself. She was dangerous—too dangerous—and he feared what would happen if he didn't get his hands on her. Syra could take everything from him. No, she would. She was the real enemy.

"Your Majesty," a voice called. Morei raised his head to see a young boy with long, dark hair standing in the doorway of the library. A messenger.

"Yes?"

"The princess wishes to see you. She is on the public terrace."

The timing couldn't have been worse. He was torn between obligations and wants. Morei knew the issues with Rhys wouldn't be resolved today, and he wanted to talk more about the Infernol, but he also didn't want to miss this opportunity to try to talk to Isla about her future. The discussion of her bloodline couldn't wait any longer. A glance at one of the windows confirmed the sun was past high noon. The council meeting was soon, and he didn't want to rush things with her. The chancellor had already taken up too much time.

"Very well. Thank you," Morei told the boy. "Rhys, how often does that hawk arrive?"

"Sporadically," he answered. "The letter was received this morning, but the hawk is nearby. They've been trained not to go anywhere without permission."

"This evening, I want to send a letter to Syra. She is our key to this empire. Do you understand?" Rhys nodded. "I will find you after the council meeting."

He was already turning to leave, but Morei was not done. "One more thing, Chancellor."

Rhys didn't even turn around.

"I still don't believe you about the transaction. But I'm willing to overlook this because of your connections. Don't make me regret that."

The threat was clear. Slowly, the chancellor nodded.

When he left, Morei closed the books up and stacked them to the side. He would return to these later when he was done with the day. Everything was coming together. Rhys was a high risk, but what he offered was more than any God had provided. Information on the redhead who stalked his dreams was the first part. Sekar would come next. The more he had on the two, the stronger he would be. The politics of Caster were volatile—Rhys, Isla, and the council gave him more headaches than he needed—but they'd proven their worth ten times over. This was the closest Morei had ever felt to purpose, and he wouldn't let that go now.

The Beast with the Crimson Gaze

Syra braided her hair to the side, relieved not to smell like mud and sweat. The bath had given her a fresh start, but try as she might, she couldn't shake off the earlier conversation. Sekar's words haunted her, and when she tried to sit, she couldn't. His touch was different, less gentle, and his attitude was resolved.

Everything that could go wrong was going wrong. She'd seen how everyone looked at each other—the chasm caused by Chaos had ruptured any sense of peace. She couldn't forget all the other problems piling up, either. Her mind was racing.

Zane was still missing, though she'd been gone awhile now and hoped good news had come in. Dryl was hoping to lead a battle against Raveer and capture the city, Zarek could hardly converse with her, and she was an expert at driving wedges between herself and Sekar. Elyas wanted her by his side, and a fracture was threatening the existence of all the realms. Cornered, she felt that any decision she might make was wrong.

Syra tried to shake herself of the thoughts, but they were deafening. Hand on the door handle of the bathroom, she stood there, motionless. Alone now, she couldn't keep her thoughts straight. Here, confined to the brightly lit chamber with too many pillows and not enough space, she felt the weight of the world on her. Between the detailed molding along the ceilings, she felt the hands of this realm slither through, holding her in place. The floor, polished and devoid of the run-down appearance of the rest of the palace, was a bottomless pit. She stared, searching for the chains that kept her bound her e.

Her life had changed so fast. Syra realized that now. When Elyas had asked why she did what she did, it was easy to answer all the wrong things. But a season ago, they hadn't been the wrong things. A season ago, she was running, to find freedom, driven by the morals she'd been raised with in a mundane city prone to violence. Do the right thing, be kind, don't steal—those were the values of her earliest summers, and she'd clung to them in a fleeting attempt to hold on to some normalcy. But she was wrong to do so. Her life was different, and she'd been forced to change fast. Syra hardly recognized who she was becoming. The woman from Caster would never have spoken the way she had to Zarek.

Syra wanted to do good—she used to give bread to the homeless, help the elderly carry heavy baskets, aid neighbors who needed a hand. More than anything, she never wanted to hurt or disrespect someone intentionally. Syra craved peace, but only because she could find the routine she needed in that.

That was all changing. The Soul Realm, lone heir, and a group of dwindling Guardians looking to her as their future. Syra was no ruler, though, never had been. She was a girl who sold fish at Caster's Port.

Dryl. She needed him. He'd always grounded her. Zarek was ideal, but it was wrong to dump her issues on him when he was already struggling to cope with what she'd done to him. He was in this mess because of her. Confused, angry, resentful—and he had a right to all those emotions. He was bound to countless souls because of her.

Carefully, she tightened her grip on the handle, gaining more courage. She wasn't sure when she'd have the luxury to be alone with her thoughts again.

Syra opened the door and found herself face-to-face with Zarek. Those otherworldly eyes met hers instantly, his hand still reaching up to knock. He was dressed as he had been earlier, but his stiff expression caught her attention.

"Is everything all right?"

He lowered his hand. "Can we talk?"

She stood there, a bit dumbfounded.

"I want to start over." After their earlier encounter, she'd assumed he would avoid her. His voice was cautious, shameful, which felt foreign from a man like him.

"Okay." She stepped out, shutting the door. She could only conclude that they needed to get over this obstacle to deal with the realm fracture. He was the most knowledgeable person here, and she had a wild theory that everyone seemed to support. They needed to work together. "Is there anywhere we can do that? Do you have some place in mind?"

He nodded and motioned for her to follow. They walked the hall in silence. Their boots echoed, and twice, they had to evade a large crack in the floor. This was a section of the palace she'd not seen before. Yes, the walls and floors were damaged, and gouges ran the length of a few areas, but they were polished, pristine, and well-loved. The black was vivid, complemented by white and silver fissures, while gold imprints of ravens appeared every other few steps. Old Tongue gold engravings decorated the floor with an obvious pattern that was lost to Syra. Fine red linework garnished the gold.

"This place was once the greatest palace of the realms," Zarek said. Even with a low tone, his voice carried through the grand hall. "As our numbers weakened, the aggression of our enemies grew. These"—he pointed to a pair of deep gouges—"were done by a Yalahnder. A beast that we almost wiped out completely but failed to after Shevana stopped the Guardian Order. The beast wanders in this realm. We've been lucky not to have an encounter in at least a decade." He snorted, but it was strained. "There was a time when even a Yalahnder wouldn't come near a Guardian. How things have changed."

They took another turn down a similar-looking hall, this one a bit narrower. The ceiling was arched high with chipped and faded paintings of great beasts Syra had never seen before. They passed a few tall pots, holding plants long dead but that once must have been as tall as the man next to her. Vines peeked through crevices on the wall to their right, dark and stained with the ailment of the Soul Realm. Zarek stopped next to a single wooden door that didn't belong in a place once so magnificent. He slid the lock back and opened it.

Inside the large chamber was a fountain. Water ran freely from it, creating a rhythmic sound. Stone was carved upward like hands reaching for the sky, with water pouring out between the fingers. All around, vines with wide leaves grew out of the walls. Syra marveled. In a place full of death and decay, this was the liveliest thing she'd seen. Before the fountain were several benches carved to look like feathers. Vines and stone gave way to massive windows overlooking the rotten landscape. On the horizon, the red stain filled the sky. Ice stretched across some of the windows.

"This is the one place we've done everything in our power to keep untouched," Zarek told her, and sat. "It is the closest thing any of us have to peace. Sit."

Syra did so, with some space between her and the Guardian. Warmth seeped into her bones, a welcome reprieve from the constant chill. The water ahead was crystal blue, looking almost surreal in this realm. She wanted to reach out and touch it. "Did Shevana know of this place?"

"At one time, yes." The man next to her shifted. "This was originally built for her when she wanted a place to think. All rulers need their space. Those were once her words in the early summers of her reign. She used to love the sound of water."

Syra sensed a "but" in there. "And then?"

Zarek shrugged. "She changed, just like we all do. Just like the winds of the north do when they grow tired. The season changed, and she stopped coming here, but my men and I didn't. As this realm grew less and less like home, we came here more often. Just to sit."

Tragic. To be tied to a realm that didn't feel like home. To be forced into a role that nobody was sure they could justify. Guardians of Death. Perhaps the name Death Seekers was truer now than ever before.

"Ve'hem," she muttered. "The burdened ones."

Zarek's hands were laced together as he leaned forward to rest his elbows on his legs. He shook his head, and she could practically feel the weight of whatever it was he was carrying. It sucked the air right out of the room, and she found herself staring at the water, desperate to escape.

"It's not fair of me to place everything on you," he said, unmoving. "You did what you did because it felt right in the moment. I awoke different, but stuck with the same memories." His chest rose and fell. "There's little to describe how I felt at the mercy of the one person I dedicated centuries to.

Even fewer words to explain the agony I felt when I learned she was killed. Even after everything, I still couldn't hate her."

Syra sat stiffly, unsure of what to do. She didn't want to say the wrong thing.

"In the end, though," he continued, "it's a relief for her to be gone. Her death has released me from promises I couldn't break. Do you have any idea why I brought you here?"

Syra swallowed, hands clamped tightly together in her lap. "No."

He looked at her now. Underneath all the newness was the Guardian who had protected her since the day he showed up at Roman's. "I was wrong to speak as poorly as I did about the Soul Realm back at the Infernol. I said those words out of frustration because I didn't want anything to happen to you. I thought if we could avoid this realm altogether, you would be given the choice you want."

His words made her brow go up. "What do you mean?"

"The choice to choose," Zarek answered. "We all want what's best for the Soul Realm, but I never wanted you to feel forced into a position you didn't want. This"—he motioned to the world around them—"should have never been your problem. Our mistakes centuries ago cost us everything. But no matter how much I tell you that you have a choice, you won't see it that way anymore, because you're Syra."

That forced a shaky laugh from her. The Guardian was right. Her obligation to her friends, to what was important, far outweighed whatever she wanted. "I don't know what I'm doing," she confessed.

Zarek smiled, but it did not reach his eyes. "You don't have to."

That meant everything to her. Syra wanted to grasp his hand and squeeze it with all she had, but she didn't. The harshness of their encounter stung, and it brought an air of awkwardness that wouldn't budge.

The Guardian sighed. "I dreamed of Caster. I walked the port and endless streets, dug my toes into the sand, and watched the sunset. I lived your memories, didn't I?"

Numbly, she nodded.

"I thought so. My mind feels . . . different. Like I'm not all there. I can't tell when I'm in control, and when I'm not."

"How can you be so certain?" she asked.

Shifting to face her, he motioned with his hands. "Imagine you're making tea. You know you want some sugar and milk in it—you've always done it that way—but as you go to boil the water, your mind slips from your grasp. Now, you don't want it with any sugar or milk. In fact, you don't even like tea anymore. So you go on with your day, but that familiar piece of you wanders back, and you start to wonder why you never finished making the tea." Zarek's shoulders slouched. "That is how I feel. Like my mind is being split in half."

The awkwardness made Syra feel like she couldn't get a full breath of air. Their encounter had left such a fractured sense of self, and now he was sitting here, speaking like he hadn't said all he had. She wasn't in the right either—her behavior was uncalled for, and Zarek didn't deserve to be treated like his feelings were less. He'd lived centuries longer than her. And now, in her one act to save his life, she'd done something to him that nobody could explain.

Syra opened her mouth to reply, but he raised his hand.

"I failed you, Syra. I spoke in frustration, but you earned the brunt end of it all. You saved my life. If the roles were switched, I would have done the same." Relief flooded her. The air between them shifted, and she knew he was sorry. She was too. "It would be unfair of me to abandon you when you have not done so for me."

A loyalty tethered them together, one that she'd never put into words but that had always been there. His anger toward Sekar was not from hate, but rather protection. This was far more than just a Guardian trying to secure the future of the Soul Realm, and she understood that now. She felt like a fool for ever thinking otherwise.

The words bubbled up in the back of her throat, clawing for release. She wanted to apologize for ever saying the wrong thing, for challenging his integrity, for thinking anything differently of him. Her allies never swayed, even when the winds grew fiercer and more relentless. When she should have been thanking him, she'd been cruel and ungrateful.

A long pause sat between them, marked only by the sound of the falling water. Syra couldn't find the right way to broach the topic, and in the end, she realized she wasn't sure there was a way. Shame for her selfish actions and words weighed on her, but she was unwilling to pass that burden on to the man next to her. In time, perhaps. But not today.

"Would you do it again?" she asked.

"Do what?"

"This." She motioned to their world. "If the option was that you could have lived a normal life in Barnăl, would you have done so?"

Zarek didn't answer right away. He and Dryl had been given no choice on the matter. The White Horn pirates had killed their parents and ransacked their village. The two boys were never granted the right to a typical life. On the other hand, Syra had been raised long enough in the living realm to resent change and the possibility of her life being stripped.

Zarek inhaled loud, coming to life. "My life would have been so mundane in Tyrik Village. I would have helped rebuild what was destroyed. With my brother, of course. We likely would have sought work from those who needed it most—fishing, baking, trade work. I imagine we would have rebelled a lot. Without our parents to guide us, we would have acted out. If not from lack of discipline then from the trauma we'd experienced. That changed us. As I am sure it changes all." He leaned back, resting his hands on his legs, finally looking comfortable. "In answer to your question, no. I wouldn't have changed my destiny. We can change what we eat, but we can't change who we are meant to be."

No doubt. No hesitation. Syra respected that. Still, she doubted everything. From the day she'd fled Caster to the day she agreed to let the Guardian across the Sorréleian River help her—Sekar in disguise—to this very moment. Life had made her wary of even the smallest gestures. She envied that confidence.

"I hope to feel that one day," she said. When he raised his brow, she shrugged. "That certainty. Every day, I question everything."

He scoffed. "Want to know a trick?"

Syra wasn't sure what he was getting at. "What?"

The Guardian shifted in his seat to face her more. "It's not a matter of believing but rather of convincing. If you can wake up and convince yourself of one thing—no matter what that is—sooner or later, you can convince yourself of anything."

Quietly, she toyed with a thread on her oversized sleeve, glad to have conversations like this. So much still needed doing, but having his support meant everything to her. The world felt a little more manageable.

"Raid is right," Zarek said. "We need to rebuild the Guardian Order."

She nodded slowly, recalling the Guardian's words. "He spoke of Rü'shane."

"Of course he did. Get him a drink and that's all he'll talk about." He shook his head, the tension seeping from his brow. "He's a good man. A bit proud and forgetful of his place, though."

She snorted. That was apparent in just the few times they'd interacted.

"Guardians are bound to a Duraloc," Zarek said. "That's one of the ancient demons of this realm. But only a Herän can execute this ritual because it requires immense strength and energy. We haven't had a Herän in centuries. Shevana killed the last one."

Syra had never been privy to information about the Commitment Ceremony. "This Herän"—she hoped she'd pronounced it right—"do they summon a Duraloc when they perform the ritual?"

"Yes, which requires incredible control." He leaned back and rested an arm over the back of the bench. "When a Herän is chosen, they aren't done so by a vote. They must prove themselves worthy by restraining a Duraloc."

That forced her brow up. "How?"

"The only weapon we have is harvesting energy." To make that point, he raised his hand. "The strongest Harvester wins the title. Sometimes these choosings can last days; others, an evening. Our last Herän held his title for four centuries."

"And so this Herän summons one of these Duralocs and . . . what? Infuses it into you?"

He shrugged. "More or less. Duralocs can be solid or not. They prefer their mist-like form. Once the Herän ties a Guardian's blood to a Duraloc, it becomes solid, but that's where the battle begins."

She nodded slowly. It was all coming together. "Nobody wanted to speak about the actual ceremony when I asked."

"Because it is agonizing. We are locked in a war of control over our body, weakened by the Duraloc's toxicity, and tortured. Guardians-in-training die—far more than we would ever admit to—because the ability to wield control over this creature when it is tearing you apart from the inside out is indescribable. But once you master the Duraloc, you master yourself. It takes days, and then at least a moon cycle before you recover."

Syra was putting the pieces together and didn't like what she saw. "So we need a Herän first, and then we need to train and create Guardians. Do we even have that kind of time?"

"Maybe." Zarek sounded unconvinced. "Maybe not. But we know for sure that if Elyas charged right now with his army, we would never stand a chance. So we have to try."

She bared her hands to him. "I'm here. Sekar is too."

"To leave the realm's fate solely in your hands would be cruel," the Guardian remarked, then tilted his head. "It's nice to see Zari again. I thought something happened to her."

This day kept getting stranger. "You know of her?"

"Every Guardian knows of her. Zari is in some of our oldest tales about this place. She is as integral to the realm as a Duraloc. The younger Guardians are a little uncomfortable at the idea of an Onye—our fault after what Shevana did—but the older generation knows they are important to keep balance. They were the eyes for us in the living realm, watched over the questionable, and warned us of danger in their prime."

Sekar's involvement with this realm stretched beyond a few centuries. The deity's entire self-worth seemed wrapped up in how it existed. His insistence on keeping this realm alive and restoring it made more sense now.

Zarek stood then, and she followed. "Why don't we get something to eat before the others leave nothing left?"

"I already ate," she said as they approached the door.

"Next lesson: when there's food and you don't know the future, eat."

Scales and Blood

Nerves turned his muscles into stone. Cyrus's hands shook as he latched the bracers and greaves on. The small horns along his arms made the bracers heavy. His armor was made of leather and metal, covering his chest, arms, and legs. Hyle had told him that only a foolish or aged Rider went to a fight without armor, and until that day came, Cyrus would always dress for a fight. It was not worth dying for by going out there in a rush. Still, he double-checked the clasps of his leather tunic. He couldn't get a full breath of air, and he was certain it was because it was too tight, but it wasn't.

He clipped his sheath clasp closed. Another lesson from Hyle. If Sozar had to make a sudden twist or turn and his clasp was unhooked, his sword could go flying. He triple-checked that one, not trusting his judgment. Breeches with flexible leather armor plating hugged his calves, allowing his boots to be worn comfortably. He leaned over and tightened the sheath that was tucked into his boot. A backup dagger in case he lost his sword—another lesson. Hyle's words were racing through his head at a speed he could hardly keep up with, but he tried. The Crescent Blade was on the other hip, latched and secured. When they'd returned, he'd had the sheath looked at and reinforced for flight, and he'd only gotten it back late the night before. Another backup, but he'd hardly done anything with it since his return, so he could only hope it proved reliable when and if the time came.

Now, under the sun, sweat coated his brow, and he hadn't even taken off yet. The saddle was heavy in his arms as he hauled it over to Sozar. The dragon twitched, anxious to go. Stone lay in ruins where talons had cracked it. Above, Dameon and Ashtir circled the city, dropping fire bombs whenever they pleased, searing the sky. Sozar only grew more antsy at that, not afraid.

Clips and clasps were done by habit. If not for the hundred times he'd put Sozar's saddle on, he would have been paralyzed, but the motions came easily. He slipped his fingers between scales and leather, checking for tightness, before moving to the next. Hyle had polished this, and it showed. The saddle looked brand new, which he was only just now noticing under the high stress of what lay ahead. The smallest details made themselves known to him, like the crack in the leather flap that he hadn't seen before but was thinner than a strand of hair, or the sound the leather made as Sozar adjusted his weight. Gore between the dragon's talons indicated he'd recently eaten but had yet to take time to clean himself.

Cyrus adjusted the second strap of the saddle, unsatisfied. He'd moved fast once the decision was made to meet the Dragon Rider in the air, but he felt like the entire world was passing him by. The only thing he could hear clearly was the beat of his heart in his ears and the way his breath came out ragged and uneven.

Alaric was out with his men to meet any possible threats on the ground. Soldiers and the king armored up, though, and left the palace. Wherever they were now, he hoped they remained as safe as they could. No matter how hard he tried to keep his head straight, he couldn't shake the overwhelming knowledge that this was all because of him. Whoever died today was his fault. He wasn't used to having blood on his hands, and it forced bile into the back of his throat. He didn't know how much of this was preventable, or if this was destined to happen all along.

Let us be off, Sozar urged. Another explosion. Cyrus didn't know how many times he'd adjusted the straps, but he was stalling. Swallowing, he nodded and pulled himself into the saddle. Muscles that he hadn't felt in ages strained against his weight. He couldn't remember being this heavy. As he settled himself into the saddle, Sozar swung around and broke off into a run. Cyrus latched on to the horn in front of him, instinct taking over, just as the dragon flared his wings and launched himself into the sky.

Fear was not an option. Not anymore. As the wind tore at his clothes and hair, he knew that he was the only thing standing in between Delion and the Dragon Rider. Cyrus had spent his whole life wanting to be someone. Now was the time.

Sozar worked fast to gain altitude. The city grew smaller and smaller. Fires were everywhere, but they remained isolated. Tiny specks—people—moved about in a frenzy. Few exchanged swords, but by the looks of it, few enemies were on foot. They didn't appear to be working together with how spread out they were. It made no sense.

Ashtir, white as snow, stuck out like a sore thumb against the blue sky. Building fast over the sea, a storm hung dark and ominous. Dameon saw him looking already and waved as he dropped another fire bomb. The Rider had his iconic mask on, but it had been upgraded, with a skull's mouth instead of the makeshift one he'd had when they first met. At this point, Cyrus was certain it was for looks, and it worked. Dameon looked menacing with his dark hair and armor, even from this distance.

Sozar moved closer to Ashtir, leveling out so that no dragon was higher than the other. Each flap of the dragons' wings sounded like thunder, and when Dameon raised his gloved hands to remove the mask, he froze.

Black veins etched their way across the Rider's exposed skin just where the hem of shirt pulled. He knew that ailment anywhere. It was the same one that Morei had worn so proudly when they first met. Fear turned to worry. Dameon was compromised, and the wicked grin he flashed when the mask was removed confirmed he liked this new version of himself. The corrupted always found ways of damning themselves further, motivated by all the wrong doings they felt mistreated for. It was a shame that Dameon would take this route, but not unsurprising.

"Cyrus," he called over the rush of wings. They kept their distance, but the word carried as clear as if they were standing nose to nose. "So good to see how much Sozar has grown. And you've got yourself a saddle too."

That statement held more—a dare. Cyrus kept his voice calm, but his hands shook, so he squeezed the saddle's stubby horn. "What happened to you?"

"I grew stronger and faster," he answered harshly. "Did you not believe me when I told you I would build an empire?"

He had, but seeing it in this way made his skin crawl. "Henry will kill you when he doesn't need you anymore. You're only a tool to him."

One large red eye locked itself on him. Ashtir's gaze was violent, wild. Whatever Henry had done to Dameon had affected his dragon too.

"Did you come to meet me just to tell me what I already know?"

Cyrus was caught off guard. Dameon soaked it up.

"You see, he needs me as much as I need him. Reputation and strength. That is what we give each other." In response, Ashtir rumbled and curled his lip. "I know there is something here. It's the only reason you've stayed so long." A beat of silence passed. "Or is it because you're afraid?"

Cyrus bit his tongue, choosing not to answer. Both questions were bait, and he wanted to give Dameon nothing. Sozar, on the other hand, growled. His body shook, and he opened his maw to let fire escape, drenching the surroundings. The heat seared Cyrus's legs. *What are you doing?* he demanded.

The dragon was enraged, hardly reachable. *Staking my claim on the sky.*

"Hm." Dameon looked around, making a dramatic motion to peer over his saddle to the destruction below. "I never liked Delion much. It's nice to see a fresh look on it."

"I know who you are," Cyrus told him. Dameon's silver gaze met his own. "The prince of Saveen. You could have come back and claimed your title as king. I'm sure the council would have allowed it given what you are now. Why not?"

The Rider dug into the pouch on his saddle and pulled out another fire bomb. He studied it, and Cyrus wanted to reach out and snatch it from him, but he couldn't. Not from this distance. He silently prayed that he could talk Dameon out of whatever mad game he was playing. Sozar, on the other hand, was a brewing storm.

"I could say the same about you." Dameon let the fire bomb go, and Cyrus averted his gaze, unwilling to see where it landed. "Why have you spent so much time running when you have the chance to be the change the world needs? Henry wants you. He sees in you the potential to lead a new era." The last words were said in hatred. "You're all he talks about."

If Cyrus had felt more certain, he would have replied with something witty, but he couldn't. Finding the right thing to say was already a monumental feat. "Why are you here?"

"What's it look like, Rider?" Ashtir snapped his jaws together. Sozar tensed under him. "I came for you."

The last bit of confidence was draining from his fingertips. "Why?"

Dameon reached over and tightened the leather strings of his pouch. As he did, Cyrus watched him discreetly unclasp the sheath of his sword. "Why don't we settle this like the Dragon Riders did all those summers ago?" His hands wrapped tightly around the horn in front of him. "With a proper *fight.*"

Cyrus never got a chance to respond. Ashtir lunged. Cyrus ducked just as he felt the wind ripped from his lungs. Sozar tucked his wings and rolled sideways. Cyrus held on to the dragon's horn as tight as he could, muscles straining to keep him in place. Sozar flared his wings to stop the rolling but immediately dropped into a dive. Behind, the snarl and heat of fire came close as Ashtir unleashed on them.

The ground fast approached. Cyrus looked behind, seeing that the pair weren't letting up. Dameon had come here for one purpose only: to kill him. It was obvious, and he felt foolish for thinking he could talk his way out of this. Mind scattered, he desperately tried to grab fragments of all the training he'd done, but everyone's words were mush. A slim, logical part of him knew he was freezing, but the other half couldn't think straight. He'd trained for this, but he couldn't even figure out what to do.

Sozar took a sharp turn left. They were just over the city, and passed through a plume of smoke. Cyrus held his breath. Reaching out, he tried to contact Sozar, but the dragon was locked up. His mind was a furious cyclone of anger, violence, and blood. Hyle's warnings were gaining ground fast. If they couldn't communicate in a fight, they might as well be dead.

Another turn to avoid a bell tower, and Cyrus spied a group of soldiers below. It was too fast, but he heard the dreadful roar close behind. Too close.

Cyrus looked behind and saw that Ashtir had gained enough ground to pounce. They were running out of time. Panicked, Cyrus slammed his hand against Sozar's shoulder. The hard scales stung through the glove, but he did it several times.

"Talk to me!" he insisted. *You'll get us both killed.* He spoke with both his words and mind, with everything he had. The dragon shuddered, and his mind shifted. Instead of shying away, Sozar's presence engulfed his own. He was no longer aware of just his surroundings, but he could also feel, see, and sense like Sozar. Wings, the wind, the strong smells of fire and sea, and the overwhelming sense of danger that filled him. The immediate change made his head spin. Cyrus could hardly decipher what was his and what was the dragon's.

Trust me, Sozar said.

Cyrus couldn't answer. His mind had been violated, even with the familiarity of the dragon. This was different. Sozar was everywhere, and he impulsively wanted to draw back, but he tightened his grip on the horn. Their lifeforces, once separated by thin boundaries, merged. He knew the dragon's intents before they happened, and the same was returned.

Sozar flapped hard, making a sharp ascent, straining against the building wind. He moved fast, tucking into the saddle and securing his weapons. He intended to get above Ashtir. Lowering one hand to the hilt of his sword, Cyrus waited, preparing for the worst. Fear was not welcome in battle.

High enough, the dragon swung around and collided instantly with Ashtir. The impact jarred Cyrus. He squeezed his legs tight, keeping his head low. Above, the snarls deafened him. Sozar scratched with his back legs, talons slashing through the soft underbelly. Ashtir screamed—a sound that made Cyrus's entire body go rigid—and Sozar reached for the dragon's neck.

But his own scream reached Cyrus's ears. Dameon had stabbed the dragon under his front leg.

They were falling. The ground was fast approaching as they tumbled, talons interlocked, each dragon tried to gain the upper hand. Ashtir landed lacerations, Sozar tore scales free from the dragon's front leg, and Dameon was doing everything in his power to be involved. Neither Rider could expertly navigate this death fall, though. Sozar's agony was palpable through their bond, but the dragon ran off pure adrenaline.

We're going to crash. He could now see the details of the ship flags. Sozar roared and unleashed a stream of fire at Ashtir. The heat and flames licked Cyrus, singeing leather and skin. The dragon tried to break free, but Ashtir's talons locked onto Sozar, not relenting. Sozar tried again, but the white beast refused to let go. Panic flared, and the dragon roared in frustration. The ground was too close.

"Dameon!" he cried, hoping the man would hear. "We will die!" Nothing. The sea looked restless from here, sending waves of white froth to the shore. The storm was moving in fast, and they would have to worry about harsher winds before long.

Sozar lashed out without warning. The dragon's incisors locked onto Ashtir's neck. At this angle, Cyrus got a full look at Dameon, whose face had twisted into something hideous. The sword in his hand wavered, and he met Cyrus's gaze. They were locked, falling to their death, in a terrible game of dare.

Ashtir struggled, but Sozar wouldn't let go. The size difference was just enough to give Sozar the advantage. If the dragon bit down any harder, Ashtir's spine was at risk of being severed. Cyrus could already taste the metallic tang of blood on his tongue, and he grimaced. He could imagine nothing more horrible than being responsible for something this dishonorable.

Dameon sheathed his sword just as Ashtir finally relented. Sozar let go and launched himself off the belly of the other dragon. He flared his wings, catching air as fast as he could, but they were already dangerously low. Cyrus watched the ground approach, preparing himself. Trees and dirt were in perfect detail, and a flock of birds took off in fear of the collision, feathers brushing over his face. Sozar never faltered though. The strain of his wings was felt throughout Cyrus's entire body. The dragon finally stabilized just as talons grazed the tips of trees, and he started flapping to gain altitude.

Cyrus surveyed Sozar with both his eyes and mind. A stab wound under his front leg pinched but was manageable. The lacerations along his stomach where Ashtir had got him bled freely, agonizing. They were deep and would require intervention. The white dragon hadn't fared much better, barely catching himself from colliding with the trees. From here, the pearly scales were now crimson along his neck and shoulders. His own cuts ran along his underside, raining blood, as he gained some altitude once more. Dameon tossed another fire bomb, undeterred from his original plan.

Sozar, he pressed, *are you all right?* He'd never felt this much pain from the dragon. Sozar was the tough one, always had been, and now that the roles were reversed, he felt angry. Dameon was at fault for this. Him and his foolish recklessness to prove a point. All of this should have been avoided.

I will be fine. Sozar's reply was labored and slow. He was losing blood too fast and lacked the experience of fighting. Cyrus did too. They were grossly unprepared. The other pair, on the other hand, appeared in far better control despite the heinous injuries to Ashtir. The dragon's motions were slow. Dameon reached over and placed a hand on Ashtir. Healing, perhaps, but he wasn't sure.

The clouds turned the sky dark gray. Cyrus urged Sozar into them. His mind raced, no longer bound by terror but by survival. If they didn't act, more fire bombs would be dropped, more lives would be lost, and he knew that Sozar could only stand so much before he made a mistake.

Higher, he ordered. Up here, they were silenced by the clouds, and he intended on utilizing it. The decision was made before he admitted it. Confidence overcame him, driven by the pure and untampered need to put an end to this. Nothing else crossed his mind, not even doubt, and he quickly acted on it. If he hesitated, he would never make it.

Cyrus swung his leg around, sitting sideways in the saddle now. The crisp chill of the clouds stung his face and made his hair stand on end. He forced deep breaths in, concentrating. Locating the other Rider's lifeforce was easy—it burned with a ferocious hunger that made Cyrus cringe. *A little closer*. He only had one chance at this.

Stay underneath, Cyrus instructed, but Sozar already knew that. He rested a hand on the scales. This would be the biggest decision of his life—and the riskiest—and he knew of only one way to make sure this was successful. "I trust you," he told Sozar.

Then he slipped off the saddle.

His skin was damp, the wind cold. The fitted leather kept his clothes from being tousled with the fall. He kept his arms out, focused on the target that came into view as he exited the clouds. Dameon didn't show any sign of being aware. He dropped another fire bomb. Ashtir, from above, shook. He was struggling more than Cyrus had originally thought. The city was a disaster. Plumes of blackened smoke and flames rose all over, even from the palace. People and soldiers were rushing about.

The free fall was euphoric. In the midst of the tension and madness, he felt alive. Nothing in his life had come close to the bliss that rushed him, save for the time he jumped off the cliff in the Releuthian Mountains.

Cyrus was nearly on him, and it was only then that Dameon stopped and looked. But it was too late. A slight shift, and he collided with Dameon, latching on and tearing him right off the saddle. The impact jarred every muscle and bone, and he hit his head on someone or thing, he didn't know. They were entangled, and Dameon was furiously trying to get his sword unsheathed. Cyrus punched him, and he went still. Grabbing the collar of his leather tunic, he brought him close and yelled with everything he had.

"Is this what you want? We will die like this!" From above, Sozar was already in a steep dive, gaining ground quickly. Ashtir was close behind. The ground below was approaching at a nauseating rate, but he kept his eyes locked on the Rider.

The mark from Cyrus's punch was already blossoming into a red rose across Dameon's cheek. The Rider blinked, and he wasn't sure if anything was heard. They didn't have time to discuss this now. Sozar passed him, and Cyrus shoved Dameon away, hoping his point was made. Ashtir passed on his right, heading for his Rider, while Cyrus widened his arms and turned his focus on not getting impaled by the horns that ran along the dragon's back. Sozar's mind consumed him, hugging every thread of reasoning and thought. This time, Cyrus was prepared.

Easy, Sozar rumbled, sounding more like himself. Cyrus adjusted his angle. They were nearly upon each other. The dragon shifted to the left and slowed just barely for him to reach out and grab the horn. He wrapped his fingers around it as hard as he could and forced his legs down, tightening his grip and tensing his body. Sozar made a sharp turn to narrowly avoid colliding with Ashtir. The white dragon snapped out, agitated, and Sozar spit fire in response. Both missed.

Cyrus glared at Dameon and pointed to the ground. This needed to be settled there, not in the air when both their dragons were wounded. This was between them, not Ashtir and Sozar. Dameon flashed a wicked smile and reached for his sword. He agreed.

On the outskirts of the city, Sozar made a rough landing. His front leg was sore, and he struggled to keep weight on it. Cyrus jumped off as fast as he could, watching Ashtir make a poor landing and groan. Dameon made no motion to sheath his weapon. He knew where this was going, even before words were said.

The first raindrop fell as Cyrus pulled free the Rider's Sword. Dameon was on him in an instant, metal meeting metal with brutal force. Cyrus shoved him back, taking the opportunity to strengthen his position. Boots dug into the soil, and he swung down. Dameon deflected and kicked out, but Cyrus saw it coming and sidestepped. The rain fell heavier now, soaking through their clothes and drenching the ground. Around, Ashtir and Sozar circled, poised and ready to lunge. Blood dripped freely from their wounds, but their snarls told Cyrus they were starved for another fight.

Cyrus lashed out, almost landing a strike on Dameon's shoulder before he narrowly defended himself. He punched, shoving Cyrus back. The Saveen prince attacked again, gaining ground and forcing Cyrus to push back for fear of running right into a dragon. Primitive survival took hold of all his senses, and Cyrus fought with everything he had. He pushed Dameon back, dragging the Rider's Sword until it struck the hilt, then shoved. The Rider stumbled backward, and Cyrus saw an opportunity and took it. His sword dug into muscle and skin as it sank its teeth into Dameon's side, just where the leather edges met.

The Rider pulled back, sinking into the deepening mud. Cyrus circled him, adrenaline making his blood hot and his mind clear. Dameon wanted a battle, so he would get it. He'd trained many moons for this moment.

No mercy. That was what he'd learned, and now he understood why. Cyrus teased a lunge, and Dameon took a step back, hand pressed against his side, where blood poured between his fingers. Guilt was unwelcome, even as the bile threatened to choke Cyrus. This was not the man he wanted to become—one so willing to cause pain—but Destiny had an awful way of forcing his hand. And if it was between Dameon or Sozar, the choice was easy.

The Rider stopped moving. Sozar felt it first. Energy. Cyrus cocked his head, warning the Rider to play fair without saying a word. They'd already tumbled to kicking and punching; this didn't have to go further.

But Dameon's wrist twitched, and Cyrus acted. He crossed the handful of steps as he felt ice claw at his legs, sucking the strength and forcing his knees to bend. Drawing on the energy around him, he tried to counteract the ambush. Dameon didn't move, and Cyrus collapsed, the tip of the sword burrowing into the mud just shy of where the Rider stood.

They were locked in a battle of wills. Dameon was desperate to get the upper hand and exploit his mind while Cyrus did everything he could to defend himself from the assault. In the cold rain, he was flush as if standing under the desert sun. Breaths came ragged. His sole focus was on the barriers he kept up in his mind. When one cracked from Dameon's relentless blows, he reinforced it. Over and over, they went back and forth, but he could feel his stamina waning. He'd hardly trained for this kind of battle of minds, and he couldn't keep this going much longer before Dameon took advantage of a vulnerability that Cyrus missed.

The Crescent Blade. He'd never had a chance to check the weapon, and now he reached for the blade's lifeforce with a single thread of thought. There, in the war that raged in his head, he both saw and felt the icy energy. An abundance of it—more than he could ever need. He submerged himself in it, letting the energy soak into his veins, muscle, bone, everything. When he was certain he had enough, he channeled it all to Dameon.

At once, he was thrown backward, back striking the ground and skidding through mud. Ashtir broke from the circle, turning his attention to his Rider. Sozar approached Cyrus, standing next to him and dropping his large head in front to defend. Carefully and on wobbly legs, Cyrus stood. The energy harvesting had stolen far more from him, but he did everything he could to conceal the fatal exhaustion that settled into his bones.

Dameon dragged himself to his feet and picked up his sword. Rain still poured, and the stench of blood filled the space between. They stood there, two Dragon Riders driven by different wants. Cyrus gave the faintest shake of his head. They did not have to end this here, and he hoped Dameon took his warning. Cyrus was not the same Rider he'd faced in Eiyrǎl, and that meant he was willing to stop this once and for all if Dameon forced his hand.

Ashtir tilted his head, a sure sign that a conversation passed between them. Heartbeats slipped into centuries. The more time that passed, the more he realized just how badly he hurt. The impacts of the fall and collisions made his body throb in places he didn't know existed. His head pounded, and he could feel a lump where his head had slammed into something. Maybe scales.

And then, in a moment of sanity, Dameon sheathed his sword. He did not say a word as he jumped on Ashtir, nor did he turn his head as the dragon launched himself into the air with far more effort than needed. The dragon's body shook as his wings caught air. That would be a long flight in that condition.

They stood there, watching, certain the two would turn around and finish this once and for all, but they never did. They grew smaller on the horizon, grains of sand against the vast sea, and only when Sozar turned one fiery eye on Cyrus did he finally look away.

Far too many emotions bombarded him in that single look, emotions that Cyrus couldn't quite put into words. Relief, fear, affection, disappointment—the list went on. Things that they'd done right, but so many missed opportunities and mistakes. He wrapped his arms around the dragon's meaty neck, grateful to feel the hard scales and warmth. Sozar hummed, returning the same feelings.

The shock bled from him freely. They'd done it. They'd managed to live through their first fight. Their wounds were manageable, and Cyrus quickly got to work inspecting Sozar. "Tell me where it hurts," he insisted, grazing his hand along the dragon's scales and forgetting his condition. Sozar was his priority. He knelt, studying the wounds underneath. Where Dameon had gotten him, blood had slowed. The stab was shallow compared to the thick lacerations across his stomach. Ashtir had narrowly missed the leather straps, but they were still stained red. He pressed his hand near the wound, wanting to help ease the agony.

There is no need, Sozar insisted. *I will be fine.*

You don't sound fine, Cyrus countered. The dragon was trying to withhold the discomfort, but Cyrus could still feel it seeping across their bond. He rested a hand on the Crescent Blade. He was too tired and weak to draw from himself, but perhaps he could try and take the edge off with some help. The Light Energy was plentiful, and he let the force sink into his fingers, race up his arm, and turn his innards icy. He never waited for Sozar to answer him. Instead, he directed the energy to the dragon, focusing solely on easing the pain and staunching the bleeding. Cyrus wasn't trained to heal wounds entirely, but he knew enough to grasp the basics. His head swam, and he leaned against the dragon to catch his breath. Beneath him, pools of bloody water gathered in the mud.

He wasn't sure how long they stood there, locked in the same position, caught up in the aftermath of the battle and paralyzed by the reality of it all. But when Sozar shifted his weight, he came to life. The rain let up just enough to be a drizzle, and it dawned on Cyrus then what a blessing the storm was. The fires would surely be extinguished. The battle was over. For now.

"Come, friend," he told Sozar with a pat. "Let us go help."

Madness Courts Power

As promised, Morei found Isla on the public terrace. This was where staff members went to enjoy the sun, eat, and relax. Her royal chamber had a terrace, just like his, but he'd found her here more times than he could count. Old habits died hard.

With her back turned, she didn't see him approach. He slid into the seat across from her. This close, he could see Caster's and Ferguson's financial reports, along with her write-ups. "Need I remind you again where we should and shouldn't review these?"

Isla pursed her lips. She held a quill and was making a quick note about a family. A small bottle of ink sat to her right. "You missed the meeting with Lady Yara."

He winced. He'd forgotten about that. It was a financial review for the funding for the city's recovery. "I know. I figured you could handle it."

She finished her note and dipped her quill into the ink. "Where were you?"

The king wanted to tell her that he'd had his nose stuck in a book, but he also wanted to tell her that he was suspicious of Rhys. The woman across from him didn't know his personal vendetta with Syra. That before he'd set foot in this city, he'd been sharing dreams with people he'd never met. Or that he was speaking to deities and falling apart. She didn't know that underneath all the political strategy was a soul-driven need to prove his worth as a king.

"I was caught up in some research on the Red Queens." It was a half lie, but he still regretted it. She was too innocent for this world. For him.

"Huh." The princess set the tip of the quill back onto the parchment and scribbled something. "It's not like you to forget things. You're usually the one reminding everyone where they need to be."

She was prying. "What did I miss?"

The princess set the quill aside and flipped through some documents. "I'll spare you the bickering between Lady Yara and me and get straight to the point." She pulled a parchment out from the handful before her. On it were scribbled numbers, starting with the largest at top and getting smaller. "We were doing some breakdowns," she explained as she handed it to him. She pointed to the numbers as she spoke. "That big one is all the Krye that Caster has available for recoveries. The rest is for payment of soldiers, staff, food, clothes—you get the point. But we're stretched a bit thin. See this one?" She tapped the one below it, which was dangerously close to the top number. "That's total repairs for homes and such in the city, drawing strictly on Caster's reserves. That doesn't even include the palace construction, which is a separate report. The next number is the coverage for all the burials and ceremonies for those who lost someone in the battle. I think it's only fair we cover that, given many of these people have next to nothing. Plus, some of those who lost their lives actively picked up weapons to defend Caster. We would be cruel if we asked for payment for those who died protecting us."

When she didn't say more, he nodded. "Okay."

Isla looked reinvigorated. She'd likely expected him to push back, but she was right. "Another thing." She tapped the number at the bottom. "This is the cost to cover the dozen or so citizens who want to move out of the city. They have no quarrel with you or the politics, but they have young families and would feel more comfortable raising their children away from—"

"Done." Morei pointed at a separate number. "What's this?" It was the lowest cost, only several hundred Krye, but he couldn't figure out what it correlated to.

"Oh, this?" The princess's mouth twisted, like she was fighting back a storm of words. "I, um, well, to be honest, I was hoping to provide every family or individual who lost a loved one in the battle with a special stone with the passed one's name engraved. Just a little gift from the royal family to them. A way to honor their names. It doesn't have to be out of Caster's finances though, I could cover—"

"Isla," he cut in. The woman stared, cheeks flush. "I think it's a wonderful idea. It's covered. Is there anything else?"

There was a reason he put her in charge of the people. Isla showed a level of compassion he would never come close to. He loved what he did, but he lacked the touch of a woman. These small gestures were things he'd never have considered. Geral certainly hadn't seen that from him after the battle with Diemon.

"No," she replied, and tucked the parchment under the stack. "Right now, those were the largest things."

"What else?"

The princess sifted through some parchment before she pulled out a formal document with the Caster stamp. "This is just for formal recognition of the ship statue being done. Rhys had it drawn up, so that we could document the work."

Morei took a quick glance over it and saw nothing he needed to worry about. This was a piece of parchment that would mean nothing to a king or queen ten generations from now. At least the chancellor had done one thing right. "Great."

Isla placed the document back, rushed. "Then that's all. I'm sure Rhys or Lord Varun will have something to tell you the next time they see you." She stood, parchment clutched close to her chest. "I should go—"

"I want to talk to you." He left no room for argument.

Her eyes flashed uncertainty. "No fighting," he added, although he wasn't convinced. "I just want to talk."

"That sounds promising," she commented dryly, and slumped lower with a huff. "Go on. I'm waiting."

And just like that, the tension was back. Morei couldn't figure her out, and that drove him mad. The people he'd regretfully and gratefully met over the summers were easy; he could decipher them over a meal. But Isla was like reading a stone wall sometimes.

He was determined to have this conversation now. "My intention was always to give you the title of queen." She tensed. "You are of Caster blood. Your rightful place is on the throne, not as some princess."

Morei gestured at the parchment still clutched to her chest. "You are clever and compassionate, two of the best qualities a ruler could have." And they would complement his deteriorating tolerance and compulsive acts. "The people adore you, the staff are loyal to you, and you deserve more than being chaperoned. You've proven to me you are capable. The question is if you want to embrace your bloodline or walk away from it all."

Slowly, Isla's hands relaxed, and she placed the parchment bundle back on the table. Several staff members walked onto the terrace before turning away at the sight of them. Good. He didn't want anyone to overhear this.

"Walk away?" she asked.

Morei didn't hesitate. "Having a queen is politically the right thing to do while we expand our territory. If you turn this down and wish to deny your heritage, I won't stop you, but you will be asked to leave. All documentation of your Caster connection will be destroyed. It will be your word against mine."

He'd done a lot of consideration about his options and knew those were the best. If Isla left, he couldn't afford her running to a kingdom and proclaiming her bloodline with documents to back it up. That would make her a risk. While he was not opposed to killing her if she posed a threat, he was trying to choose the lesser of two evils. What really mattered was that she took her place as queen, so that he could strengthen Caster's political stance.

"What about me?" The question was hardly audible.

"What do you mean?"

The princess kept her gaze low. "It sounds great in theory, doesn't it? Give me a second chance at life, reinstate my royalty, then make me queen. That's what you want, what the people would love, and when I first agreed to all of this, I was too caught up in the dream to think about what this all meant for me ."

Morei leaned forward. This was more than just the council and the battle. A frigid thought traced the back of his mind, and he clenched his jaw.

"Do I become your wife?" she asked.

He cleared his throat. "Formally, yes."

"Formally," she mused, voice hollow. "Doesn't that bother you?" She regarded him fully. "To marry someone out of obligation, not love?"

Isla wanted a family, children, *love*. She wanted to be desired, not a tool. That introduced doubt into this decision he needed to make. Isla's avoidance wasn't because she didn't want the title—it was because she was thinking about a future that Morei couldn't fathom.

"I want you to be at peace with your decision," he insisted. "If this isn't what you want, then I'd rather you go."

She shook her head. "That's the problem. I don't want to go." This was not what he'd planned. "I suppose that's cruel of me, isn't it? To want what you don't. You've gone above and beyond, taught me everything, and given me a second chance at life. That should be enough."

Morei could hardly get a full breath of air. He was the ex-king of Ger-al, who'd slaughtered his citizens and then stole a throne that wasn't his. Nothing about him was kind or compassionate. Yet, this woman wanted something genuine. He wasn't even sure he knew what that meant.

"We can arrange something," he countered. "Formally, we'll rule together, but you can have your family. They can live here, be considered royalty—"

"That's not sustainable, and you and I both know that. People will talk. The tradition of a married king and queen has been around since the Vorelian Empire, and you're suggesting we break it. The people of Caster would never accept that."

"I know." Now it was his turn to avoid her gaze. The king loathed love. It was foolish and made people weak. Isla didn't want something real with him, she only wanted the idea of it. Nothing he could offer her would make her happy. She was a cornered animal, too afraid to run but terrified to let go of the little bit of life she'd been given, even if that meant dealing with him. She was a helpless fool. One day, she would learn just how cruel life could be. Until then, she was desperate.

"I'm willing to try," she said. "I want to be a part of this all, but I need you to try too. We can compromise. I don't need the magical happy-ever-after, but I need you to be more than just the man who gets mad at me because I want to help."

The words stung. After all that he'd done for this city, that was how she saw him? "What do you want from me?"

"I want to be your friend." The answer was so simple, it was painful. "I want to get to know you—the real you, Morei—and I want you to get to know me. No romance, no love. No public displays of affection. Just genuine friendship."

The king couldn't admit to her how much that horrified him. Very few people had ever entered his inner circle, and those who had were dead. The panic that bubbled up inside him was crippling, and he hoped she didn't see how hard he was trying to hide it. Isla wasn't asking anything serious of him, but he felt like she'd just demanded he hand over his entire kingdom. He wanted to squirm, get up, scream, anything.

Morei swallowed his temper and gripped the seat of the chair, squeezing as hard as he could to still the shake. If a promise like this was all she needed to take her place, then he would do it. She didn't have to know that he had no intention of being an honest man with her. She would never know the real him. If she feared him now, she would never look at him again.

"Your bloodline," he said. "Are you willing to accept it?"

"Always a trade with you, isn't it?"

He tilted his head, loosening his grip on the seat. "Formalities, Isla. This is what this is. I need to know you're reliable and will be so moving forward. If not for me, then for yourself. You are a Caster. I want you to act like it."

She shuffled the papers around, a nervous habit. "Okay."

Relief drenched him. This was good news. After everything they'd dealt with, securing a queen was a monumental step—and she was a Caster. He'd had several backup plans, one being Krystal from Diemon, but knew that was a far reach. After killing the woman's mother on the battlefield, a marriage like that would end in bloodshed. Convincing Krystal would be like taming a wild beast with one hand tied behind his back. It would never work. Isla was his safest and most secure option, and now he had it.

"I can't promise anything," he told her. "This"—he motioned between them—"isn't something I know how to manage." To *control* was what he really wanted to say.

Unbelievably, she laughed. Her voice carried across the terrace, and he wanted to crawl underneath the table. "You don't know how to be a friend?" she managed to say.

"I've had friends."

She was still chuckling. "You sure don't act like it."

The tension was melting. It was nice to share a moment with her that wasn't obligated, but he didn't want it taken too far. "Do we at least have a deal?"

"Do we need to shake on it like *formal* partners?" she teased.

Morei's lips tugged upward, uneasy, and he reached out his hand. "We have to start somewhere, right?" If she ever spoke like that to him in front of anyone, he'd cut her tongue out.

Isla took his hand. Her grip was firm, warm, and they shook. "All right, now we hug."

He stopped halfway out of his chair. "What?"

She gave him a pointed stare. "We shook like partners, but friends hug. Come on," she insisted, and approached.

"I've never hugged my friends," he remarked, but he still stood.

"Then today we start." Isla wrapped her arms around him and buried her head into him. He assumed it would be a short hug, but when she didn't move, he wrapped his hands around her. Her frame was petite, and his arms engulfed her. They stood there uncomfortably. He didn't know how long, but it was awkward.

The king hadn't hugged someone in ages. He'd shared a bed with women, kissed them, danced with them, but those actions were formal. They usually got involved because they wanted something from each other. In sex, it was pleasure. In dancing, it was because nobody could dance by themselves at a royal event. A hug, though, was intimate. The act made him feel vulnerable, exposed, like a rabbit poised to run. The emotions that rushed through him were foreign, and he didn't even know what to make of them, except that he wanted them to stop.

When the princess finally pried herself from his body, he was relieved. He stepped away, needing space. "Start thinking wedding attire. I'll speak to Rhys about the documentation and scheduling."

Isla nodded. "I'll do it immediately and find you later." She looked lighter, while he wanted to bathe himself free of the encounter. "And the announcement?"

"I'll have Rhys work something up and get it posted in the next few days." The words came fast, shallow. He still felt dirty. "How does that sound?"

"I like it."

They went their separate ways. He'd gotten exactly what he wanted. The council meeting was nearly upon them, and he needed a moment to collect himself before he saw her again. He'd been prepared for the conversation of making Isla queen, but hadn't calculated in her proposal. The king knew the value she would add to the city and his reign. Selfishly, he'd considered children because it would secure the Geral bloodline, but no more. He was a king, and that was where he would remain. If Isla ever proposed a situation that was more than friends, they would have a problem.

Some Journeys Are Walked Alone

Sekar was missing. He was there one moment, gone the next. Zari trotted along, not a care in the world, while Syra and Zarek sought him out. He was important. The God would be able to help them address the realm fracture. His connection with Chaos was vital. They were preparing for their final meeting, and she refused to go there until she had him.

But it was also more than that. After their last encounter, Syra couldn't shake the finality of this all. Like he'd told her those things in his twisted way of goodbye. Anxiety blossomed. They couldn't leave things like that—he couldn't just leave her. She refused to accept that, which had spiraled her into a mindless mess, searching the palace.

She stopped at another door that looked like it hadn't been touched. This had to be the tenth one she'd tried, but the longer this dragged on, the more frustrated she became. She knocked. "Sekar?" No answer.

She knocked harder. The Onye sat back on her haunches and watched. When nothing came of that, she slammed her hand against the wood. It stung. Their last encounter mocked her. Every word she should have said screamed in her head. She should have followed him, demanded they speak more, anything. Instead, she'd stood there like a blubbering fool and watched him walk out that door. And now, amid the growing tension of their circumstances, she couldn't ignore the suffocating feeling that they were on their own. That Sekar had said his piece and was letting her go.

Syra tried the door. It gave, and she shoved it open. The small chamber was hardly impressive, but it was cozy and untouched. Syra entered, but Zari didn't budge. Not even the chair looked sat in. The small bed was in perfect condition with too many threaded pillows. A layer of dust covered the sheets and made the air smell musty. But to her right was a small, folded note. The parchment was yellowed, and when she picked it up, it crinkled with age. She opened it and found the most elegant handwriting staring back at her.

Syra,

You are where you need to be.

She stared at the words, certain she was misreading them. But they were still there and had the same meaning as when she read them the first time. She was where she needed to be.

"Syra." Zarek's voice was low but confident. She looked at him, disappointed as he approached. Her shoulders slumped, and her hands hung limply at her side. He took the note from her.

When he was done reading it, he set it back on the table.

Syra wanted to crawl underneath the table. Anything to get away from the stare he delivered. He could have made the dead shiver. Disappointment, yes, but no surprise. As if he'd predicted this from day one.

When the Guardian didn't say more, she asked, "What?" Her tone betrayed annoyance.

"We are supposed to meet Raid and the rest of them."

She gestured at the spot where the note had been. "And what of that?"

Zarek's demeanor hardly shifted. He didn't seem to care. "There are few things I involve myself in. A God's problem is not one of them. You should learn to separate yourself more."

"Far easier said than done." She raised her wrist. "In case you forgot—"

"I haven't. I won't," he bit back sharply. Despite the changes, the same fierce, hotheaded man was there. "You will learn rather quickly, or so I hope, that if you want to involve yourself in Sekar's doings, it is best to do so at arm's length. He is neither trustworthy nor reliable, even if he is loyal to you. That does not mean he doesn't have other conflicting obligations."

"You're so stubborn." Sekar's actions were cruel, devious, and harmful, but he'd shown her that sliver of loyalty that she was terrified to let go of.

The Onye sneezed, but neither acknowledged it. "I've lived half the life that God has, but in the summers I've been alive, he's been responsible for more deaths than I can possibly recount. He has executed Gods, committed massacres, and twisted the words of kings and queens for a war he could win. That is not a man I want to share a meal with."

"He helped me save your life," she countered.

"You're asking me to trust a God that has spent lifetimes betraying those closest to him." Zarek's tone never fluctuated. "The answer is no."

"Dryl?" she challenged. "I didn't say trust, either."

"Eventually," the Guardian said. "When Sekar no longer has use for my brother, he will betray him."

"Me?"

That deadly gaze met hers, and she flinched. "You know that answer already."

She did, but she'd hoped he would change his mind. Even after everything, he still couldn't trust Sekar. "We need him." *She* needed him.

"No, we don't." Zarek crossed his arms. "We have you."

She threw her hands up. "I am only what I am because of him. Chaos isn't that easy, and I hardly know enough to address the chasm."

Zarek made a noise in his throat. "You've become dependent on him. That is your mistake."

"Can you blame me?" she shot back. "He's been with me since the day I ran. Since all of this started. Whether I adored or hated him, he was here. And now, when I need him most, he leaves."

The Guardian didn't even attempt to sound sympathetic. "You don't know him like you think you do. He's one of the ancients. His obligations go beyond anything we understand. This man doesn't choose sides, stay, or do right. Sekar has no concept of right and wrong, and if you thought he did, you're the fool."

She was grabbing on to strings now. "But his deal with Henry—"

"Is a pathetic sob story," Zarek interjected. "You have no idea what that man is willing to do." His voice rose now, finally showing some emotion. "His deal with Henry involves things beyond a Guardian's knowledge."

Humiliation and shame competed for the right to rule her head. "Then why would he do any of this?"

The Guardian scoffed. "How am I supposed to know? How are any of us supposed to know that? I fear not even Death herself knows what Sekar plans." He took a single step forward. "You need to make a decision, Syra. One that you won't like."

She looked at him, unable to find her tongue.

"You need to learn to let him go." Zarek spoke slowly, as if luring in a deer from the woods. "You cannot continue to chase a man who has spent lifetimes running from the world. You will always lose."

His words deflated her. Syra knew he was right, even if she wanted desperately to believe that Sekar wasn't that man. They'd shared laughs, traveled, and managed to intertwine into each other's lives in a way that could not be undone, and while the God had admitted to feeling something for her, it was likely not in a way she could ever return long-term. He'd spared her that trauma when he said his piece. They had proven their friendship to one another, but how long could that last? Destined for violence, trouble, and with a head full of voices he couldn't silence. Syra wasn't sure what to think of him. She wanted to believe in him, wanted him to be a hero, but she couldn't tame a wild beast that had spent centuries alone.

And that was her problem. Syra expected too much from Sekar. Every God earned their scar. He'd said those words to her. What she hadn't considered was that some scars never went away; they grew thicker, uglier, and no amount of oil could ever hide the grotesque reality of how they came to be.

"Syra." Zarek's voice was closer, reassuring in this hollowing void in her head. "You're a good person, and I know he's shown you kindness, but don't let that be the only thing that guides you."

Under different circumstances, she would have laughed at the audacity of it all. Her heart and mind could only take so much in one day, and she was already overloaded. But to be faced with a decision that would force her to relinquish all expectations from Sekar was almost too much. This was not what she'd wanted. They couldn't afford this. An unreliable God in the face of this growing disaster was unacceptable. And underneath all that, she couldn't fathom moving forward without him. She blinked back a single tear.

She wasn't surprised. Deep down, she'd known for a while this day would come—that she would need to stop caring so much for him. And it finally had, but at the worst time. The choice Zarek laid before her wasn't an ultimatum, it was for her good. Sekar practically threw this at her earlier. Everything he'd said was for their good. Yet, as she stared at the note, she couldn't bring herself to accept it. Every memory lived, both the bad and good, submerging her in a sea of torment.

"I thought I could change him," she confessed, hardly above a whisper. "I thought in all this madness, I could be the one to show him consistency and compassion."

"You're not the first to feel that way," Zarek said. "And you will not be the last."

But she would be the only one he ever regretted. She blinked, long and slow. "When he agreed to train me, he only asked that I give him friendship. I thought that he would try and take more. But now I wonder if he even understood what he asked of me."

"If he knew what he was taking advantage of, he wouldn't be such a fool." The Guardian wrapped his arms around her, engulfing her in warmth and affection. She burrowed her head into him, relieved to close her eyes from the world, even if temporarily. "You give too much, Syra. You think too good of people. Sekar doesn't know a world without suffering, but he's made his peace with that, and you have to accept him for what he is."

"I know," she mumbled.

Tension clung to the study's walls. Syra shifted her weight, considering taking a step back and disappearing. She would have if she could. Sekar's abandonment made her hardly interested in the world. She'd relived their last conversation a hundred times already, knew every expression and word by heart, and it still didn't appease her anxiety. So she tried to keep busy by doing everything but focusing on her thoughts.

If Zarek and Raid could have stabbed each other with looks alone, they'd have started a fight. Words must have been exchanged before this gathering, but she didn't know what. Syra leaned on a small desk, eyeing the scratches and the aged dark wood. She was curious about whatever was in the drawers. Her fingers trailed down to the nearest handle, which was shaped like a raven's head. The silence made it impossible for her to open it without risking drawing attention, but she pulled ever so slightly.

It gave with a squeak. Syra grimaced and didn't need to look to see them all staring. She shrugged, trying to feign that it was an accident, but didn't close the drawer. "Please, continue." She hoped she sounded as serious as the rest of them.

She thought she caught the faintest curl of Zarek's lips, but it was gone before she could confirm. "What's your plan, Raid? Talk to me."

Syra was impressed. The last time they'd all met, the young-looking Guardian appeared to be in control, but an obvious shift had occurred. Zarek's back was straight, his jaw locked, and his words sharp. The men gave him space, and Syra made sure to stay several steps from him. He was the embodiment of authority, and it fit him well.

Raid's jaw worked, chewing on the next words. The Guardian to her left crossed his arms, and Syra offered him a small smile. He looked as cold as Death herself.

"Ten men to resurrect a realm." Raid shook his head. "We need men in the living realm and here. I've given it some thought, and I think six here, four in the living is good enough. Our scouters gave word while we were split up that there's a small army of Geíons and Cer'hans guarding the realm fracture. Ruins the bit of fun I was hoping we could have."

"Scouters?" Syra prompted. "I thought you said there were ten of us." By the looks of it, assuming she still knew how to count, they were all here.

"The dead," Zarek answered without much thrill. "Watchers, scouters, our eyes and ears when we're not around. Souls who are not ready to pass and wish to be of service. We give them purpose here."

She stared, reminding herself where she was. "Can't you use them then?"

"No. They can scout the Soul Realm because their lifeforce is now tied here, but they cannot cross into the living realm. Small tactics here and there for distraction, possibly, but they are not fighters. Energy works differently here, Syra, and that means souls do too." Zarek leaned on the desk, hands splayed out. "Keep the scouters on the realm fracture. I want to know every-thing happening. Raid, I'm assuming you're staying here?"

The Guardian nodded. "Me and Eril are going to return to the outskirts of Ashýon, investigate the chasm, and see what else is there. Sazi, Jerun, and Xair will remain here to continue the natural order of things. The rest—Meril, Zeryl, Razer, and Vaeke—will cross to the living and survey the realm fracture from there. Reports will come in every evening. We're tasked with intercepting if mortal lives or souls are threatened but will remain hands off." Raid appeared to spit those last words, and she didn't blame him. It was unlike a Guardian to sit out a fight, but they had no choice. An army of beasts and demons against ten Guardians and a Goddess who hardly knew her abilities felt like a fool's errand. "The realms' survival is in the hands of that Rider. Don't make me regret this."

She chewed on her bottom lip, peeking at the contents of the drawer. Only a sliver, but she could see an ink bottle and a wax seal. That wasn't too interesting, so she pulled a little more. This time, the drawer gave without a noise.

"The plan sounds good in theory, but we need to address our numbers," Zarek replied. "The *Leangé*. Dryl had it before it was taken, although I don't know where. We need that book to secure some of the original Guardian practices for the Commitment Ceremony. It's been centuries since our last one. Many of you were the last to be trained. Without a Herän, we don't know the proper ritual for the bonding."

The man to her left spoke up. "All due respect, when and how are we supposed to fit that into our plan? You said do it all, but we hardly have enough numbers in the living realm to fight off a Cer'han."

"Minimize attention," Zarek insisted. "I don't care how you do it, just do it. One or two of you need to address the *Leangé*. We are nothing without that book."

"We're nothing without a Herän," another said. He looked even younger than Raid.

"Razer, I don't want to hear it." Zarek sighed. "We'll address appointing a Herän when the book is found. If we can find the book, we can begin building our numbers. Until then, Sazi, Jerun, and Xair, I want you all to start pulling reports on any tragedies in the last five summers. You know the deal—no survivors, we want the boy. Young men if everything looks right, although we increase the risk of death during the Commitment Ceremony. We'll address that if we must later on."

Men across the room nodded, some even meeting Syra's gaze for the first time. She returned it, pleased to be acknowledged and see their respect. They wanted this to work as much as she did. They couldn't afford any deaths.

"And you," Raid interjected. "What will you do?"

Zarek gestured at Syra. "We will return to Dryl at the Infernol. We need to inform him of what's happened. After that, we'll come back here. We need to determine how to slow the effects of the energy imbalance. If we don't figure that out, we won't have a realm to protect."

The Guardian didn't need to tell her for her to know what he was trying to say. They would need to move fast after departing the Infernol. Syra needed to claim her place as heir and the Gods' Death Keeper to please the realm and restore *some* semblance of order, even if it was small amid this cataclysmic disaster.

The Zyulë Bond itched. Syra snuck her fingers over to give a good scratch, sensing the familiar burn. The men continued to talk, oblivious, but Zarek's gaze swept over her in a fleeting motion. Just enough to confirm he was always watching. The itch intensified, and she rubbed the raised skin harder, concealing the action behind the desk as best she could. The Guardians knew what she was but were unaware of her bond to the man they deemed the God Killer. Those who had known were dead, and she wasn't in the mood for a show-and-tell.

She looked at Zari sitting in the corner and noticed the beast's ears were folded back, watching. She stared, stressed that she was supposed to be picking up on some silent sign. Of course he would leave and get himself in trouble. That was all Sekar knew how to do. Heat washed over her, and she felt a cold sweat dampen her neck. She rubbed the scar harder, the skin tugging and pulling uncomfortably.

And then it stopped. All of it. The beast's ears returned upright. The Onye was connected too, she realized. Either that, or it was an awful coincidence, which she highly doubted. Whatever had happened was over. She was fine, which meant he was too. He had to be.

"Syra."

She whipped her head around. "What?"

Zarek didn't look entertained. "Are you good with that?"

"Yeah." She didn't know what she was agreeing to, but she didn't want to admit to all these Guardians that she was elsewhere. Based on Zarek's unwavering gaze, she wasn't fooling him.

"Great." The Guardian nodded at everyone. "Let us remember the Order and why we are here. This realm needs us as much as we need her. Get going, and I hope to see you all soon. Syra"—he turned to her, and she pushed the drawer closed—"it's time."

The Choice of a Hero

Mud sucked Cyrus's boots in as he made his way toward the city center. He walked, slow, with Sozar by his side. The dragon's talons carved out deep gouges in the mud. The ground gave way to cobblestone, but they left a grimy trail behind them. The rain had since washed most of the blood from the dragon's scales, but he still walked cautiously, sore and hurt. Cyrus wished he could do more healing, but his skills were slim in that field, and he'd ignorantly thought he had more time to learn. He would not make that mistake again.

Clothes soaked, he couldn't wait for a hot bath. The light drizzle and low clouds made the city look straight out of a nightmare. Blackened pieces of wood and stone, bodies, and soldiers dragging people out from buildings that had been directly hit. Mothers, children, lovers knelt over some, screaming for a response or sobbing uncontrollably. Burn marks splattered the majority of the dead—hideous blisters and skin peeled away to reveal bone and charred muscle. The rotten smells of burning skin and ash made his nose wrinkle. A head turned toward him, the skull visible where hair was seared away. No eyelid protected the round orb staring at him, and the skin around was dark and blistered. Blood seeped freely in some portions, and the woman over the man tried to keep him still as he started to seize.

Cyrus turned away, his stomach twisting as she started to scream.

This is not your fault, Sozar rumbled. Cyrus wanted to believe him, but he couldn't. Dameon had come here for him. The Saveen prince wanted his attention, and now he had it. Deep down, he wondered if all of this would have been avoidable if he'd upheld his bargain with Henry. The mad king was trying to prove a point. Wherever Cyrus went, destruction followed.

Soldiers pulled more bodies from up ahead. He watched as a mother grappled with the death of her newborn, her own face unrecognizable. The physical scar would not come close to the emotional one that would stay with her forever. The faces that did meet his own did so with charred skin and gaping mouths. Cyrus couldn't tell if they despised him, and he couldn't stand looking long enough to figure it out. They crushed him. If this was war, he wanted nothing to do with it.

Shouts from behind caught his ear, and he turned in time to collide with a body. Alaric embraced him in a hug, pounding his back. "Are you and Sozar all right?" he asked, breathless. When he pulled away, Cyrus saw grime coating his face—a mix of ash and mud—but he couldn't ever misplace the gaze that was so similar to Raj's. Every now and then, it felt like the dead king was staring at him.

A handful of soldiers continued forward, aiding the others. Cyrus had never seen so much devastation in one place. He'd done everything in his power to avoid this, to run from the haunting reality of his existence. But this had happened because of him.

Numbly, he nodded, but his lips were already moving. "I failed you." His throat was scratchy, his voice hoarse from the yelling.

The king looked between him and Sozar. Alaric's hand wrapped around his neck, drawing him close so their foreheads touched. Cyrus didn't fight it, grateful for the brotherhood. Water dripped freely from their faces, and the king smelled of putrid smoke and sweat.

When he spoke, the words came out proud. "We are here because of you." He laughed, mad. "Do you not see what you are? What the world sees you as?" Alaric pulled his head back and squeezed his shoulder. Crevices of skin peeked through where rain had washed the soot away. "What you did up there is no less the most impressive thing I've ever seen. The Vorelians will speak of you for centuries to come."

Cyrus shook his head, unable to listen. "How many died today because of me?"

The king frowned. "What war does not have casualties?"

"I never wanted this."

Alaric sighed and looked at Sozar, his façade slipping and revealing the horrors he fought to hide. The dragon blinked, regarding him thoughtfully. A long moment passed, only noted by the screams of those mourning and the shouts of soldiers still working to remove bodies. Each sound dug a little deeper, and he desperately wanted to disappear. Delion had no right to call him a Dragon Rider when he couldn't even protect them.

When Alaric looked back at him, his shoulders slumped. "No hero is ever innocent, Cyrus. The greatest leaders have blood on their hands. But you want to know what defines you and the enemy?" He shoved a finger into Cyrus's chest. "You stayed to face the result of today. The enemy fled, a coward. The people know that. I know that. Loyalty is what makes a hero, not who they save or what they do."

Alaric was blind. Maybe he didn't want to accept the glaringly obvious: that Cyrus being here had put innocent people in danger, and would continue to now that Dameon knew he was here. Or maybe he knew, but as a king, he'd learned the art of never telling the full truth. He wanted Alaric to blame him, curse his name, any acknowledgment.

Sozar hummed, thoughtful. The dragon spun his head around and nudged Cyrus in the shoulder with his snout. *We cannot hide from our actions, but we can learn from them.*

"Will they forgive me?" he whispered, addressing the dead and dying. This was his fault. No matter what anyone said, blood was on his hands.

The king knew what he meant. He squeezed his shoulder again and then let his hand fall. "You can't blame yourself." If he blamed Cyrus for the damage to his city, it didn't show, and he wasn't sure he'd ever get that answer. "Come, let's help where we can."

Staying close, they walked toward the nearest casualties, who lay on the cobblestone, clothes ripped and skin blistered. A woman had a cloth over her eyes, her face eaten away by char. The man next to her had his hands soaking in a bucket of water. He looked up to Cyrus and the king, but Alaric waved him off before he could try and stand.

"Don't," he ordered. "Can I help you with anything?"

The man looked to Cyrus and Sozar, brown eyes complemented by a harsh redness. "Is it over?" His voice croaked.

Cyrus nodded, the action stiff. "Yes," he answered. For now.

"Thank you," the man said, and turned to look back at his hands. Alaric motioned for them to move forward. Before they made it even a few steps, Sozar stopped again and lowered his nose to the man and woman. Their home was ruined, their fear palpable, but an overwhelming silence fell between the three with Sozar there. The woman couldn't see, but her chest hardly rose in the dragon's presence. Gently, Sozar rested his nose against the woman's forehead. Then he did the same to the man. Cyrus watched relief bleed from the two as they said something in return.

Sozar approached him and Alaric with no rush. *What did you say?* Cyrus asked.

I apologized. This was not their battle.

Alaric nodded. He was privy to that answer and moved on to the next group of injured people. Sozar repeated that message, and each time, the people, no matter how hurt, acknowledged it. Cyrus helped lay damp cloths on burned skin, wrap bandages, and carry people. Alaric was right there the whole time, telling the injured they would be compensated and their homes rebuilt. Nobody tracked his promises, but Cyrus knew the king would manage.

He found himself inside some homes. Wood had turned to ash, furniture was destroyed, roofs collapsed. Some homes had fared worse than others. So many had been about their mornings, baking or cooking, folding clothes, or working on projects. A fire stove still burned with a pot full of biscuits overdone. The tops were hard, brown, but Cyrus pulled the dish off the fire and staunched the flames with water. He cleaned the less damaged homes by folding clothes, remaking beds, washing dirty laundry, or wiping soot off walls. One household had been in the process of chopping ingredients for a stew, so he continued with it, cutting onions and vegetables before piling it all into the pot with meat. He placed the lid on the pot and set it aside. Another family was kneading bread, so he did his best to help, although he was less skilled.

One by one, they tended to each home or business, helping where they could or noting damages too great to be fixed. It gave Cyrus fulfillment to help like this, and the soreness in his muscles felt less and less an issue and more of a reminder of his commitment to protect the innocent. Sozar dragged heavier items, offered condolences, and blessed a few who passed into the Afterlife with a dragon's touch. Cyrus respected Sozar for being a part of such a raw and intimate moment, knowing well enough that he didn't have the strength for it. His dedication to helping people restore their homes gave him all the reward he needed to smother those negative thoughts.

As the day grew older and the clouds parted, Cyrus found himself chuckling at the jokes soldiers told to one another. They were trying to lighten the mood where they could, and he appreciated their effort. They only stopped to rest when a citizen offered food and drinks. Those capable cooked meals and fed the weary. Citizens and soldiers started pulling wood and stone from reserves to fix the homes that could still be repaired.

The high sun dipped lower to the horizon, racing toward sunset. Cyrus accepted another drink. This one was an ale, which he was grateful for. Water and tea had been handed out all day, and if he had more water, he'd gag. The warm ale burned on the way down, and he drank half of the mug in one go.

Alaric approached. Most of the ash was gone, but his hair was still streaked with grime. "It's getting late. Why don't we head back to the palace and clean up, call it a day?"

Cyrus looked at all the work that still needed to be done, almost telling the king to go without him. Alaric must have sensed this. "There's only so much that can be done in a day, Cyrus. The people are slowing down. We all want to rest. Tomorrow, we'll continue."

"All right." Cyrus dreaded leaving. "Tomorrow," he promised.

A group of them broke off, making their way back to the palace. Sozar followed behind, choosing to walk instead of fly. The dragon had already feasted, his belly full of sheep, and he was tired. Cyrus knew by the sluggish movement of his thoughts. He was in the same boat. As the city was left behind, he realized just how little energy he actually had. Still dressed in the gear from his morning, the belt strung around his hips, and the boots he'd put on just at dawn, he couldn't wait to change into something more comfortable. The moisture stuck in his bracers had caused a rash from all the rubbing, but he hadn't said anything. It felt inconsequential compared to the rest of the city, and he was certain the other soldiers had similar issues with their armor. None of them had changed or removed pieces. They'd carried on, so Cyrus did too.

The palace came into sight, and a part of him was selfishly relieved to see that the building was in good condition, but he was ashamed that he didn't have the heart to turn around and look at the destroyed city. People would talk, and it wouldn't be in glory or praise that his name would be spoken in, it would be devastation. His actions cost countless lives today, and he would never forgive himself.

His identity had finally caught up to him. If he didn't act in the best interest of the world, enemies like Dameon and Ashtir would see to it that more would die in his name. Alaric could tell him anything, but he was not a fool. If these people were killed under a commander's protection, the king would have his head. But because he was a Dragon Rider, Alaric wouldn't lift a finger. Instead, he'd have to face the people's judgment.

It was his responsibility to protect the people, and he'd failed them. Never again.

"The city was the primary target." Alaric slowed his walk, clearly exhausted.

Cyrus couldn't believe only this morning he'd been standing in the hall, staring at Asher's body. "It's been a long day," he said. The bloodied and burned stained his mind. No matter how hard he tried, he couldn't shake their agonizing screams. Helping had given his thoughts a place, but now the void of frustration that threatened to swallow him whole remained.

"I want a woman and a good drink," Alaric said. "I'm not asking for much tonight, save for a good bath."

Others muttered their agreement. His thoughts drifted to the egg then. "Alaric, the egg."

"Is fine," the king assured him. "I had men down there for the whole day. If there was a problem, they would have come to me. If they were killed, someone else would have alerted me." He wagged his finger, oblivious to Cyrus's troubles. Perhaps it was a king's duty to shrug off casualties, or maybe Alaric didn't know how else to cope. "Speaking of, Markus is supposed to have names for me." He flashed a wild grin. "What about you? Feel like being a chancellor?"

"No," he answered, forcing a snort that got caught in his throat. Too much was on his mind. "I wouldn't last a moon."

Alaric patted him on the arm. "You say that now, but you've got politics in you. You just don't know it yet. Just you wait and see."

Cyrus shook his head. Politics wasn't for him, but he understood the need for them. Without rulers and councils, there would be no order. Without order, madness ensued. People, for the most part, thrived with structure and guidelines, no matter how small. Zorya knew that. She'd also know the right thing to say in the face of all this horror. In the season he'd been here, he could relate to the comfort of routine and expectations. Now, though, it ended. Comfort had put blood on his hands. Today marked a new beginning. It had to.

Cyrus chuckled roughly. "Maybe one day."

Married to the Crown

R hys was late. Morei stared at the empty chair across the table, willing the chancellor to appear. The council fiddled their thumbs, drank, and passed a few words. Isla sat to his left, but he tried not to acknowledge her. Their arrangement was formal, nothing more, and he didn't want to give her the wrong idea. There hadn't been much time since they'd made it, and when he'd sought out a drink, he'd found the Kendell's Milk was gone. Between his increased drinking and the single night of the festival, the supplies had dried up. Esme was quick to explain the shipment was coming in later that day, and offered another type of liquor. Fang's Revenge. It was a drink inspired by one of the extremist groups centuries ago. The red, creamy liquor was made with berries and spices. It was good—not Kendell's Milk, but it would do.

The king took a sip of it now. A different fiery burn seared his throat and warmed his stomach, a refreshing change. Maybe it wasn't so bad after all. Lord Cayden sipped on some hot tea, which Morei couldn't fathom doing in this growing heat. He'd arrived when the cool air touched the evenings and had enjoyed a pleasantly chillier winter than what he was used to in the Hazar Desert, but he had yet to experience a sea summer. It was by all accounts brutal.

Isla tapped her fingers on the table, filling the silence. He watched, unsure if he was annoyed by the distraction or relieved. Lady Yara fanned herself, tucked into a corset too small, and Lady Genesa kept her gaze fixed outward. She'd been King Drexis's mistress but had proven invaluable. He liked the older woman, even if she occasionally looked at him like a future meal.

Lord Malachi cleared his throat, flashing a handful of silver rings with different engravings. His salt-and-pepper beard was neatly trimmed, and his dark hair fell to his shoulders. The man looked like he was stuffed in clothes that didn't belong, like he should have been working the port or captaining a ship. "Shall we begin?" he offered.

"Let's be on with it," Lady Yara agreed. "He's never reliable."

Morei took another drink, gathering his thoughts. The last time they'd spoken, there'd been no indication that Rhys would be late or not show. They still had a conversation to finish too, but he'd never found the chancellor unreliable in this way. "You think poorly of him?"

The woman scoffed. "He's nothing but a scoundrel."

Isla kept drumming her fingers.

"What do you mean?" the king pressed. "Why are you bringing this up now?"

Lord Varun opened his mouth to speak, but Morei raised his hand to halt him. He pointed to Lady Yara. "I want to hear from you."

"Well." She looked around, questioning. "I eavesdropped on him talking to some attendees at the festival. He was talking about some deal." Lady Yara sat a little taller, proud. "I got a little closer, didn't want to let him or the guest know I was listening, you know? Anyway, he passed some coin. I saw it, but didn't get any more details than that."

Everyone looked at her like she'd just confessed to murder. Morei leaned forward. "And you just now told me this?"

Isla's fingers stopped.

Lady Yara's lips turned to a thin line, and she set her hand fan on the table. "Your Majesty, if you think I overheard this conversation and thought he was working outside your terms, then I would have said something. Based on your reaction though, I would assume you had no idea."

Her attempt at innocence was pathetic. "Spare me the façade, Yara. The last people who thought they could outsmart me wound up dead, and they too sat as councilmembers." The woman sank into her chair, pale. "Now, who here has a problem with Rhys?"

A few hands shot up. All this time, he'd thought the chancellor was worth keeping around because of his knowledge and reliability. Now, he was starting to believe he'd misread the entire situation. He gestured to Lord Eli. "What's your problem with the chancellor?"

The young man shrugged and laced his fingers together. "He's a liar, if you ask me. Makes promises, doesn't always deliver. I've had several instances where transactions fell apart because he failed to follow through. Would tell me the buyer changed their mind or whatever, but between us, I just never quite believed it."

The king motioned to the next hand. Dread blossomed in his stomach, turning his innards cold.

"A few summers ago, I firmly believed he was forging documents. I tried to press the matter with Drexis, but he didn't believe me." Lord Varun shook his head and snorted. "I couldn't figure it out. Documents disappeared and reappeared on my desk multiple times."

Morei stood. The chair slid, screeching. "Guards!"

The doors busted open. The handful of soldiers who waited outside rushed in. Before they could say anything, he ordered, "Fetch the chancellor. Find him at all costs. I don't care if he says he's meeting the queen of Diemon, I want him brought to me immediately."

"Yes, Your Majesty," one said. They left without another word. Morei stared at where the soldiers had been, infuriated. All this time, he'd been wrong. The chancellor was playing a far bigger game. Morei had known he was a criminal, but now he believed that Rhys was working on overthrowing him for the throne. Their last conversation haunted him. His intuition had told him the chancellor couldn't be trusted, but he'd been too worried about the political ramifications to act, as well as what he could gain with Syra.

He stood there, unable to just sit and wait. Edwin wasn't here. The commander was working with the city's recovery efforts, and had been excused from the meeting. The council stared at him; he could feel Isla's eyes burning a hole into the side of his head. Time stretched for an eternity, and he leaned on the table, hands pressed against the cool surface, stilling the tremor and displaying his ailment. Nobody dared speak. Morei's temper was on edge. Everyone here was a potential victim. A single push was all he needed.

The doors finally opened again, and one of the soldiers stepped in. "Your Majesty, we can't find him."

This couldn't be happening. "Have you looked everywhere?"

"Yes, Your Majesty."

"Keep looking," he snapped.

"We don't know for certain—" Isla started, but Morei spoke over her.

"I want soldiers on steeds immediately to search the city. Check ships first, and get men outside our territory in case he fled west. No Man's Land too. I want scouts in the north."

The man stared at him, mouth agape. "Your Majesty . . . can I ask what this is about?"

His answer came drenched in disdain. "Treason."

Silently, the soldier nodded and started to retreat, but Morei stopped him. "I wasn't done yet."

"Yes, um." He turned and stood at the door's entrance. "Apologies."

"You have permission to enter his study and chambers and pull all information you can find. I want his desk ripped apart, bookshelves emptied, every book sorted, you name it. I want it done. Bring everything to me." He would execute Rhys and make him a public example of what happened when anyone crossed him. The crows could have his eyes. He'd let the chancellor's body rot under the sun until nothing but bones remained. And when that was done, he'd take Rhys's skull and display it on his desk.

When the soldier didn't move, Morei motioned at him. "Go."

As the doors closed once more, he still couldn't find the ability to sit, so he resorted to a slow walk to the window that overlooked the sea. He hated this as much as he had the day Ezra's announcement came through.

"His family has been a part of the Casters for as long as this city has stood," Lady Genesa whispered from behind. "His family has connections outside this country. Powerful connections that could cause a political war if they found out what you did."

"Political war?" He turned to face the council. "My family has ruled the Hazar Desert since the founding of this country. My bloodline has sat on the throne for centuries. My people took that all away. They didn't care about who knew who or titles. They only cared about what they wanted at the moment: to be right." His voice shook with rage. "And now you want to tell me what is and isn't political war? I don't care who Rhys knows or who his grandfather served. I care about proving a point."

"His family is linked to the Lirallian Empire," Lady Genesa continued. "And before that, the Raveers. He comes from royalty. You kill him, and you start a war."

Between being lied to or having information withheld, he didn't know which was worse. The cold kiss of violence pressed against his cheek, and he tried to swallow the sensation. He couldn't risk making a scene with Isla here. She was far too valuable to lose in the long run.

"Then I want everything we can find on him and his family." He pointed to Lady Genesa. "You seem so informative, so here's your task: document everything you know about Rhys and his family, and when you don't know something, find it. I want his connection's connections. I want to know why someone with a Raveerian bloodline is serving as chancellor in Caster, and why they have anything to do with Liral."

He would need a new chancellor, but that wasn't a priority. The king could leverage Isla to fulfill certain duties until then. Replacing the position would be no easy feat. It required extensive questioning, strict requirements, and time that he didn't have. The council could have led the chancellor's selection, but Morei preferred to be hands-on with the person he was supposed to trust so much. Royal blood should accept the position, but he wasn't sure he trusted any of the councilmembers or their families for that.

"You have my word," Lady Genesa said.

He appreciated people who didn't challenge orders. He turned to the rest. "Regarding the battle with the Red Queens. I am aware there are some questions about how things were handled."

Lord Cayden leaned back, meeting his gaze. "Well, perhaps we've worded this a bit wrong." As if to confirm, he looked to his fellow councilmembers and nodded. "We were unaware of your . . . capabilities, shall we say?" A nervous chuckle followed.

Morei understood that tone. The council had spoken behind his back. "What are your concerns?"

Lord Eli cleared his throat and bared his hands. They were all obviously uncomfortable based on the fidgeting. "I think I speak for everyone. Well, almost"—Eli glanced at Isla—"and I think we're primarily concerned with your, uh, reliability?"

The last word came out as a meek whisper. Morei stared *hard* at the lord, trying to decide the best way to deal with this.

"I mean, many of us here understand the implications of Dark Energy. It's a bit dangerous, yeah? Can kill the Harvester?"

"It brings with it bad luck," Lord Varun rushed to add, as if his clarification made it all the better. With all attention on him, he shrugged. "You know the taboos, Your Majesty. We don't need to explain them to you."

"No," Morei said. "I'm well aware of your ignorance."

He watched the council squirm. He couldn't believe he was here again. The city was saved, the Red Queens dispelled, and their concerns were related to bad omens and taboos. So insulting. Standing here now, he remembered clearly how the Geral council had treated him. They'd practically spat at his feet and cursed his name. He was tired of traditions, obligations, and cultural beliefs. Sorréle was pinned by their practices, unable to see beyond what they'd told themselves. A shame to be faced with this again. They were all alive because of him.

"You think my ruling short-term," Morei continued. "You believe that I'll get myself killed before this promised empire is yours to take." The council shifted. This was what they wanted. "I can assure you that won't happen."

"Your ailment," Lady Yara pointed out. "The curse of the dead. Or—"

"The mark of the damned," Morei finished. "I have heard the names, and I don't care what you call me, so long as you share the same vision I do."

Lord Cayden wrapped his large fingers around the tea, engulfing it. "How can you be certain that you won't die before then? History has never spoken of a Dark Energy Harvester to live beyond a few summers."

Morei knew the facts and swallowed the small pang of uncertainty. He was not like the rest of them. His condition was different, and he'd so far managed to create a relationship with the energy that kept him alive. That was more than the rest of the Dark Energy Harvesters could say.

But he couldn't put that in words. These people, in all their normalcy, would never grasp the complexities of harvesting. They were meant for trade and talking. Isla hadn't moved since he'd gotten up, and he wondered what she thought of him right now. Her expression was unreadable—a skill she'd perfected from all the summers working as a staff member.

"I have outlived the majority who ever tried to harvest Dark Energy," the king boldly stated. "I have done things that nobody has read about in history, mastered an element untouched by anyone." They stared, unmoving, and he let the next words go for the first time since he'd harvested fire. They'd hollowed out a small piece of his chest for many moons now. "Death will come for me one day, as she does for us all. But I will be ready then, and there will be an empire in our name to remember me by. As well as a bloodline." It was a bold lie, but nobody needed to know that. If a promised heir kept them satisfied, then he would say it, even if he never intended on fulfilling that. "My intention was never to live forever—I am just a man—but I will ensure that even the Gods know who to fear. That is my promise to you all."

Nobody spoke right way. They likely didn't know what to say, and he didn't either. Confessing to Death was harsh when he felt like he still had so much life to live, but then again, he didn't know who to be after building his empire. That was always his end goal. Beyond that, he didn't know who or what his purpose was.

Lord Cayden put his fist to his chest, just as the citizens had in honor of him. "What we've done since your arrival is more than this city has done since its birth. Taking Ferguson is a testament to our capability and strength. You've shown us that. My loyalty is to you."

The confidence in the lord's words brought a smile to the king's face. This was why Caster was the optimal location. The people were tougher, more prepared to fight, and hungry for control.

More nods. He had their dedication. Morei's willingness to do the impossible was starting to pay off. "As this empire grows, we need to unify the people under a common message. Something that all men and women can carry forward. It will represent everything that we stand for."

He thought for a moment, sifting through ideas and motives. He couldn't declare a statement that meant nothing to the commoner, but he wanted something strong enough to capture the attention of the world. Mumbles passed among the council as they too thought of ideas. This would be a statement that would embody everything he wanted the new era to be.

"An empire to end the reign of Gods." As the words left his tongue, they felt right and tasted sweet. This was what he wanted. It was time to end the power of deities once and for all. "Tell this to everyone. Let word spread like wildfire. I want the world to know what's coming. I want citizens in the southernmost cities to know our call before we show. Sorréle will be ours before the winter."

Nods and agreements. Lord Eli pounded his fist on the table, loud, and others followed to show their support. All but Isla, who still looked uncertain, though her head moved up and down in the slightest motion. In time, she would understand that to be strong, one had to be cruel. He motioned to her, and she gripped the chair, ready to stand. He indicated for her to do so, and the room fell silent again.

"Another announcement," he declared. The thrill of the council's eagerness seeped into his bones. Rhys felt leagues away. "An empire cannot be superior without proper rulership. Because of this, I have asked Isla Caster for her hand in marriage, and she has graciously agreed." Councilmembers exchanged looks before turning their attention to Isla. They knew what this meant. Tradition only meant so much in the name of power. He let the next words sink in, speaking deliberately. "The Caster bloodline will sit on the throne of the most powerful empire in history."

The Currency of Trust

Zarek took a single look back and then nodded, obviously satisfied. Ahead, Syra stared at what she could only describe as the closest thing to a real portal she'd ever seen. The silver and blue, cloud-like substance spiraled, taller than she and oval-shaped. The air around the portal rippled like waves lapping against the shore. They were standing in the courtyard, or what was left of it, in the Soul Realm. Crumbled stone made up a once prestigious wall, and a sheet of ice covered a portion of the palace. Pieces of metal reflected the purple hue from the sky above, and a massive fissure stretched across the courtyard, wide enough to suck Syra's leg in if she wasn't careful.

She stood beside the Guardian, who held Death's Sword. Zarek had led her out here right after the meeting, leaving everyone else and the Onye behind. She was glad to be dressed and ready; they hadn't even stopped for water. Once they'd passed the worst of the courtyard's destruction, he'd gotten to work. Zarek recited a script in Old Tongue as he raised the sword and tore right *through* the veil between realms. The blade's tip sank in as if slicing through butter, disappearing, and he twisted it. The air rippled, and the sigils along his blade shimmered brightly. When he removed Death's Sword, a puff of blue mist appeared, and the weapon returned to its normal appearance. There, it grew, chasing its own tail, until it became what she saw now. The mist became more substantial, shifting to silver when it pulsed. The border of the portal fluctuated, unstable, and she halfway suspected the entire thing would collapse on itself.

Ahead, she saw nothing, just a swirling vortex of the substance.

"So"—Syra struggled to use her tongue—"that's how you travel?"

Zarek passed her the faintest of amused smiles. "The metal is tampered with. Volkeri Island is where the veil is thinnest between realms, which means the soil there is rich with enhanced elements, including the metal we use for our swords. When we forge them, there is a ritual that happens—"

"Dark Energy," Syra interrupted. Mist from her breath billowed up between them.

He nodded. "It is only a portion of the process. One day, you may see it for yourself. Combining the metal and the ritual provides a conduit for the energies to merge between realms. When they do so"—he pointed to the portal—"this is what we get."

Syra weighed his words, intrigued. The Guardians had always just been there, especially when she needed them. She knew they traveled but had never gotten around to asking how. Life hadn't granted her that opportunity until now.

"What about the realm fracture?"

"These are temporary tears." He sheathed his weapon. "Small enough that the realms correct the intrusion before it becomes anything more. A realm fracture is large enough to fit four dragons through, sometimes more. Portals are within the threshold these realms can manage. Anything greater, and we risk disrupting the balance."

Another reminder of how little she knew. The Guardians had been practicing this for centuries, experts in realm hopping.

"Are you ready?" Zarek prompted. They were partners in this mad plan to save the realms. "It doesn't hold long. We need to go, or I have to open a new one."

Syra's fingers trailed over the hilt of her sword. It was a comfort to have a weapon on her. The chilly air, the smell of decay, and the colors all struck her at once. Faced with the living realm, she was no longer sure she wanted to cross but knew she had to. Dryl needed to know they were okay—and she hoped that he was too.

"And after this," she breathed out, "we leave?"

Zarek stepped toward the portal, raising his hand so that his fingers were submerged in the mist. "Destiny has not been kind to you, Syra, but I hope you can trust that I will do everything I can to keep you alive."

When he looked at her, she had no doubts that he meant those words completely. And she needed to hear that. Her world had changed so fast. No longer was she the girl on the run; now she was the one saving the realms. She could feel the tension in her shoulders and neck with each movement. In a matter of days, everything had been flipped upside down, and she couldn't even recall the last time she had laughed hard and well. The Infernol, Keryn, the run from Jasper Village to the outskirts of Raveer . . . all felt so far away. Syra should have been grateful to be alive, but instead, she was ashamed that she couldn't even recall the most basic memories.

"Okay." The word was hardly audible to her ears. If there was one thing she could rely on, it was that she couldn't imagine doing this with anyone else.

Zarek gave her a single nod and stepped through. The mist engulfed him. She surveyed the realm, taking it all in. One day, if they managed to stay alive through this all, this realm could be something extraordinary.

With that final thought, she stepped forward. The mist was cold, sending a chill through her, and the hairs on her arms rose. Her boot disappeared, and she panicked. What if she was stepping off a cliff? She bit her cheek, letting her weight carry her forward, and was relieved when she felt the hard-packed promise of ground. The rest of her passed through, and she blinked. This was the same room where Sekar had ripped Keryn's heart out. A place she'd actively avoided since that day. Even now, with a freshly polished floor, repainting, and several furniture pieces, she could still see the dead lying about

.

Ahead, Zarek stood with a young woman she'd come to know and rely on. Trish was a refuge from Assane, and her ebony skin and amber eyes made her look like a deity. She'd never once looked at Syra any differently, and they'd become fast friends. Trish helped with the inner council meetings, and in the last moon cycle, she'd become more and more of an advisor with her knowledge of the country.

"Get Dryl, please," Zarek told her. "Tell him we need to speak immediately. No exceptions."

Trish nodded, not moving. People didn't see portals like this every day.

"Hey," Syra managed.

"We don't have much time," Zarek said before any questions could be asked.

Trish's head tore between them, even as the portal dwindled. The mist shifted, and the tail started to recede. Syra tried to open her mouth, to say something that would put the woman at ease—this was not the finest entrance—but she was tired and lacked the strength to sympathize. Zarek didn't move, watching Trish with an unreadable expression.

The woman finally got it. "Yup," she mumbled. "Got it. Yeah. I'll get him." She scrambled to the doors and slipped out.

Syra looked around. The furniture looked comfortable, and she was tempted to sit while they waited. The air was different here. Having been away from the living realm for as long as she had, she could taste the life—metals, spices, roasts—and feel the warmth on her skin.

Shouts came from somewhere beyond the chamber. Syra stiffened, and she and Zarek both reached for their swords.

The doors opened without a sound. The hard step of boots echoed, and Dryl entered. He was dressed in armor, and Syra's heart jumped into her throat. He held a sword that he looked ready to swing. At the sight of them, he didn't slow. He walked right up to Syra and studied her as if reviewing a document, then turned to Zarek.

"Your eyes."

"Long story," the Guardian said. Syra knew Dryl wasn't satisfied with that answer—he was a man who liked information. A Guardian trait, she'd concluded. But now was not the time to talk about having been dead. "What's with the armor?"

Dryl's tone was tense. "Liral has paid us a visit." Zarek opened his mouth, but his brother halted him. "Tell me, what happened? I had scouts out for you two, but you just vanished."

Syra wanted to say everything at once. She wanted to say that she'd been a fool to think she could ever outrun Destiny, that she regretted taking the option to die from Zarek, regardless of what he said, that she was scared. Scared of what might become of her, uncertain of what the future held, and terrified that she might make a mistake that could cost everyone their lives.

Instead, Zarek answered, "Shevana is dead. Elyas is driving demons into the living realm. Brother . . ." He shook his head. "The Soul Realm is in grave condition."

The door opened behind him, and Bane stepped in, dressed in armor. "Gonsín." The commander didn't even seem to see the others in the room.

Dryl looked back at Bane. "I'm coming."

More shouts came from the hall, and a resounding ringing vibrated the chamber. A bell from somewhere, although Syra hadn't even seen one in the Infernol's halls that she'd wandered. The buzz was back, the air charged with anticipation. She could practically taste the bitter flavor of battle on her tongue, and she grimaced.

The Guardian she knew so well scanned the small trio. His crimson gaze betrayed the fierce nature of his order. The softness there moments prior was gone, replaced by the look of a warrior who had seen his fair share of battle. "We should have killed that demon when we first met."

Zarek agreed, but Dryl was already heading in Bane's direction. "I have to go. If Liral takes this place, we have nothing." At the entrance, he stopped, and his head spun back. "Syra, remember what I said about Raveer?"

Numb, she nodded. How could she forget? The world wanted to weaponize her—he needed to weaponize her—and now was it. He wasn't demanding or begging, simply stating. But it was enough to make her stomach twist.

Dryl's sword moved as he shifted his grip. "Ve'hem," he told her. With that, he was gone.

His brother was next to her. "The praise of a Guardian does not come lightly."

Only earlier today, if time could be measured like that in the Soul Realm, he'd awoken. Zarek was barely a day out from being resurrected, and she worried about his stamina and strength. "You, though—"

"Don't," Zarek warned. "I will not be treated like a lame horse. I am and will be fine."

She nodded. He'd told her he didn't want sympathy, and she needed to remember that. The man who shoved, pushed, and spared no mercy when it came to training her, who would rather drive a blade through her heart than watch her make excuses. She'd learned a lot from him, and she needed to embrace that. If he was willing to set everything aside, to swallow the uncertainties in the face of Death, then she needed to as well.

Guilt for the Wary

Cyrus rested his head against the wall. The night sky was lighting up with another storm, this one angry. It ravaged the sea and shook the ground, and rain pelted the windows. Sozar was tucked up in an unfinished dragon hold, sleeping soundlessly through it. After they'd returned and determined that everyone was safe, the dragon slept. Cyrus didn't bother reaching out or checking on him. He knew Sozar was secure and comfortable, and that was all that mattered.

He'd sought a bath out and sat in it for the entire evening, hoping to ease the harsh newness of his frustrations. No matter how hard he scrubbed his skin, blood still remained. Blood from the dead, as gruesomely slick and red as when he first saw it earlier on the faces he passed.

He replayed the fight with Dameon constantly, wondering where it went wrong and what could have gone better. A different swing there, another word he could've said. Maybe he'd been too caught up in his emotions. But what was he supposed to do? Sozar was injured, Dameon was reckless, and Ashtir's close brush with Death was bothersome. He hoped the dragon was okay. Cyrus didn't want to be the cause of any dragon's agony—that was no honorable way to live—but he also understood certain actions were necessary. If Sozar hadn't done so, Ashtir would have, and the roles might have been switched.

Peeling the leather off had been the greatest thing he'd done all day. His body was sore, he had bruises in odd places, and he'd learned later of a cut on his head from hitting it. Blood matted his hair, and he was gentle when washing it out. His ribs hurt, and the hand that clung to the Rider's Sword was tender to the touch. He'd held it with far too much stress. If Hyle knew that, he'd scold him. That was a mistake he couldn't afford to make again.

He wanted to talk to Hyle. Nobody else knew what it was like up there, save for the man he exchanged the fight with. He couldn't sit with the commander and talk about what it felt like—the fears, the pressure, all of it. Soldiers understood the battle on foot, but an entirely different layer of complexity occurred when his life was in Sozar's ability to catch him. Or the fall that had happened when Ashtir wouldn't let go. His heart tripped at the memory. In the heat of the moment, fueled by pure survival and instinct, he hadn't thought about the monumental risks of anything going wrong. He'd just acted.

Cyrus wasn't sure if that made him lucky, or a fool.

The egg was okay. Cyrus had asked again when he'd finally emerged from the bath. Once again, he was assured that nothing was amiss. The palace had never been attacked directly, confirming that Dameon and Ashtir had no idea that an egg was here, or that Üg'ahn lived and protected another dozen. Cyrus grimaced. It was, indeed, luck.

His stomach grumbled. By the Gods, he was starved. The small meals he'd eaten throughout the day hadn't made an impact. A fight like that had sucked all the strength from him, and it felt like he couldn't get enough food. Cyrus weighed stopping by the galley and seeing what leftovers they had from the day. He'd failed to meet Alaric for supper. The council had demanded an explanation, and the king had obliged under the promise that he could eat while they spoke. The invite was extended to him, but Cyrus denied it. The last thing he wanted was to listen to the councilmembers turn this into a political argument. Add alcohol to that, and he was certain it would turn into a disaster.

Sozar had told him that his mind was different after interacting with Üg'ahn, the Forgotten. He still didn't feel it, and when he poked around in the silence of this chamber, he couldn't find anything out of the ordinary. Cyrus tried to seek out Üg'ahn, testing their connection—if one was still there—but he found himself aimlessly meandering through his thoughts and memories.

Beneath all that, though, something caught his attention, like a small crack that one might feel when running their hand over a wooden door. A strange energy lived there, neither dark nor light, and he tried to investigate it more. But nothing came as a result. The crack, hardly worth noting, didn't fluctuate or react to his insistence.

Cyrus's mind was no longer entirely his own. With Sozar, he'd always believed them a pair. Their feelings and thoughts intermingled, unified, but this was different. Üg'ahn could find him anywhere. A mark, tracker, whatever he wanted to call it, confirmed the ancient dragon's strength.

Pulling himself out from the depths of his mind, Cyrus pushed his leg out. He was nestled in a chamber meant for guests who waited to see Alaric. It was smaller, cozy, with several chairs, a table, and a large window. A plant to his left was taller than him with wide leaves. It looked similar to some of the life he'd seen in Venkar City. Tucked up on the windowsill, he raised the drink to his lips. Orange tea, but it was nearly gone and growing colder.

He really needed to pull himself together and go to the galley.

Lightning streaked through the sky, and thunder immediately followed. He could go to bed, but that thought was unfulfilling. Sleep was not welcoming him tonight like he'd thought she would. After the day he'd had, he'd hoped to be like Sozar and pass out before he made it out of the bath. Instead, he'd sat there, entranced by thoughts that he couldn't shake himself of, no matter how wild or grotesque. And he was doing it again.

Cyrus downed the rest of his cold tea and hopped off the windowsill. He moved too fast, and his muscles screamed in protest. Stopping, he let the discomfort pass before he started his walk. The galley was close. Cup in hand, he made the quiet journey through the servant hall. He could have used the primary one, but he was hoping to avoid attention after today. Most servant halls ran parallel to the main ones. They were narrow, a little less glamorous, and generally quiet this time of night. He found the door to the galley, which had a knife carved into the wood to signify the location, and opened it. Only one woman was there. She greeted him, kneading dough. Next to her were a dozen baskets full of dough ready to proof for the rest of the evening.

"Good evening," Beth called, cheerful. Nothing to betray anger for what happened today. But he wasn't sure she would reveal that. Her gray hair was up in a bun, and she wore the usual staff attire—plain blue and tan clothing. He liked Beth because she always had a smile on her face. She didn't ask him questions or pry. She treated him like anyone else.

"Is the hot water still available?" he asked as he approached. The use of his tongue felt foreign to him after a night of silence. The strong smell of yeast met his nose. Behind her, a fire still thrived.

"Funny you would think it wouldn't be." Beth chuckled. "You almost always stop by this time of night, so I've learned to keep it going for you."

Cyrus stopped at the hearth and set his cup aside. As promised, a water pot sat ready for him. After everything, the predictability brought him peace. "Thank you."

"Tea leaves are in a cup just to your right."

Sure enough, he saw a large cup with the leaves bundled in a cloth. "Have I really become that predictable?" He grabbed a mitten and then the hot water, making sure not to splash any on himself as he poured. He'd done that several times in the past. The pot was bulky, with a wide spout, and he was still getting used to it. This time, he was successful in not making himself look like an imbecile.

Beth laughed and reached for more dough. She floured the wooden surface and started another round of kneads. "A bit," she admitted. "I'll tell you what, though, I spoke to a young gentleman yesterday, and he said that his family have created a new selection of teas. He was hoping to have them available here. Charming young man, really. He was selling all day to the markets and got the courage to come talk to me."

Cyrus grabbed a spoon and stirred the tea. It would be ready soon, but he would have to let the water cool off. Steam billowed up. "Did you say yes?" Conversations like this would have made him feel normal under different circumstances. She was the first person he'd seen all night, and he'd prepared himself for judgment and questions he didn't know the answer to.

Beth pinched the dough to start shaping it into a ball. "Of course I did. You were the first person I thought of who would appreciate a new selection. You and Luke are the only two I know who would tell me if the leaves aren't good. You'll do that, won't you? I would hate to have tea available that you don't like."

She reminded him of a grandmother who worried constantly about her grandchildren. "Of course," he said. "Let me know when we get the tea in. I'd love to try it." The cup was still hot to the touch. "Have Luke and us sit down and we could do a taste test. See what we like."

"Oh, that's a fantastic idea," Beth said. "I'll be sure to fetch you both."

Cyrus nodded. He was eager to return to his place on the windowsill and be alone. "You have a good night, Beth. I'll see you tomorrow."

The woman had started humming a song, and she stopped to reply. "Goodnight, Cyrus."

He took the servant hall back to the guest chamber. His room was on the third floor, but he didn't feel like going there tonight. Not yet, anyway. Cyrus would have to face his bed, and he wasn't in the mood to be reminded that he would probably not sleep.

The side door opened just next to the guest chamber. No one was in the hall, and he quickly slipped into the room.

As the door closed, he heard Alaric say, "You're a hard one to find when you don't want to be found." Cyrus turned to see the king standing there, dressed simply. Alaric motioned at the table between the two chairs. There, a plate of pastries invited him. "These were made a bit ago. I had Beth prepare a small batch."

She knew. Cyrus shook his head. The woman was in everyone's business without even trying. "I was enjoying the silence."

"Or you couldn't sleep," the king observed. He sat in the plush chair. The leather strained under his weight as he reached for one of the pastries. "I couldn't either. Hard to lay your head down after such an eventful day."

Eventful. It implied exciting and new, nothing close to how he felt. Cyrus made his way to the windowsill, which was only a few paces away. He wanted to watch the storm, but he snatched a pastry as he went. As he got comfortable, he set the cup between his legs and asked, "Was the council meeting eventful?"

He bit into the sweet. It was filled with apples and cinnamon, buttery too. Alaric answered, "The usual. Concerns about the financial impact outweighed those about the loss of lives. Lady Treza was a nightmare, and I nearly stabbed Jexton. I tell you, one of these days I'm going to replace my council with people who care."

"Did they say anything about me?" Cyrus asked. He needed to ask. Alaric might be able to feign ignorance, but the council would reveal the city's true nature. Not often was there a Dragon Rider fight—at least not in the last eight centuries. That was sure to get anyone's attention.

A pause, and he stole a look to see Alaric chewing. He knew without confirmation that they'd spoken about him and Sozar. Who wouldn't? The king's words came out slowly.

"War is ruthless. Politics can be the result of such things," he began. "The council is concerned about your loyalty still, especially after seeing another Dragon Rider—"

"Do they think that was all for show?" Cyrus interrupted, annoyed.

Alaric reached for another pastry. "Don't worry, I didn't budge. Delion has pledged itself to you, and I would not expect you to pledge fealty. You've made that clear, and I reminded the council of that. Your actions were clearly for Delion. They're just finicky. Change scares them, but dragons scare them more."

Cyrus drank his tea, mulling things over. This was why he struggled with politics. All his actions were always on thin ice. One wrong move and the council questioned him. "I don't know what I can do to help them see that I'm a good person. Sozar too."

"You don't do anything," the king replied. "Let me worry about that."

The tone caught his attention. "What do you have in mind?"

"Delion has pledged itself to you," Alaric said. "In return, you have pledged yourself to the Rider Federation. Tomorrow, I intend to announce fealty to the Rider Federation."

Cyrus looked at him like he had five heads. "How can you convince a city to believe in something that existed centuries ago? That city is in ruins."

"But their purpose still lives," Alaric said through a mouthful. He swallowed. "The Rider Federation stood for world peace. It was the most powerful city this world has ever seen, even compared to empires. You bring back an egg, declaring more, and I have seen a God more than I have in my entire life. Times are changing, Cyrus. I intend to make it clear where I stand, and the city will follow. Forget what the council says, the people see you as a hero. In time, the council will have no choice but to follow. Anyone who denies it will have consequences."

That word "hero" made his mouth dry. He took another drink of his warm tea. The king was acting foolish, making claims that blurred the truth. What happened today couldn't ever happen again. "So I will be world peace," he whispered, drumming his fingers over the cup. Chavi and the others had called it Eei'on Rü, but it sure didn't feel that way. The pastry lay half-eaten next to his leg. "I don't even know what I'm doing."

"Yes, you do," Alaric told him, stern. "Everything you do was a choice you had. You could have left this city after what my father did to you, but you didn't. You could have refused training, but you didn't. When Dameon showed up, you could have tucked your tail and run for the trees, but you chose to put your armor on and face him. You say that, but you continue to do incredible things. One day, it'll be your name people worship, not the G ods."

Cyrus raised his hand. "Too far."

Alaric shrugged, unconvinced. "There was a time when the Dragon Riders were more revered than the Gods. I once laughed at those stories, but now I'm not so sure they were far from the truth."

"Eei'on Rü," Cyrus breathed. Alaric raised his brow. "That is what the Dragon Riders called their cause. Peace of the world, or something like that." He picked up the pastry, eyeing the apple filling. "I hope to bring honor to that one day, but it will not happen overnight. We need Riders, to train them, and to hope they all agree on the purpose of what the Rider Federation once stood for. And fast." Two eggs remained in Henry's possession, and he feared what the man was willing to do with them. If they hatched and bonded, whether naturally or by force, he risked facing multiple Dragon Riders. That was a battle he and Sozar would never survive.

"Use Delion," Alaric offered. "I told you once, this city is yours, and I'll say it again. Delion is at your service."

Cyrus nodded. "I know, and I am forever indebted to you for that. But what will the world think when Dragon Riders call Delion home? It will be a political war. Hyle was right." Alaric pursed his lips. "No, the Dragon Riders will need a place to call their own. Perhaps Delion can serve in the beginning, but not forever." The answer came without hesitation. Cyrus had known this for a long while, even if he wasn't entirely certain of the logistics. After the God's insistence on the federation, he knew he couldn't approach this any other way.

When the king didn't reply right away, he gained the courage to look. He didn't want to offend or disrespect Alaric, but he wouldn't lie about his intentions either. Cyrus knew the Dragon Riders needed a city of their own. They would not have to worry about politics, deals, or pissing off the wrong king or queen. Much as Alaric would do tomorrow, cities would pledge themselves to the Dragon Riders. It would never be the other way around. He had spent this long a free Rider, and he would continue to embrace that.

Alaric smiled at him, pastry still in hand. "You are a good man, Cyrus. I am honored to call you a friend."

Relief swept over him. "I could say the same about you."

With a wave, the king shook his head. His cheerful expression fell. "I'm not the man you are, Cyrus."

"That's a bit harsh—"

"No, let me explain," Alaric insisted. Cyrus raised his hand in defeat and picked up the pastry to finish it off. "You've taught me a lot, far more than I could ever put into words, but most importantly, you taught me that there are genuine people out there. I was raised by a man who gave me a scar because I tripped while he was in the middle of an announcement. That was my normal, and I admit that when I look in the mirror sometimes, I see my father looking back at me. I hated him, the man he was, but I'm just like him."

Cyrus held his tongue, knowing he shouldn't interrupt, but he wanted to tell Alaric how wrong that was.

"I raise my hand too quick, my temper is short, and when I become upset, it's far easier for me to raise my sword than speak," Alaric continued. "I know that I can't change entirely. The violence my father taught me is all that I know, but I can try." He chuckled to himself, but it came out strained. "I should be thanking you for saving my life, Cyrus. And please, listen to me, will you?"

Quietly, he nodded. Rain continued to pelt the window.

"I've watched my father beat men and women until they lost their lives, and they begged—by the Gods, they begged so loud. But you didn't. You never once pleaded for him to stop. When I saw what he was doing to Sozar, what he was willing to do, something in me snapped. Here you were, a Dragon Rider, and he was treating you worse than a murderer. How could anyone justify that?"

Alaric sighed. "When I killed him, I thought Sozar would burn me right there. I was prepared for it, but instead, he thanked me. It felt almost unfair to be rewarded with those words when my blood was the same as my father's. And then, before I knew it, I was dining with a God and a Rider." He scoffed. "I ask myself every day where I'll go wrong. I certainly don't deserve the kindness your friendship has offered."

The king didn't continue. Cyrus jumped off the windowsill and walked to sit in the chair next to him. Cup in hand, he settled. Seeing this side of Alaric unnerved him. This was a king who never faltered. Alaric hadn't even flinched when he saw the chancellor's body. But here he was, speaking like he'd failed to be a better man. It was unfitting.

"We've helped each other, then," Cyrus said. "You taught me that not every ruler wants to weaponize me, and I've taught you that there are good people who can occasionally have poor luck." The king laughed. "I appreciate our friendship, Alaric, and I hope you know that regardless of what the future holds, you always have my and Sozar's loyalty."

"Thank you," Alaric replied, clearly relieved. "The same for you."

Cyrus could sense the shifting tone. He looked around the chamber, confirming what he already knew. No alcohol. "Why don't we have a drink? Just one for the celebration?"

The king shook his head and stood. "No, no. What I should do is get some rest. The same for you. Tomorrow, we'll return to the city once the announcement is over. And for your information, that statue is certainly happening now, after what you did." He made his way to the door, making no motion to pick up the rest of the pastries. "Try not to get used to that. I feel disgusting sharing so much already."

Cyrus laughed. That was more like it. When the king left, he made no motion to go to bed. Alone again, he was more aware of his thoughts than ever before. Alaric was, indeed, a trustworthy friend. It felt good to call him that, and he would do everything in his power to make sure Delion was safe. This city had given him the world, and Alaric had taught him that people were complicated, ruthless even, but they could still have a heart.

He reached for another pastry.

The King of Monsters

Life hadn't been easy for Morei, but he was starting to see it all come together. His father taught him everything he knew—to fight for what he believed in, to stay stubborn, and that strength was a choice. The king of Caster had chosen to keep those values close. Morei was relieved and satisfied to see everything coming together after so much hardship, but he was unwilling to forget his bloodline or the man his father raised him to be. Even if he didn't recognize who he was becoming, he had a sliver of hope that he would someday earn the title of a peaceful king.

The council was pleased, the citizens acknowledged, and the deal with Isla was an annoyance but worth the investment. Morei was willing to put in a little work with the princess to secure an empire. He also knew that she deserved that. A lonely queen would kill him faster than any war.

Ferguson was theirs, and soon, Geral would be too. He was confident in what Edwin would come up with, and looked forward to their discussions on how to proceed. The commander had shown no mercy on the shore against the Queens. Having him by his side was invaluable. The effort in Geral would be focused on finding Ezra, and he hoped they succeeded—for their sake. If not, he'd massacre the city like he'd done before. Only this time, he wouldn't stop until ash fell from the sky. Anyone who opposed the new empire and what it stood for would be killed.

Diemon would be next, but timing would be everything. Too fast and he risked losing stability. Too slow and someone would likely attempt an assassination or to overthrow him. The king knew an insider threat was the highest risk, so he kept soldiers paid well, and a handful had their ears open for anything out of the ordinary.

Morei took his drink with him back to his study. Fang's Revenge was growing on him, and he was tempted to have a decanter brought to him before the end of the day. The issue with Rhys crawled underneath his skin. The wretched thief. There were signs, plenty of them, and even more opportunities where he should have just discarded the chancellor, but he'd been too worried about politics. Now Rhys was running, guilty. Where the chancellor intended to hide out was a mystery. Rhys would be foolish to stay in the country when it would be his by the winter, but Morei would stop at nothing to find the chancellor.

His pace slowed as he neared the study. Soldiers were stationed there. "Men?" he asked. "Is there something I need to be aware of?"

They shook their heads. "Given the circumstances, Gerald ordered us here."

He nodded, hoping they didn't see just how tense he was. "Very good. That's appreciated." They shifted out of the way, and he opened the door. "I will be fine in here."

The one to his left had a neatly trimmed beard. "We are going to stroll this hall, keep a watch. Is that okay?"

"If you hear anything, let me know."

Morei stepped in, pleased to finally be alone, but the man standing at the terrace's entrance disrupted that. The doors were open, allowing a breeze in and tousling the man's crimson cloak. He was bald, his neck and hands covered in red ink, and he had crystal-blue eyes.

They stood there, locked in silent battle. Morei wanted to beckon the soldiers, challenge this man's unwelcome arrival, summon Dark Energy. This red-cloaked bastard was just standing there, daring him to speak first. No, Morei concluded, he wouldn't. Quietly, he removed his hand from the door handle and waited. He would not show any fear or surprise; his face was wiped clean of all expression. If this was Destiny, he was ready.

A small smile crawled across the man's thin lips. Morei hated it. "You've come a long way, haven't you?" His accent was not Sorréleian, instead something faintly like Emerald's and her soldiers'.

Morei kept his position by the door. Immense energy radiated from this man. His lifeforce could have fueled a city alone, and Morei decided it would be reckless to prod his mind. Based on how this man carried himself, he knew exactly who the king was.

He decided to play along. "You're from Diyrặ?"

"Good ear," he remarked. "Have you been?"

"No." Morei approached his desk. The basket full of gifts sat, ready for him to review. "I suppose it would be a waste of time to ask how you got in here." A quick look confirmed his decanter was still empty. The drink in his hand wouldn't last long enough for this. The king was tempted to take the rest now, but he chose to look at the man again. By the Gods, he didn't like those eyes. He was dangerous. "So let's make this easy for both of us. What do you want, and who are you?"

He chuckled, amused, but the sound took a blade to his spine and twisted. "I've watched you for a long time, Morei." At the sound of his name, he tensed. The man took several steps forward, then stopped—he knew the impression he'd left. "I must say, I'm impressed with your work. You've managed to take a city in less than a season of being king here." He gestured to the grand room. "And now, you intend to stomp Geral out."

If Morei had been a praying man, now would have been the time to start. That was not public information. Not even the council knew of his and Edwin's discussions. "How do you know about Geral?" Closer, he recognized the markings as Old Tongue sigils.

"I know a lot of things," the stranger continued, unperturbed by his astonishment. Morei hated this lack of control. "I know that your chancellor in Geral was named Peter, that you can harvest fire, and that your ailment was from an ambush from several seasons ago. It looks like it's progressed significantly."

The last was said without judgment. Morei didn't find the need to deny anything. This man had done his research, knew things he shouldn't, and was here for unknown reasons, but that made him curious. He took a drink, finished the glass, and set it on the desk to his right.

"Okay," Morei replied quietly. "You have my attention."

"I thought that might." His fingers trailed over several books on the table before he straightened. "You will take Diemon once Geral falls, as I am sure it will under your rule. But what happens then? Will you stop at Sorréle?"

"No," Morei admitted. "A world empire is what I seek. But you probably knew that, didn't you?"

He bared his hands. Even the palms were inked red. "Not entirely, although I suspected, because you and I are alike." The stranger kept his distance, which didn't ease Morei's concerns. Energy Harvesters didn't need to be close to strike, so he barricaded his mind and stayed attuned to the shifting energies in case he struck. "I'm here to offer a deal. One I hope we can both benefit from."

So, he wasn't here to kill Morei. Yet. "Go on."

"A world empire requires work, and most importantly trusted allies. You couldn't possibly be everywhere, could you?" He paused, maybe waiting for Morei's response, but he gave none. "You would need allies in each country—Creitón, Eiyrạl, Diyrạ—while you would be here. They would report to you, enforce the laws you find reasonable to instate, and act out punishments for those who disobeyed the king's ruling." The stranger regarded him, intentionally quiet. "I want to offer my place in Diyrạ as a par tner."

This was a conversation Morei hadn't dreamed of having for many more summers. Of course ruling the world would require partners, people of equal power and respect, placed strategically across all the countries. All who wanted the same thing, stood by the same message, and enforced laws agreed upon by all. He'd toyed with the idea about who he could ally with in the different regions, like Kalic in Eiyrạl and Saveen in Creitón. But as far as he was concerned, this man was no king. "Who are you?"

"I suppose I should tell you about me, no?" The man raised a brow, gleaming like Morei was saying exactly what he wanted to hear. "You and I want the same things. I have committed and am willing to continue to commit crimes to get what I want. There's a saying out there. Become who you need to be, and you'll never spend a day wondering what you could have done differently. When I carried out the Diyrạllian Massacre, I did so under the belief that the country needed unification. I still stand by those beliefs."

Shock ripped through him, leaving him completely hollow. Never had Morei ever felt so small as he did now. This was not just anyone he was speaking to.

"I've waited for the right time," Henry Junok said. "The timing was important. Your ruling in Geral was unstable at best, and after Diemon, I decided to wait and see." He motioned to the sea behind them. "And I'm glad I did. You've come so far. You've earned these people's trust, given them something to latch on to—*hope*." Henry said that last word like it tasted sour. "But it's time to start thinking bigger. It's time we both started thinking bigger."

Morei swallowed, trying to find his tongue. He felt cold and flush, and his heart beat erratically. Countless questions came to mind, the biggest being how a man like him could cheat Death for so long. Before him stood the most dangerous Energy Harvester in Vore history, a master of the Dark Energy element, metal. He'd become a man of nightmares, stories told to frighten children into behaving or to advise young rulers to act fairly.

Instead, in a whisper, he asked, "How can I trust you?"

Henry's smile could have stanched a fire. "We need each other, Morei. You think I'm untrustworthy because of what I've done, but I could say the same about you, couldn't I? You slaughtered your own citizens, and for what? To taste revenge?" His expression faltered, and he looked to the Merrél Sea. "You think I'd kill you, but why would I do that? You are the anchor for Sorréle, just like I am for Diyră. Together, we could build a world empire."

The king needed a strong drink. He couldn't ignore the fact that Henry might just be using him. A man as powerful as the one standing before him didn't need anyone to get what he wanted. But Morei had proven he could be just as resourceful and brutal. A snake and a lion, poised and ready to see who would strike first, but the outcome of the risk was enthralling. A partnership like this would change the world. Nobody would challenge the Casterian Empire. Not with power like this. It was risky, he knew, but so was crossing the Sorréleian country and taking the Caster throne.

"I am close to taking Diyră." Henry spoke nonchalantly, studying the large chamber. Always, he kept some distance from Morei. "Junok is under my rule, and Raveer is fragile after the Firóle attack. The harsh winter in that region has kept my men and women from making progress, but that is to change."

War strategy was easy for the king to cling to. It stabilized him. "You speak of Junok, but I received a threat from King Nerius just days ago."

"Hm." Henry's calmness betrayed a shift. Annoyance. "That shall be addressed after today. You must understand that for some, family is all they have."

He nodded slowly, his head heavy. "After Raveer, you'll turn your resources against Assane. Am I correct?"

"Unless they pledge themselves," Henry said. "That is a matter I intend to look into once Raveer is taken."

"And then what?"

Henry looked at him. "And then we address Eiyrăl. Two cities stand in our way there, although I firmly believe Kalic will support our plan. Perhaps even be the partner we need to secure that country. It will be an easy taking."

He approached. Morei stiffened, tempted to grab for his sword, even as Henry reached into his cloak. If he showed fear now, he was as good as dead. The king was tense, arms crossed, ready to defend himself at any point. But instead of attacking, Henry removed a small red bundle.

"Your favorite color," Morei remarked.

"It is a prestigious color," Henry said. "And one my people have spent centuries wearing. It would be foolish to change things now." Slowly, he unwrapped the cloth from the item in his hand. "This has always been my intention. So long as you accept our partnership, I wish to gift you this as a sign of my faith in you."

Before him, pristine and polished, was the most wanted blade in Vorelian history. It was the blade Syra Castello had been alleged to have when she fled this very city, and he'd never stopped thinking about it, but he'd believed that it was beyond his reach.

The Demon Killer was far more beautiful in person than he could ever have imagined. The metal was darker than midnight, engraved with Old Togue sigils, the black leather hilt encrusted with rubies, and the pommel garnished with another ruby. Just looking at it, Morei felt a wave of euphoria. Rumors and grand tales spoke of this blade as if it were a God itself.

"It is only fitting you possess something that will help you along this journey," Henry observed. "The blade is forged with the blood of a dragon and Dark Energy. She will serve you well."

A hum met his mind, piercing and raw. It was the dagger's lifeforce, volatile. Morei looked between Henry and the Demon Killer. After all this time, to be blatantly handed this weapon felt wrong. The world wanted this relic, and now he would have it. But it would require a deal he wasn't sure was smart to make. Henry would try and kill him eventually. It was foolish to think either of them was willing to go into this partnership innocently. Henry had a motive, and he saw Morei as a tool he could leverage to get what he wanted. But so too did the king. Henry was exactly who he needed to make progress, to dominate and expand the empire's territory. Yes, it was risky, but it was necessary.

It was just a matter of who would try to kill each other first. Morei would act the first chance he got. They had time. Dominating the world would take a few summers, and that gave him a chance to grow stronger, identify replacements, and determine how to kill without disrupting the empire's stability. He would be a fool to think Henry wasn't considering the same.

He reached for the dagger, knowing that this simple act confirmed they agreed. Henry grabbed his wrist, the touch cold. He studied the black veins, but only briefly before those dead eyes met his. "You're a clever man, Morei. Embrace yourself, and you'll have no problem becoming what the world needs you to be."

"What's that supposed to mean?" the king asked. The Demon Killer was within his reach, but he didn't want to struggle against Henry's grip.

"Centuries ago, they once spoke of a prophecy so vile that it was hushed and all books associated with it burned. The Rider Federation was the last to possess information on it, and even then, their text was limited." Henry let go of Morei, who cautiously wrapped his hand around the hilt. The blade was comfortable, and the hum grew louder—addictive. Where his hand met leather and ruby, skin turned to ice. It felt as if the weapon was made just for him. He studied it up close. This was made by the man who now stood before him.

"They called it the Díanzon Prophecy," Henry continued as he folded the cloth and set it on the desk beside them. "It spoke of a man who would have the strength of Gods and the lust for Death. He would be the birth of a new era, the master of beast and man. They called him the King of Monsters, but over time, as word evolved, he simply became known as the Demon King."

Morei looked at him fully now.

Henry regarded him as if seeing him for the very first time. "When I built the Lirallian Empire, I was certain it was me, but I was wrong." Henry lifted his chin, his next words were drenched in purpose. "I believe it was you all along."

Morei smiled. He didn't want to be the hero.

Even the Dreamless Weep

Syra wasn't equipped for battle. Zarek had trained her relentlessly in the passing season, but that was a much different experience. In training, the Guardian was merciless, but she'd never be fatally wounded. Eyeing the sea of red, she knew this was the real threat. All her training would come to this. Syra couldn't afford a mistake or misstep.

The cliff she and several archers were on looked over the valley below. Trees crisp in color towered high, oblivious to the bloodshed they would soon witness. Birds had gone silent only moments prior, when the Lirallian army sounded off a horn. Syra saw a doe bolt from a thick bundle of bushes well beneath them, followed by a rabbit. The sky, vivid blue and alive, didn't have a cloud. It was a stark contrast to the unforgiving climate of the Soul Realm.

The Infernol looked ill-prepared compared to the Lirallians. Syra could see that, even without summers of strategic warfare. The crestless red armor filled the valley, organized and moving in unison. They held a red flag with a single white Old Tongue sigil—a group of lines that intertwined in an endless knot. Peace. What a mockery. She couldn't see any large cannons being pushed, which offered some relief, but she worried an Energy Harvester or two was among their ranks. Syra knew she was expected to harvest Chaos, and while she'd done so on several occasions now, she was anxious to be put up against an enemy.

Their men, dressed in armor without any consistent coloring, lay crouched in the crevices, rivers, bushes—anywhere they could hide. They were scattered along the valley, intending to ambush the Lirallians from either side once Bane gave the signal. Dryl was down there, among those lying in wait, and Zarek was waiting on the front lines, where they guessed many of the soldiers would run to once they realized they were being squeezed from either s ide.

She and the other two remained on their stomachs. Syra did not have a bow like the others did, but she wasn't there for that. Her goal was to scout for vulnerabilities and try to exploit them with Chaos. Dryl hadn't given her any clear guidelines. His only advice had been to cease the Lirallians' movements.

Along the mountainsides, others lay with their bows drawn and ready. Arrows would be dipped in a bucket of poison before firing. The scent was pungent, even from here, and she had to restrain herself from gagging when she first smelled it. The poison was somewhere between a carcass decaying in the sun and rotting milk. The archers advised her to be careful—coming into contact with this would cause hallucinations and body paralysis. She didn't need to be told twice. The Infernol elegantly called it the Kiss of Death.

Syra wasn't sure if this poison would have the same effects on her, but she was unwilling to take the risk, so she opted to be on the outer edge of the two, farthest from the bucket. She'd added leather greaves and bracers to her attire, along with another sword and a dagger. Zarek had insisted on it, and she didn't argue. It was always best to have multiple weapons in battle.

The woman next to her quietly adjusted her bow. Her dark tan skin complemented a head of blond hair that was braided down her back. The other woman was identical—sisters raised in the Infernol. Kayla and Illy were their names, born and bred for war.

With her chest pressed up against the warming stone, Syra's heart slammed itself against her ribcage. The thump rang in her ears, and she was certain the other ladies could hear it. They showed no fear or nerves, and she envied that. Her hands shook, and she could hardly get a full breath without feeling like she was drowning. If Zarek had been here now, he'd scold her for letting her emotions get the best.

Quietly, she wished he were. It was far easier to face the unknown with someone she knew. Being up here, nestled with two women who hardly knew her beyond the rumors, was both humbling and terrifying. They had to rely on her as much as she relied on them.

Another horn, and she tensed. That one was much closer. She peeked out over the cliff's edge and saw several Infernol members move through the trees to get closer. They darted with silent grace, swords already drawn. Ahead, the Lirallians stood motionless. Movement indicated orders being given. A handful of the red soldiers flared outward to protect the front where, she assumed, the commander was.

The action was obvious. They could smell an ambush.

Syra nudged Illy. When the woman looked her way, she whispered, "They know."

Illy nodded. "Agreed." She placed her hands to her mouth and made a bird-like sound. Silence followed, but nobody moved. When Syra heard the sound returned, she swallowed the last bit of fear.

Shouts and roars followed. Tree branches snapped, swords clashed, and the sound of metal scraping against itself filled the air at once. Illy and Kayla moved quickly, plucking arrows from the pile on the ground and dipping them into the poison. In unison, as if this had been rehearsed a dozen times, they strung the deadly arrows and drew their knees up to get in position. With steady precision, they let loose the arrows and repeated the action.

Syra looked again at the carnage. Men and women were locked in fights throughout the valley. The Lirallians in the middle, where the Infernol had yet to penetrate to, were pushing forward, exactly as predicted. In the midst of it all, she saw Dryl. It was hard to miss him. He moved with the confidence of a warrior who knew Death personally. He was aggressive, shoving himself into the middle of the Lirallians and slashing anyone who attacked.

To her left, where the front lines lay, she could see the Infernol launch their attack on the Lirallians who had made it to that point. Only a handful, and they were quickly cornered and dispatched. She caught sight of Zarek as he drove his blade right through the neck of one soldier. The Guardian didn't show any sign that he'd been dead only the day prior. And if he felt anything at all, she knew he would never say.

This was the first time she'd ever seen the Guardians in action. Their centuries of experience overshadowed the mortals they fought next to. They stepped and swung as if they knew exactly what the enemy was going to do before they did it. For every Lirallian that the Infernol defeated, Zarek and Dryl killed four.

But she needed to act. Syra was so caught up in watching that she hadn't moved since the battle started. Illy and Kayla, along with the other archers, were sending arrows toward the hundreds of enemy soldiers. Lirallians swarmed around several individuals who bore no weapon.

Instantly, a large chunk of the mountain above them broke free. The deafening crack echoed through the valley, and Syra acted without thought. "Move!" she yelled, and grabbed Illy and shoved her back as she was in the middle of letting loose another arrow. The giant bolder slammed against the cliff's edge, taking the rock with it as it fell below. Kayla scrambled to keep the bucket of poison upright. Illy nodded at Syra before she strung another arrow.

"Wait." Syra pointed at the red army. "Energy Harvesters. They are trying to take down the archers. If you let them know you're here, they'll turn their attention back on us."

Illy and Kayla stared at her, awaiting instructions. It dawned on Syra that they believed she would do something about this. She'd walked herself right into that one, and as another large chunk of the mountain broke free across from them to wipe out more archers, she knew she needed to act. Without the twins, she was one of the only Energy Harvesters they had. The Guardians, while they shared the gift, were too busy, and she didn't know another Harvester in the Infernol who was strong enough to counter these Lirallians.

And she was more than just a Harvester. She was a Goddess.

Syra turned her attention to the trio of Liral Harvesters below. Without Kayla and Illy sending arrows, the enemy wouldn't know she was up here. At least yet. Syra tucked herself up against the broken cliff, just where the shadows of the looming mountain ended, and concentrated.

She needed to locate at least one of the Harvesters. Practice with Zarek gave her the confidence to do that. Their auras were larger, brighter, and volatile. The moving lifeforces all around were hardly noticeable against theirs. Syra chose the one closest to her, then hesitated. This lifeforce wasn't normal, not even remotely close to a standard Harvester's. Elyas's mind was sinister, but this was different from even that. The volatility lashed out with intelligence, and a pulse that rendered the brightness dark radiated outward. Syra dug deep, harnessing Chaos that burned in her veins. She sent a small amount to the Harvester and saw their lifeforce lash out. Syra retreated. Too close and she risked the Harvester figuring out where and who she was. Her mind was not protected enough to get too close. It was an amateur mistake.

With distance, Syra reinforced the barriers around her mind. She thought of steel doors, thick and impenetrable. Goddess or not, she was at risk of having a strong Harvester break into her mind and do horrific things. Zarek had proven it over and over again during their training, and she could practically hear his voice now advising her to never go into a fight without protection.

With the barriers up, Syra approached the Harvester again. From somewhere, she could hear another large boulder fall and short-lived screams follow. She ignored them, burrowing deeper into herself to remain concentrated. She would have to trust Kayla and Illy to protect her if needed.

She closed in on the Harvester. The volatile lifeforce sensed her coming, but she lashed outward. Chaos burned the surrounding energy, turning it into dust. The dark pulse quickened but recovered. The Harvester lashed out at her in return, slamming against the barriers she'd placed. The impact jarred her, and her head throbbed.

The Harvester did it again, and again, she kept the barriers up. And then, they stopped. Syra waited, knowing better than to lower those barriers. But she never had a chance to evaluate her plan. The Harvester's lifeforce swallowed her whole. Limbs reached all around, and her defenses dissolved instantly. She was isolated in her head, cornered.

Hm. The voice echoed from all around. *You are different.*

Syra could see herself, arms wrapped around her knees, tucked up against a wall that led nowhere. All around, a dark mass sat. The Harvester, confident, let his mind wander through hers. She caught glimpses of Henry, the Demon Killer, and even the slightest memory of his childhood. Voices came and went, their words lost to her. It was Dark Energy, she realized. His mind was twisted with it.

Have nothing to say?

She wanted to ignore him, but she couldn't. The words were ripped right out of her. *Does it feel good to fight for a man who will kill you in the end?*

He laughed, the sound filling every corner of her mind. His lifeforce intensified, and she realized that he was going to suffocate her from the inside out. Heat filled her, thoughts strayed beyond her grasp, and the dark mass squeezed her. Zarek had warned about this—if an enemy conquered her mind, they could kill her by taking control of organs, sucking her lifeforce dry, anything they wanted.

As the walls around her closed in, Chaos bubbled up with burning need. The energy worked with a mind of her own. The black substance reached for Syra, but Chaos lashed out. Hesitation bled from the Harvester's side as he sensed Chaos—an energy no mortal could harness—and she leveraged that. Syra directed the force right into him. As she did so, she shoved him out of her mind and seized him. The brightness of Mother was blinding, tearing apart the very fabric of his mind. It all happened before she could stop herself. His mind fractured, his thoughts ceased, and his lifeforce disintegrated before her. The Harvester collapsed.

Voices echoed all around her, growing louder and angrier. She retreated as fast as she could, but not before she felt the frigid claws of Dark Energy latch on to her. Syra tore the hands off with the help of Chaos and opened her eyes.

She was covered in sweat. Her head pounded.

When she looked again at the battle below, she saw Lirallian soldiers around the body of the Harvester, pointing at their surroundings. She should have felt proud, but she didn't. She felt ashamed. Murder was not something to brag about, even when it was necessary.

Illy slapped Syra on the arm. "You did that?" She was elated.

Numbly, she nodded. "Two more to go." The words made her sick.

With a wave, she turned her attention to the next Harvester. This time, she was more prepared. These ones were using Dark Energy, but they were not fully immersed in it like the first. Never had she seen so many in one place draw on the pure energy. This had to be a historic event, but she knew Henry had something to do with it. Whatever he was doing was enriching their capabilities.

The second Harvester dropped faster. Syra let Chaos channel right through her, suffocating the lifeforce of the woman. She grimaced as Death took her next victim, but she removed herself before the hands of Dark Energy could grab her again. The headache radiated through her neck, making her nauseous, but she swallowed the food back where it belonged.

She was preparing to dispatch the last one when Illy shook her. "Syra!" She didn't even try to whisper. The jarring call forced her to look at the terrified woman.

"What?"

The archer and her sister both pointed to the ground below. Syra looked, and felt bile rise up in her throat at what she was witnessing.

The dead were getting up. Slowly, but with stubborn determination. Blood coated their armor. Some had limbs partially torn, others were missing eyes. But it didn't matter. They raised their weapons and turned on the Infernol, who were still trying to defend themselves against the living Lirallians.

She watched in horror as a large group ganged up on the Infernol members where Zarek was. Dryl and his small group of soldiers remained untouched by the dead, but they would learn soon enough as more and more were resurrected.

Her mind raced for any idea on how to reverse the effects, to kill the dead for good. The undead soldiers fought as fiercely as the living, and she watched several Infernol members go down by surprise. When she called on Chaos, she found the minds of the undead soldiers empty, their lifeforces drained to nearly nothing—they were corpses. She didn't know how to fight against something she didn't understand.

Thinking would get her killed. It was time to act on instinct. She grabbed the bucket of poison. It sloshed onto her hand, but she didn't stop to think about it. Instead, she poured some on the group of Lirallians below her. The living panicked, struck by a substance, while the undead didn't flinch. The living soldiers started to gag, convulse, and drop with paralysis, but those who were resurrected were not bothered. Not even the Kiss of Death could deter them.

Frustration squeezed her from all sides, and she kicked the bucket off the cliff. The pungent smell wafted up to her, and she saw the poison coating her hand. Her body did not react—she felt nothing—and she glanced toward the ladies, who watched in awestruck horror as she didn't have the fatal reaction. Their creased brows made them look more like twins.

Syra didn't want the questions. She jumped up. "I'm going down there." As quickly but carefully as she could, she descended the side of the mountain. The path she'd taken up felt more precarious going down, and she clung tightly to the jutting rocks, but that didn't slow her. Sheathed swords scraped against stone, her boot slipped more times than she could count, and she slammed her knee into the side of a rock she didn't see until it was too late.

More of the dead were rising, and she was still trying to figure out a way to counter them. An idea was teasing her, and she couldn't shake it. Infernol soldiers tried to stab, but that did nothing to stop these undead warriors. She saw people shout back and forth, panicked, and she didn't blame them.

Syra grabbed a tree branch when she was close enough to the valley floor and hopped off the narrow path. The fall was short-lived, and with the adrenaline pumping through her, she hardly felt the impact. Syra unsheathed Death's Sword and laid a hand across it. This was her plan—half-assed and reckless—but it was all she had. If this didn't work, then she didn't know what would. Only once in history was there mention of the undead sea of red, and millions had lost their lives. This would not happen here.

The metal pulsed with life as she channeled Chaos into it. She didn't know if the sword could handle such raw energy, but she was betting on it. If it shattered, she didn't think she could rely on the basic sword strapped to her hip. Not with Chaos. At this point, she was running off hope.

It worked.

The dirt was soft, and her boots sank in. A decoration of shadows littered the floor from the leaves above, garnished with the blood of the once fallen. Now, the undead stood, approaching her. Syra wasn't sure what she was going to do. She raised Death's Sword, which hummed loudly in her head—an extension of her lifeforce—and slashed. The Lirallian to her left deflected the blow, but his weapon shattered. The jarring impact reverberated up Syra's arm, and she felt a slight pull of strength from the recesses of her mind. Without hesitation, she drove the weapon through the armor, and it obeyed. Metal sliced right through metal, sinking deep into the chest of the undead, beneath his previous stab wound.

The soldier stopped moving, spasming. His lips turned gray, and she watched as the skin on his face crinkled and started to peel off in thin layers. His bloodshot eyes sank inward, and the skin that remained tore as it dried, like fruit under the brutal sun, to reveal bloody muscle and bone underneath. Then he collapsed for good.

Syra still had the sword burrowed in his chest. She sensed the furious swing of another enemy before she saw him. Ducking, she saw the blade's shadow sweep above her, and she yanked free Death's Sword. The reality of what she'd just done didn't have time to make itself comfortable in her head. She swung the weapon. Once more, the sword made contact and shattered the enemy's. The sound of fractured metal was ear-piercing, like nails dragged against stone. The Lirallian tried to pull free his dagger with a hand that was missing three fingers, but she drove the blade right through his chest. Once more, the undead soldier's skin peeled and shrank, turning grey, before he too collapsed.

Chaos was the weapon. Death's Sword was the conduit. Syra felt the merciless yank of exhaustion and blinked. The swarm of red coming toward her was overwhelming. She counted at least two dozen—too many. Syra was not a warrior. Despite all the training, her muscles burned, and her head pounded.

Ignorant and foolish. She knew this was reckless, but she couldn't stand by any longer. Syra had their attention and hoped that gave the Infernol a chance to plan, get away, anything. Not that she had a plan herself.

Syra took a deep breath, trying to calm her nerves. They screamed, and her hands shook, but she squeezed the hilt tighter and raised it. To her right, she heard the pounding of incoming boots. The pale blue skin was the first and only thing she saw.

"Got a plan?" Zarek asked. He didn't attempt to lower his volume. The undead soldiers were closing in on them.

Syra gestured at the heavy sword in her hand. "Infused with Chaos. It seems to work." To prove her point, she pointed at the two dead soldiers who had not yet risen.

The Guardian was splattered in blood, his gaze wild, nearly unrecognizable. The leather armor was now stained red. "Fantastic in theory. Do you intend to kill the whole army?"

The sarcasm dripped from his words, and she shot him a glare. "Got a better idea?"

Zarek never got a chance to reply. The Lirallians were on them. He kicked and slashed, while she did her best to try and dispatch those already distracted by him. One went down, and as she burrowed her weapon into the chest of the next, his eyes caught her attention.

They were bleeding.

The soldier's body went limp before his skin peeled, and she watched him cry blood even in true death. The droplets rolled down his cheeks slowly, then picked up pace. Syra stepped back and scanned the others. They'd stopped too, blood pouring from their eyes.

All around, a silence fell over the valley. A tree branch cracked, whispers from the confused echoed, and the Lirallians remained motionless. Hundreds of them stopped what they were doing, swords hanging at their sides. Syra stared, watching their irises and pupils disappear, sinking into the murky whites. Dead or alive, they all fell victim to the spell.

Syra looked at Zarek, hoping he had an answer, but he shook his head.

The visual took her adrenaline, crumpled it up like old parchment, and tossed it aside like it was nothing. The sword in her hand felt like it weighed as much as the overfull baskets of dead fish she used to haul from ships. The stench of blood combined with that of the spring soil and fresh-bloomed plants worsened her nausea. Chaos, which had infused Death's Sword and burned through her veins, dissipated. With it, her strength went too. The overuse of the energy made her knees weak, her muscles heavy, and she would have sat if not for the Lirallians.

And then, from a distance, she heard the thump of bodies as they collapsed to the ground. Life breathed itself back into her, and she tightened her grip on the hilt, readying herself for the next wave. Zarek tensed next to her, taking one step forward. The Lirallians closest to them didn't react—it was like they didn't even see them anymore.

Beyond their small clearing, she saw the figure, dressed in a black cloak with the hood drawn back. The short dark hair was unmistakable. He moved meticulously through the crowd of spell-bound soldiers. Blood seeped, dripping free from their chins and garnishing the blades of grass and dirt below. Like a parent comforting a child, the man raised his hand and rested it against the side of a soldier's face. They stood there, face-to-face, for only a moment before the soldier collapsed. And then he moved to the next soldier, repeating the same action.

He neared, and Syra knew who it was before he ever turned his head. Sekar. The God's eyes dripped blood, the color gone and replaced by a milky white. Silvery veins stretched up from his jaw, reflecting the sun. Startled, she stepped back, horrified by how twisted his features were. This was not anyone she recognized. He looked fit to court Death.

This was the God of Dreams. This was the real Sekar.

"What is he doing?" she whispered.

"Agony shares many faces," Zarek mumbled next to her. "This is Sekar's."

Her questions died. All the answers lay bare before her. The scars he'd referenced, his intimate relationship with Chaos, the Gods that had died by his hands, and his ageless existence all made sense. He was Chaos's lover, intertwined in a dance he'd never be able to escape. He served her, enforced order when none existed, and brought wrath to those who threatened his existence or Chaos's control. He yearned for the grace of normalcy, of peace, and Syra was that, but he could never sustain that life when he belonged to M other.

The Zyulë Bond, the deal. Bold attempts, or perhaps reckless promises to outsmart Chaos, to remain in touch with a realm he'd once called his own.

Soldiers continued to collapse for good. Vacant eyes stared back at her, but she didn't see terror. In those colored irises that now returned, she saw contentment. He was releasing them from a prison they couldn't get out of, and in doing so, he drank what little lifeforce remained.

Sekar passed Syra and Zarek without looking their way. Healing wounds discolored his tan features. He worked as a blacksmith would on a blade—careful, thoughtful, and with no ear for the world beyond the one he focused on. Ahead, an army of Lirallians. Behind, countless bodies. The Infernol saw what he was doing, and slowly, they examined the fallen. Zarek studied the soldier next to him. The Guardian checked for a pulse, tapped the face, anything to try and get a response, but none came.

Sekar would move his way through the valley until every last one of the soldiers was gone for good. She didn't know if the God would return, but she didn't expect him to. The madness to commit such a heinous and yet peaceful massacre would corrupt even the most twisted minds. And who knew how often Sekar had done so already in his centuries alive?

But she also knew that what she was witnessing was monumental. These were Henry's men. Sekar, in his crooked way, had chosen a side. At least long enough to give her a running start to save the realms. She didn't know Sekar as well as she thought, but she knew enough. Underneath all that madness was a man driven by loyalty.

"Come," Zarek said. He stepped over several dead Lirallians. Neither he nor Syra sheathed their weapons. Not yet. "Dryl will need us."

Syra nodded and fell into step with him. For once, she was confident about what needed to be done.

The Age of Dragons

Cyrus still wasn't in bed. The last four pastries were eaten, the storm continued, and he'd gotten too antsy to sit in the room any longer. Poking at Sozar, he found the dragon still drained, although he acknowledged him this time.

The palace at night was magical. The lanterns cast a warm glow, the colors were vivid, and certain plants bloomed. Staff explained that some of these plants had been in the palace for generations now, a few as old as the city. The one he passed now had a nocturnal flower called the Maid's Kiss because the petals were pearly white and as soft as silk. It only grew in places like these, where humidity was abundant, and the weather was relatively nice. This particular plant had been in the palace for at least 250 summers. Then there was the silence. Less people, less questions.

Murals on the walls he passed depicted ancient beasts of the sea and ships. This was as old as the palace, he'd learned, and regularly managed by a family line of painters. Much of the palace had been remodeled over the summers, save for a few things, like murals and plants. Petrified wood in the shape of ships was everywhere, with precise detail. Cyrus always managed to find his way around the place by figuring out which ship he'd passed. They were all named after the real ones. He'd spent much time surveying the carvings. The creator had even made little figures that stood on the main deck or at the wheel. While he'd never been on a ship, he constantly wondered what it was like.

Now, he passed *Victory*, one of the oldest ships of Delion. One of the soldiers had told him that one afternoon after he asked. Cyrus gave it a nod and descended the stairs. He wanted to see the egg himself. After enough thought and inability to rest, he decided he would visit and check himself. Not that he didn't have faith in Alaric, but he needed something to do. If that didn't do the trick, he would end up walking the halls all night. Maybe stop by the galley again for more tea. He hoped Beth wasn't there. Not that he didn't adore her, but he wasn't in the mood for conversation. The longer he went without speaking a word, the more content he became in not opening his mouth for the rest of the night.

These walls were too familiar. Rough, dark stone stared back at him as he left the main floor and descended into the dungeons once he passed through a large iron door. It still wasn't easy being here, not after what had happened, but Cyrus was getting better at managing his anxiety. The one place he'd refused to visit again was where he'd been locked up. The small cells forced his thoughts into places he would spend a lifetime avoiding.

The smell was still the same—sour, moldy, and wet. He wrinkled his nose. The moisture was trapped, and mixed with the blood, sweat, piss, and shit of those who once called this place home, it created a smell that made him want to gag.

Cyrus took a right, happy to avoid the cells, and made his way toward the area of the dungeons dedicated to supplies. A handful of rooms were large enough for soldiers to use for resting at a table. A weapons room, which wasn't as big as the one attached to the main floor, offered all the tools one needed to torture, beat, and kill. Cyrus had seen it once and didn't need to again. The whip used on him had been cleaned and put back next to a wide blade. But he didn't request it removed. Alaric would have done it, but Cyrus didn't want to be defined by the weapon. It was easier said than done.

What stood out to him, though, as he walked was the lack of soldiers. Cyrus peeked into the rooms, finding them empty. The last time he'd been down here, soldiers mulled about, mostly here for the egg. Ahead, in one of the wide rooms—that was where they'd placed it. The location wasn't obvious, and after many questions, Cyrus realized this was the last place anyone would look if they knew an egg was here.

Men should have been on guard. Agitated, he opened another door and found a lone soldier, middle-aged, with dark skin complemented by a trimmed beard, picking at his fingernails with the tip of a dagger.

"Where is everyone?" Cyrus asked.

The soldier raised his brow. "In bed, Master Rider. Why?"

"What about the egg?"

The soldier frowned, blade still stuck under a fingernail. "Taken care of. I thought you knew."

"Nobody told me," Cyrus said, and left the man there. He couldn't afford another mistake this massive. If Henry managed to wiggle his way into his life so bluntly again and take an egg, he was going to hunt the man himself and kill him.

Cyrus stopped, startled at the anger that flourished in him so freely. He was not hot-headed. wasn't even an angry person. But he couldn't help it when he'd poured so much of himself into making this work, into staying alive. The door in front of him was closed, and he shook his hands out. So much for trying to sleep tonight. Adrenaline poured into his veins, and his heart pounded. When he looked, he saw the soldier staring at him from down the hall, as if he had a front-row seat to whatever entertainment lay ahead.

He opened the door. The usual met him. A beaten-up table was covered in cuts from blades, a few chairs, two lanterns, and the makeshift nest made to store the egg. At this angle, he could see part of the bright silver egg sticking out of the dingy straw it was nestled in. As relieved as he was to see the egg unharmed, he was surprised by what else he saw.

Hyle was sitting in the chair, his back to Cyrus. He'd have recognized that mop of blond hair anywhere. The God carried himself with so much authority that a blind man could have seen him.

Hyle didn't move. "Close the door, Cyrus."

He did as he was told, but he didn't move further. The God's tone made him cautious. "Is everything all right?"

Hyle laughed. He didn't sound entirely like himself. "I'm fine."

He didn't offer more, and Cyrus weighed turning around and leaving. The egg was okay, and Hyle was here to guard. He trusted the God's intentions, even if he didn't fully know him. Hyle's dedication to seeing Cyrus succeed was enough proof that he was authentic. But he wavered, hand on the handle. Something felt off. His instincts kept his feet grounded, unmoving.

"You accomplished something that Riders spend a decade training for today," Hyle observed, voice soft. He still didn't move. "When Vikter and I trained the upcoming Riders, we waited until the season prior to induction to teach them the trust fall and death spiral. But there you were, doing both, and Sozar isn't even a summer old. Remarkable."

Cyrus swallowed, feeling hollow. "You saw?"

"I watched the whole thing." Now his words came out with haunting certainty. "You did the right thing out there today. For a Rider with as little exposure as you have to fighting, what you and Sozar accomplished was no short of a miracle."

Cyrus nodded, though the God couldn't see him. Hyle had spent many summers as a Dragon Rider. The praise made him want to crawl out of his skin. The Rider-turned-God wouldn't lie to him.

"How's Sozar?"

"Sleeping," he answered, glad his voice didn't sound as small as he felt in the presence of this man. "He was injured during the fight."

"I know." Hyle's head tilted. "I spoke with him this evening. Not to intrude or overstep, but because I wanted to make sure he didn't require more serious care. In the future, I will give you more information, so that you are better prepared to manage his injuries and what to look out for. I thought we had more time before a battle like today, so for that, I apologize."

"That's unnecessary." He wanted to move, but he still found his legs unable to cooperate. "We are only alive because of what you taught us."

"Hm." Hyle sounded unconvinced. "It's a shame that the Dragon Riders are so young and already at odds. Vikter fought tooth and nail to avoid that problem toward the end. It was the one thing he regretted the most when he died."

"I hope to avoid that with the others," Cyrus insisted. "I want to give the future Riders a chance to choose right and not be corrupted. Dameon is compromised. I saw black veins, and his dragon, Ashtir, looked wild. I think Henry did something to them."

"There is no doubt that he did," the God replied, slower. "Dameon is so starved for recognition that he would do anything to have it. Ashtir hatched for him because he felt the Rider's urgency for freedom. They were always meant for each other. Under different circumstances, they could have taken that and channeled it into something productive—being ambassadors or world explorers—but we are not granted such a luxury at this time."

To be as confident as the God. No questions, no doubts when he spoke, and he wielded centuries of knowledge. In the presence of Hyle, Cyrus realized he knew so little, but he had hope, and he clung to that. "I want to see the Rider Federation for myself."

Silence. "Are you certain?"

"Yes." Today's harrowing reality gripped him, forcing the words out with an urgency that made his hands shake. "I want to bring the Rider Federation honor. I know the future Dragon Riders will need a home, and we can't use Delion forever. Cities will question loyalties, and I don't want the Dragon Riders to be born for war. There is no other place I see fit. I know the federation lies in ruins, but in time, it can become home. No treaties, pledges, nothing. We don't have to start completely from scratch."

In a quieter voice, Hyle asked, "How can you be so certain these Dragon Riders aren't born for war?"

"Eei'on Rü." He prayed he was pronouncing it right. "That is what the Yavinks spoke of when I was there. They said it was what the Dragon Riders used to speak of. Peace. I want that."

Hyle didn't reply, and Cyrus wondered if he'd said something wrong. Peace felt practical, reasonable, and more importantly, the right thing to do. It might not happen overnight, but the more he thought about it, the more certain he was that he wanted to establish peace. A world built on violence was no place to live, and he couldn't imagine living centuries constantly looking over his shoulder. That was unfair to Sozar and everyone who lived now and would be born.

When the God spoke again, he sounded somber. "I have done horrible things, Cyrus. Mistakes that would make you hate me." He sighed and looked down. "And I'm going to tell you them now."

He leaned against the wall, not willing to approach. This was it. This was what he'd been waiting for. Faced with that realization, he felt like an intruder in Hyle's space, so he decided to keep his distance back here, afraid that if he got any closer, the God would change his mind.

"The Rider Federation didn't fall by accident," Hyle began. "The politics were tense, yes, but it was so much more than that. Vinfali resurfaced—an extreme belief in controlling bloodlines. Riders were killing each other over it, and a lack of trust started to mount. Our council made decisions without us, which only fueled the tensions. Nobody knew who to trust. You couldn't associate with a Rider if you two didn't agree. Our city became divisive, a breeding ground for deception. If you were caught talking to the enemy, even if that was a fellow Rider you shared studies with, you were ostracized and punished by other Riders. It didn't matter who you thought you knew, what mattered was whether you sided with the ideology or not. I started digging, searching for answers to all the madness. The more I uncovered, the more I realized that the Rider Federation had become the heart of something much more sinister. Some of our councilmembers were working against us, targeting Riders who didn't support Vinfali. The war was inside our walls, not out there."

Cyrus didn't say anything. Couldn't.

"I got too close to the truth, and it cost me everything. Kelise and I were sent on an exploratory flight, but it was a setup. In what is now known as the Hazar Desert, we were ambushed. I watched them kill her. Three dragons against one. Merciless. She never stood a chance." Anger burned his words. "That's the day I earned this scar, and it was the day they shoved a sword through my heart. I thought that was the end of it, the end of the agony. But I was wrong. It was only the beginning."

Cyrus swallowed, pained. To watch his dragon die—Cyrus couldn't imagine a worse horror than that. The lump in the back of his throat grew, and a response failed to come out. But Hyle continued, unbothered by the silence.

"I was reborn into what I am now. Enraged. Of all the tricks Destiny could have played on me, this was the one thing I hated her the most for. I wanted to die. No Rider wants to live if they can't live with their dragon. But now, bound to serve the only true God of the realms, Chaos, I let the rage win."

Hyle's head bobbed, but he still made no motion to look at Cyrus or move. The next words that came out were a pained whisper. "I went after them. I made it my sole goal to kill those who took Kelise from me. I killed Ny-gals, Riders, dragons. I made a mockery out of them all. They turned on one another fully, believing their enemy was inside the city. It's because of me that the Rider Federation fell."

Cyrus's lungs held no air. He could hardly breathe, too caught up in the admission to think straight. He was angry, yes, but he made no motion to show it. The shock tore everything out of him. Adrenaline, emotion, motivation. Nothing was left.

"Vikter got caught up in it all, certain he could change me. That man wanted to see the good in me, but I couldn't. He worked tirelessly to ensure the survival of the Dragon Riders, and it's because of him you stand here today. In all the war and destruction, he still saw good in me, and I hated him for it. This was a man who was supposed to loathe me. It was because of me that his world was crumbling, but he still couldn't stop believing in me. I dug in harder, committed unforgivable crimes, and when it was me standing over him with a sword pressed to his heart, he only had one thing to say to me. You want to know what that was?"

Cyrus nodded, though he knew the God couldn't see him.

"He asked that I protect the city for when the age of dragons returned. Vikter didn't hate me, didn't beg for his life. He didn't even try to stop me. Vikter forgave me for everything because he understood my torment. And like a fool, I took his life in a desperate attempt to prove that I was worthy of my revenge. I wasn't. I never was. The only thing revenge gave me was regret. I spent so many decades screaming into the ruins, certain Vikter would walk out from some abandoned home and scold me. That was my brother in all but blood, and I tore him from his dragon. Aythen went mad. The stories speak of the Rider Federation falling at her talons, and they're right. The only thing they're missing is that I was the reason it all happened."

Hyle's shoulders rose and fell, and he raised his head. "So, now you know the real story, Cyrus. I don't ask for your sympathy or your forgiveness. You can hate me, ask me to leave, or take a sword to my heart. I will not stop you."

Sozar stirred. *I do not hate him for what he did.* The dragon had listened to the entire conversation, and hearing his words brought Cyrus to life. Hyle *wanted* the hate, the anger, the frustration. The anguish in his voice was crippling, as if he'd just committed the atrocious crime yesterday, but Cyrus couldn't bring himself to that. Faced with his emotions, sorrow was the only thing he felt. He'd earned the answers he'd wanted, but it had cost this man everything.

"No," Cyrus said, finding his tongue. "I can't do any of that to you. You have shown me more than I could ever ask for." Finding words to explain how he felt was more difficult than he realized. He wanted to tell him it was okay, but that felt cheap, but he couldn't exactly say that what he'd done was fine either. "You did what you felt was right in the moment. I cannot judge you for something you've spent centuries agonizing over. There is no bigger torture than living with a mistake you know could have been different." He shook his head. "That is not my place to judge when I don't know what I would have done in the same situation."

The God made a sound in his throat, a mix of a hum and a pitiful scoff. "Vikter once said the same. You two grow more alike every day." Hyle finally shifted his legs, the most he'd moved in this entire encounter, and leaned forward as if to stand, but he stopped. "I stand for the Rider Federation, Cyrus, I hope you know that. Everything I've ever done was to ensure we could have a future."

"I know." He didn't doubt it. He hadn't before, but hearing that story made him certain.

A nervous laugh followed. "I have spent centuries wondering if I was good enough to be a man, let alone a God. I accepted long ago that I would never feel the wind in my hair like a Rider does on the back of their dragon again." He turned then, revealing the rest of the egg, broken. "What I didn't consider was that I might be given the chance to do things differently."

Curled in his lap was a small dragon, scales as white as snow. She blinked, revealing eyes as blue as the sea.

The Dance of Destiny

The Demon Killer. The blade the whole world wanted now rested on Morei's desk. He'd spent the afternoon staring at it, unable to look away. The midnight blade, the rubies, the *power*—it all symbolized everything he'd worked so hard for. This path was rightfully his. Morei knew that without a shadow of a doubt. When Destiny became cruel, he became crueler. Every challenge he'd faced, he'd overcome. The only way forward was to ensure his name would be spoken about for centuries.

The king had the city's devotion, and he couldn't have been more pleased with this. They would do anything for him. His plan of raising an empire was now more obtainable than ever before. Ferguson was theirs, and Geral would soon crumble. The final plan would be Diemon. The mountain kingdom had extensive finances from their mining and jewelry-driven economy. He intended to draw on the desert city's resources to seize Diemon.

His fingers grazed the relic's hilt. The hum was back, inviting. The blade was responsible for the Diyrąllian Massacre. This weapon had spilled more blood than anything else in history. This was power. His attempt to distract himself lay to the right. *The Vorelian Scrolls*, his home for his thoughts and perspectives, was unrolled and new ink was drying. Although there hadn't been much added, not when he stopped after every other word to stare at the weapon.

Dark Energy vibrated off the metal, coaxing him. Morei couldn't deny that he wanted to know just what this relic was capable of. This was what he'd use to assert complete control. Nobody would dare question him or his abilities now.

His fingers tightened around the hilt, the leather cold to the touch. The tremor in his hand had silenced for the first time all day. Sitting here now with no one to oversee or interrupt his thoughts, Morei let them wander. They poked at the volatile lifeforce of the blade, certain one misstep would cause a disastrous result. The storm that brewed underneath the relic's surface was monstrous—*incredible*.

Morei checked his study again, certain Henry would show up. It felt wrong to have this blade in his possession, and beneath the thrill of it all, he knew the man had intentionally given him this. No one escaped Death's grasp without some payment.

The king leaned back, taking the blade with him. He kicked his boots up and placed the relic between his hands. Closer, he could *feel* the Dark Energy's fingers caress him like a lover would. Death knew him well, and she was pleased to have even more of him to herself.

Heat obliterated all senses, searing the skin that made contact with the relic. Morei hissed and dropped the Demon Killer, stunned. It struck his leg, and he fumbled to grab it before it clattered to the floor. The king snatched it by the metal, finding it scalding still, and dropped it on the desk. A strong stench of burning wood met this nose, and he shoved the blade back more, finding the desk blackened where it originally sat. A small puff of smoke rose before dissipating.

Morei stared at the relic, waiting for flames to burst to life, but nothing came. He shook out his burned hand. It stung, and when he studied it, he found the skin red. Shock consumed him. Never had Dark Energy treated him so. Carefully, he took his other hand and nudged the weapon, expecting the searing pain to return. Nothing.

Exhaling, he snatched the weapon back up, finding it devoid of any heat. "Hm." The king brought it close again, trying to read the sigils on the metal. It was an oath dedicated to—

A knock startled him, and he lowered the weapon, covering it with the red cloth. "Yes?" he called. He wanted to explore this relic's lifeforce more and try to figure out why it had burned him, but that would have to wait.

The door opened, and Darryl, one of his personal guards, stuck his head in. "Your Majesty, there is a gentleman here to see you."

Morei rubbed his temples, restraining his annoyance. He had only left so much time before duties required his attention. "Now? I'm due to see Isla. Tell him to come back tomorrow." He paused, soaked in the earlier disaster. "Is there word of Rhys?"

Darryl's face twisted. "No, Your Majesty. Although men have yet to return."

"Dramatic, isn't he?" the king mused. Their last confrontation had ended poorly, and now that he knew the chancellor was working behind his back, he couldn't get his hands on him fast enough. If he wanted to be a coward, Morei would let him do it while he burned to death.

"Yeah," Darryl mumbled. "The other piece you mentioned is not here either."

He gritted his teeth. The hawk was missing. Of course it was. Rhys had fled. This had been the chancellor's plan all along. While he wanted to ask questions, now was not the time. "Thank you."

Darryl pulled his head back and exchanged some muffled words. Morei was baffled. It was uncommon for a visitor to arrive without an escort to his study. It certainly wasn't Henry—he didn't need to play by the royal rules.

"Yeah." Darryl poked his head in again. "I'm sorry, Your Majesty, he says it's urgent. Says he's been trying to get your attention all day."

Morei sighed, knowing he wouldn't get out of this one. "Can you talk to the men at the doors about letting people in? This isn't a habit I want to keep. It's unsafe and obnoxious." He didn't care if the visitor heard.

Darryl nodded. "Of course, Your Majesty." He stepped back out, and Morei took the chance to finish the rest of his drink—Fang's Revenge—and top it off. He hoped the shipment for Kendell's Milk would come in soon. The decanter hadn't even made it off his desk this afternoon. Isla would probably give him a hard time about it. She wasn't an avid drinker. She preferred her teas, which he found bitter and boring.

The king summoned the last bit of strength he had for dealing with people. He stood just as the door opened, so that he could properly greet the visitor. The man was tall, and as he drew back the hood on his cloak, Morei froze.

He knew those eyes anywhere.

Loyal as the Guardian

One Day Later

Syra had never considered herself brave. She was, at best, lucky. When life got tough, she had all the right people. When her life was in jeopardy, she'd always been saved. Now, everything was shifting. She had to be brave. If not for herself, then for everyone depending on her.

In the day that had passed, the Infernol had collected all the Lirallians' bodies and set them ablaze. A potent message for anyone even leagues out. The dark smoke billowed upward, filling the sky, releasing a sickly smell that made Syra gag. She would gladly go the rest of her life not inhaling that rotten stench.

Sekar had left just as quickly as he'd arrived. News of his massacre had reached every ear in the Infernol. Some revered him; others feared him. Syra kept her mouth shut. Certain topics were hard for her to engage with—discussing how the world saw the deity who'd ripped her life apart was one of them. Words traveled through the halls. Some people were still dressed in their armor from the day before, desperate for a bath but too busy with the cleaning and frenzied with anticipation. The Infernol was moving.

But she wasn't going with them. Zarek either.

The long walk to Dryl's chamber from the training area took most of the morning. She'd left just before dawn, relieved that most people didn't acknowledge her, to get fitted for new leather. Gloves, boots that reached her knees, Krye, a cleaning on her greaves and bracers, which were placed back on her, a check on Death's Sword and the belt to ensure they were in good condition, and a new dark green cloak with pockets. She was already dressed for travel in simple pants and a tunic, but she was glad to put the cloak on. It would serve her well in countering the chill in the Soul Realm.

Zarek would be fitted similarly, if he hadn't been already. They'd gone their separate ways late the night before for some rest, and now they were due back at Dryl's for a final farewell. Carl, the blacksmith who'd helped her, wished her good luck. He was made aware of the situation—Bane too. The less the people knew how perilous their situation was, the better. The realm fracture was common knowledge, but Dryl had done his best to keep discussion on it light, so that they wouldn't stir up a panicked mob.

Each step closed in on a destiny that Syra was nervous about. Each hall or door she passed, she studied a bit more. Every person who slipped by, oblivious, was a victim. She took it all in as if seeing it for the first time. The love for the paintings, small figurines carved from stone along the back of the large dining hall, the precision of carving the stairs, and the smells. Baked apples, bread, and roasts. The staff were cooking their last biggest meal before many of the Infernol left for Raveer.

This place would house only a fraction of the remaining Infernol members until Raveer was stabilized. Then the rest would move into the city, taking whatever remained.

Syra was coming up to the door now. Despite how long she took the walk back, she still didn't feel like it was enough. She didn't know when she would see any of it again. If ever.

She raised her hand and knocked. In all the madness, she'd managed to get little rest, and the usage of Chaos weighed on her. In time, she hoped to recover faster. This would not work forever.

The door opened fast. Zarek. He was dressed just as she'd imagined. A bit more leather along his shoulders—a pauldron—and a blue cloak that looked far lighter than the one she wore. Death's Sword was comfortably fitted, and from here, she could see that his belt had been freshly oiled like hers.

"Carl?" she asked. It was the best she had.

He nodded and motioned for her to enter. The door closed behind her, sealing their fate. Ahead stood Dryl, still dressed in his armor. The Guardian's fingers were laced together, and he was propped on the desk, leveraging it as a chair. Blood stained the leather, now dried, and Dryl hadn't even bothered washing the grime from his hands.

The longer they went without speaking, the more Syra wanted to turn around. Fleeing across the Merrél Sea had been far easier than this. Shifting her weight, she swallowed the last bit of bile. These were the two strongest men she knew.

Dryl cleared his throat. The ring she'd carried for so long rested on the desk. "When we see you again, let's hope it's in Raveer." He straightened and approached. "Do you have everything? Sword, leather, coin—"

"You know we do," Zarek interjected. "We've got enough Krye to pay our way for the next two summers."

His brother chuckled. "You'll be jumping between the realms. The last I want is either of you having to worry about a place to rest or eat when you're in this one." Dryl met her gaze then, looking more like the man she'd known in the Nighthunter Federation. "How are you?"

"Ready." She hoped that sounded as tough as she was trying to be.

The Guardian saw right through it. He closed the space between them and forced her eyes up to his with his hand. "There is nobody else I would trust you with. Zarek will do everything to protect you, but in return, I ask that you do the same. You are not the same woman you were all those moons ago. Follow your instincts, Syra. They will never fail you."

He hugged her tightly, squeezing every bit of fear and worry out of her. She returned it, grateful for the connection. Muffled, she said, "I don't know when we'll see you again." As the statement left her lips, tears burned. She was trying not to cry, but the gravity of all of this was getting to her. She didn't know if she would ever see Dryl again.

"Syra," he hummed. "Don't." He said it with affection. "Give Zarek some credit, okay?"

The brothers laughed, and she couldn't help but follow along. When Dryl let go of her, he reached for the ring and offered it to her. "A little something," he said, and grabbed her hand. He gently laid the item down and folded her fingers over the cool, familiar metal. "I don't need it anymore."

More tears fell, and she wiped them away. "Why make me haul this around for you when you were just going to give it back to me?"

Dryl laughed. "It'll be our thing. When the time comes, you can give it to me." The Guardian turned to his brother then and embraced him. Dryl whispered something, too faint to be heard. Zarek nodded, and then they pressed their foreheads together. The ring in Syra's hand was as familiar as it had been all those days she plucked it out of her pouch while traveling. The chip and scuff marks displayed its age, and as promised, the same message stared up at her.

When dawn breaks, strike me, pull me, drag me, but I am what I am. My skin is soaked, but my will is stronger.

"Make them proud," Dryl told Zarek. "I'll see you soon, brother."

Syra wiped away the remaining tears that were struggling to hold on and tucked the ring in its rightful pouch. It was time. Dryl stepped back, and Zarek unsheathed Death's Sword. They would leave in privacy, without the Infernol's knowledge. As the Guardian did before, he softly incanted the Old Tongue and brought the blade to life. Syra watched him work, slowing her breathing and letting her mind drift. Their plan, if it worked, would resolve the realm fracture and restore balance, sealing the chasm too.

If they failed, there would be nowhere to call home.

Vore Terminology

Ashýon (*Ash-ee-on*) – Outer region of the Soul Realm. It has become the home to the majority of the demons and is the most dangerous region of the realm. No Guardian will travel to this territory. Beyond demons, great beasts roam the area that are not seen anywhere else.

Assane *(Ah-sane)* – Northeastern city of Diyrǎ. One of the only major cities to still allow for smaller territories to be ruled by tribes, the tribal territories make up the vast landscape of Assane. The primary income varies between tribes, but eccentric and unique gods are well known to come from this region.

Barnǎl *(Bar-nahl)* – Eastern city of Creitón. A brutal past with strong armed forces. Historically remembered as the city that enslaved its princess. Supplies cities with ships, gathering supplies through a deal with the ancient Venkar City.

- Tyrik Village – Small and quaint, but best known as the village massacred during the White Horn pirate raid approximately 434 summers ago.

Binter – Often confused for Yavinks. Tiny creatures with translucent wings that live in the tropical forest of Creitón. They are attracted to humid climates, fruit, and wherever they can hide under leaves. They are known to be grumpy and prefer to be left alone.

Caster – Eastern city of Sorréle. Known for its high crime rates and violent culture, the city's economic income weighs heavily on the production of wines and trading. All goods, exported or imported, must pass through Caster's Port, giving the city a significant advantage over all others.

Cer'han (*Ser-hahn*)– A flying creature that comes from the Soul Realm. Many have referred to it as a 'demon dragon' because it embodies similar characteristics, such as wings, snout, powerful jaws, and talons. They live for decades and can be as small as a hand or as large as a home. Aggressive, territorial, and hard to kill.

Chaos – Often referred to as 'the mother of energy' or 'Mother.' Without Chaos, there would be no Vore World. Dark Energy and Light Energy are both sub-energies to Chaos. All things, including the realms, are linked to the mother of all energies.

Creitón (*Cre-ton*) – Nicknamed 'pirate country.' There is no clear record of whether Creitón or Eiyrăl came first, and the answers will vary by individual. This country is well-known for its ports, ships, and the cultural significance of the sea. It is true that most of the pirates Vorelians meet consider Creitón their home, but it is certainly a well-established country with strong values. Main cities: Barnăl, Saveen, and Delion. Lesser cities: Venkar City, Ruby Village, and Tyrik Village.

Crescent Blade – An honorable dagger forged out of gemstone, harvested from the depths of Crescent Lake. This blade isn't meant to be fought with but to store mass amounts of Light Energy. It is a ceremonial weapon presented to those identified as invaluable by the Yavinks. Very few are made. The hilt is narrow, made of dark leather and braided leaves, and the pommel is flat. There's no handguard. The blade is pink, translucent, and wavy.

Crystónity *(Cris-ton-ity)* – Branch of Drügalism. This monotheistic religion only celebrates Sekar and does not consider the other deities significant. Crystóns are secluded worldwide, but the City of Liral is the only location to practice openly.

Cu'cel *(Su-sel)* – Sinister illness responsible for the deaths in Geral. Old Tongue translates to 'evil' or 'ungodly.' Refer to Grënyl for a description.

Dark Energy – A more prominent form of energy, sometimes referred to as 'the sister of Chaos' or 'the dead's power.' This energy is raw, untampered, and pure, derived from the souls of the damned locked in the living realm and unable to pass into the Afterlife. Dark Energy is nearly impossible to master by an Energy Harvester, given the incredible power of the force. This power is often known to consume and kill the harvester and is considered a bad omen by most Vorelians. Dark Energy is embodied in the purest elements: water, wind, metal, and fire. Historically, only two have mastered the energy: Selena Delcate (wind) and Henry Junok (metal). Morei Geral (fire) is now the third Vorelian to master it.

Death's Sword – The blade of the Guardian. This weapon is forged using metal harvested from Volkeri Island. The creation requires Dark Energy and the blood of the selected Guardian, creating a customized weapon that will not break under high stress. It can withstand the strength of Chaos, as proven by Syra, and acts as a transportation tool for Guardians to form portals. This sword is highly prized in the living, with some extreme underground traders willing to kill to obtain the weapon. The actual process of how the blade is forged remains a secret, but it is akin to a God's sword, able to kill a Guardian, slay ancient beasts, and end souls.

Delion *(Dee-le-on)* – Northern city of Creitón. A quiet city that keeps to itself. It is commonly referred to as the heart of Creitón because of its central location, although the city remains compact and smaller in stature, unlike Saveen and Barnǎl. Do not be fooled by the city's quiet demeanor, as the toughest citizens live here, with many working the sea as their source of income.

Díanzon Prophecy *(Die-an-zon)* – As old as time itself. This prophecy focused on the rebalancing of the realms. It spoke of a man born with the power of a God, but with the violent tendencies of a monster—a delicate symbolic dance between the living and dead. Centuries of stories have been passed down, which have tampered with the literal meaning of some terms. The one who would act as the catalyst for this change is known as the King of Monsters, but due to time, has come to be known as the Demon King.

Die Cux'erial *(Dee Cuk-er-al)* – An ancient belief that a series of specific deaths would lead to a world-ending event (i.e., Diyrǎllian Massacre, the Great Fall, and the fall of the Vorelian Empire are a few). There is confidence that all lives are interconnected somehow, and that decisions lead to certain outcomes. This belief is often shared with Ghrynál, although they are not related. Hyle is a firm believer in this ideology.

Diemon *(Di-mon)* – Northwest city of Sorréle. The city of gems, or as some refer as 'the gem city.' Stationed up against the Releuthian Mountains, its primary income is from mining and jewelry.

Diyrǎ *(Di-rah)* – Founded over 1,500 summers ago and well-known for its gruesome history. At the height of the Lirallian Empire over four centuries ago, Henry Junok led a bloody domination that slaughtered millions, now known as the Diyrăllian Massacre. Main cities: Assane, Raveer, and Junok. Lesser cities: Nighthunter Federation, Jasper Village, and Whale Village.

Diyrăllian Massacre *(Di-ral-lian)* – The largest massacre in Vorelian history that occurred over four centuries ago. The Lirallian Empire carried it out under the guidance of Henry Junok. Millions of lives were lost across Diyră, and the summer has become known as the 'Blood Summer.'

Don'sul *(Dawn-suul)* – A ritual that restricts Energy Harvesters from harvesting. This ritual is considered dark and is prohibited across all four countries. Most successful when performed on a child less than five, but it is still used on adults, although results vary.

- This was performed on Cyrus by Henry Junok.

Drügalism *(Druug-al-ism)* – The primary religion of Vorelians, embodying all five Gods: Helyna, Greve, Hyle, Eazon, and Sekar.

Duraloc *(Der-ah-lock)* – One of the original demons of the Soul Realm. This demon is bound to a Guardian of Death during the Commitment Ceremony, and is what gives these warriors their features and enhanced abilities. The demon lives in cave systems and is a soul eater. Also used as part of the eternal punishment provided by Guardians.

Eazon *(E-zon)* – God of Luck. Ritual of Contact: a bundle of Krye placed on a cloth and surrounded by candles.

Edanzín Blade (*E-dan-sin*) – The blade used in the Commitment Ceremony of the Guardians. While the vast amount of information surrounding the process of the Commitment Ceremony remains a secret, this blade has been confirmed. The user of the blade is specially trained and must undergo a mental evaluation after each use to confirm that the power of the blade has not negatively impacted the person (in this case, Guardian). The master of this blade is called a Herän (*Her-ahn*).

- Only one Herän can exist at any point in time. The blade is bonded to the chosen individual until they relinquish it. In any case, relinquishment can be through death or by choice. In unique cases, by force.

Eei'on Rü *(Ee-I-on Ruh)* – 'Peace of the World.' This is the core value of the Rider Federation. It is referenced as 'the code of all codes' or simply the Code and represents the overall goal of the Rider Federation: achieving world peace by any means necessary. This philosophy was expected to be adhered to by every member during the federation's reign. Failure to abide results in punishments and formal hearings.

Egunsar *(E-goon-sar)* – Pesky and aggressive rodent-like creatures that have an appetite for eyeballs. They live in the Soul Realm and can attack in hordes.

Eiyrặl *(Eye-ral)* – An ancient country with conflicting settlement records, although many agree it was well over 2,000 summers, with some estimations as high as 3,000. With no clear indication, it is well-known as the Dragon Riders' home. The ancient country holds traditional Vorelian values that are entirely lost to many outsiders. More interestingly, Eiyrặl is withdrawn from many political movements and is independent of a lot of activity with other countries. Main cities: Kalic, East Razan, West Razan, and Rider Federation (destroyed in the Great Fall).

Ferguson – Northeast city of Sorréle, more commonly referred to as 'the silk family.' Ferguson's economic income is primarily from clothing, specializing in silks. An eccentric group of people that remain withdrawn.

Firóle *(Fur-ole)* – Giant serpents that once ruled the lands of Diyrặ and traveled openly. One of the ancient beasts. The Firóle were hunted for their scales and fangs during the height of the Dragon Riders, driving them to extinction. Very few remain and stay in hiding. They are ancient beasts and possess many characteristics like a dragon, such as telepathic communication and intelligence.

Fräurune (*Fraah-rune*) – Translates to 'Lady of the Dead.'

Geíon (*Ge-ee-on*) – A highly evolved and intelligent species of demon. They are violent, bloodthirsty, and constantly seek control. They are active users of Ön'grusah with theories stating they have evolved because of their use of this force. They loathe the Honuyál.

- Ka-Geíon (*Kah-Ge-ee-on*) – A higher and more powerful Geíon. Have the capability to conjure their own bodies, so they can look like anything. Many of these Ka-Geíons take the body of people because it allows them to walk among the living.

- Gor-Geíon (*Gore-Ge-ee-on*) – A lower and less powerful Geíon. They cannot conjure bodies like their brethren, so they possess the living. Any possession or soul bondage with a person is not permanent. This is because their own lifeforce slowly devours the lifeforce of their victim.

  ○ Morei Geral, prophesized Demon King, is soul bonded to one.

Geral *(Geh-ral)* – Western city of Sorréle and nicknamed 'the blacksmith's city.' Geral's economic income weighs heavily on the trade of metals, including armor and weapons. A city that takes pride in its strength and independence.

Ghrynál *(Ghrin-all)* – A philosophical belief quite literally translating to '*the path forward.*' Everything has a cause and effect; every action dictates a different path. The mother of energy, Chaos, knows all paths forward. It was once revered in traditional Vorelian culture but has since become less known, specifically in Sorréle and many parts of Diyrǎ. Guardians of Death adhere to this philosophical approach.

Gods' Realm – The original name for the living realm.

Gonsín (*Gone-seen*) – Translated from Old Tongue to 'leader.' A high form of respect when this term is used.

Gray Realm – The space between the living and Soul Realm. Often believed to be the realm closest to Chaos. Given its vast and uncontrollable environment, no one goes here, and it is acknowledged by Energy Harvesters or Vore scholars. Very few cultures address the Gray Realm. Sekar is believed to be the only God who freely travels to and from the Gray Realm, using its volatile and secretive nature to his advantage. With so little knowledge of this realm, no one truly understands what or if anything lives there.

Grënyl (*Greh-nal*) – Ailment associated with Sekar. Old literature discusses Grënyl to be the mark of the Dark Lord and how he identifies his next victims. Symptoms include black rotting pieces of flesh, fever, and mental deterioration. Sekar utilizes this tactic to weaken the life force and bring them to the Gray Realm, a space between the living and dead realms. Ancient texts theorized Grënyl only came to those with fractured loyalty to the Gods, such as Greve, Hyle, Eazon, and Helyna.

Greve (*Greeve*) – God of Strength. Ritual of Contact: wooden posts with letters nailed to them, followed by a hand gesture over the heart.

Guardian of Death – Warriors that belong to the Soul Realm. They are responsible for the guidance of souls from the living to the Afterlife. Guardians are also responsible for the protection of the Soul Realm against all forms of threats. They are mortal boys taken before ten after a tragedy and raised in the realm of the dead. Countless summers of training and mastery of their skills and emotions make them savage competition in a swordfight. Upon training completion, they undergo the Commitment Ceremony, which involves the bondage of a lesser demon to their soul. The ultimate test is surviving this ritual, and those who do are honorably gifted Death's Sword and become a Guardian of Death. Details of the Commitment Ceremony are not shared; Guardians do not speak highly of the seven-day ceremony and a few have emphasized that it is unbearable. The iconic characteristics—pale blue skin, red eyes, black hair, and Marking—all result from the ceremony. In cultures where they are less accepted and perceived as bad omens, they are called 'Death Seekers.'

- Shevana ceased all further training of Guardians, and the numbers are now the lowest they've ever been.

Gýshin *(Gee-shin)* – The purest form of the Old Tongue language. Spoken by the Yavinks. Translated to 'true tongue.'

Helyna *(Hel-e-na)* – Goddess of Love. Ritual of Contact: a glass of wine with use of the phrases 'Love is endless' and 'Helyna bless you.'

Honuyál *(Hon-u-al)* – A grotesque and ruthless species of beasts. They are power-hungry and feed off souls. They follow traditional values and place a high emphasis on female rulers. Noted traits include leathery skin, large and strong bodies, dagger-like teeth, slit noses, and tusks. They have amassed numbers in the Soul Realm.

Hyle *(Hile)* – God of Courage. Ritual of Contact: silver beads with a small wooden sun, widely named 'Hyle's Beads.'

Indül *(In-duul)* – A flower harvested on the outskirts of Venkar City. The flower produces a toxin that can be fatal in high doses. Ingestion of the toxin will create hallucinations and other symptoms. Only a master herbalist should work with a flower this dangerous.

Inere (*E-near*) – One of the ancient beasts of the Vore World. This giant beast is covered in shell-like armor. Large pincers, a dozen beady eyes, and ten legs. The Inere burrows underground and comes above ground only when threatened or curious. Can live up to 400 summers.

I'num *(E-num)* – The sigil of the Dragon Rider. Translates from the Old Tongue to 'loyalty,' and was used to symbolize the dedication Dragon Riders held for one another during the Rider Federation. Acts are made in the best interest of the Dragon Riders. Failure to uphold this was considered punishable. I'num is considered closely tied to Eei'on Rü.

Junok *(June-oke)* – Northwest city of Diyră. The largest territory of all Vore cities and best known for its gory history and rich Energy Harvesting bloodline. The Junok family is most notably known for Henry Junok, despite the family's expulsion of the prince and his title from the family lineage. Junok's Port is the major port of all trades for Diyră, making up a significant amount of city income.

Kalic *(Kal-ick)* – Eastern city of Eiyrăl. One of the smallest cities in the world. Well known as one of the only cities to enslave people still. Its brutal punishment system and predefined roles make the city ancient in its practices. Primary income is weapon and armor production.

Kan Sëri *(Kahn-Sar-e)* – Translates from Old Tongue to 'Master of the Sea' or 'Sea Master.'

Krakí *(Kra-kee)* – One of the ancient beasts of the Vore World. Eight tentacles, larger than any ship, and territorial. In some cultures, like Creitón, these beasts are revered. They live deep underwater and occasionally come up out of curiosity. Highly intelligent and hold grudges. Can live up to 1,000 summers.

Krisár *(Kris-har)* – One of the dark rituals of old Vorelian practices. Involves the consumption of the participant's blood and the recital of an ancient text spoken in Old Tongue. A blade of power must be used in the ritual for it to be successful. It is forbidden in most cities across the Vore World, given its highly dark association with the dead and curses. The ritual was outlawed after the fall of the Lirallian Empire and all books associated with Krisár and equally dangerous rituals were said to be burned.

Kultón *(Kuhl-tune)* – The most prestigious title a Guardian of Death can be given, similar to a commander in the living. Dryl held this title for many summers before it was stripped from him.

Ku'sar *(Kuh-sar)* – Old Tongue for 'Death Dancer.'

Leangé (Lee-an-gee) – One of the most important books of the Soul Realm. This book possesses all sorts of information regarding the history and creation of the Soul Realm, along with natural laws. This book is one of the few that was saved when Shevana, the current and longest standing ruler, set fire to all material in an attempt to withhold information and increase her political power.

Lifeforce – More commonly known as soul. This is the energy that makes up every living thing or object. Depending on what region of the Vore World visited, one will hear either soul or lifeforce.

Light Energy – The weakest but most malleable form of energy, as it is impure and tampered with. All life is made of Light Energy. All Energy Harvesters lean heavily on this form, as its ease and stability make it reliable. Commoners often refer to this form as 'magic,' which indicates a lack of education in energy.

Lih'rel *(Lie-rehl)* – An ancient religion that worshipped the Vore beasts, including the dragon. Followers of this practice believed the Gods were not in control, only servants to the original masters of the realms.

Ly'rün (*Lie-rune*) – A potent mixture of chemicals that combusts into a deadly fire when used. A fatal gas is released during this, which can spread for half a league in all directions. Anyone who inhales this will experience swelling of the lungs, hallucinations, and bloody tears. No records exist of any survivors.

Móermism *(More-mism)* – Spiritual religion. Followers place their value and respect in energies and are considered extremely spiritual, often praising Mother, or Chaos, as the ultimate deity. This old practice is seen rarely but is scattered throughout the world, and followers are known best as Móers.

Mo'lüre (*Mo-lah-ure*) – The commoners call it a unicorn. The creature is created with pure Dark Energy and has been nicknamed the 'Walker of Realms' because of its ability to dissipate and reappear wherever it wants. Nobody can touch the creature without permission. Doing so will cause the Mo'lüre to consume the lifeforce of the person. Ancient stories say that to see one is a good omen for this creature does not show itself to anyone without intention. There are only a handful of sightings throughout Vore history.

Nighthunter – The best assassin in the world. Trained for up to eight or more summers under the guidance of skilled assassins and must earn their sword in training. They hold tremendous value in the Old Laws and will hunt anyone.

- Upon the formation of the Nighthunters, a deal was made with Junok. In return for land, the Nighthunters would never take a bid against the Junok family.

Nighthunter Federation – A southwest city located on the panhandle of Diyră. The city is well known for its zero-crime tolerance and is the only city in the world to offer asylum to all refugees. However, the Nighthunters are more than just soldiers, but the best assassins in the world. An underground market allows travelers from around the world to come and bid for a Nighthunter. The federation is a hotspot for illegal trade.

Old Laws – Old text written over 200 summers ago. These laws were the original promises of the Nighthunters and define the guild. To break one of the Old Laws is to break the oath of a Nighthunter.

Ön'grusah (*Ohn-gru-sah*) – Translated to 'evil energy.' This is a form of energy that has been abused, contorted, and twisted into an all-consuming force. While many of the Soul Realm believe the Ka-Geíon are responsible for this, it is still unconfirmed which species of demon is to blame. However, it has been confirmed that Ön'grusah is responsible for the current state of the Soul Realm.

- Studies on Ön'grusah are few. Those that have spent time researching this malicious power have theorized that it is alive and moves with the intelligence of Chaos. This could be the result of evolution—the force growing stronger and smarter when faced with any form of threat. Although one theory is that Ön'grusah was created with the use of a God's heart, which would explain the theory that there is a direct link to Chaos. There are no confirmed reports. To study Ön'grusah, one would have to venture deep into Ashýon, where it is believed the heart of this evil energy lies. This is extremely dangerous.

Oth'al (*Ahth-al*) – The book dedicated to the Guardians and their laws. All information regarding the Commitment Ceremony, their order, and training is covered in this book. As of current, the book is lost.

Rauna (*Raw-na*) – In old stories, she is the ancient queen who fell in love with the God, Zyne. She was killed by her own citizens.

Raveer *(Rah-veer)* – Eastern city known for its brutality and ancient values in Diyră. The city has become revered for its armed forces; they are trained for twice the number of summers than the standard soldier observed in other Vorelian cities. The primary city income is metalwork.

Regule *(Reh-ghoul)* – A large, four-legged beast from the Beutóne Mountains. Incisors that extend past the jaw, and white fur speckled with orange stripes. Infamous for its iconic glacier-blue eyes with slit pupils. Prone to lashing out when it feels threatened. Can live up to 300 summers.

Renuri *(Ren-yuri)* – An expert in poisonous explosives. An outlawed practice by most cities, but that does not stop rulers from seeking out these experts.

Rider Federation – North city of Eiyrăl, or the remains. The city was destroyed over 800 summers ago during The Great Fall. The city's remnants offer sanctuary to strange beasts, volatile energy, and secrets. Often, citizens of Kalic and Razan come to offer gifts and say prayers.

- When it stood, the Rider Federation was glorious and home to some of the most influential people in the world. The federation kept peace among the cities worldwide and led massive explorations.

Rider's Sword – A prestigious and irreplaceable weapon custom-made for each Rider who passes the rigorous summers of training. Once inducted, Riders are gifted this as a symbol of their status. A Rider's Sword is forged with the blood of a dragon and meticulous ceremonial work. They can't break and they possess a lifeforce. Cyrus carries Darrin's, once a Master Rider who soared the skies with Vikter and Hyle during the reign of the Rider Federation.

Rubal *(Ru-ball)* – A desert flower that, when crushed into a paste, can cause near-fatal reactions in the body. It is used in the underground market as a method to fake deaths. It is risky to use because, at times, too high a dose can be fatal.

Rül'Cril *(Rah-Cril)*– Translates to 'Crown of Gods.' This relic was one of the three forged by Henry Junok in his reign. It earned the name because it has the power to make any beast a mindless slave to the user of the crown. Sekar remains the only God with the knowledge of how it was forged. Henry Junok never got the chance to use it.

Rü'shane *(Ruh-shane)* – Translated from Old Tongue to 'God's Soul.' This is the proper term for a raven. Souls unwilling to pass into the Afterlife for one reason or the other. Once bound to the Soul Realm but managed to break free. These souls are forever bound to wander between the living and dead, too stubborn to pass.

Saveen *(Sa-veen)* – Western city of Creitón. Saveen drives global trades of jewels and unique goods. The city is known for its exquisite architecture and attitudes, but they are masters of the seas and should not be misunderstood.

- The prince of Saveen, Dameon, is the second Dragon Rider to soar the skies in over 800 summers.

Sekar *(Seh-kar)* – In traditional culture, known as the Dream Walker or God of Dreams. More recently, heavily regarded as the Dark Lord, God of Darkness, and unacknowledged by some cultures altogether for the belief that such action brings bad luck.

- Ritual of contact as Dark Lord: blood sacrifice and recital of cursed text. Punishable by death if caught performing this ritual in most cities.

- Ritual of contact as Dream Walker: prayer before bed. The method of contact is through dreams, so many would pray to Sekar for him to visit and guide them while they dream.

Sorréle *(Sor-rel)* – The youngest country of the Vore World, founded over eight centuries ago. The establishment of this country originates in a political dispute between families in Diyră. Main cities: Geral, Ferguson, Diemon, and Caster. Lesser cities: Gamer's Village.

Soul Realm – The realm of the dead. Commoners refer to this location as the 'underworld,' but this is inappropriate, as the Soul Realm lives parallel with the living—not above or below. Souls pass into the Soul Realm and exist until they are ready to be guided to the Afterlife. It is ruled by a select family who the Gods chose to uphold the responsibility of caring for the dead. The Soul Realm is critical to the living—it brings order and balance to the energy system. If the Soul Realm fails, the living will follow, and vice versa.

- The Soul Realm was notably once beautiful, with flowing rivers and vivid colors. It has since become the embodiment of ghastly and horrible imagery. The malevolent forces entered with permission under the guise of promised power and slowly devoured the land.

Soul Speaker – People who have a connection to the dead. They see, hear, and speak for the deceased. Some cultures regard Soul Speakers as bad omens, while others revere their gift.

Syckl Blade *(Sick-ill)* – One of few weapons that can kill a Guardian of Death. It is forged with the toxin of a Cer'han, and it is known for its yellowish-colored blade. This is the execution weapon used on punished Guardians, though that was a rare ceremony. The blade was held on to for more hideous purposes.

The Great Fall – The fall of the Rider Federation. Upon the death of her Rider, Vikter, Aythen went mad with rage and destroyed the city. It is said only a handful escaped the carnage, but what happened to the survivors remains unknown.

- Prior to The Great Fall, two Dragon Riders fled in the middle of the night with their weapons and gear. What became of them remains undetermined—no further dragon sightings were reported, and no one by the iconic silver eyes was documented following the destructive events. Cyrus is believed to possess one of the Rider's Swords that was saved before The Great Fall.

Trembar *(Trem-bar)* – Originally from the Dark Forest. A four-legged creature with spiral-like horns that cover its jaw and head. It has tan fur, hooves, and four eyes. Will chew through anything except iron, and is known for its voracious appetite.

Tsu'Ran (*Su-ran*) – Shapeshifters of the sea. They live in hordes and call the Grave their home. They transform into anything their victim most desires. Souls are what they consume. Powerful creatures that in their natural form look closer to a small Krakí.

U'can *(You-can)* – A fierce and territorial mouse found in the Releuthian Mountains. Also the name of an obscure and small tribe of pirates.

Ve'hem *(Veh-hem)* – Old Tongue for 'the burdened one.'

Vor'gal *(Vore–gal)* – Old Tongue for 'the pit' or 'underworld.'

West and East Razan *(Rah-zan)* – Western city of Eiyrăl and second largest in the Vore World (primarily referenced as West Razan). Rich in ancient culture and values and is considered one of the oldest cities. One of the only cities in the world where people will walk without a weapon in the streets. Energy Harvesters are welcomed and highly regarded. The Razan family occasionally opens their gates and allows citizens to explore the vast palace. An extensive underground tunnel system accommodates the palace. Income varies, given the city's adaptability to economic changes.

- West Razan was once known as Suniyr (Sun-ear), a city of occult followers. Approximately 1,100 summers ago, Suniyr was dissolved by Razan after a political war. The Suniyr family was executed publicly.

Wurok *(War-ak)* – Massive and ghastly worm-like creatures that live in the Starved Sands. They sense through vibrations, noted by the ripples left in the sand when they move. Described as having hundreds of incisors and black. Extremely territorial and stalkers of their prey.

Wynzer *(Wine-zer)* – A creature created through mass experimentation and Dark Energy. Similar build to a dragon, small, and with an abnormally long tail. No scales, extremely intelligent, and observant. Only one exists, which resides in Caster, and is endearingly named Savage after he bit the head off a mouse.

Xaxer *(Zax-er)* – A bird-like creature that lives in the Soul Realm, once believed extinct. It has long, scaly legs and a disproportionately large body. Its dark, orb-like eyes and white beak starkly contrast with its black wings tipped in purple. Curious and passive.

Yalahnder *(Yah-lan-der)* – A violent beast with the bulk of a dragon but the body of an Onye. Bred for blood, thrives off destruction, and is infamous for the gouges left behind at the Soul Realm palace. Nearly driven to extinction but has since disappeared. The last whereabouts remain unknown.

Zimbórism *(Zim-bor-ism)* – Branch of Drügalism. This religion identifies Greve as the primary God and is heavily recognized in Diyră, although there are a small number of Zimbór followers across the Vore World.

Zyne (*Zine*) – A Vore God who many believed was the moon in ancient Vore beliefs. He fell in love with a mortal, Rauna.

Zyulë Bond *(Zule)* – A type of energy bond that doesn't identify a master. The equal relationship that results is often referred to as a God's Bond. Both individuals must remain alive; the death of one will result in the partner's death. This peculiar characteristic makes it both dangerous and extremely useful. Both participants must adhere to the rules of Krisár. Individuals of Zyulë Bonds possess a silver raised scar on their wrist and are extremely valuable in some traditional cultures.

Acknowledgment

There aren't enough words to describe my appreciation and gratitude to those who have made this possible. Dylan, Cherie, Eve, and the countless Vorelians who have joined this Empire. Dylan, the Emperor, is always in my head and is the best editor I could ever have. Eve brought to life the Vore World in all her map illustrations with incredible precision. Cherie, the visionary, has captured this world perfectly with her cover design work. This has been an international project from the start, and if not for the dedication of each, I don't know exactly what *The Vorelian Saga* would have become.

I want to give a few shout-outs to the Vorelians who have made this journey truly fun and rewarding. Bryan Kamtsios—you crafted an illustration that captured the heart of what it means to be a part of this Empire. That's an unforgettable gift. #Vorelian4Life. Micah Campbell—the chapter *Immortal and Exhausted* is dedicated to you. I expect to see my chapter title in your book too. It's our deal. JB Caine—you made my day by taking the time to create laser-engraved bookmarks. I will cherish these and likely ask for more.

Brian Lynch—you went above and beyond to ensure this book was the best version it could be. You have an insane eye for this stuff. Your help means more to me than I will ever be able to put into words. HD Bergen—you've taught me what pursuing your dreams really means. The long hours, the restless nights, and the many cups of coffee are all worth it if we know what we're working toward. All of you are exceptional storytellers who make this community special.

Five years ago, I was struggling to justify pursuing this wild dream. Ten years ago, I thought it was impossible. Now, as I wrap up *The Scars of the Wicked* and pursue other projects—both inside and outside the Vore World—I am constantly humbled by the journey. There is no textbook to tell you how to pursue your dreams, and there's even far less out there that will tell you the best approach. Nobody's way is right or wrong, although many believe they have the answer when, in fact, they only have the answer to what worked for them.

So, while I can sit here and give you a story about some random event that shaped my life, or drone on about how much I love the Vorelians who have supported me—you know who you are—I want to acknowledge all the budding storytellers out there who are thinking about making their dreams come true. It's terrifying to make that first leap but trust me, it's worth it.

Keep your swords sharp, Vorelians.

www.ingramcontent.com/pod-product-compliance
Lightning Source LLC
Chambersburg PA
CBHW030327010826
48973CB00004B/898